CW00859868

An Invitation To Kill

An Invitation To Kill

Lainey Quilholt Mysteries Book 2

Lorelei Bell

Acknowledgments

To Justin Pletsch for help on the use of rubber band slingshots and various projectiles.

Dedicated to

Angela Landsbury aka Jessica Fletcher of "Murder She Wrote"
(my mentor in mysteries)
And to my husband of 30 years now.

Journal entry by Lainey Quilholt

I woke from a dream one morning—maybe it began as a dream, but turned into a nightmare. Anyway, the dream began with me in the back seat of a car with my parents (now dead), driving. I don't know where we were, or where we wound up, but I had a sense of traveling, much like when we were on that fateful trip in Colorado. The beginning portion I couldn't remember very well, but the ending I could remember with great clarity. I was in swift water, struggling to keep my head up, trying to get to shore when a dark hand reached down to pull me up to safety.

I didn't understand the meaning of this dream until weeks later.

Chapter 1

"This is not rocket science, folks, but it's close," Mr. Taylor said as he paced the front of the class, black marker in hand, ready to pounce on the white board as he had during the last forty-five minutes to jot down basics of writing. "Writing a novel isn't like writing that essay for English in fifth grade where you fill in a lot of bullshit description just to fill pages."

Some of the students around me chuckled, as did I. There was a certain energy which Mr. Taylor threw off like a Yorkshire Terrier in a room full of people. I grew fond of him within the first five minutes of my seven o'clock class in my first ever-college course. Everything he said I agreed with and he said a number of new things that had me excited about starting that novel of mine.

He stepped up to the white board where he'd written out several headings with a number beside them. He'd been going through these for the first portion of the hour, pausing to make a point, questioning us for our ideas and input, and to add his own to each sub-heading.

His marker poised at "Describe Character's Physical Appearance". He wrote *blue eyes* in an almost illegible downward scrawl.

"Now, I don't know about you, but if a writer goes into great detail about what a character looks like, what they're wearing, that they have a mole on their right cheek, green flecks in their otherwise brown eyes, I'm outa there," he said. He turned to us. "Jane Austen's description of Elizabeth Bennett was that she had 'fine eyes'. It's up to the reader to figure out the meaning of that and use their own imagination. If your character has brown eyes, or blue eyes. Fine. Write that, but don't waste a whole frigging page on the color of their eyes. Unless you've got a vampire with all black eyes, of course, I'd like to know that."

More chuckles.

He turned back to his list on the board and tapped *Protagonist & Characters*. "No one is perfect. And if your protagonist is perfect, then, they're boring. Saints are nice, but, I'm sorry, their boring. Unless you behead them, of course, then you have a story." Laughter. "A new writer makes a lot of glaring mistakes, and this, I can say, is one of my pet peeves. Give your protagonist a trait that might be considered a little wacky, or off. He, or she, can have a scar, or a tattoo that stands out, just to make them memorable. In any case, make them marred, on the inside, as well as outside. No one is perfect." He gave everyone the eye. "And don't give your detective a drinking problem. That's old hack." Chuckles all around the room. "Find some other maladjustment. Maybe he's OCD, you know, like Monk." This was met with a few chuckles from the older students. The rest of us just stared. Leaning on his desk, he shook his head and sighed. "Once again, I'm dating myself." He smiled at those who knew what character he'd meant. There were older students—over thirty—sprinkled throughout the twenty-five or so students. For the most part, all were sophomores, around eighteen or nineteen. I was the only freshman in the class. I'd gotten special privilege because of recommendations from my English teacher in high school. I'd been so excited about this class, and happy it was the very first class on Monday, Wednesday, and Friday.

Stopping at his desk Mr. Taylor grabbed a pile of papers. "Let's see a show of hands. Who's writing what genre. How many of you are writing suspense?" He held up his own hand. A few hands went up around the classroom. "How many are writing science fiction?" Again about four hands went up. One guy who reminded me of the character Hagrid, held up a hand as big as a catcher's mitt. Shaggy hair and beard obliterated his features, and he seemed to take up a large amount of Real Estate at the table behind me.

"Horror?" More people raised their hands. I counted six hands. "Okay, good." He counted and then handed out the stapled sheets as he went from row to row in the room. "How many are writing romance?" There were a few timid hands. "Don't worry, if you aren't sure about it. If you like to read that sort of genre, raise your hands." He looked down at the girl second from the front and smiled at her. "Writing romance has big rewards. It's got a huge audience, and usually a writer worth her salt can net six figures, especially if she gets a good agent and they can get her into one of the bigger publishing houses." The girl's face turned bright crimson and she turned to her friend next to her. Both giggling with hands to their mouths.

While the hand-outs were passed back, I looked over mine. I loved hand-outs. He'd already handed two out before this. One was called *How to Write your Novel*, in which were xeroxed pages from writing magazines and was at least thirty pages in length. Another was called *Goodbye Writer's Block*. I decided I had a lot of reading to do later on, and happy about it. In fact I couldn't wait, I became slightly distracted by some of the subjects in the most recent handout. From the sound of pages being riffled through, others were just as itching to learn what was inside as me.

"You'll find that each genre has sub-genres. Take for instance mystery." He looked around the room. "Anyone here writing a mystery?"

I raised my hand half-heartedly. I hadn't committed anything to paper. My summer had been too busy, what with graduating, my aunt getting married to Sheriff Weeks, and moving in with us. Oh. And the murder that occurred, in which I played some minor part in solving, working to unravel who had, and who had not murdered Arline Rochelle. Admittedly, I wanted to write about that, but worried about lawsuits. I was strongly advised not to.

Mr. Taylor stepped over to engage me. "What type of mystery are you writing? Or do you know?"

"I guess I hadn't thought about it," I said, clueless.

"Do you have any favorite authors?"

"I've just switched over to murder mysteries, so I don't actually have anyone."

"I'll give you a list, next time. But you'll see under Murder Mysteries in your handout—" he tapped the paper he'd just handed out in front of me "—you've got the Classic Whodunit, Cozy, Courtroom Drama, Espionage, Historical, etc." He had stepped away from me with long legs and walked back to the front of the room and chose a blank area of the white board. "Let's take the cozy mystery. Normally, they take place in a small town, where all the suspects are present and familiar with one another, except the detective, who is usually an outsider, but not always." He wrote out the general headings.

In my case, Weeks hadn't been as much an outsider as he wasn't quite yet a family member. But I reminded myself I would have to change the whole story, as well as names.

"And then there's the amateur detective. This is like the Jessica Fletcher character, or Agatha Christie's Miss Marple. Those are both interesting characters to read." He turned and our eyes met. "The trick of writing a mystery is knowing who did it, how, why and then write backwards." He smiled and amended, "Well, not literally backwards." Chuckles again rose from our classroom. I smiled, enjoying the fact he wasn't dry as a November leaf like my past English teachers had been.

I thumbed through the hand-out. Finding my genre and the sub-genres, I pressed the pages open.

"At the end of this handout there are some questions I'd like you to answer in the space provided. I'll ask for these back. Just tear out that sheet and hand it in on Wednesday. And, I see that it's time to let you guys loose, so see you all next time." As he said this, he shuffled papers and tapped the edges on the desk, and putting them into his briefcase, getting ready to leave himself. I couldn't believe the time was already up.

The whole class stood, and like someone had shot a starter's gun, everyone filed out and were all gone in 5.3 seconds. My movements jittery, I tried to gather my notebooks, pens and multiple hand-outs, and kept dropping things on the floor. I always had trouble getting out of the room in as quick fashion as my classmates.

Mr. Taylor held the door open, waiting for me with a smile while I pulled the backpack onto my shoulder and felt suddenly weighted down with fifty pounds.

"You might want to check out our library for some books in the mystery section," he suggested.

"That might help," I said. "I was writing romance before this, but I just couldn't get into it."

"So, murder holds your interest. I can get behind that." I placed Mr. Taylor at mid-thirties with not too short-cropped, coffee-colored hair, and stood about six-two. He towered over me and was about the same height as Weeks. I smiled and was too shy to look into his handsome face or into his eyes for more than a few brief seconds. I couldn't say what color his eyes were. My gaze fell on his left hand where a wedding band rounded his finger. I don't know why that disappointed me.

"My aunt owns a bookstore, too. I should just check out what she has as well," I said.

"By all means! One of the things I stress in my class is read as much as you can."

I nodded. "Well. I enjoyed your class. Have a good day," I said in parting.

"Thank you! See you on Wednesday, Ms Quilholt." Wow. He remembered my name. We had filled out 3x5 cards with our names and interests on them at the beginning of class. He'd filed it into his memory so quickly. Impressive.

I waved, and watched his tall, somewhat athletic body turn a corner. Face warm, I turned away, trying to curb my thrill over this first class under my belt in something I hoped I would excel in. What I would not excel in was my next subject. Math.

I looked over my syllabus, found the line for this subject, which would begin in less than ten minutes.

ROOM 335 - LEVEL 3 – EAST WING

I puzzled on this for a moment. For the life of me, I actually didn't know where I was. East Wing, or West Wing? Before seven o'clock this morning, I'd stepped into this gigantic, sprawling white cement and windowed building known as Whitney College for the very first time. I had found this class only by asking around. I had gotten here early in order to make sure I got to it on time because I didn't want to miss my first creative writing class. I couldn't miss my next class, however.

A rotund man in a dark suit and pink shirt and dark tie approached down the hall. Smiling, he said brightly, "Morning!" to the few people he passed. Balding with a fringe of dark hair over the ears and back of head, he had the air and look of a man who owned a Fortune 500 company. I put him in his fifties, his suit looked expensive. Shoes—wingtips—immaculate with a high shine on them I didn't doubt would show his reflection, that is if he could bend over to see himself.

"Excuse me," I said, moving into his path.

"Yes, young lady?" His cologne assaulted me, but it was pleasant enough at maybe a football field away. I always wondered if people who smelled this strongly of cologne were covering up bad BO and maybe I should buy stock in the company that made it.

"I'm looking for the East Wing," I said, holding out my map of the building. The print was really small, and I couldn't really discern one wing from another. The numbers printed on it would require a magnifying glass. This map was a joke.

The balding man looked down at my map briefly. "Ah. East Wing. It's east, of course." He chuckled at his little joke. I sort of knew that, thanks. But I didn't know which way was east from where I stood. He pointed over my shoulder and said, "It should be down to the end there, and take a left. What class?"

"Math."

"Third floor. You'll find the elevator or the stairs at the end." He still pointed and I noted a large gold watch on his wrist as well as a diamond ring on his ring finger of the right hand.

I thanked him and headed in that direction. Of course, this was Level One, and looking around I found a sign on a wall which announced WEST WING. This should be easy, but it wasn't. The way the building was set up was like spider legs growing out from a central main section. Plus, the hallways were placed on the outer sides of the classrooms with a lot of glass. Looking out, their various sports fields filled my view on this end. Beyond that were corn fields, and the small town of Cedar Ridge in the distance. Interesting concept, and the view was spectacular, but I had to wonder what the cost would be to heat the thing during our ferocious Iowa winters.

Heading back toward the center of the building where a series of balconies and staircases descended or ascended, I paused. Below where I stood, I looked down on the commons, which was situated in a sort of large oblong pit. A number of students sat, or moved through taking breaks between classes, some of them studying or eating. Music from some speaker eddied up from this subbasement break room. Taking the stairs, I moved up two levels to find myself on Level 3. As I moved along the hallway, classes were filling up. Doors were being shut. I glanced at my watch, thinking it couldn't be that late. It was now five minutes before the hour. Five minutes and I hadn't even found the east wing yet.

Panic setting in, I rounded the end of the hallway, and found myself in the Arts Building. Wonderful. Where was the Arts Building on my map? Unfolding my map I studied it. Everything looked confusing on the map. I turned it around and around, trying to find the Arts Building. It was at the end of a wing and in its own square building called "Fine Arts Building". Finally looking up and locating another one of those signs I hissed.

SOUTH WING.

Great. If only I'd taken art next, I'd be fine. But that wasn't until this afternoon. I'd decided to take an art class as an elective.

Moving along, I came to a juncture and found the bathrooms. Convenient. But where was I? I referred to the map once again. At this rate I might make it to my next class by Christmas.

Screams burst from down the hallway ahead of me. I looked up to see three girls running toward me, screaming something inaudible because their voices overlapped. They flew down the hall in my direction like the Devil himself were chasing them, long hair flying behind them. I saw nothing at all in the hallway that would invoke such behavior.

Maybe they were late for class, like me.

Their loud screams made me cover my ears as they fast approached me.

"Clown! Evil Clown!"

What the hell? I didn't get a chance to ask them directions.

Did they say "clown"? Or was it something else? Surely they weren't screaming about a clown. Here? Unless the theatrical studies were somewhere down here. Fine Arts would include everything from music to theater to art. But why were they frightened?

I moved back toward the juncture again and finally found a small sign showing an arrow pointing to the East Wing. Finally!

Looking down through the glass I spied a nice little outdoor courtyard with trees, small pond with a central water fountain, benches and flowers growing in large pots, and professionally landscaped with tall grasses and wild flowers. Immediately, I thought of having lunch there later on. If I could find it again.

I heard a very solid door shut and paused to listen. Clown or not, I needed to get to class. The sound wasn't from a wooden door, it was more like a solid one made of either glass or metal. In pausing to take in the sound, I tried to figure out what it meant in relationship to what those girls were so frightened about. In today's world, one never knew when someone might be wielding a gun or machete.

Below where I stood, down in the little courtyard, movement pulled my gaze. A man strode to the bench near the pond. He paused and pulled something off his head. It looked like a sort of wig of wildly curly hair—not unlike what a clown wears—in a rainbow of colors. I made out a mask with clown white and a red bulbous nose. He stuffed it into a backpack. The man looked around as though making sure he had not been seen. But he had been. By me.

That's when he looked up. Startled I stepped back from the window, but I wasn't about to run. If he had just scared a bunch of girls with a clown mask, I wasn't going to let him intimidate me. I fully expected him to run. He was the one up to no good, not me.

He didn't run. Standing straight, he stretched out his arm and pointed right at me, then pointed two fingers to his own eyes and repeated the pointing fingers at me. Message received. I was dead meat.

I stared down at him. I was not going to become a victim. I wasn't going to run. Unless he had the afore mentioned gun or machete, of course.

He collected his backpack and charged through the trees and bushes and disappeared somewhere beyond the side of the building.

I quickly assessed he had to be at least a sophomore for him to know the building inside and out so well to have found an exit so quickly after scaring a couple of girls. I figured he may have been in one of the empty rooms along this hallway when he appeared to the three girls, jumping out to frighten them. What his point was, I wasn't sure.

Shrugging this off, I continued down the hallway and finally found room 335. Upon entering I noted my math class was already in progress. The woman with graying curls on the very top of her head sent me an icy glare that told me I was in hot water from that point on with her. Her name was Mrs. Ratner. I already had a pet name for her, and assumed I was not the first to give it to her.

Chapter 2

By eleven my stomach was turning inside out. I'd forgotten to bring some sort of snack, and I only had enough money to buy myself lunch today.

Texts from both Brett Rutherford and Nadine Shaw said they'd meet me at lunch around eleven. I found that all the rest of my morning classes were in the East Wing—which made my life easier. And I knew that my last class of the day was in the Art Building. Assuming I could find it again.

The cafeteria was down the hall from the commons, which I'd had a bird's-eye view of earlier. The cafeteria was buffet style, thankfully. I could choose from whatever I wanted and pay at one of two cashiers. Spaghetti was always my favorite, but not without meat, and this stuff looked and smelled generic with too much garlic. I went with roast chicken and mashed potatoes with gravy. I was starving after four hours. The green beans had once been green, but not since they'd clung to a vine. Chocolate pudding with whipping cream on top would lift my spirits and keep me going the rest of the day.

I text messaged Brett where I was so he could join me while I found a table next to a brick wall and no sooner sat down than heard Brett saying from three feet away, "Hey, Lainey. There you are. Been looking for you." He put his tray down and sat across from me.

"Me? I've been lost most of the morning," I said and made a half-hearted chuckle.

"You have a map app, don't you?"

"Yes. It's confusing. But I found my classes. Nearly all of them are in the East Wing. But my writing class is all the way in the West Wing. It takes a half hour to get from there to my math class. And she's a bitch, by the way." I shoved some food into my mouth and looked up at his reaction. "What?"

"Wow. Rant much," he said, placing his tray of lasagna opposite me.

"Sorry. I'm starving. I'm bitchy when I'm overly hungry."

"Good to know. By all means eat something," he said motioning to my plate, and tucked into his own food.

"Where'd you find the lasagna?" I asked, miffed.

"You gotta know your way around. Plus have friends deep in the system." He was joking, of course. Maybe.

"Apparently." I grabbed my chicken drumstick and snarfed it down in four bites. Holy cow I was hungry. I vowed I wouldn't utter another word until I had half my plate gone.

"Who did you say you had math class with?" Brett asked.

Chewing, I wiped my mouth with a brown napkin and said, "Ratner."

"Old Rat Face?" He chuckled.

I snorted and nearly choked. "I knew I wasn't the first to give her that nick-name."

He chuckled. "No. There are others, of course, but not ones I should say in front of a lady."

"Oh, thank you sir," I effected a British accent. We had been dating for about three weeks and had been slowly learning our likes and dislikes. So far our likes matched, and we were still working on our dislikes. Agreeing on which teachers we hated was one subject we warmed up to and began comparing notes from the past to now.

"Oh my god! Did you guys hear about the clown?" the excited voice belonged to Nadine who rushed up to our table and dropped her tray like a bomb. I noticed she had lasagna as well, plus a milkshake. Where on earth did you get a milkshake in this place?

"What clown?" Brett said. "Go ahead and sit down, please." His sarcasm was lost on Nadine who'd already plopped her tiny bottom into the seat next to me.

I screwed my face up, determined to hear what she had heard about it, and didn't interrupt.

"It's all over school! Evil Clown Face—he's been on the school site and Facebook spewing all sorts of nasty threats. Mostly to teachers and to girls."

"For real?" Brett said, shaking his shaggy hair out of his eyes.

"No one knows who he is," she went on, shoving a forkful of cheesy layers of lasagna into her mouth, chewed, swallowed and then sucked on the straw embedded in her chocolate milkshake. Somehow she would be able to eat and talk at the same time. I had no idea how she accomplished this, but it wouldn't surprise me if she could crochet at the same time as well.

"But if he was on the school site, he surely has an identity," Brett pointed out.

"Of course he does!" Nadine said. "They'll find him if he used his own identity. But he could have hacked someone else's identity, too."

"True."

"I've seen him," I stated. Elbow on table, looking out into the crowd, only now wondering if this guy would show his face anywhere in the school now. Or was he a total chicken after knowing he had been spotted?

Becoming quiet, Brett and Nadine fixed their stares on me.

"What?"

"You didn't!"

"I did," I said.

"You didn't say anything to me," Brett complained.

"I was eating. Besides, I'd forgotten. It was early when I saw him."

"So, you saw the clown?" Nadine wanted clarification.

"No. I saw the guy, putting away his mask. I saw his face."

"No. Way." Nadine slurped on her shake. "When?"

"Right after he scared three girls. They ran one way, he went out a door and down into the courtyard. That's where I saw him."

"Would you know him if you saw him again?" Brett asked.

"I could pick him out of a line up," I said, smiling.

"How did you know he was the clown?"

I launched into the story of what had transpired hours ago while trying to find the East Wing. My story left Nadine speechless—a remarkable feat in itself. But she was first to pull out her phone and begin tapping out something. I grabbed her hand to stop her.

"Wait. What are you saying. And to whom?" I asked.

"Just putting it on my site that the clown's been ID'd by you."

"No. Don't even say that."

"She's right," Brett said. "That could get the guy mad. Retribution would be his next step after learning who Lainey—or even you—are, and where you live."

"Crap. You're right. What was I thinking?" She bit her lower lip looking at her smart phone. "I'll erase it. Oops."

"What?"

She grimaced, teeth gritted as she hissed. "Oh, shit."

"What did you do?" Alarm went through me.

"I somehow, by mistake, hit send."

"Freudian slip," Brett sat back, eyes shifting from her to me. "Are you on site?"

"Uh, I don't know." I wasn't one to waste my time on such things. My life was full enough and I didn't need to go to the social network, or play games on-line, like Pokémon—the latest fad. Please. What a waste. I'd rather take a walk in the woods and bird watch.

Nadine was looking at her phone. "Wait. Yes. You're here, but you haven't announced yourself to the school's home site. None of your personal information is in here. And no picture." She smiled brightly. "You're good."

"That's good, isn't it?" I said, looking at Brett.

"Let me check." Brett was using his phone to check it out.

"Can anyone see who she is?" Nadine asked. "I mean not just friends, but anyone?"

Embarrassed, I didn't look because I hadn't figured out how to find such sites as yet on my new phone. The computer was terrifying enough. I'd often had things just blip out of existence on a computer. This new phone had me all a dither, worried I'd post something I really didn't want to post.

"Oh, wait. I see." He looked up. "Only your name's there but there's no picture, no description or anything."

"Good. I'll fly under the radar." At least for a while.

"But this is seriously creepy," Nadine said, showing her phone's screen to Brett. "See?"

"Demented, this one is," Brett said. "You're sure that was him?" He looked across to me.

"I saw him shoving a mask of some sort with crazy-colored hair into his backpack. If he wasn't doing anything wrong, why was he hiding in the courtyard looking around like someone might see what he was doing?"

"And you said he saw you," Nadine reminded.

"Yes."

"He might be looking for you." Brett looked concerned. I didn't need them to tell me this.

Shrugging, I took up a spoon and began diving into my pudding as if I couldn't care less.

"Says here he terrorized some girls in the East Wing," Nadine said, looking up at me.

"That's when I saw him," I said. "What I mean to say is that I saw him afterwards. He'd already gone outside, down some steps into the courtyard. I've a feeling he knows this building inside and out."

"You mean like he's not a first year student?" Nadine said.

"Yes. He's probably a sophomore."

"That would be easy to check." Nadine had a determined look on her face. "You did say you saw his face?"

"Yes." She smiled, and looked like she had a plan.

"What classes do you have left today?" Brett asked me into the pause.

"Just an art class at one."

"Do you have time after?" he asked.

"I do."

"When?"

"Two -thirty."

He turned to Nadine. "How's your schedule look?"

"I'm booked through four o'clock."

"You sure took a lot of hours," I said.

"Tell me about it. I think I'll have to drop one or two. I only have the weekend off."

"You'll burn out," I warned. She made a fist and lightly pounded herself on the forehead. "I know. I know. If it wasn't for my dad paying for tuition, I wouldn't even be going to school this year. It was like I became crazy with power."

I smiled while eating my pudding. It was just the right consistency, thick as cheese cake.

"You still have that history class on Tuesday and Thursday nights?" she asked me.

"Ugh. Don't remind me." I swirled my chocolate and whipped cream into an ugly mess.

"You have night class?" Brett asked, surprised.

"Unfortunately." I rolled my eyes. "I couldn't fit it in anywhere else."

"When's your music class?" he asked me.

"Piano," I corrected. "On Tuesday and Thursday, nine AM. You'll have to show me where the music section is in the Arts Building." I pulled out my map and unfolded it.

"Wait. What's that?" He pointed.

"My map of the building. I got it in the mail."

He made a hissing sound. "No. Bring up your app."

"What app?" I blinked up at him.

"Your map app." I stared at him blankly. "You don't have the map app?"

I shook my head. I was a total idiot with my new phone.

"Hand it over. I'll get it up for you." Brett held out his hand to me. I put my phone into his hand and he worked on putting up the map for campus and showed me how to use it. I was wary of this. I've lost such things before, and it wouldn't be the first time I messed up something on my phone as well.

After lunch we all had to part ways. Nadine was taking drama class. I didn't know she was into drama, but her brother was. Maybe he talked her into it. When I had chosen my classes, my aunt told me this was the opportunity for me to "find myself". I actually liked that idea. Finding myself—or whatever interested me. Music and art had always been something I wanted to dabble in. I had been told when young that I was a talented artist. My interest in writing had come when I took the creative writing class in my senior year of high school. The need to explore everything made me feel like a spinning top, but I could only take so many hours. I had decided to see where my interests lie by dabbling in a few things in my first year.

I looked at the map on my phone and experimented with moving the map around. "Oh, there it is. And there's my art class." I looked up. "Speaking of which, I've gotta go get my art supplies out in my car."

"Now?" He checked the time. "You've still got a half an hour."

"Oh. Yeah. I keep forgetting I get a whole hour off for lunch, now.

"Let's go to the commons," he suggested.

We found our way back to the commons. It was similar to, but ten times larger and a hundred times better than my high school cafeteria. I'd heard people refer to it as "the pit" because that's what it was. It was lower than the main floor, about ten cement steps down on either end. People gathered in groups around the many tables. Some were round, some square but all were the dark brown fake-wood laminated tops. Lined up all along the wall were a variety of vending machines. I found I still had some money on me and bought a candy bar from one machine while looking down at my phone. Meanwhile Brett joined a large group of people around two tables shoved end-to-end.

"That clown was terrifying," a woman's voice turned me around to two women behind me. I faced someone from my past.

"Brianna Bryde?" I sputtered. We both made the little screams of realization and delight, and threw our arms around one another for a hug.

"I have not seen you since I lived in DeWitt," I said, drawing back to look at her. She was what you would call beautiful. Her dark hair was more styled now than I remembered, and I remembered the large mole on her neck. It made me think of my writing class in how to make a character stand out in the memory of your reader.

"I thought that was you, Lainey!" she said. We both laughed.

"Are you going to school here too?" I asked.

"Yeah. I also work here. In the Bursar's Office."

"Oh, really? Congrats!"

"Just part time." She shrugged it off.

"But it's a good job, right?"

She made a delicate snort. "You wouldn't believe how office people are. Some of them are absolute sharks. But I don't mind Mrs. Taylor. She's nice to me."

"Mrs. Taylor? She must be married to my creative writing teacher," I said, wondering what she looked like.

"Might be. They have the same last name. What's he look like?"

"Tall. Handsome. Probably thirty-something," I said.

She nodded. "Yep. I've seen them together. They make a cute couple." We chuckled.

She grasped my arm and said, "Lainey, I'm sorry about your parents. I wanted to come to the funeral," she said. "But I had something come up I had to go to. Sorry."

"No problem." I looked away. The mention of my parent's accidental death always put a downer into my day. I was getting better at riding over my emotions after two years, but it was still difficult when someone out of my past said something to me.

"But wow! How crazy to run into you like this here," she said, brightening.

"What did you say a moment ago about the clown?" I had to confirm something.

"Oh. Wasn't that you in the hallway?" she asked.

"And I take it that was you running past me like a ghost was chasing you, along with two other girls?"

"Yes!" She chuckled lightly. "This guy in a clown mask popped out of nowhere and scared the poo out of us. Didn't you see him?"

"I did. A guy with a mask playing a stupid joke," I said unimpressed.

"You haven't seen what he's been posting on-line?"

I shook my head. "I've heard."

She looked down at her phone. "I can't seem to stop looking at it." She looked up and said, "He's been threatening specific teachers as well as students as a whole. This was the first time anyone saw him. I tried to get a video, but I just couldn't work the buttons fast enough. I just wanted to get the hell away from him."

"I saw him," I said. "I mean without his mask."

Her eyes popped. "Really? What did you do?"

"I watched him take off his mask."

Her blue eyes still huge, her perfect mouth became unhinged. "You didn't!"

"He went outside, right afterwards. I watched unnoticed from above. I know what he looks like." I didn't get a chance to say he'd seen me, too.

"You should go to someone in the main office and tell them!"

I put up my hands. "If things get out of hand, then I will. So far he's just made threats and scared a few people." I still didn't know *who* he was.

"Well, I should go, my break is almost up. My schedule is brutal. I'm here all day, have classes in between work." She stepped away. "Nice to see you, Lainey."

"Yeah. Nice to bump into you again, Brianna, we should get together!" I called after her.

"Hey, that would be great!" She was in a hurry and so I let her go. Checking the clock on the wall I now had twenty-three minutes before my art class, and it lasted a total of an hour and a half. I would have to go outside to get my art bin and sketch pad. I wondered what we'd do in art on the first day.

Someone said my name and I twirled to find Brett at a table with Moon and a few other people, two of the guys towered over everyone. Brett motioned to me and I stepped over.

"Lainey," Moon said as I strolled up and Brett put an arm around me. "So, how are you liking college life?" Moon's hair style had changed drastically since I'd last seen him. Shaved on the right side, the longer left side was died black and about four inches long. He constantly had to shake it back, or left it hanging over his left eye. The real color of his hair was more like his sister, Nadine's, a mousy brown. He also had added black plastic rimmed glasses. I wasn't sure if he actually needed glasses, but it was stylin'.

"Well, give me a week to decide. I haven't even finished up one day, yet," I said on a chuckle.

"By then you'll hate it and will have become as cynical as the rest of us," he said.

I laughed. "We'll see." I looked up at Brett.

"You know where your art class is?" he asked.

I'd bitten into my candy bar and could only nod as I chewed.

"No, you dumb shit. That's *not* a banana spider. That's a Wandering Brazilian Spider. A full grown can wrap it's legs around your head. It's bite can kill you in two hours!" Someone's voice made me turn around to find it was the large hairy guy who had been in my creative writing class. He was with a slightly shorter, thinner guy, but anyone would look short compared to him.

Brett and Moon turned to the two. "Ellwood! Ham!" Moon greeted the tall, thin guy and went through some sort of weird hand bumping and hand slapping with him. The large hairy guy wore a Stephan King T-shirt with all the titles of his books. Obviously a fan.

"This is Ellwood," Moon said, motioning to the largest guy. "You have him walk anywhere beside you and no one will bother you." He leaned over and in a lowered voice said, "I sometimes slip him money just so that happens."

"Oh, good to know," I said, smiling as the others chuckled. I could definitely see why and wondered if he wasn't serious. Ellwood had to stand six-six, was as wide as a redwood, and the fold in the middle of his brows made him look like an ogre.

Ellwood looked over at me and pointed. "Oh, wait. You're in my creative writing class. Wait. I thought you were a freshman."

"I am," I admitted shyly.

"Only sophomores can take creative writing. How did you get in?"

"My English teacher wrote a letter to Mr. Tyler." Warmth in my face told me I must have been turning a bright shade of pink.

Ellwood smiled. "Aw, she still blushes!"

21

"Nickel for your thoughts," Ham said.

Ellwood turned on him and said, "Being a dick won't make yours any bigger."

Ham made a fluttering hand gesture. "What-*ever*." Then stepped away.

"Good that we understand each other, motherfucker!" he yelled at Ham. I had been under the wrong impression they were friends. Ellwood turned to me. "Don't mind me. I don't go crazy. I *am* crazy. I just go normal from time to time." He laughed and a few others around the table chuckled possibly to avoid the same sort of verbal abuse.

I was finding that the color was gradually going out of my face. In fact it was probably going white with shock. I hadn't been around guys like this before. In fact, I did my best to avoid them. The rough language was something I would have to get used to here. I wasn't in high school any more where teachers monitored us.

"But let me warn you, Mr. Taylor is tough," Ellwood said to me.

"I'm sure he is," I said. "But he's easier to look at than Ratner."

Everyone chuckled at that. Chalk one up for me. I knew if I wasn't accepted into this rough crowd I'd become the target. I'd seen it many a times in high school. Girls who are teased mercilessly by guys like Ellwood, who, for whatever the reason, chose to pick on them.

"Oh, yeah. The last time I saw something like her, I flushed it down the toilet!" The others agreed with hilarious laughter. I stepped away, having had enough of this crowd. I noticed Moon and the one who'd taken Ellwood's insult, Ham, both now sat at a separate table.

"I hope they don't decide to do *Romeo and Juliet* again," he said to Moon.

Moon rolled his eyes. "God, give me strength!"

"Hi, Moon. I don't believe I know your friend," I said, my glance going to the taller guy with the red bow tie.

"Brad Hamilton," he said. I thought his white button shirt and red bow tie was a bit of an oddity, but maybe he wanted to look as nerdy as possible. "Everyone calls me Ham."

"Nice to meet you, Ham." I shook his hand, since he'd extended it. His hand was cool and the handshake was weak.

"Oh, by the by, Lainey, Nadine told me you saw the clown," Moon said.

I wished he hadn't said that so loud. Several people from nearby table looked over at us.

"The clown?" Ham burst. "You're kidding me! I heard he chased a bunch of girls earlier."

"I was there—"

"Really? Did you scream and run?" Ellwood had turned around, his voice challenging. He chuckled demoniacally, throwing his head back.

I met his eyes. "No. I actually watched him run in the opposite direction and take off his stupid mask. I know his identity."

"No shit?" Ellwood looked impressed.

"Uh, guys, let's hold it down a bit, okay?" Brett's caution brought the other's voices back to a lower key.

"You mean you know who he is?"

"No. I don't know *who* he is. I only know what he looks like. If I get a picture of him, I'll be able to match his face with a name."

"That should be easy enough. I've got a Whitney graduation book from last year at home," Moon said.

"That would work," I said. "How do I get it from you?"

Moon thought on it for a beat. "I think Nadine has a night class. So, I can't give it to her."

"Are you working tonight?" I asked.

"Yeah. From five till closing."

"Perfect. Maybe I can meet you at The Huddle?" I looked up at Brett hopefully.

"I've gotta work," Brett said. I made a disappointed sigh. He worked at Pizza Wheel.

"Bring the book to work with you, I'll come by and pick it up," I suggested.

"Why are you thinking he'll be in last year's graduating book?" Ellwood asked.

"Because he knew his way around really well. Not like someone who's never been here. This place has a lot of hallways. He knew exactly where to scare the girls and then went out an exit door, down into a courtyard below to escape being seen when he took off the mask."

Moon smiled up at Ellwood who's brows had disappeared underneath his unruly dark hair. "Lainey here is our resident Sherlock Holmes," he said proudly.

"Really?" Ellwood wasn't convinced.

"She solved two murders just this past summer," Brett added with a beaming smile.

Embarrassed, I let my gaze drop. "I had help."

"Sure, but if it weren't for your bringing everyone to the scene of the crime, we wouldn't have found out who really killed Arline," Moon said. "Wish I'd been there." Looking wistfully, he shook his head. "I heard you got Comb to confess all."

"It sort of was a given, since she had Arline's phone and her jewelry right there in her car and was wearing her gold bracelet. But both Lisa and Bridget killed her," I said, feeling the heat of stares from Ellwood and Ham.

"Too bad about Wendy being somewhat homicidal, though."

"That's a bit mean," I said. "She has schizophrenia, and now she's being treated."

"Wait. This schizoid killed someone?" Ellwood said, his interest obviously heightened.

"No. She stabbed her in the back. Just once. It was the other two girls who took turns stabbing her repeatedly, and then robbed her." Moon rattled off. *Thank you Moon.*

"Jesus. How didn't I hear about this?" Ellwood wondered.

"You were working on your book," Ham said. "It was hard to pull you away to get you to even watch the Cubs win the pennant."

"Not into sports, dude," Ellwood said without looking down at him.

"God, this is depressing. I need to go and get my things for my next class, anyway." I turned to Brett. "Walk me out to my car, and then walk me at least halfway to the art class so I don't get lost, please?"

The fact that our menacing clown lurking about had me a bit nervous, since I not only saw him, but he saw me, wasn't lost on Brett. Arm around me, he headed me out to the parking lot. Whitney College stood in the middle of countryside, with farms on two sides, a main road that went east and west, and one that cut north and south. It was the only large building four miles from the nearest town, thus, no one had any business parking here unless they had classes or worked here. The parking lot was conveniently close to all exits, and wrapped around the large building on three sides. The first row we walked through had reserved signs posted for those I presumed worked here. Yep. I found the president's spot was closest to the door, naturally. The vice president's was next to his, and on either side were the reserved signs. My car was parked three rows back.

"Are you really going to try and identify him?" Brett asked while I grabbed my art box and sketch pad out of the back of my car.

Straightening, I said, "Why? Shouldn't I?"

"Maybe you should hold off on it. I mean, he hasn't really done anything bad, yet."

"No. But, what if he does?" I said. "I don't need to remind you of the numerous shootings on campuses all over the country, do I?"

His head leaned to the side with agreement.

25

"What's he been saying on social media?"

"He's threatened teachers."

"Just teachers in general? Or were there specific ones?"

"A couple. One was Ratner, and the other was Taylor," he said.

I squinted at him. "Mr. Taylor? That's my creative writing teacher."

"Yeah. Well, the names are out there."

"I think someone has to know who this creep is before he does something horrible," I said, shutting my car door and pressing the auto-lock button on my key fob.

Brett's silence either meant he agreed or didn't agree with me. I hadn't been able to read him yet, after these few weeks of either talking to him on the phone, or going out for something to eat, or just hanging out.

We went back inside, and took the cement stairs up to second floor. "This is it," he said pointing. "From here on is the Art Wing. Didn't you say you had a night class?"

"On Tuesday. History—Western Civilization. I get two credits for it." I sighed. "I don't relish the idea of coming out here at night."

"I don't either," he said. "Anyone you know have night class that night too?"

"No." But I didn't know if there was anyone I knew from my high school who might be. I hoped there was.

"What time are you done with classes today?" Brett asked. Had he already forgotten?

"At two-thirty. This is my last class of the day."

"I'll try and meet you back at your car, okay?"

"Sure." I smiled up at him. "What class do you have?"

"Business management."

"Oh, I had no idea you wanted to get into management," I said, teasing him a little bit.

"Well, you know, I can't lean too much on my band and music to take me anywhere."

"That's what I like about you. You're practical." We passed a series of shut doors.

His arm slid around my shoulders. "We're just two practical people."

We turned down a corridor and heard some sort of flute music.

"Sounds almost ethereal," I said as we pulled up to an open door.

"Sounds like Native American flute," Brett said.

Peering inside, we saw a guy sitting cross-legged on top of a desk. His black hair was in a long braid, a red bandanna tied around his head. At first I was transfixed on the spot, wondering why the man seemed familiar. I knew him, and had to remember from where I knew him. Then, when he stopped and looked up at us, it hit me who it was.

"Sorry to interrupt," Brett said.

"Nate?" I said, taking a step inside the room. "Nate Blackstone?"

"Lainey?" Nate Blackstone hopped off the desk and strode forward.

"Yes."

"You know each other?" Brett said.

"Yes. I met him over the summer." Well, that didn't sound good. "You remember? He was there at the park, you know when we did that reconstruction? Him and Lassiter?"

"Oh. Right. Right," he said thrusting a hand out to Nate and they shook hands briefly.

"I didn't know you played flute," I said, admiring the unusual instrument. It was about as thick as an oboe but not as long. It had an eagle feather attached to it by a leather thong.

"Yeah, man. That was great," Brett said, being admiring of another musician.

"Thanks." Nate held up the thick wooden flute. I must admit I'd never seen anything like it. "This was my grandfather's. I'm trying to learn to play it." He shook his head. "Can't seem to find the right time or place to do it."

"Are you taking music classes here?" I asked.

"No. Not music." He smiled. "They don't teach Native American flute here, I'm afraid. But I am taking automotive mechanics here, along with a few other courses."

"That's good," I said.

"Listen, we didn't mean to interrupt you, man," Brett said, a possessive arm around my shoulders.

"That's alright. I've gotta go to my next class, anyway." We all moved out into the hall working to part company, him going one way and us going another.

"Nice seeing you, again," I said, raising my hand in a wave.

"Same here," he said and strode off down the hallway.

Once he was gone we continued our way around a corner and finally came to the art rooms.

"Well, this is where I will leave you," Brett said. We kissed and he was gone.

I opened the door and stepped into a large room with large heavy tables big enough to spread all your art crap on, arranged in a circle. About a half dozen students had already claimed their tables, so I found a vacant one. I wasn't sure if the teacher was in, or not. There wasn't a desk where a teacher would sit. A door that may have been used as an office was situated in the far wall, beyond some easels and clutter.

I spotted a dark haired woman in faded jeans and frilly top moved around the room. Possibly in her forties, she reminded me of my Aunt Jessica a little bit. Her long, brown hair was braided down her back. She had an earthy look to her, as did my aunt Jessica.

"Go ahead and take out your drawing pencils and sketch pads," she said. "Today we'll be considering shading."

That was a good thing to consider for an hour and a half.

Chapter 3

"So, how was your first day at college, Lainey?" Uncle John asked.

"I guess it was alright," I said while sitting at the table eating dinner with my Aunt Jessica and her new husband. I'd lived with my aunt after my parents had drowned in the flood in Colorado, two years ago. Now John Weeks, the sheriff of Montclair, was my new uncle.

Weeks looked at me a little put off by my teenage detachment. I wasn't sure why I didn't want to share my day. I was exhausted when I got home that afternoon and had tried to begin reading one of the three chapters assigned by three different teachers, only to fall asleep on my bed for nearly an hour. Poe, our cat, had decided to nap with me, and when he woke and stretched, pressing his front paws against my face, I came to as though I'd been in a coma.

"Okay, Poe. Go on." I'd encouraged him off my bed, and opened the door to let him out into the hallway. And in cat fashion, quickly skittered down the stairs for whatever his destination—most likely a food bowl.

I'd forgotten how a long day at school affected me. And college was a longer day than high school by a long shot. I still had one night class to get through two nights a week, yet. Gag me!

"Is it me, or does it seem like you and I are the only ones sitting at this table who want to carry on a conversation, Jessica?" Weeks said, looking first at my aunt and then at me.

"She's tired." My aunt shrugged, fork lifted to her mouth. His gaze drifting to me.

"The spaghetti is really good, Aunt Jessica," I said trying for a cheerful, yet aloof tone. It was definitely one hundred times better than what they served at the college cafeteria.

"Thank you, dear," she said.

"Have much homework?" Weeks asked.

"Gobs. Already have a test on Wednesday," I said through a yawn.

Weeks laughed. "No rest for the wicked."

I glanced up at him without moving my head. I must have had a startled look on my face because he said, "What?"

I shook my head. "You reminded me of something."

"Well?" he said when I didn't continue.

I swallowed. "I have to go to The Huddle tonight."

"Why's that?" my aunt asked.

"Uh." I put a mouthful of spaghetti into my mouth to stall for an answer, which wasn't coming to my lips for some reason. Finally I knew what to say after I'd swallowed and drank some milk. "A bunch of my friends are going there to study." In reality, only Moon would be there. Brett had to work, and Nadine had her night class. If there wasn't the promise of finding out who Evil Clown Guy was, I wouldn't even venture out. I didn't plan on staying long.

"I thought that's what the library was for," Weeks said with a knowing grin. My aunt sent him a warning look.

I wiped my mouth, then chugged down my milk. "Do you need help with dishes?" I asked my aunt.

She looked up. "No. You have homework. Go ahead." I was getting all sorts of breaks from my aunt. I had no time to work in the bookstore, except on weekends, and only a few hours then.

Not having to do dishes was a blessing, but I would do them once in a while so I didn't feel like a worthless slug eating and sleeping under the same roof.

"Thanks." I was up and out of my chair, taking my plate, silverware and glass into the kitchen. Looking at the time, I felt six thirty wasn't too early to get to The Huddle. I would look through the school graduation class of last year to see if this guy wasn't in there. It wasn't that I didn't want to share my day, and what happened with my aunt and uncle, but since Weeks was sheriff, he would read too much into the clown business. I just didn't want to get him involved in something that was a silly stunt done by some moron.

The Huddle was a hangout mostly for teens since no alcohol was sold or consumed. On occasions older women came in for fancy coffee and some sinful-looking deserts. The Huddle was also known for certain creative salads and bistro sandwiches made to order for a fancy price. A few times a week local talent would show off their talents, get up and either sing or read poetry. Thankfully they'd gotten rid of the karaoke years ago.

Light Jazz music played on speakers as I walked into the almost theater-dark interior. Tables and booths were made of dark wood. In fact, the booths looked like the bench seats from an old church. Sconces hung over them with small, flickering lights mimicking candlelight.

Moon stood behind a service counter. Sighting me, he waved. I waved back and settled at an empty table. I hoped he hadn't forgotten about bringing the yearbook. The tables were all empty, so I had my choice of seating. Monday was a slow night, apparently. About three or four weeks ago, Brett and his band had played here. I had not seen him for two years, but knew him (we had been in the same class), from my old high school. That was prior to my becoming involved in investigating Arline's murder. I was still convoluted about the outcome of that. On one hand Arline's murderers were behind bars, but waiting on their trial. Wendy, who had been my friend—but more of a BFF to Nadine—was in a mental hospital trying to get better after being found incompetent to stand trial.

Moon swept up to my table cutting off my dreary memory. "What can I get you?"

"Oh, snap. I forgot to bring money," I said. "Sorry. Maybe I should just get the book from you and leave."

Moon looked toward the serving area where the food and drinks were made.

"Nah. It's just me and Justin tonight. Justin's cool. But I'll bring you an ice water."

"You do have the yearbook, don't you?"

"Of course! Water and a side of yearbook, coming right up," he said and slipped away.

In a few moments Moon was back, the yearbook tucked under his arm and a clear glass with ice water, and a straw.

"On the house," he said, wry smile in place.

"Perfect. Thanks. You're probably expecting a tip for this," I said.

"You can owe me." He chuckled and set the yearbook on the table. Opening it, he flipped through the pages. "The freshmen pictures start here." He had the book open to the A's.

"Thanks."

"Take your time." Something in the back pinged. "Oops, the panini is up." He darted back to get the order. I hadn't seen anyone else in the place when I'd entered, but apparently someone else was here. In a few moments, Moon brought the tray out with the panini on the plate and surged to a booth in the back where I couldn't see the patron.

I returned to looking at the photographs, skipping the girls, of course. Page after page, I didn't think I'd come across him, thinking that maybe he hadn't had a picture taken, which would be my luck. I sipped my ice water and kept flipping pages. Finally I came to the S's. And there he was. Shorter hair, wearing a suit looking out at the camera with a slightly self-satisfied smile. Tyler Sinclare was the name printed underneath.

Right at that moment, Moon sidled up and I pointed to the picture. "That's him. That's who I saw today shoving a clown mask into his backpack."

"You sure?"

"Positive."

"Hang on a minute. I'll be back." He went back behind the counter, iPhone in his hand. The other guy who was working with him, Justin, exchanged some words with him. They both laughed, so I had to assume a joke was involved.

Then Moon said in a slight gasp, "Look at this!" They now both looked at his phone. Justin nodded and said something again—sounded like a swear word. I couldn't hear over the piped-in music. After a moment, Moon and Justin walked out from behind the serving counter. Moon's attention still on his phone. Justin was heavy-set, medium height, brown hair cropped short, wearing an apron. He had an amicable face.

"Justin remembers him," Moon said as they came up to my table.

"Yeah. Sinclair was kicked out of school for cheating on his finals," Justin said.

"Really?" I said.

"Oh-h, yeah. It was a big scandal," Justin said with a big head nod, which made his whole body move. "Then, about mid-summer this clown guy shows up. Show her," he said to Moon. Moon placed his smart phone down and I saw the post on social media.

"See? He even has an evil clown emoji," Moon said.

I looked at the post and the picture was a clown with sharp teeth. "Cute," I said sarcastically as my lips drew back with disgust. The post said, "*I will kill everyone who is responsible*".

"He might be serious," I said. "Do you have Tyler Sinclair's page?"

"No. It was taken down right after they banned him from the school," Justin said.

"I can certainly see why."

"Are you going to tell someone in the office about this?" Moon asked.

"You think I should?"

Moon and Justin exchanged looks.

"I think you definitely should. Yesterday he posted that." Justin pointed at the post about killing those responsible on a social media page. I was surprised it hadn't been blocked or something.

"He seems to be serious," I said. "But why come into the school and scare a couple of girls? What does that prove?"

"Just to show that he can get into the school at any hour. Who can stop him?" Moon said. "The school is open campus, and it's all one building."

"True." I thought for a moment. "You don't think I should tell my Uncle John, do you?" Moon looked confused. "Sheriff Weeks," I added. "He married my aunt?"

"Oh. Right. Well, that's totally up to you, but you should definitely tell someone at the school tomorrow."

"Who should I go to?"

"Dr. Cooper Smith is the president. Maybe you should try and see him. If not him, anyone in the office. Just tell someone in the main office. They'll listen to you. They're pretty nice," Justin said. Then looking at Moon added, "My schedule was so screwed up, I didn't think they'd help me fix it. I had classes over-lapping. It took two of them an hour to work on it, and got it straightened out."

Moon chuckled. "That'll teach you to try and take Spanish and Latin in the same hour, dummy."

"That wasn't my fault," he defended. "It was the effing computer."

I got up, holding up Moon's yearbook. "Okay if I take this with me? I'll need it to identify him to the women in the office."

"Sure."

"I'll try and find time tomorrow, and give it to your sister when I'm finished." I said, thinking of my own schedule, wondering when would I have time.

I drove home, still in a quandary as to whether or not this merited Weeks' involvement, what with the new information about his threats. Probably not yet. He could do nothing about a guy in a clown mask terrorizing girls in a hallway. After all, it was questionable as to whether it was Sinclair who was posting the latest threats on-line. It would take the police to hack in and find out, but if Sinclair had done his own hacking, and used someone else's account, could they find out who it was? I didn't think so. The guy would have to be caught red handed. My only hope was that his death threats would not be carried through, if the Evil Clown guy was Sinclair.

* * *

"You didn't study very long," Weeks said as I strode into the house.

I twirled to find him seated in the living room with the TV on low volume. It was weird having the sheriff in the house, never leaving to go to his own home, after visiting my aunt. He now lived here. His things were here. Mainly his clothes and a few pieces of furniture, including the large screen TV and the cabinet it came in, now taking up space along one wall. But the other totally weird thing was him following my Aunt Jessica up to bed. Don't get me wrong. I liked him, trusted him with my life, and I knew they loved each other, etc., but it was going to take a while before I could get used to him being part of the household, and related to me by marriage.

And his questioning me at every turn, like tonight.

"Oh, ah, I forgot my books," I said, making a goofy face to sell it. I wasn't sure if he bought it. Being a cop he could probably sense my ruse. In fact I had no doubt he could read my lie a mile away.

"So I gather," he said evenly. His keen blue cop eyes settled on the yearbook I had in my hand. "And yet you've brought one back with you." He sounded more suspicious than curious. I had to make up my mind right at that very second whether or not I was going to share this Sinclare business with him.

"I'm working on something and had to borrow this." I said, hiding the book's cover and swiftly marched to the stairs.

He didn't stop me, or challenge me further, and I made it all the way to my room at the top of the stairs where I closed the door softly. Somehow I felt so sneaky about all this. I sat on my bed and opened the yearbook again to the page with Sinclair's picture on it and pondered my not telling Weeks about this. I worried I was wrong not to. I hate second guessing myself. Was I certain this was the guy? Yes. Was this the guy who had threatened people—teachers and students alike—on social media? The jury was out on that one. But Moon's friend, Justin, had the story, or the motive, behind his traipsing around wearing a clown mask, assuming the emoji of "evil clown" and threatening people at Whitney College on social media.

I made up my mind, before hitting the books, that I would wait and speak to someone in the office of the president at Whitney. If they knew who was behind the threats all along, then it would only be a waste of maybe five or so minutes. If they didn't, they would know through me tomorrow, and maybe they could head off any problems or foil his threats by informing the police about it. I just hoped I wasn't too late in telling them, and Sinclair decided to do something really stupid beforehand.

Like go through with those threats.

* * *

I studied until eleven-thirty-six, and was the only one up, burning the proverbial midnight oil, working to stay quiet in my room by studying in bed with all my books spread out around me. My room was at the top of the stairs, and my aunt's and uncle's room was at the end of the hallway with a bath in between. Yawns began while reading in my psychology book, the chapter on "Morality and the Brain". Good reading if one wanted to become comatose. When the words began to blur because my yawning induced tears, I was unable to continue, and closed the book. I rolled out of bed, stood and stretched. My back ached. Would this be my life for the next eight weeks?

I changed out of my sweats into my nightgown—not even sure why I bothered changing out of my street clothes. Something bumped outside the hall. I heard my aunt's small voice whisper something, and Weeks' deeper voice reply in a hoarse whisper. He was out in the hallway, near the stairs.

Swiftly, I went to my door and opened it up. Weeks was fully dressed in his uniform.

"What's going on?" I asked, thinking some crises had come up and he had to go into work. My mind automatically conjured Sinclair's threats.

At the top of the stairs, Weeks turned to me, hand on the newel, he twisted his upper body. "Two of my men came down with the flu. I've gotta go in."

"Oh. Alright. 'Night," I said.

My aunt floated out of the dark toward me. She had a blue nightie on under a bathrobe she now just tied at her narrow waist. "You're still up, Lainey?"

"Yeah, but I was just going to bed, then I heard your voices and the creak of stairs," I said as she came up and put an arm around me.

"Will you be up early again tomorrow?" she asked.

"Yes. I've got another early class. I don't know what I did to deserve this," I said. She laughed and then kissed me on the cheek.

"Then, you'd better get to bed," she said.

"I'm heading there now," I said on a yawn.

Lights in both our bedrooms went off two minutes later almost simultaneously. I peeked out my window to watch Weeks' vehicle back out of the drive and rolled quietly down the deserted street. The street light silently keeping watch over our quiet neighborhood. My eyes scanned the perimeters, knowing clowns might be lurking in the shadows, but I was too tired to care.

Chapter 4

I'd over-slept. Of course, talking to Brett until two a.m. had not helped. He had gotten off early (because of lack of anyone ordering pizza) and had called me, so we recycled the events of the day, including my finding Sinclair's picture. Seven a.m. came way too soon and my alarm clock was the enemy and I wanted to throw it through the window.

Note to self: no more talking on the phone in the wee hours to boyfriend on school nights.

My aunt sipped coffee at the table in her blue robe.

"Good morning."

"Mornin'," I slurred, trudging through the kitchen, backpack feeling like a load of bricks, over one shoulder. I located my keys on a peg.

"No breakfast?" she said.

"No time."

"There's toast," she said. I grabbed a buttered corner of toast and jogged out the door. I hopped in my car and turned the key and at first it sounded like it wanted to roll over and die. But then the engine finally caught and started, albeit half-heartedly, much like me. My heart throbbed in my throat with dread. What I did not need this morning was car problems.

Note to self: have Weeks look at my car. Later.

The college was fourteen miles away, and if I took I-80, I could make it in ten minutes because I could go 70, instead of the snail-slow 55, plus slowing down for all the little towns in between I'd have to drive through. So, I took the Interstate until I got to Rook Road, and took this road through Cedar Ridge to Whitney College, about a mile beyond that.

At seven-forty-five in the morning, parking was at a premium. I had to park in a back area and trudge up three sets of steps (they were only three risers each), like a Sherpa to the front door. Inside was a sign directing me to the main offices. I figured if they weren't open, I'd try during my nine o'clock break.

I climbed yet more steps, wondering where the hell the elevator was as I breathlessly ascended into a blue carpeted hallway (much better than the slate gray of the classrooms and hallways). I turned, and to my left I found the elevators. Well, shit. Before me stood glass doors to the main offices. I noticed no one inside. I tried the door, and found it locked. On the door the hours were posted as 8AM – 4:30PM Monday – Friday.

I twirled around, stepped up to the elevators stabbed G for ground, and rode it down to what I thought would be the main floor, grumbling to myself out loud, "I should have figured that office hours would not be open this early. Duh."

The elevator doors slid open and I stared down a long dim hallway that looked nothing like where I had started out. In fact it looked nothing like any place I wanted to be. Round recessed lights dotted the ceiling giving the look of subbasement. The smell was possibly locker room mixed with mold. I looked at the elevator panel, hit 1 and tried to get back to where I needed to go. A short ride up had me back to the main floor. I strode out, lugging my fifty pounds of books and necessities. Although I only had morning classes, I'd brought a snack for later (having planned my day more thoroughly than the day before), and more money, just in case.

My first class was Psychology, in the East Wing. At least I knew where that was. I was excited about this class. Learning more about the psychology of the mind would be handy for understanding certain personality disorders, I reasoned, and jumped at taking this class.

Without realizing it, I found myself in the right corridor and in a few steps, I found the correct room, #103. My luck was changing. I went in, found one seat left in the back of the class room, which was made up of eight foot tables with seating for four bodies along one side facing the front. I dug out my psychology book, remembering the wacky cover. It would have cost me $165 new, but my aunt bought it for me used for only $51 through Amazon. Everyone was still situating themselves at their seats, pulling out notebooks and such.

I busily pulled out my new pen and a fresh new notebook, and was ready. The teacher was Mr. Udall, a tidy blond man with glasses who I put at forty-something, the sleeves of his lavender shirt were rolled up three quarters of the way exactly, as though he'd measured it and had creased them with a steam iron. Gray slacks were also creased with precision only a steam iron could achieve. He wore no tie and top button undone. Interesting. I had to admire the fact that the teachers in college could pretty much decide what to wear and how to wear it, without worry of some rigorous conformity.

"Welcome to Psychology 101, my name is Mr. Udall," he pointed to his name on the white board. "I'll pass out the syllabus for the class while you pull out your books and open them to page twenty-one."

While Mr. Udall passed out the syllabus I had already opened the book, and now turned to the first chapter "Why Do We Do the Things We Do?" I read the first paragraphs while the syllabus was passed down. The first chapter was basically asking why some people, like Mahatma Gandhi, and Mother Teresa do the moral thing, devoting their lives to great causes, while others, like Adolf Hitler, Saddam Hussein, etc., are their exact polar opposites in morals.

I took in the guy seated beside me who had leaned his chair back on two legs, his back against the wall, big arms crossed, making it clear he was bored. Walls were handy for such things, I guess. Before I even looked I knew he was a large guy, the size nineteen or twenty black shoes told me that. My gaze traveled up thick legs, torso and his folded arms across his thick body, and finally a face full of hair.

"Mr. Blake, would you please place all four chair legs back on the floor, before you go through that wall. It's not really a wall, but a floater," Mr. Udall said in an even tone. I think he meant it was a partition wall.

Blake obeyed. "It'd be an improvement," he said low, darting a glance at me.

"Thank you." Mr. Udall ignored his comment and went about face to the front of class.

I met Ellwood Blake yesterday, he was also in my writing class. Turning his head, he graced me with a smile. His beard spread out with that smile while one giant hand rose in greeting.

"Hi."

"Hi," I said. "Looks like we have another class together."

"Don't worry. I'm just your basic stalker," he said, still grinning.

Well, this should be an interesting hour.

* * *

Turned out I liked my psychology class and the teacher, but I did not like Ellwood being there. During the last twenty-five minutes of the hour the teacher put forth a hypothetical question asking how we would stop a run-away trolley car to keep it from running down, and probably killing five people who are (for some reason) on the tracks. We had only two choices. Would we throw the switch and kill only one person who also was on the tracks? Or throw someone onto the tracks in order to stop the car, killing only one person? The teacher asked which would we do. It was a moral question and we were expected to answer as he called upon us. I thought it was a stupid question, but kept that to myself, like all the other people in the room, with the exception of one.

When the teacher came to Ellwood, he answered that he didn't really like any of the people on the tracks better than his buddy next to him. This got a rise out of everyone, and the argument went in circles about this for a while, especially between Ellwood and Mr. Udall.

It was one of those hypothetical situations you would never have to deal with in real life, and should you have to, you might react differently when it came right down to it. I learned Ellwood was a cynical bastard. In the end, he told Mr. Udall that he would throw his friend onto the tracks, not so much to save the five—because he didn't know them—but because the friend had been "an asshole", giving rise to yet more chuckles, mostly from the males in the room. I didn't find it amusing at all. And from his expression, Mr. Udall shared my opinion.

I didn't know how to answer and kept watching the clock, hoping he'd never get to me. Nearly everyone said they would throw the switch and yell out to alert the one stupid guy on the tracks, and that would have been my answer if he'd gotten to me. Fortunately, we ran out of time and the teacher never got to me. I had changed my answer, however, after enduring Ellwood's waxing on friends in general. I would have said I'd push Ellwood into the path of the oncoming car. *Ha, ha.*

When class ended, I had all my junk put away, grabbed my backpack, and was out the door, almost racing to get the hell away from Ellwood. In five minutes I was back in the main lobby, ready to jump on the elevator when someone else pulled up beside me and hopped on. I looked at the man who had stepped on with me and was surprised.

"Hi, Lainey," he said.

"Good morning, Mr. Taylor," I said smiling, heart thumping wildly. I think I had a crush on him.

"Beautiful day," he said.

"Yes." I hadn't really noticed, but if he said so.

"Going up?"

"Yes. Second floor," I said. "I need to go to the office."

"That's where I'm going." He stabbed the correct button with a manicured finger and the doors shut and away we went. I slid my backpack to the floor wishing we had at least ten floors together.

"You have influential friends, Miss Quilholt," he said as the elevator slid upwards.

I glanced over at him with a little surprised expression.

"How do you know Dr. Lamont?"

I gave him what was more of a confused than startled look. "Who?"

"Dr. Ed Lamont," he repeated, and my brain finally engaged. "He was my English teacher some years back."

Ed Lamont. As in my aunt's uncle. I called him Uncle Ed. I wasn't used to hearing his name with "Doctor" attached to it. He had a PhD in English, and had taught at the university.

"Oh, yes," I half-laughed to cover up my embarrassment. "He's my great uncle."

"Really?"

"Yes. Why—or what does he have to do with—" The doors of the elevator opened and we stepped out, pausing in the lobby.

"He was in touch with me regarding your entering my class. He highly recommended you, by the way. Glowing terms, I might add," Mr. Taylor said.

Sudden realization dawned on me and I barked a small chuckle. "I'm embarrassed. Uncle Ed heard how much I wanted to take your class. I was disappointed that I had to wait another year. I wanted to take it so badly. I apologize. I'm so embarrassed."

His hand came up, palm out. "No need, Lainey. He thinks a great deal of you."

My face was burning by this time. I imagined it had to be beet red by now. "I know he does. He's pretty special to me, too." Uncle Ed and I came to know each other very well over the past two years I had lived in Montclair. I trusted him with secrets I shared with no one else. He was more of a friend than an uncle.

"What's he doing these days? Enjoying his retirement, I would think."

"You have no idea," I said. "He's a Mark Twain impressionist, and does shows on his own river boat."

"Really! I'd love to see that." Mr. Taylor's eyes lit up. "My wife and I have been talking about taking a riverboat cruise. What's the name of his boat?"

"*The Miss Twila*. Docks at Montclair. That's where we live."

"Wonderful. I'll have to look that up." His cell phone rang and he pulled it out, glancing it. "Oop. My wife." He said putting the phone to his ear. I was happy he hadn't called her "the wife", as some men do. Weeks wouldn't call my aunt that, I knew this for certain. We both moved toward the glass office door. He opened it for me while speaking on his phone. "Yes. I'm here... right outside in the main office. Right. See you." He closed his phone. "Well, Lainey, I'll see you in class on Wednesday."

"I look forward to it," I said, watching him nod to the women in the front office, saying good morning to each one by name. They returned the greeting. His first name was Chad, I learned from the various greetings. Chad Taylor. A nice sounding name for such a handsome man.

"May I help you?" a woman behind the counter said and I had to tear my eyes off of Mr. Taylor as he rounded a corner and disappeared.

"Actually, I hope to help you," I said, and bent to dig out the yearbook in my bag. I plopped it on the counter. The woman, who looked to be in her forties, waited patiently as I flipped open to a page I'd marked with a ripped piece of notebook paper. "I saw this person wearing a clown mask who scared some girls yesterday."

"Yes. We've had that complaint. You said you saw him too?" she asked.

"I did and I can positively identify him."

"What do you mean you can identify him?" The woman gave me a perplexed look. The other two women in the office had looked up from their desks. A fourth woman was at the xerox machine, and I definitely had her attention as well.

"I saw him pull off the mask when he thought no one saw him. I stood above him inside, while he was outside in a small courtyard. His name is Tyler Sinclair." I pointed to his picture in the class yearbook. I turned it around so she could see the picture. By this time the other three women had gathered at the counter to look at the picture.

"Oh, yeah. Him," one of the women said. Her gray hair was cut shoulder length, she poised her glasses on her nose while peering down at the picture and then up to me. "He was dismissed last year."

"I've heard that he was caught cheating on his finals," I said. The women slid glances at each other.

"That's correct," the blonde woman said as she pulled over a post-it note. "What's your name?"

"Lainey Quilholt."

The gray-haired woman said, "Any relationship to Ellen Quilholt?"

"She was my mother," I said, a little startled. I looked into her large, dark eyes. She was thin, and wore a black and white dress that formed to her rather well-endowed chest. I wasn't certain how to proceed with this, or where this would go on her end. I had to pull up my resolve to not let my emotions out of the box I'd put them into long ago.

She reached over to cover my hand with her thin, cool one. "I worked with her at Darby Insurance, years ago," she said. "I was so sorry to hear of your parents' death. It was a terrible tragedy."

"Thanks." I nodded, my gaze lowered to avoid seeing how her face had crumbled into sorrow-filled lines. I pushed the memories of the flood as it rose over our car out of my mind. Being the only survivor of your family was a difficulty I could not have handled if it were not for my mother's sister, Aunt Jessica, taking me in and loving me as though I were her own.

The other three women went back to their various jobs, answering a phone, feeding a xerox machine.

"Do you have a cell phone number, some way to get in touch?" the blonde woman asked.

I rattled off both my cell phone number and our house number, figuring somehow they'd be able to get in touch with me. She wrote this down, and I noted she had put Sinclair's name down as well.

"What will you do?" I asked. "I mean, I've been informed that he's making threats to certain teachers on social media. He might be serious about going through with his threats."

"I will pass this along to Mr. Smith," she said with a closed-lip smile.

"Uh, okay. Who is he?" I asked.

"He is the president of the school," she said.

"Oh. Sorry," I said, thinking I'd been told his name by someone, and I'd forgotten who. "Thanks. I hope this helps."

"I'm sure Mr. Smith will be happy to have this information," she said.

I put the yearbook back into my bag and thanked her as I strode out into the lobby and stood in front of the elevators. I wondered if any of them took this seriously. I rode the elevator down, definitely distracted, and found, once again I had pressed the G button, instead of the 1 button on the panel. *What is wrong with me?* There I was standing looking down that dismally quiet hallway. The silence was broken by chipper whistling further up the hallway. A custodian in jeans wearing a green shirt appeared only five feet away.

"Oh, I'm sorry. I must've hit the wrong button," I said.

He smiled. "It happens a lot." Until that moment I hadn't recognized him. His voice stirred a memory of many years ago in grade school.

"Mr. Bean?" I said, surprised.

He closed one eye and peered at me through thick glasses. "You're the Quilholt girl."

"Yes." I stepped out of the elevator and shook his hand. Mr. Bean used to be a custodian at my grade school. His hair was a bit grayer, now, maybe shorter too, but he looked essentially the same. He'd always been kind, and had played Santa on the day before Christmas break, and gave out candy canes during lunch. "It's been a while. How nice to see you again!" I said. "So, you work here now?"

"Yep. There was a position open, and I applied." He leaned slightly toward me. "I don't mind saying I beat out sixty-three people for it."

"Well, congratulations!" I said. "I'm glad to see you here."

"So, you're going to school here, now. My, my." He shook his head. "Time just flies."

"Yes."

"Sorry to have heard about your parents. That was a terrible thing. I just want to say it about broke my heart. But sure am happy you're still on this earth."

"Oh, what a sweet thing to say," I said, feeling tears biting at my eyes. I forged on. "And I'm super happy to see you here, probably making better money."

"And a better pension," he said, winking. "The work's the same, no matter what."

I nodded. "Right. Right." Realizing the time, I said, "Oh! I need to get back."

"Sure. Sure," he said with a nod. "It was real nice seeing you again, Lainey."

"You too. I stepped over to the doors of the elevator and pressed the up button. Over my shoulder I asked, "What's down here, anyway?" I asked.

"Oh, this is the older section. Used to be offices, there's bathrooms, and down the hall you can get to the locker rooms, and eventually the gym."

The elevator arrived and the doors split open. "Ah. Good to know," I said. "Bye."

"See you around."

* * *

My next class was Rhetoric and Composition. I knew I could get through this class without too much problem, but worried upon entering that Ellwood would also be there. Thankfully he was not.

An hour and a half later I burst out of the building, looking forward to going home for the day, but not looking forward to my night class. Not that I had anything against sociology, it was more that when I got out, it would be dark.

Making my way through the lot, my mind wasn't on watching for anyone who might be following me, particularly Sinclair. Then I heard the scrape of shoes behind me and I twirled, my back pack over my shoulder swung like a wrecking ball and hit me in the ribcage. Ow.

I saw the tall guy walking in a bouncing steps, you wouldn't guess the man was six-six, weighing in excess of 250 pounds. He forged ahead like a Mack truck, and reminded me of a bad dream I would have in my future. Like tonight.

He smiled as he pulled up nearby. "Told you I was your stalker."

"Good thing there isn't a train track or a runaway car nearby. You might throw me in front of it," I said, turning to my car and pulling open the back door. Oven heat blasted out at me. I didn't look forward to sitting on a hot seat, waiting for the air conditioner to cool things down.

"Give me a break! You're upset about that?" He gave a breathy sigh. "First of all, that was an unrealistic situation. No one would ever have to face that, especially since there are no trolley cars in Iowa. Secondly, the teacher, who by the way is your basic psychoanalysis, is trying to get into our heads." He pointed to his own head with two thick fingers. "Come on, Laney, you can't be serious. I sure wasn't. I was yanking his chain back."

I open my front door and slid behind the wheel with my door still open, letting all the heat out.

"Well, you're right about that whole situation being bogus. Why did he ask us such a stupid question?" I asked.

"He wanted to make us all squirm. There was no right or wrong answer. Remember that when he asks something like that again. Just go with your gut. He grades on participation, not on whether or not you come up with something brilliant no one else has thought of."

I blew out a breath between my parted lips. "You're right. I'm sorry."

He leaned an arm over the open door. "You done for today?"

"I've got a night class."

"Hate night classes. I avoid them like the plague. Be careful to park close to the building, if you can. It'll be dark out when you get out of class."

"Yeah. I know." I plugged the key into the slot and the chime kept pinging.

"See you around."

"Okay, stalker," I said and he laughed as he turned to go. I shut my door, if only to shut off the stupid annoying chime. I turned the key and heard clicking.

"Oh, crap!" This wasn't good. I turned the key again. Same clicking. I opened my door to get out of the hot and stuffy car. A beater dark blue car rambled up behind mine. Ellwood's big head and arm hanging out the window.

"Car problems?" he asked.

"Yeah. Won't start."

He shoved his into park and left it running while he got out and walked over. "What's it doing? Or not doing?"

"Just this funny clicking noise. This morning, I didn't think it would start."

"Let's hear it."

I sat back down in the seat and turned the key. Again clicking.

"That sounds like battery trouble," a new voice sounded behind Ellwood. He turned and there was Nate standing beside him.

"Indian dude," Ellwood said. I was mortified by what he'd called Nate, but when they clasped hands in that upward way where the thumbs hooked, I knew they were pals.

"That's what I was going to say."

Nate said, "Pop the hood."

I reached down and located the leaver and pulled, releasing the hood, rather proud I knew at least that much about my car.

Nate and Ellwood both went under the hood and I came up beside them, clueless.

"Yep." Nate pointed to my battery, which looked pretty corroded. "You've gotta replace that, or you ain't going anywhere."

"Where's the closest garage?"

"Garage? Five miles," Ellwood said.

"They'll charge you an arm and a leg to put it in," Nate said. "A better idea would be to go and buy one, and I'll put it in for free."

"Really?" I gasped.

"You got money, or plastic?" Ellwood asked.

"Yes." I did have a credit card. I wasn't thrilled about using it for a battery, though, but what could I do? I had few alternatives, and one was not leaving my car here waiting for my aunt to come and pick me up, and expecting her, or Weeks to help me out. I was an adult, now, after all. I could do this myself. "But I have to get the right battery. How do I know which one—"

"Don't worry," Ellwood said, one bear paw jarring Nate's shoulder. "This guy is a great mechanic. I'd trust him with my own pile of junk."

"Alright. If you have time, that is. I really appreciate this," I said.

"Lock it up," Ellwood said, slamming the hood back down.

"I'll grab my stuff." I didn't want to leave my backpack in the car while I was gone. Not with my laptop and all my books in it. I locked my car up and we all converged on Ellwood's car. I opened up the back door, which made a horrendous creaking noise, then I had to move junk off to the other end in order to create a space big enough for me to sit. There was everything from fast food containers, empty pop cans, to books and notebooks back here. It looked like a personal junkyard.

"You guys are all done today, too?" I asked from the back seat.

"Yep." Ellwood said.

"This is crazy," I said. "If you guys weren't there I'd have to call my aunt and she'd have to find someone to come out here with a new battery."

"Or, they'd tow it and it would cost you even more," Nate said.

"Yeah. They do like to tack on more expenses," Ellwood said as he drove out of the parking lot, using one hand to steer, turned out of the lot, and zoomed off down the road. I rolled down my window to get some air.

"Nice wheels," Nate said to Ellwood.

"At least it works."

"So far."

"Not everyone can drive a Harley."

"I'm still paying on it," Nate said.

Amid the banter between the two guys, I called my aunt, telling her what had happened, and that I had to buy a new battery. She was going grocery shopping, and Weeks was still at work. I would have had to handle this myself, anyway. She suggested I call her mechanic, and I told her I had two guys who knew what the matter was, and would fix it for free. She was happy to hear that.

Ten minutes later we arrived at an auto parts store, Nate showed me the batteries, and suggested I not buy a too cheap of one. I was shocked at the price of a battery, but glad that I had a credit card on me for just such emergencies like buying clothes, books, or batteries for my car.

The whole affair took a little over an hour before my battery was replaced, and I was waving goodbye to my two male buds.

Returning home, I found that my aunt was still out. Expecting me to be home by ten, she had left me a note on the bulletin board saying she'd gone shopping, and would be back in time to make lunch. But I knew she had gone to the larger grocery store and it sometimes took her a while, because she talked to every living soul she knew, and some she didn't, while she shopped. I was still amazed I'd beat her home.

I drank a can of soda as I moved through the house, working on zoning out for a few minutes while it was still quiet. I was also happy that today my aunt's bookstore wasn't open. Not on Mondays or Tuesdays. Otherwise I had offered to work on Thursdays, after my morning classes.

I sat on the couch, feet up on the coffee table—something I wouldn't do if my aunt were around—and nearly fell asleep when my phone vibrated in my back pocket. I took it out and saw the read out.

"Nadine. Hi," I answered. "Where are you?"

"I'm still at school. Where are you?"

"I'm home. You wouldn't believe it, but my car battery went dead."

"Oh, wow. How'd you get home? Did you have to get it towed?"

"No. Ellwood Blake, and Nate Blackstone were there. They gave me a ride to buy a new one and they put it in for me for no charge."

"That's good. My life is hell, by the way," she said and off she went ranting about her first math class with the infamous Mrs. Ratface.

"Well, it only figures," she went on. "After all Mercury is in retrograde. Everything will be a disaster."

"I can't believe you follow a horoscope," I said. She only laughed.

"Yours said today would be a three. And friendships would definitely play a part in solving a problem or two," she said. "So, you wanna eat crow now, or later?"

"I don't put stock in that stuff. You know I don't."

"I know you're not a believer, but whatever you do, watch yourself tonight, after class."

"I know. Everyone's saying that to me."

"No. Really. I mean you're on Evil Clown's hit list," she said.

Chapter 5

"You actually bought a battery for your car?" Weeks asked as we sat down for lunch. I was surprised he was taking lunch with us but he'd been up since eleven last night. His normal hours were six am to six pm. But because he'd been called in to cover last night, his hours were screwed up.

"Yep."

"How'd you know which one to buy? I'll have to look at it. Later."

"I had two guys to help me."

"Who?"

That was his second favorite question. His first favorite was "Where are you going?".

"Ellwood Blake and Nate Blackstone," I said.

He chewed his sandwich, washed it down with the iced tea my aunt had made, and said, "I don't know who Ellwood is, but I know Nate Blackstone. Steer clear of him."

"Why?"

"He's got a police record."

"He's going to school on a grant," I said by way of making him an okay guy to hang out with. "Besides, I don't think it's possible for me to steer clear of everyone who's ever gotten themselves into trouble. And he was willing to help me out. Is that such a bad thing?" I felt I had a good argument.

He made his usual belittling bark of laughter. "Any guy would want to help a defenseless woman, and for all the wrong reasons." His gaze shifted from me to my aunt and back to me. "Any woman stranded somewhere with car trouble is target for a guy who might be up to no good. Women have disappeared because of trusting a stranger."

I blinked my eyes for a strength-gathering moment. "I understand that not all guys are altruistic. And knowing this is strength."

"Just be careful. No woman should trust strangers."

"They weren't strangers," I said. "I know them."

"How long have you known these guys?"

"I just met Ellwood, and he's friends with a bunch of my friends." He looks scary, but I had a feeling he was a pussy cat underneath all that hair and girth.

"And you know Nate how?" he asked, lacing his fingers, and leaning arms on the table, giving me his total attention as though I'd impart some big secret. His radio gave a belch of static, which he ignored, waiting for me to answer.

He was trying to trap me. I knew it. "I met him in the homeless shelter when I was there with Aunt Jessica." I took the last bite of sandwich.

"When?"

"I don't know," I said through a mouthful. "A few weeks ago. Back when I was looking into Arline's death."

He made a harrumph and gave my aunt a look of disdain.

To my aunt's questioning look, I said, "He was that Native American guy."

"I remember him. He seemed nice," my aunt said.

"First impressions notwithstanding, he's still bad news."

"What's wrong with someone going to school to learn a trade?" I argued.

His eyes went wide as he pulled in a breath and looked at my aunt. "There's that young adult righteousness. I'll just pass that along to you, my dear."

"Well, she's right. Not everyone is perfect, and when they know they've made a mistake, they've got every right to try to go straight."

"Ah. I knew I should have kept my mouth shut," he said. "Two women against one man. The women will always win."

"That's right," My aunt winked at me and I smiled.

"Well, it's good that you were able to get the battery, Lainey," my aunt said. "John, she had no choice."

"If I had called for a tow they would have charged me an arm and a leg. And that's before I got it into a place that would replace my battery. I only spent a few hundred."

Weeks wiped his mouth and said, "First of all, towing's covered by insurance," he said. News to me. "I'm just glad nothing bad happened and that you were able to get it fixed. Next time call me."

I glanced at my aunt, squeezing my eyes. She had her game face on, which was neutral. She knew me and Weeks were feeling out our territory here. He had just become the head of the family, and I had to respect his new place in the household. It had been awkward at first, probably for both of us. Everything from getting our bathroom schedules adjusted, to hearing him in the shower—yeah, he sang—and seeing his undies in the laundry (fortunately my aunt took care of laundry duties).

He stood, looking at his phone quickly and then tucking it away. "Well, I'd better get some sleep." He yawned. "I haven't done these sort of hours in ten years."

My aunt slipped an arm around him and kissed him on the cheek. "Sleep tight. I'm going back to the shop." She wasn't open today, but she sometimes went in and worked on orders, bookkeeping, and displays.

She and my uncle moved out of the kitchen into the hallway, their voices hushed. I tried to ignore their little words of endearment, wondering if when I married would I carry on like these two. Probably.

Week's last words carried to my ears, "Had some moron last night driving erratically all over the road while on his cell phone and caused an accident. It was a mess out on I-80. I guess people don't get why it's a law to keep off the thing while driving. Luckily no one was badly hurt."

I looked at my phone after it made that silly tone that said I'd had a text message.

"DID U C ANY CLOWNS 2DAY?" The message read.

This was from Brett. It sounded like a tease.

"N.U?" I keyed my response.

"HE MUST B SLEEPING IN LOL!"

"MUST BE!"

"U HAVE CLASS 2NT?"

"Y! I NEED 2 STUDY CU"

"L8R"

We had not said those three little words, "I love you", to each other as yet. I wasn't sure about my feelings toward Brett. I liked him a lot, but it was too early in our relationship to be committing to each other like that.

I cut our messaging short, wanting to hit the books. I was slightly miffed that he'd brought up Sinclair, reminding me that I was on Evil Clown's shit list (posted in his site according to everyone). I hoped my telling the office ladies who was masquerading as a clown both on social media and now in person would help in curtailing his threats. Wondering if now wasn't the time to mention Sinclair's threats to Weeks and my aunt, since he now had zeroed in on me. Agitated, I went to my room and focused on homework. After the other studies I don't really excel in, I dove into my homework for my creative writing class. I filled out that sheet for Mr. Tyler, which had several questions pertaining to what you like to read, write and who your favorite authors were. I so looked forward to Wednesday's class.

* * *

Weeks woke up later in the afternoon. He looked at my battery and deemed it good, and left it at that. Whoever usually worked night shift was still sick with the flu. He was doing what he called "a split shift". I didn't know how he managed to stay awake, but somehow he did.

I ate dinner with my aunt and uncle before leaving for my night class. I was still debating on telling Weeks about Sinclair, but I didn't think there was much he could do about him, since he hadn't actually broken any laws. And if the school had wanted to do something about it, they now knew who was behind it, thus, I had done my duty, and felt it to be enough.

That evening, I drove around the three parking lots of Whitney, trying to find a close spot to the building, but it looked like it was futile. I guess I wasn't the only one who needed a closer parking spot. I parked several rows back and went inside and, according to plan, met Brett in the commons. He was through with classes for the day. We visited for ten minutes, and he walked me to my class, again in the east wing upper level. He told me he would try and meet me after class in order to escort me back to my car.

"Oh, I'll be okay," I said, certain Sinclair wouldn't know me from any another girl at Whitney. "I'll walk out with other people."

"I'll still try and get here. I just have to tell my boss I'm coming in late," he said.

"I don't want you to get fired."

Arm around me, he squeezed my shoulders. "Don't worry about it. I'll be here." The promise seemed genuine. I went to my class and the hours dragged. I yawned the whole time, took notes and wished I could just put my head down and close my eyes. The teacher's droning on and on was good white noise. Somewhat like a distant radio tuned to one of those all-talk stations.

Walking out of class after nine pm was weird because the sky was dark, and stars were out. Air was much cooler than when I'd gone into class, and I'd forgotten to bring something warm to wear after dark. It reminded me of going to a matinée in the afternoon, and coming out of the theater when it was dark. I didn't see Brett. I checked and found he'd sent me a text saying he would be late. My only thought was to get home and go to bed. Another day had wiped me out. I hoped that after this first week I'd get used to the drudge of classes, especially night classes. I knew that was too much to hope for.

Two other girls who had been in the same class with me were leaving at the same time. "Where are you guys parked?" I asked, jogging up to them. "I don't want to go hunting for my car alone."

"Oh, me either!" the one I thought whose name was Jill said.

"I don't even remember," the other one said.

"Does that look familiar?" her friend said, pointing.

"They have the lots marked with letters, like A, B, C, etcetera," I said.

"Now you tell me."

We all chuckled like it was fun to have to find your car in a sea of other cars at night when someone named Evil Clown might be lurking around.

"Wait, over there. We parked by a light pole," Jill said, pointing again.

"I hope it's the correct light pole. There seem to be dozens," I said as we stepped off the curb and ventured into a nomad's land of lot with fewer cars than when I'd arrived. The three of us crossed several rows of parking lot amid car doors slamming and engines starting. Vehicles began vacating the lot.

"Wait. I see our car," the friend said to Jill. Bidding me good night, they moved in that direction. My car was not far away, as I spotted it in a pool of light a few rows away, nearly all by itself. I'd been told repeatedly to park underneath a light, if I couldn't park close. I kept a vigilant eye out for moving shadows or suspicions characters walking around. I'd also already dug out my keys. I would not be one of those imbeciles you see fumbling for her keys late at night in movies or reenactments.

Moving in the direction of my lone car, I heard screams back where those two girls had gone. Looking back, I saw the oddest sight of someone in a full clown's suit and wildly colored hair, jumping out from behind a parked car. Flopping his arms, jumping up and down and screaming crazily. The two girls ran off screaming. I didn't know if they'd made it to their car, because I turned and ran for mine, which might have only been thirty feet away, but it might as well have been a mile. I knew he was looking for me.

That was when the clown (I was certain it was Sinclair), turned and came bounding after me, making his weird yell. Keys out, I raced toward my car, aiming and pressing the lock button on my remote. I had to hit it a couple of times before the lights all flashed on. Breath raged, I pulled the door open. My screams came at the price of pulling in precious air, but I couldn't help myself. The crazy sounds of Sinclair's cries, "*Yee! Yah-ha! Yee!*" sounding so close I could feel his breath. I barely pulled the door shut when he was at my window. The nasty clown with razor teeth and horrible eyes and hair, banged against my car, his hands pressed against my window. The second I'd engaged my locks, he tried to open my door. At the same time, my keys fell out of my hand. I tried to calm myself. I was safe, he couldn't touch me. I had to find my keys and get the hell away from him.

Something banged loud on the top of the car. BANG! BANG! BANG!

I screamed again, jerking in my seat. I didn't know what he was hitting my car with, but it was something hard. He hit my window with what looked to be a baseball bat.

Panicked, I reached down trying to locate my keys, which had fallen between my seat and door, somewhere. I couldn't reach them because my hand wouldn't go any further underneath the seat. With shaking hands, I tried to locate my phone. Where was it?

Meanwhile, Evil Clown, aka Sinclair, was now on top of the hood of my car. I saw the baseball bat in his hands and had renewed horror that that's what he was going to swing at me and now swung at my poor car. Down came the bat and bashed my windshield making a large spiderweb of cracks, but he didn't break through. I threw up my hands in front of my face, fully expecting the window to shatter. Somehow it held. But for how long?

Thinking quickly, I hit my horn, and kept hitting it over and over again, hoping the noise would either scare him away or bring someone to my aid. Calling someone at that moment would not get him off my car, or stop him from bashing in my windshield. Besides my phone was in my purse, which I'd thrown across the front seat and it was somewhere on the floor. Cracks in my windshield spread so bad, I no longer could see through it, as Sinclair kept bashing at it. His movements on top of my car wiggled my car as if it were no more than a baby cart. He would be through it in a matter of minutes, but I kept honking the horn.

Suddenly movement flashed before me. Sinclair's attack stopped. There was a scuffle off to the side of my car. Swear words exchanged all out of my visual as I could see nothing out the windshield of my car. I leaned down and fished for my keys again, feeling the metal at the very tips of my fingers. "Damn!" Even if I could get it started, I doubted I would be able to drive it home because I couldn't see out of the windshield now.

A rap on the glass beside my head made me jump and cry out. I looked up into Nate's face.

"You alright?" he asked through the glass.

Realizing Sinclare was gone, I opened up the door tumbled out, tearfully saying, "Yes, yes." Before I knew it I had my arms around his neck, and his were around me loosely.

"You're alright, Lainey," Nate said, pulling me from himself. "You've survived worse."

His words made me gape at him. I wondered how he would know this. I'd only let a few of my closest friends know what I went through when my parents had drowned. Maybe he'd seen it on my Facebook site.

"How'd you—"

"Ellwood and I came here to make sure that asshole didn't get to you. We were almost too late."

That wasn't what I was going to ask, but I blinked back tears. "Thank you."

"That asshole got away," Ellwood's booming voice arrowed through the parking lot. I turned away from Nate to take in Ellwood as he trudged back, panting after running my attacker off. "Too bad, I would have fed this bat to him." He held the bat by the thick head.

"Don't touch it!" I cried, pointing.

"What?" Ellwood asked, still holding the bat up.

"Fingerprints!"

Ellwood dropped the bat. "Oh."

I turned to Nate. He was gone. I didn't see him anywhere. It was as though he'd vanished like a ghost.

A white van drove up with Brett at the wheel. He jammed it into park at nearly the same time he threw open the door and jumped out and ran up to me. "Sorry I'm late." We wound arms around one another. "Are you okay?" he asked, worry etched across his face.

"Yes. Rattled, but I'm fine. My car windshield has seen better days." I pointed. And I'd have to have that fixed now, thank you. I'd be sending the bill to Sinclair.

"Fuck," he said, leaning to have a look. "That guy's crazy."

"He ran like a lunatic," Ellwood said, looking off in the distance. "Cops are coming." He turned back and smiled. "As always they're too late to the dance."

Sirens sounded in the distance. Out on the highway several blue, red and white lights flashed from emergency vehicles.

"Who called 911?" I asked. "I couldn't even get my keys. All I could think of was hit my horn over and over."

"That did the trick," Ellwood said. "Nate called police."

"Nate did?" A smile broke out on my face thinking of the irony of that.

"Thanks for getting here," Brett said to Ellwood. "I knew something was up when I called and you didn't answer." He looked down at me. I bent into my purse, yanked it up and found my phone from a zippered pocket. It was nearly dead. "Oh. I forgot to recharge it."

"Why am I not surprised?" Brett said on an exasperated sigh. It wasn't the first time. It wouldn't be the last. But this was not the moment to debate that oversight.

Within a few minutes a squadron of police came roaring into the lot, wheels kicking up dust as they screeched to a halt, parking nilly-willy in the nearly empty lot. Men in dark brown uniforms jumped out and strode forward. Ahead of the pack was, of course, Weeks barking orders, pointing this way and that. Two men jogged back to their cars and turned on their search lights. I blinked and had to put my arm up to block the glare until they lowered them.

"Lainey, You okay?" He rushed up to me.

"I'm fine. But he got my windshield." I pointed.

He swore under his breath. "Describe him to me," he asked.

"Hah! Easy. Look for a man in a clown outfit, mask and all," I said.

He paused, hands at hips. "Really?"

"I'm serious."

"It's true. Evil Clown Guy has been all over social media threatening people. Including Lainey, here," Brett said. Okay, thanks for that.

Weeks' eyes popped as they fell off Brett and zoomed over to me.

"It just went up today," I said.

"And you didn't tell me?"

"I don't know what I was thinking," I said. Rather than lie to him. "Anyway, his name is Tyler Sinclair. You might have better luck in finding him that way."

"You know who this creep is?"

"No. I don't *know* him. I know his name. I was the one who identified him after seeing him remove his mask," I explained. "It's why he was threatening me."

"Did you see which way he went?"

"That a-way." Ellwood pointed, but he pointed to empty lot and darkness beyond.

Weeks spoke into his mike as he stepped away. "Put out an APB on a one Tyler Sinclair. Wanted for assault." He stepped up to his men. After speaking to them, they all hopped into their vehicles and chased out of here with lights and sirens going, each unit going different directions. Hunting down the clown.

Weeks stepped back over to us. "I'll call a tow truck for this." He looked over my head to Brett. "Can you take her home?"

"Sure," Brett said.

He pointed to me. "I'll be at the house later, and you and I are going to talk."

My lips pressed into a flat line knowing then shit had definitely hit the fan. I nodded and let Brett lead me to his van. He opened the door and I hopped in.

"Boy. He sounded pissed," he said as he got in behind the wheel.

"You don't know the half of it. I should have told him about Sinclair. I just thought this guy wasn't serious," I said after we climbed into the still running van.

"He's real serious," he assured.

I couldn't help the laughter that bubbled up in me.

"What?" He looked across at me, unable to keep from smiling.

"The police have an APB on a clown." We both laughed. I guess the tension had lifted. I needed something to laugh at after all I'd just gone through.

Chapter 6

How to Make your Characters Memorable & Likeable was written across the white board in front of class.

Mr. Taylor paced the front of the class. All of us quietly expectant of what today's lesson would teach us. You could hear a pencil drop on the carpeted floor it was so quiet.

"If you've built upon a character who is so very real there will come a moment when he, or she will say or do something you hadn't planned on them saying or doing." He looked up at us with a smile. "That's the moment when your character has become a living entity outside of the confines of a sheet of paper, or your computer."

He took the marker and wrote as he spoke, "Plot is nothing without character. No character, no plot, it's that simple."

He wrote: What makes your characters likable, or hateable?

"I'm pretty sure that isn't a word." We all chuckled as he pointed to the word "hateable".

Hands went up. He pointed to someone.

"You have to have them do something that makes the reader like them," the guy said.

"Like what?"

Someone else raised a hand and he called on them.

"Maybe something happens to the character that makes us feel sorry for them?" the young lady said. I liked that answer.

"I think you're saying that you need someone a reader can relate to," he said. "If they're witty, that's great. Maybe they have courage beyond measure. Go up against insurmountable odds."

"But how do you do that?" someone asked.

"Very good question. First of all—" he went to the board and wrote: Don't Cop Out. He tapped the board with the capped pen. "You have to give your main character major problems. Some little ones that he, or she, can overcome, and at least one big problem that seems unsolvable until the end. Like I said; seemingly insurmountable." He paused again and then said, "What happens to Harry Potter in every book. Or movie?"

Someone answered timidly. "He faces Voltermort."

"Right, but what else?"

I raised my hand and Mr. Taylor pointed at me.

"He finds he has enemies nearly at every turn. At one point, even his own friends turn against him."

"Right. Good point, Miss. Quilholt!"

"He and Snape aren't the best of friends," someone else said, and we all chuckled.

"Exactly. Good one, Mr. Field. Come on. Give me more. How else does J.K. Rowling give Harry problems?"

"Like learning magic, only in his case, he gets into trouble when he uses it outside of Hogwarts."

"Ah! Good! Very good!"

"And trying to live with the Dersleys," Ellwood said.

"Yeah. They made him sleep in the place under the stairs," someone said. All of a sudden there were more suggestions. We were having fun with this.

"Very good!" Mr. Taylor said. "Now, you see my point? Even though Harry is magical, not everything is wonderful in Harry's life. Of course he's far better than a muggle, but even sorcerers have problems in day-to-day life."

The class went on like this until the end. We were all excited about learning how to write about an interesting character. Too soon the class came to an end. We all turned in the questionnaire from our last class as we left.

"Lainey, can I speak to you?" Mr. Taylor said.

"Sure."

"Uh-oh!" Ellwood teased as he filed out with the rest of the students. I smiled at him.

When everyone was gone, Mr. Taylor said, "I heard about last night. That you were attacked. I just want to know that you're okay." He looked worriedly into my face.

"Yes. I'm fine. I have a lot of friends who came to my rescue," I explained. Not to mention my uncle was sheriff.

"I understand that it was Tyler Sinclair who was behind this."

"Yes."

"Did they catch him?"

"Not yet." My uncle said they'd looked everywhere. He hadn't gone home, nor was he anywhere else. It was as though Sinclair had disappeared.

"That's too bad."

"I understand he cheated on his finals?" I prompted. I didn't know if he would confide in me.

"He somehow was able to lift answers to the final in my English class and another class. We aren't sure how this was done. Maybe he stole the answers from a file, or he hacked the school's computers and got them that way. But his answers were word for word perfect."

"Maybe he just knew the answers."

"No. Mine was a written final. No one can write exactly some of the answers I had. Besides, he wasn't an 'A' student. Even my top A students had trouble, and none of them had answered verbatim. Same thing in Mrs. Ratner's math class."

I considered this as I nodded.

"He wanted to go on to a much bigger college, and needed a better grade point average than he was going to get. He was caught cheating, and the school expelled him."

The explanation made sense, Sinclair's reaction to it didn't. I had pondered this throughout the night and had gotten little sleep. It wasn't the attack on me, nor my conversation with Weeks after I'd gotten home that had me upset. It was why Sinclair had reacted so violently, wanting to blame everyone for his mistake. I certainly didn't hold a gun to his head and made him cheat.

"Lainey," Mr. Taylor said, placing a firm hand on my shoulder and looking soulfully into my eyes, the other hand over his heart. "I want you to know that I'm deeply sorry this guy attacked you simply because you came forward and identified him." A pleasant cologne drifted to me and for some reason I wanted to sniff at it for a moment longer.

I made a half shrug, still under the spell of his cologne.

"No. Really. If there's anything I can do, let me know."

I smiled up at him. "Sure, Mr. Taylor."

The hand over his heart dropped and he made a pointing finger. "I expect to see some good writing from you, however. You're not off the hook on that."

I chuckled, then snapped my fingers. "Darn. I thought I could just coast through your class and do nothing."

He laughed at my joke. "I'll see you on Friday, if not elsewhere."

"Right," I said and exited his classroom.

Once again I was late—only by one minute this time—for Mrs. Ratner's math class. I edged along the side of the room to find a vacant seat, and heard my name called from the front.

"Miss Quilholt, may I see you in the hallway, please?" Mrs. Ratner said.

Every cell in my body went cold, and my stomach tumbled.

I obeyed and followed her out into the hallway. When I faced her I was surprised to see the woman's usual sour countenance turned soft, even her icy-blue eyes had become watery puddles.

"Lainey, I had word this morning that you were attacked by Tyler Sinclair."

Once again, her softer mien caught me by surprise. "Yeah," I said.

"Very sorry to hear that. Are you okay?" Her empathy overwhelmed me.

"Yes."

"I heard he had a baseball bat, that he went after you and two other girls," she said. "Is that true?"

"Yes. But he was after me because he'd seen me when I saw him without the mask," I said. "Last night I got into my car and locked the doors before he could get me. But he bashed in my windshield."

"I'm so sorry. I heard the police came. We were put on notice this morning that if we had to, we may go into lock down if there are any more threats."

"Wow."

"I just wanted to make sure about what I'd heard." She shook her head, blinking long and frequently as she did and went on. "You know how things get said, rumors get started. There was one tweet that said you were in the hospital."

Ah. That's why all the special treatment from my teachers today.

"No. My friends came to my rescue. And then the police came almost right away. My uncle is the county sheriff."

Her lips parted. "Ah. I see. Well, I only wanted to make sure about your welfare." She grabbed the doorknob and I stepped inside before her. All eyes were on us. You'd think I'd been given a thrashing by the way they all looked at me, their eyes following me through the room. Obviously none of them were aware of my dealings with Mr. Sinclair, last night. It wouldn't be long, though. Someone would find whatever was out there on social media and they'd all know who I was in a matter of hours. It was like living in a small town. I knew exactly how that worked.

No other teacher in the rest of my classes took me aside and spoke to me, thank goodness. By eleven I was in desperate need of refueling and headed for the main dining room, having left a quick text to Brett to meet me there. While in line, Brianna Bryde slid in behind me.

"Hi," she said.

"Hi," I said back to her.

"Heard you had a tussle with Tyler Sinclair, last night," she said.

I sighed. "I gather it's all over school by now."

"Pretty much. What happened?" We lined up to pay. I handed the woman a ten and got change back.

"You want the long version or the short one?" I asked as we walked away from the pay station to find a table.

"Oh, I need the blow-by-blow version, of course. Don't I rate?"

"Of course you do," I said. We found a booth well away from anyone who had ears, and I launched into what happened, giving her everything that led up to last night. At this point the whole thing felt like a dream, rather than an actual event. The clown mask and costume probably had everything to do with residual nightmares for me.

She gave me the sympathetic sounds at the correct intervals.

"Did the bat have his fingerprints on them?"

"Oh, yes. They did. His and Ellwood's. That's what nailed Sinclair to the wall," I said, thinking it was odd both were in the system, but Ellwood had to give them his for "elimination purposes".

But she had something eating her, I could tell by the way she merely picked at her food.

"Something going on with you, I can tell. Spill," I encouraged.

She looked around the dining room, leaned forward and said in a low voice, "Mrs. Taylor was fired today. And my head may be next on the chopping block."

"Oh, my gosh, no! Why?" I said. "What happened?"

"Well, just the other day Mrs. Taylor—her name is Carol, by the way—found a big problem in certain accounts after she wrote out a check for some uniforms for the band. It bounced!"

"Bounced!?" I said, shock coloring my face. "You sure?"

"Oh, yeah. It was very embarrassing. She gave me the check to give it to the company who supplied the uniforms. Two days later—just this morning, in fact—the bank called and told us it bounced!"

"Oh, my god. How embarrassing."

"Right? She said she was certain the account had more than enough money in it to cover the expense. I mean, the bill came to just a little over eight hundred dollars, and she said the account had over two thousand in it, last she knew." She leaned closer again while scanning our surroundings and lowered her voice so low I almost couldn't hear her. "Carol said something fishy was definitely going on because when she called the bank to check on that account, and a few others, the bank's totals and hers didn't agree. Not anywhere near what she'd had. They were far lower amounts in the bank than should have been there. She'd done an audit over the summer and everything was fine, then. Now, this." she sat back for a moment, but leaned forward again, eyes darting around as though we had spies everywhere. "She and I went through the bank accounts, and we could see amounts were being withdrawn at regular intervals."

"Wow!"

"She went as far as saying it looked like someone was skimming. She went to Mr. Smith about it, of course, about a half an hour ago, maybe an hour—I don't know. This morning was just a disaster—she came back, her face was as red as your shirt. She told us she'd been fired. She's clearing out her desk as we sit here."

"Wow. That's terrible. Didn't Mr. Smith believe her?"

Brianna shrugged. "You accuse someone of skimming, and they aren't likely to take it well."

"Skimming? Don't you mean embezzling?" I said.

"Same thing. It's just that it's small amounts. Less than two thousand." She looked around again and then leaned forward. "I heard that she's going to talk to someone. I don't know who or where."

"To report it, you mean?"

"Yes."

"That's a good idea, she needs to tell someone right away." I couldn't think of who she'd speak to. Police? Maybe a lawyer? "But isn't it likely that Smith thinks she's lying about it? That maybe he thinks she's the one who skimmed? That's why he fired her?"

"That's sort of what the other women in the office were saying."

A figure loomed up. "There you are!"

I smiled up at Brett. "There you are," I echoed.

Another person zoomed in behind him like a bird on a mission.

"Lainey!" Nadine squealed, dumping her tray on the table and suddenly her arms were around me squeezing me. "I tried to call you last night! What an awful, awful thing to happen to you!" She finally let me go and looked at me.

"I'm fine," I said.

"Oh, you won't believe what happened to me!" her eyes went skyward and her hands went over her heart.

"What is it?" I asked.

"I met a guy." She plopped into her chair and tucked her short hair behind her ears. "His name is Franklin Dunn. He's a sophomore, and a fourth generation farmer. He's taking agriculture classes here."

"That's great!" I managed to say before she went on about him, and told me she had a date with him on Friday night. It was why she hadn't called lately. I told her that was fine, and I was happy for her.

Three more people, all of them tall, like trees, moved into the area and settled at a table nearby. The tallest one leaned into our circle.

"The clown hasn't been caught yet?" Ellwood said to me.

"No word on it, so far," I said.

"Lainey is the hero of the school," Ham said, shaking a fist in the air.

"Hey. I chased him off, you moron," Ellwood said, batting Ham's arm as he moved back to their table, claiming a chair from another table. He twirled it around and sat astride it like a horse. I saw no food before him.

"Anyone who would run after a woman with a baseball bat deserves to be beaten up by you, Ellwood," Moon said. He had lasagna today. I had found it only passable. My aunt made the best lasagna in the world. Even Weeks said so. But would follow that by saying "Don't ever tell my Italian grandmother that I ever said that."

"Unfortunately the bastard ran faster than I could," Ellwood said as he pulled out a large candy bar from his pocket and chomped into it. I made note that his bite was large enough to inhale half a large candy bar.

While the boys were taking turns verbally bashing Sinclair and thinking up various horrifying ways to eradicate him from the Earth, I introduced Nadine to Brianna. They made nice noises at each other. I explained I knew Brianna from when I lived in DeWitt.

After a few minutes Brianna stood. "I'd best go and see if I'm still an employee."

"Okay," I patted her arm as she passed me. "Let me know, okay? I'll be home later tonight."

Brett and Nadine had tucked into their respective meals at my table.

"She works here?" Nadine asked between bites as usual.

"Yes. In the office," I said. I looked at Brett who was checking his phone. "Any news, good or bad, on the Internet?"

"Nothing from Clown Boy." Brett had given Sinclair that nick name last night while he drove me back home. "Have you heard anything from your aunt or uncle?"

"No one called, or left any messages, so I'm assuming he's still at large." I then told them what Mrs. Ratner had told me about the school being prepared to lock down, in case he made any further threats.

"Lock down? Seriously?" Nadine looked from me to Brett and back again. "Why?"

We were a little shocked at her question.

"Because Sinclair has threatened two teachers with death, and now Lainey, who is a student, has been attacked," Brett said, somewhat miffed she couldn't get the why part.

"But what would a lock down do? Aside from keeping everyone trapped inside. I mean, what if he's somewhere in here, hiding? Waiting to spring his trap?" Nadine said. I didn't like the way her mind worked.

Brett was about to answer when I touched his arm.

"She's right. There's some places in this building that people don't ever go," I said.

"Like where?" he asked.

"Ever been to the ground floor?" I said, looking at them both.

They looked at each other repeating "Ground floor?"

"I've pressed the elevator button wrong twice my first days here. I ran in to a janitor down there yesterday. He says no one uses it. It used to be—"

"I've been there," Ellwood said, interrupting me. I looked over at him.

"Why would you go down there?" I asked. "It's spooky down there. And it doesn't go anywhere."

"I go there when I want to be alone."

"I vant to be alone," Moon said humorously, dramatically thrusting his arm over his forehead.

"Don't scoff," Ham said. "Writers and composers often seek quiet solitude in order to compose."

"Whatever," Moon said, and went on with his meal.

"So, Ellwood, you've been down there? How did you discover it?" I asked.

"Like you, I discovered it by accident. I found it last year. I wanted to know where it went and did some exploring to see what doors were open and stuff. Had this awesome scene I was writing for my current WIP—a science fiction novel—and it was so quiet down there I just began going there to write. No distractions. No one coughing, or talking, like in the library. No one knows where I am. I even use the john down there." Chuckling, he looked at his pals. "I can make as much noise as I want when I have to take a dump."

A roar of laughter burst from Ellwood and company.

I was glad that I was finished with my meal. I noted the time. "I've got art class," I announced to my two companions. Brett stood with me, leaving his meal.

Brett walked me to the exit. "Do you need to go out to your car?"

"Yes."

"I'll walk you."

"No. You go eat. I'll be fine."

"You sure?"

"Clown Boy wouldn't show up in broad daylight to attack me, would he?" There were plenty of people around.

"You hit your panic button if you need me, okay?"

My "panic button" was a fast dial to his number. I had two others, which reached Weeks or my aunt.

"I'll do that if I so much as see brightly colored clown hair," I said. He chuckled. We kissed and I was off. Thing about being alone you begin to play back every conversation. The last thing was Ellwood's admitting he went down into the subbasement for solitude. If he knew about it, how many other people knew about that place below ground? Did Sinclair know about it? How many other students would have stumbled upon it, I wondered. For myself, it was a place that was not on my list of places to go. Not even to get away from anyone. My own room at my aunt's was a sanctuary of sorts. No one bothered me, unless dinner was ready, or someone came to see me.

My mind went to last night, after I'd gotten home and I had that "little talk" with Weeks. I had expected it to go really badly. I was surprised by what happened.

Weeks had stood in the kitchen, my aunt had left the room to allow him to make his little speech.

I'd decided to make my opening plea and said, "I didn't know the guy would become a lunatic. He started out by scaring a couple of girls in a hallway. I saw him take the mask off, and I was able to identify him to the office people the next day."

Weeks nodded, hand held up to hold back any further words from me, but I didn't have any more to say in my defense. It was his turn.

"Lainey, I understand that college is a special time of your life. Things go on that you'd rather keep to yourself. I'm not saying what you did, or didn't do, was wrong. But I want you to know that if anyone threatens you ever again, I want to know. Not because I'm trying to invade your space, or whatever, but because I love you."

It was an odd moment for me to hear him say this. Sure, he would say it now and then, just like my aunt would, but saying it in this way, in this situation just threw me emotionally, and I couldn't hide my tears. We hugged and that was the end of it.

* * *

My afternoon went by without any further problems. Art class was almost therapeutic for me. Quiet sonatas and quartets played in the background while we drew a still life that the teacher had set up with white balls, cones and blocks. Easy stuff. My left brain could relax while my right one took over. We were learning how to shadow. Having an hour and a half in which to complete it for a grade, or we could turn it in on Friday. I chose to work on it further at home, as she had told me I needed to darken my shadows more. Apparently I hadn't gotten the darkest of pencils when I'd gone shopping for art supplies, which had me stopping in the small store in the school before leaving for home. My teacher gave me suggestions like "Ebony" and "5 B" for the darkest shades.

After I drove home, being extra careful, since I'd had to borrow my aunt's car while my windshield was being fixed. Brett left a message saying he had the night off and wanted to stop by. Maybe we could do something. We might get a bite to eat. But after that I really had to work on my homework. I was already behind in three subjects, and I still hadn't read very far into my psychology book. I wanted to explore the chapters further in, look into personality disorders. But this was going to have to wait.

* * *

Psychology class Thursday morning wasn't something I looked forward to.

Mr. Udall had decided on a lecture today. Which was fine. Maybe everyone was too shocked over what had happened the other night. We all quietly took notes.

Ellwood was wearing another shirt with a snarky saying on it: IF STUPIDITY WAS AN ILLNESS, YOU'D BE DEAD BY NOW.

I had time before my piano class to take a break and joined the usual crowd in the pit.

"Where's Ellwood?" I said. I could have sworn he followed me out of psychology. I hadn't noticed when he'd disappeared. And a guy as big as him couldn't disappear that easily.

"He needed to go to his bat cave," Ham said.

"Bat cave? Who is he today? Batman or Robin?" Moon said.

"I think we've got the wrong show. He's more like Lurch of the Adam's Family."

Laughter burst from the others.

Nadine swooped in, gave me a hug and said, "No news on Evil Clown's site. Which is incredibly odd, since he usually posts a hundred things a day."

I was certain she was using hyperbole in this case.

"Maybe the police caught up to him," Brett said. "I wouldn't be surprised."

"It's sort of hard to drive around in a clown suit all the time and not get noticed," Moon said, eyes on his phone.

That was when Ellwood walked up, looking pale, eyes vacant. I watched him and waited for him to make some sort of comment to Ham, or spout a cruel or crude joke, as he usually did. He just stood on the outer fringe, hands down by his sides, a vacant expression on his face.

"Ellwood, you're quiet," Moon said.

"I just saw a dead man."

We all looked up at him. He still looked pale, swallowing a few times. He definitely looked a bit ill, in fact. The others chuckled, as though he were making a joke.

"You okay? You don't look so good," I said.

Ellwood nearly fell into a chair. "I was with the police."

Everyone came to attention, all chuckles faded.

"What?" I said.

"What happened?" Everyone said at once.

"Shhh," I said, batting the air with my hand. "Let him talk. What happened, Ellwood?"

"I went downstairs, you know, underground, like I always do to work on my story? And I went into the bathroom and noticed something odd in the handicap stall. I opened it and there he was, hanging from a rope."

We were all stunned, unable to respond to this.

"Oh, El, you had us going!" Ham said, batting Ellwood's arm.

"No. I'm telling you. I saw a hung man. Called the police and stayed until they came."

"Who?" I asked. "Who was it?"

He looked straight at me. "It's Mr. Taylor. He's dead."

Chapter 7

Shock went through me. "What?" I said.

Bent over, he nodded, hair flopping all over. His eyes darted back and forth, not able to focus on any of us. "I just came up from there. Police are all over it."

"You can't be serious!" Ham said. "A teacher is dead?"

Ellwood grabbed his arm. "SHHH!"

Ham yanked his meaty hand off his arm. "Stop it!"

"Be quiet, okay?" Ellwood looked around. "No one else knows about it. The police didn't want me to talk to anyone about it."

"So naturally, you've told all of us," Ham said.

"Ellwood, you're sure it's Mr. Taylor?"

"Oh, yeah."

"How?"

"I saw him hanging from a rope. It was around his neck. They said it was suicide," he said quietly.

"What!?" I almost screamed with disbelief.

"Wait. I've got this on my iPhone." He pulled out his phone and began tapping and sliding his finger across the screen. "I nearly forgot about this." Sound came from his phone. I recognized his voice. "I was dictating into my phone, like I always do. Here's a video of it." He set the phone down on the table, and we all bent, or craned, to look at it. The video had a head shot of Ellwood as he walked along a semi-dark hallway, and spoke into the speaker. His ramblings about a character named Emox, his voice echoing oddly as he entered a different room with deep turquoise tiled walls. Tops of stalls angled passed his head as he moved along.

"Uh... oh," he said as he paused. The sound of something like a door creaking came next. "Oh SHIT! Oh God! Hell! Shit no!"

The video swung wildly around, and then it came to rest on the mid-portion of a man, hands limply hanging at his sides. Wearing a lavender shirt, sleeves rolled up mid-forearm, but one had fallen loose. The camera angled upward to the face, the sight made me blink away, but I forced myself to look. Yes. It was Mr. Taylor. A rope around his neck, the face slightly bloated, lips blueish tinged. The camera angled down again to his feet and the floor. He might have hung two feet off the floor.

With a gasp, I ran from the group. Someone called my name, but I didn't stop. I charged up the steps to the main lobby, ran to the elevator doors and pressed DOWN. I had to wait what seemed forever for the doors to open. By the time they did, everyone had gathered around me.

"Here's your backpack and purse," Brett said, handing them to me. I slipped the pack over one shoulder and my purse over the other.

"What are we doing?" Moon asked.

"We're going to see the dead body," Ham said and Ellwood shoved him. Ham had to catch himself on the doors of the elevator and looked up at Ellwood with a hurt look.

"No, you stupid puke! The body was taken away almost right away. I told you I was with the police for an hour. Missed a class and everything."

The doors of the elevator opened and we all shuffled in and I punched G. The ride didn't take that long, but it felt again like forever.

"What are we doing, then?" Brett asked.

"Police still here?" I asked.

"They were when I left," Ellwood said.

The doors of the elevator slid open and I was about to step out when a uniformed man turned and held up his hand.

"I'm sorry, folks, you can't come into this area," he was in the uniform of a state cop. Wonderful. He looked as serious as a heart attack.

Somewhere in the mix I recognized Weeks' voice. Maybe I could play that card.

"My Uncle is Sheriff Weeks. Could you see if he would speak to me? My name is Lainey."

The state cop gave us all the once over, and his eyes went high and behind me. Probably recognized Ellwood.

"Just stay right there," he said, that hand up to keep us poised in the elevator.

I nodded. Brett held the door of the elevator open while we waited. I hoped nobody else wanted on the elevator because we held it hostage.

"What are we doing here?" Ham said timidly.

"I need to see what's going on," I said. "Mr. Taylor did *not* commit suicide. I don't care what anyone says."

"Lainey? What are you doing here?" Weeks strode up, his eyes taking us all in.

"Can we step out of the elevator, at least?" I asked.

"All of you?"

I turned slightly toward my companions. "These are my friends. Ellwood, here, discovered Mr. Taylor."

"Okay. But no further."

We all stepped out and let the elevator doors shut, and gathered around Weeks with the state cop holding vigil just in case a few of us had the notion to make a run for the men's lavatory. I noticed the knot of men in either uniforms or suits further up the hallway. I couldn't tell if the people in suites were detectives or what they were. I didn't recognize anyone.

Weeks went into a stance of folded arms across his chest, feet wide. "Why are all of you down here? There's nothing to see."

"That was my teacher," I said. "I was told they were saying this is a suicide."

"That's what it looks like. A suicide note was there, with him," Weeks said.

"How do you know he left it, or wrote it? How do you know his intentions?" I challenged.

"We've only just begun our investigation, Lainey."

"Make sure, then, that you look for another possibility. I spoke to Mr. Taylor only yesterday and he was fine." I looked up at Ellwood. "Right? Mr. Taylor wasn't depressed at all in class."

"No. He seemed fine," Ellwood put in.

Weeks drew in a breath, making his shoulders draw up. "This isn't my investigation," he said on his expelled breath. "I have to differ to the local authorities."

"Sheriff?" someone from behind him said. He turned. They were motioning him over. He gave him a hand up indicating to wait a moment and turned back to us. "I want all of you to go back upstairs, back to whatever you were doing and stay away from here."

I cocked my head to one side. I could think of no excuse for staying, but this wasn't over by any means. I turned away. "Let's go, guys."

We returned back upstairs, not one of us saying a word until we filed out of the elevator.

"You know that cop?" Ellwood said to me.

"That's my uncle. He just married my aunt," I explained.

"A real hard ass, eh?" Ellwood didn't miss much.

"Goes with the territory, I guess," I said as I stalked toward the commons, realizing half-way there I had a class. I really didn't want to go. How would I get into music after this?

"Oh, my gosh! I'm late for class. Mr. Williams is going to hang my hide!" Ham said and darted off like he'd been stung by a bee. Moon had already split.

"I don't know about the rest of you, but I'm too bummed to go to class, right now," Ellwood said.

I glanced up at him, "Don't blame you. I've got piano. No way I can get through the rest of my day." He strode off, his hair shifting like a banner as he walked away.

"Are you going to class?" Brett asked me.

My shoulders slumped, backpack slid from my shoulder. "No. I just can't.

"Okay, why don't you stay down in the commons, wait for me to get done with my class," Brett said, one arm slid around me. "Economy. Ugh."

"Okay. I've got things to read." I wasn't sure how I could concentrate enough to read anything. He walked me down the steps into the commons. No one seemed aware of what had happened. The police had somehow kept the death a secret. At least for now. Once people found out, it would be all over the school like wild fire.

Brett kissed me on the cheek and took off for his class.

I dumped my things onto a table and dropped into a chair. Elbows on the table I pillowed my head on my arms. It was too loud in the immediate area to fall asleep, which wouldn't be a good idea where people could steal anything from someone who had gone into Z Land. I wasn't lucky enough to even doze, anyway. Five minutes later there came this sound of a deep guttural sigh. Someone said, "Oh, no!"

I looked up and around. I figured that someone had discovered the news about Mr. Taylor. It was probably getting around on social media. Possibly one of the people in our group who had gone downstairs, or however, someone had gotten the news and leaked it. Sometimes I just hated social media. Lately I wasn't a big fan at all.

From another direction there was a sudden screech.

Someone said, "That's awful!"

My eyes darted around to try and locate the source. Other people in the Pit were also trying to discern where this noise was coming from. It had my heart hammering, worried that possibly Sinclair was behind something once again.

Someone rushed up to me. "Lainey! Lainey!" It was Brianna. I was on my feet, and met her at the end of my table.

"Did you hear?"

"I've heard," I said, but said nothing more, waiting for her to say it.

"I can't believe it!" Her eyes were moist as she dropped her purse on the table and shakily fell into a chair. I wasn't sure why she was upset. It seemed odd to me she'd be this upset over a teacher she didn't know had been found dead.

"You need something? A coke?"

She shook her head. "I just can't believe it! Someone shot Carol."

"Wait. What?" I said and dropped into a chair, looking at her. "You heard what?"

"Someone got word that Carol Taylor was found shot to death in her house. The police had gone to tell her her husband was found dead—they think he hung himself—and the police had to go into the house and found her shot to death."

"What? How? I mean—" I shook my head trying to grasp this new piece of news and put it all together. A hard knot had formed in my center, not able to grasp all this at once.

"I only know that the police found her body in the kitchen. At their house. She was shot to death. They say her husband committed suicide down in the basement, right here, just this morning." She tapped the table with a mint-colored polished fingernail.

I grasped her arm and said, "First of all, I'm not so certain Mr. Taylor committed suicide. I just won't believe it until an autopsy is performed."

She looked at me. "You knew about this?"

"I only knew about Mr. Taylor. Not about his wife. You say she was home?"

"Yes. Remember? She was fired yesterday."

"Yes. I do remember, now that you've reminded me." My mind was whirling with several things. How were the deaths of this couple related? Or were they?

She pulled in snot and said, "Someone tried to say he shot her, and then came here and hung himself."

"What? That's just ridiculous!" I said with passion. "I saw him yesterday, spoke with him, he seemed fine. He loved his wife. I could tell." Even though I'd only just met him, my intuition about people was never wrong.

"Well, it just goes to show you how much you don't know people," she said with a shrug.

Of course, I wasn't convinced by any stretch. But I wasn't going to win an argument over this, and so dropped it. The dust would have to settle first.

She looked at her cell phone and said, "I'd better go. The office people were all in shock, but with everything that's happened, there are rumors the school will be shut down. At least for rest of the week," Brianna said and wobbled away, blowing her nose into a napkin.

Brett's form loped across the nearly empty pit and came up to me a bit breathless. I stood again, wondering what else had happened.

"They've canceled classes," he said. That didn't surprise me.

"I just saw my friend. She told me Mr. Taylor's wife was shot at home," I said.

"Serious?" he said, straightening. "What's going on!"

I grabbed my things, shoving books back into the backpack. "I don't know." My brain seemed to be going in a hundred different directions at once.

"I think we should leave," Brett said. We climbed the stairs to the next level, facing the wall where the stairs and elevator were. The elevator doors slid opened and the very rotund Mr. Smith emerged wearing an olive green shirt with a matching tie, black pants, no jacket. His wingtips shinny, except for a noticeable smudge on the left one. As he approached I noted the smudge on his shoe looked more like a gray scrape. I had to wonder if he knew this when he'd put them on this morning. I noticed his shirt looked slightly rumpled, and there were sweat stains around the armpits as though he had been doing something that had put him under some sort of stress, or something physically demanding, and I wondered what it could have been.

As we turned to head for the exit, Weeks and two of his men marched toward us from our left.

"What's the meaning of this!" Smith shouted, his voice carrying through the open area of the commons, which was quickly emptying of students.

Holding Brett's hand, I stopped, as it was apparent we were angling to a point where we'd be between Weeks and Smith and it was pretty obvious there was about to be a confrontation.

"What do you think you're doing here disrupting classes?" Smith's legs carried him quickly across the commons, quicker than I'd have thought he could work his legs under such a girth.

"Excuse me, but who are you?" Weeks growled back, not giving an inch. The two men were five feet away from one another. Brett and I stood a few feet off from the center of the confrontation. Our heads moving as we watched the volley of words.

"I am Cooper Smith, the president of this college." Smith tilted his head back slightly, looking self-important, as though he'd just claimed himself emperor.

"You are aware that a death has occurred here, in your little college, aren't you?"

Smith's jowels shook dangerously as though the very mention of death had disrupted his planned day. "I have heard that, yes. A very sad thing. Very sad indeed. I was about to—"

"And are you aware the decedent has been found in the basement of this building?" Weeks said, hanging his hands at the utility belt were his gun and other paraphernalia pertaining to his occupation was.

"Yes. Of course I have!" Smith's face had turned an particular shade of crimson that definitely clashed with his olive shirt. "And I'll ask you again, why are you here disrupting classes and my students?"

"Teachers have dismissed classes for the day," I said.

Smith blinked at me as though I were a detestable rodent who'd just appeared out of nowhere. Students were heading toward the exits in droves. Unless he was blind, I didn't understand how he hadn't noticed the place was emptying faster than a theater after the last show. In fact, who had decided classes should be dismissed, if he, the president, hadn't ordered it?

Smith looked around, and seemed to drink this in for a moment. "I've been out. I wasn't aware. B-but still, you have no warrant to be traipsing through here. I demand you leave at once!" The red had suffused from his face and now was merely a pink glow in his cheeks and portions of his thick triple chin.

"First place, this is a public place. Second, I'm investigating a homicide. I don't need a warrant for either," Weeks said and looked at the uninformed man who came up the hall and stepped up beside him. A large clear bag in his hands. Inside was a gun.

"Found it in his desk drawer," his deputy said.

"Good. Tag it, take it to headquarters for the lab to look at it," Weeks said. Both men marched away to the distant door behind us. There were three exits to each lot from here.

"Wait a minute, sheriff. Homicide? A gun? What's going on here? I demand to know at once!" Smith said.

"A little while ago, Carol Taylor, wife of Chad Taylor—who was found hung in the basement of this building—was found fatally shot to death in her home."

I was mentally correcting his sentence as Smith did something akin to a double-take. Somehow it seemed over-done, in my opinion.

"My lord, no!" he gasped. One hand had produced a white handkerchief and dabbed at his sweating face.

"You haven't heard that either?" Weeks asked a little surprised by this.

"Those in your office heard all about it, just moments ago," I said, circumventing whatever Smith was about to say, because his face was turning red again, cheeks puffed up holding back whatever it was he wanted to say.

His eyes slid to me, a tight smile on his lips. "My dear child, I've just returned from town. I've had no calls, nothing about this got to me."

I somehow found this hard to believe that someone hadn't called him.

"What are you doing here, anyway, child? If you're a student, why aren't you also leaving?" While he spoked to me his arms went outward and the area where his shirt met his trousers opened revealing skin and dark hair. Slightly embarrassed, I looked away, thinking I was happy that his zipper wasn't open as well.

"Lainey, if you don't mind, could you just go on home, please?" Weeks asked me pleasantly enough.

"Oh, you know each other?" Smith said, looking from me to him.

"She's my niece," Weeks said, giving me that look that said not to push it.

Without another word, I stepped between them, with Brett in my wake.

He caught up with me. "Who told you about the murder of Taylor's wife?"

"Brianna. Just a few minutes before you came," I said, striding through the doors and out into the heat and humidity.

"Was that a gun that deputy had?"

"Yes."

We walked out into the parking lot several paces when I realized I'd parked in the back lot. I stopped. "I'm not parked out here," I said.

"Oh. Well, let me drive you around back. This heat is pretty bad on the blacktop."

"Thank you." He led me to his car. I got in and said, "You've got the car today?"

"Yeah. I don't like driving the van very much. I'm going to have to have someone work on it before we drive up to Dubuque for the next gig." He paused and looked at me. "Did you ask your aunt and uncle if you can go?"

I hadn't asked. For one thing, I didn't think it was proper for me to go. For another, I know Weeks and my aunt would simply say no. I turned to him. "The answer is no."

"That's what they said? No?" He was pushing the issue.

"Ah, actually I didn't ask them. I don't think I should go."

"What? Why?" He sounded more angry than disappointed.

I shrugged. "Right. I can just see me telling my aunt I'm going to be staying in Dubuque over night with you and your wild band members."

"It'll be in separate motel rooms," he said defensively.

"Motel rooms have doors," I said. "And beds."

"And locks." His finger went up.

I looked at him, a smile creasing my lips. We hadn't done anything more than kiss on our dates. I had told him I wasn't about to break my rule of staying a virgin until I married. Maybe I was silly to expect any modern man to respect this, but it was a logical barrier against my getting hurt after giving into a man's desires—or my own for that matter—and his leaving me soon afterward. I'd heard about many girls giving into a guy, having sex with him, and his leaving her after he was done with her. And sometimes the girl would become pregnant. Of course, there were times I'd frustrated him by stopping him before our kissing got out of hand. He'd begun to grope in places I didn't want his hand. I once had to slap him. It took him a day and a half to get over it and call me to say he was sorry. He even brought me a single red rose. I forgave him, but it seemed our relationship was on wobbly ground and at any time we'd break up because of this. My going somewhere to stay in a motel where Brett was staying was good as saying "yes" to allowing our relationship to go to the next level.

While he drove through the lot, he talked about having to call some motel to make arrangements for the band members to stay. "I haven't looked it up, yet, but it's a big city. Should be all sorts of motels."

"No doubt."

"Ask and see if you can come," he said. "Pretty please? With sprinkles on top?"

I closed my eyes briefly. "When is it?"

"Two weekends from this one."

"I don't know," I said.

"What don't you know?"

"I've got homework," I argued. I actually wanted to have a weekend without anyone bothering me so I could begin writing my book. His being gone would afford me that time to do what I wanted. Mr. Taylor's handouts had me excited. Then my brain did an about face. Who would teach his class, now? And then I replayed Ellwood's film of what he'd seen when he discovered Mr. Taylor's body. I hadn't really looked at it properly. I wanted to see it again, before I couldn't.

"Do you have Ellwood's phone number?" I asked.

"It's on my cell phone. I don't know it off hand," he said. "Why?"

I reached over and he handed me his cell phone.

"What have you got in mind?"

"You'll see in a moment." I scrolled through his contacts, didn't find Ellwood but found El. "Is it El?"

"Yeah. Don't like long names, so I shorten them," he said.

"What am I under?" I wondered.

"LQ, of course."

"Of course."

I called the number and Ellwood answered, "What's up?"

"Ellwood, it's Lainey," I said.

"Hey. What's up?"

"Where are you right now?"

"Driving into town."

"Which town?"

"Cedar Ridge. Why?"

"Is there some place we can meet?"

"Uh, sure. How about the burger place? I'm pulling in right now, in fact."

I said to Brett, "There's a burger joint in town. Do you know it?"

"No. Where is it?"

I repeated the question. Ellwood gave me directions and I repeated them to Brett.

"Okay, see you in a bit," I said and hung up. "Let's leave my car for now."

"What? Why?"

"Gotta eat lunch, right?" I said evasively. I didn't want him to know my ulterior motives.

"I guess."

When we pulled into the burger place—it was called One More Burger Place—we spotted Ellwood's dented and rusted car and pulled in next to it. I hoped out and joined Brett. He opened the door of the burger joint for me. We strode in and were blasted with heavy grease from the fryers. I felt suddenly starved. It took one second to scope out the small interior where a dozen or so tables or booths lined up along walls or the window in the narrow space provided for indoor seating. Ellwood sat at a booth, his laptop open in front of him. Food wrappers scattered around him like protective walls of greasy paper. He looked like a squirrel with his cache. We waved to him, he held up his big paw in a wave, but was too much into whatever he was doing on his laptop to hold our gaze. I hated to bother him.

"What do you want?" Brett asked as we pulled up behind a few people waiting in line to order.

"Get me a burger, fries and Coke," I said, noting they had the only beverage I liked here. "I need to use the lady's room."

After I was finished in the bathroom, I strolled over to Ellwood's table. Brett was already seated across from him, waiting for our baskets of greasy fast food to arrive.

"What are you working on?" I said as I slid into the booth.

"What I was working on this morning before I was so horribly interrupted by our teacher's body swinging from the bathroom stall." I was amazed Ellwood could go into his callous-unemotional mode so easily as though he had completely recovered from his shock—if indeed that was shock—three or so hours ago, and could now talk about it so casually.

I, on the other hand, had to muster up the courage to not only ask to view that video, but watch it. I wasn't sure if I was up to doing so on either an empty stomach or full, but I had to see it again. I was certain Mr. Taylor did not take his own life. And if that was the case, someone else did. Which would open a whole can of worms, but there it was.

"Ellwood. Do you still have the video you took this morning when this all happened?" I asked, and bit my lower lip waiting for him to respond.

"Yep." He was tapping away at his keys.

"You didn't by any chance share it with anyone, did you?"

"No. I was afraid I'd get into trouble. But my finger wanted to push SEND to about a dozen people on Facebook."

"Good that you didn't, because you might get into trouble for it," I said. Not only that, it would be so horrible people would think him the lowest form of human. "I'd like to see it again, if I could, please?"

Ellwood's gaze went off me to Brett and back to me. He couldn't hide his surprise.

"I should charge you."

I made a scathing sound and whacked his thick shoulder.

"Sure. Here." He moved his finger on his laptop. "I can bring it up on this, and the view will be much better on the larger screen. Let me just get it set up." He tapped and scrolled and tapped again, then turned it around after one final press of his mouse.

"Wow. This is great!" The screen was filled with Ellwood talking and walking down that semi-dark hallway. Turning, he entered the bathroom, a squeaking door hinge preceding him.

"*Make sure I haven't discarded that chapter on Rood. I really need to expand on that character,*" Ellwood was heard saying in the video. He moved through the men's lavatory, and now the dark turquoise tile was clearer and I could see the grout in between each square. The white ceiling swished behind his head as his camera on his phone panned awkwardly.

"*Oh shit,*" Ellwood said in the video.

Brett grabbed my arm at this point. "Are you sure you want to—"

"Shhh!" I said still watching the camera angle off of Ellwood, the picture swished and jarred the image until it stopped and now the body of Mr. Taylor came into focus. I noted his lavender shirt, with the cuffs rolled up but the right one had come partially unrolled. There was no tie. I wasn't sure if Mr. Taylor wore ties as a rule, the two times I'd seen him, only once he'd had a tie on.

The video panned down to his feet. Something about his feet caught my attention. Something about his shoes wasn't right. Then it panned upward.

"Wait. How do you pause this?" I wasn't comfortable with his laptop, as it was a little different from mine.

"Here," Brett said, reaching and he made the video pause, but not where I wanted it.

"Can you make it go back a few seconds?"

"To where?"

"I want to see his feet."

Brett put it back to the right place.

"Stop it right there." I pointed to the feet.

"What is it?" Ellwood came around to view the screen. He'd been eating his fries while I was watching the video.

"You see? Look at the shoes. They're definitely on the wrong feet!"

"Whoa," Brett said. "She's right."

"Crap," Ellwood said. "I never noticed that."

"How do you explain that?" I said, pointing to the screen.

"You don't," Ellwood said, and he moved his cursor and re-played that part again.

"Not only that..." I pointed at the screen while I looked up at Ellwood. "Was there anything he could have stepped up on?"

Ellwood straightened, eyes on the video. "Like, the toilet?"

"How far away was the toilet from where he hung?" I turned back to the computer. "Run the video again from the beginning. But mute it." I darted a look around. A woman with our food on a tray came to our table. Ellwood lifted the laptop off the table and stepped away a foot or two with it. The woman in the apron set down our baskets of steamy hot food and drinks, telling us to enjoy.

"Ready?" Ellwood asked me, now that we were alone again.

"Yeah," I said, moving our food to the side, the aromas wafting off the fries had my mouth watering. I grabbed my drink and a fry while Ellwood set the computer back down on the end of the table. He ran the video again, leaving the sound off. I took it all in, working to not be bothered, but I was. A human being was hanging by the neck in a men's stall. I couldn't help but wonder if this bathroom wasn't chosen because hardly no one went down there. Obviously the murderer had to find a safe place in which to commit his crime where no one would discover it until much later.

"That isn't a suicide," I said after seeing the thing all the way through. "The shoes being on the wrong feet is a big tell. But there's a few other things that bother me, too." There was something about the way the head was angled forward, not to the side, like I'd expected. An autopsy would determine how he died. Asphyxiation, or something else. Maybe something else had happened to him prior to being hung. I reasoned someone would have to surprise Mr. Taylor, and maybe knock him out first, then strangle him somehow, and then string him up like that.

Ellwood took his laptop back to his side of the table while Brett and I sat down to eat our meals. After unfolding my greasy hamburger, I paused for a moment, not touching my food, not because I was grossed out, as I thought I would be. The morning's events went through my head. Especially when Mr. Smith and Weeks butted heads. Smith's objections to the police being there hit me all wrong.

"Which police unit came first when you called 911?" I asked Ellwood.

"Unit?"

"Was it the sheriff's police or a local cop?" I clarified.

"He was some local cop. Sort of reminded me of Barny Fife." Ellwood laughed at his own joke. We chuckled politely.

"I thought you were hungry," Brett reminded me gently.

I picked up my hamburger in two hands. It had everything on it, and I had to maneuver it around to get the best bite. Once I bit into it I couldn't stop eating. I hadn't eaten since this morning before going to school, and that had only been toast! No wonder I was ravenous!

We were half-way finished with our meals when I said, "I've gotta go back there. I need to see that lavatory for myself. See if there's any clues. Get the feel of it, see how large the—you know—"

"—john—"

"—stall is. How far away from the toilet he was hung, all of that."

"Jeeze. Not while I'm eating," Brett complained. I glance up at him, surprised to see the irritated look in his eyes.

I looked over at a few fries left on his paper wrappings and a messy pool of ketchup to the last dregs. "You look done to me." I grabbed one of his fries—and he didn't object—and ate it.

"You're fucking joking," Ellwood said in his usual unfazed way, his gaze through the thick glasses unflinching.

"No. I need to go back there," I said, looking at my companions. "I'll go alone, if I have to."

"I'm in," Ellwood said, a smirk on his face.

"You sure? I mean, why?" Brett said, wadding up his napkins and wrappers and put them into the red plastic basket it all came in.

"I told you. Mr. Taylor did *not* commit suicide. Someone murdered and put him there. I want to get to the bottom of that."

"Cool," Ellwood said, closing his laptop, and gathered up his garbage.

"Okay, but this had better be it," Brett sighed. "I'd like to go home at some point today and crash before I work tonight."

"Fine. Could we use just one vehicle? I don't want us to be obvious when we drive back there, all three of in two cars." Of course mine was still parked at the college.

"We can use mine," Ellwood offered.

"That old bomb?" Brett scoffed gathering up our mess and putting it all back on the tray.

"It may look bad on the outside, but the engine works," Ellwood claimed, shoving his laptop into his backpack.

"Let's use his car," I said, getting up out of the booth.

"If it starts," Brett complained.

"Hey. The engine is new," Ellwood retorted.

"Oh. Alright. Talk about skullduggery," Brett said getting up.

"This is awesome. We'll park in the back lot," Ellwood said, following us out.

I retrieved my backpack from the back seat, and took it with me. I'd have to retrieve my car from the campus lot, after we were done.

We drove the ten minutes back to school, and found that the parking lots were nearly empty. We figured it had to be just office people, maybe a few teachers, and hardly any of them, if that.

"We'll go through one of the back doors," Ellwood said.

"Can we get downstairs another way, besides the elevators that we used earlier?"

"Yes. There's stairs, but I've got an even better way, so no one knows you're heading down there," he said and made a sinister laugh— "*Moowah-ha-hahhhh!*" Then he rushed ahead.

Brett and I followed our large friend through a side door. He turned up a hallway that I wasn't familiar with.

"You know, this is giving me a new idea for my book," Ellwood said, sounding excited.

"You working on a murder mystery?" I asked.

"No. I'm strictly fantasy or science fiction. Currently, my WIP is fantasy. I sort of borrow from Jim Butcher, but my characters are in a sort of Lord of the Rings type of world."

"Sounds cool," I said.

"Coming to a theater near you," Brett joked. The two went back and forth with a volley of insults (male teasing in its prime and I'd rather not repeat), as we turned a corner. Here the floor inclined slightly. We turned another corner and there was a window looking down onto a gymnasium where three guys were shooting and bouncing a basketball across the parquet floor.

"Wow. I didn't know this was here," I said, leaning toward the glass to look down.

"The stairway is up ahead," Ellwood said, already ten feet ahead of me. I caught up with Brett and Ellwood, and we went through a metal door and down the stairs, which bent at right angles twice.

We came out into a long hall. The smell of locker room was strong here. The hall turned ten feet to our right.

Pointing to the corner Ellwood said, "The men's locker rooms are down there. The women's are on the other side of the gymnasium."

"Good to know," I said.

"That explains the men's john on this end," I said.

Without a word we strode down the hallway, passing several wooden doors, some with large dark windows, some without. One had STORAGE stenciled on it. Storage for what, I hadn't a clue. I had to peer into the ones with windows, out of curiosity, but it was so dark I couldn't see much but shadows.

"Here it is." Ellwood stood next to a door, and pushed it open. The interior was walled with that dark turquoise tile I'd seen in the film. *Eau de locker room* scents wafted out. I definitely picked up faint cologne in the mix. I paused to sniff. My two companions stopped to look at me strangely.

"You getting high off the smells down here?" Ellwood teased and both of them chuckled. I couldn't help it. Odors lingered here. There might be a clue as to who was here, if I noticed that cologne again.

"Not exactly," I said, knowing he was just being flippant. "I remembered someone wearing this cologne." Mr. Taylor had worn exactly this fragrance, but it was faint, yet a musk came through, a stronger one overlapping the first one, and because of the mix I couldn't pick out either one with authority. But something about the two scents had my brain working on who wore such cologne.

I pulled my cell phone out and took a picture right away of the lavatory. Three urinals on one wall, three sinks on another and off to the left were two stalls. One was rather large and it was obviously the handicapped stall. Larger than usual, I had to guess that it was possibly a last minute construction to accommodate the handicapped. Maybe they'd made it out of two stalls? I looked at the floor. There were little round holes and imprint where the previous upright for the door had been. My guess was that it was at least six feet wide, with a larger door to accommodate a wheelchair. The overhead bar was on the hinge side of the door. I noticed it was bent slightly. Probably where Mr. Taylor's body had hung.

Brett advanced, and I pressed him back. "I'm taking pictures first." As far as I was concerned this was a murder site and anything I found here would be crucial to my reconstruction.

Looking across the white tiled floor, I noticed dusty tracks across the floor, like wheels had made it. Some were skinny and some were wider. Of course the many footprints from the police marred this one bit of evidence. There was no help for it, so I went in, stepping to one side, trying to not add my own footprints to what was already there.

"You guys stay out there and guard." I pointed to the door. "Anyone comes along tell them the toilet is out of order, and you've sent for a janitor."

Ellwood looked over to Brett and said, "What if it is a janitor?"

"Then, tell him... tell him I'll be out in a minute."

They both chuckled again. I was batting a thousand with these two. Maybe I should become a stand-up comedian?

The door closed and I was now alone in a men's john where my creative writing teacher had been hung to look like a suicide. The thought of that alone made my body quiver. I'd never been in a men's john before, of course, and ignored the urinals. I took three pictures of the floor, making sure the tire treads of each were visible. I took another one directly across from the stalls, and one close up of the handicapped stall. Carefully, I opened the door and took pictures of the stall's interior, especially above where the brace came across and where I assumed the rope had been drawn across in order to hang Mr. Taylor. I took one of the hand braces along the wall next to the toilet, where Ellwood said the other end of the rope had been tied to hold the body up. I noted how far away the toilet sat from where his body hung. I bent at the waist, studied the marks of the wheel tracks inside the stall, unfortunately a lot of it was marred with many footprints from those who had to cut Mr. Taylor down. I then realized there were two sets of thin tires, coming and going, but they were only on the outside of the stall. Something with wider wheels and a little bit of tread on the outer edge had been pulled into the stall. After a moment's thought, I realized the paramedics would have had to bring in a gurney to take Mr. Tyler's body out of here. That would explain the second set of wheel tracks.

The other set of wheels was something else. Thicker with different tread. I was sure that it wasn't a wheelchair. A wheelchair had large wheels in back and off-setting front ones. Even if it had been an electric cart, the wheels would not have been so wide apart. I surmised it to be two feet wide, and at least two sets, same width apart and same thickness for both sets of wheels. I was thinking some sort of cart.

Quickly I had a reconstruction in my mind. Mr. Taylor would had to have been killed elsewhere and brought down here, somehow. It would be a bit of a strain to carry a six-foot man down here and hoist him up, unless you were a pro wrestler. It would take a lot of muscle to take care of this task—or take two or three men, which I was certain didn't happen.

I knew what I was looking at was the method of operation—the MO—to bring Mr. Taylor into the lavatory. If there was a cart somewhere that had been used to bring the body in here, I hadn't seen it. Obviously, the killer had hidden that as well.

I trudged back to the outer door and pulled it open slightly, and it made that noticeable creaking sound I'd heard in the video. Ellwood and Brett stood on either side of the door like obedient sentinels. Ellwood looked like an immovable ogre and I doubted anyone would think twice about messing with him. They both looked at me.

"How's it going?"

"Okay. Say, did you guys see a large cart? Something big enough to move a body with?"

Ellwood snickered and Brett simply returned a look like I was crazy.

"What do you need a cart for?" Brett asked.

"I don't need it," I said. "The killer used it to wheel Mr. Taylor in here from wherever he killed him."

"Are you kidding?" Ellwood said, incredulous. Brett looked down one end of the hall to the other as though he were looking for one.

"No, I'm not. Check and see if any those other doors are unlocked along here. If they're open, look inside and see what's in there. If you find something like I described, don't touch it, but let me know. I'm going to take a few more photographs and come out.

The two began methodically checking all the doors up and down the hallway. Every one of them were locked.

"No luck," Ellwood said striding back to where I stood at the doorway.

"I need to find it. If too much time passes, the murderer might move it away from here."

"What do you suggest? We pick a lock?" As if he had a lock pick set. But then, I wouldn't put it past Ellwood to have access to one.

"No. I just wonder if a janitor might be still here." I was thinking of Mr. Bean.

"Well, we haven't seen one," Brett said.

"Ellwood, you know this place pretty good. You have any idea where the janitor might hang out? His cubby, whatever?" I asked.

Ellwood thought for a moment. "Yeah. I think I do. It's on the first floor."

"Okay, good. You don't mind going to see if you can find a Mr. Bean?"

"Mr. Bean?"

"I knew him in grade school," I explained. "I bumped into him down here the other day. He's really nice. You go and see if you can find him, me and Brett will try and locate him on the other floors."

"What's he look like?" Brett asked.

"Not very tall, sort of slight, and about fifty-something. Wears thick glasses."

"Sounds like my computer science teacher," Ellwood said.

My hope was to find Mr. Bean, explain to him I needed to find a cart that might have been used down here, and then, call the police. Or, if not call the police, at least tell Weeks of my suspicions.

We took the elevator to the first floor. I stayed on the main floor, went to look in the cafeteria, but the doors were locked tight. I didn't want anyone to know we were here, or what we were doing, so I went down to the Pit and waited.

Fifteen minutes later, Brett called me letting me know he'd found Mr. Bean and they'd be down in a moment. He'd found him on the third floor where the offices were. I called Ellwood, telling him to meet us in the subbasement. I started out of the Pit, but ducked back down,below sight, seeing someone emerge from the elevator. It was Mr. Smith. Tie gone, his jacket flipped over one shoulder, whistling aimlessly, he headed for an exit. I waited until he was gone before I surged to the elevator doors and pressed the call button. It stopped, doors opened, and there was Mr. Bean and Brett.

"Hello, Lainey. Your friend here was telling me you needed something from the basement?" He looked at me through those thick glasses as I got on and pressed the G button.

"Yes. If you could, please? There may be a cart down there, and I'm almost pretty sure it's in one of those locked rooms down there." I'd given some thought to lie some. Did I want Mr. Bean to know what I was doing? I worried it would sound like I'd gone around the bend, as they say. So, I didn't elaborate, unless he asked.

"Oh, sure. No problem." His wide smile beamed and he made a little laugh. "You'd be surprised what people have left in those rooms down there. Once I came across three upright vacuums, all of them in perfectly good working condition. After they built upwards, I guess they wanted to buy all new office equipment. Sort of a waste of money, if you ask me."

"How old is this building?" I asked, as the doors swished shut.

"Twenty-five years. Thirty-seven, if you count the older buildings they used to have on the outskirts," he said.

"Really?" The elevator went down briefly and the bump of it coming to the bottom jarred my knees some.

"Yep. They built this center section here twenty-five years ago. This was all the offices down here." The door swished open and we stepped out. The hulk of Ellwood loomed down the hall-way.

We all converged in the center of the hall, near the bathroom.

"You heard about what happened here, this mornin', didn't you?" Mr. Bean asked.

I nodded while my two friends made affirmative noises.

"What a terrible thing, too. He was such a nice man. I can't imagine anyone taking their own life when here's life and hope," Mr. Bean went on.

My glance darted to Ellwood and Brett and I said, "Mr. Bean, can I tell you something confidential?"

"Of course," he said.

"Can't repeat it though," I said.

His hand went up. "Word of honor. I won't repeat it."

I smiled. "Good. Mr. Taylor didn't commit suicide." I let my words sink in for a few seconds.

"What do you mean? Someone mur—"

"Shhh!" I said, hoping no one was around to hear us. I whispered. "Yes."

"What about Mrs. Taylor? They say Mr. Taylor shot her," he said.

"No. Someone else shot her and then killed her husband." I frowned down at the floor. "I've gotta find the motive behind it all." I wondered if one murder was to hide something major done by the murderer, and the other one was to pin it all on Mr. Taylor in order to draw suspicion off of said murderer. Sounded about right to me.

Brett made a groan, but I ignored him. I'd told him he could have gone home, earlier, since my car was parked out back.

"But how do you know about all this?" Mr. Bean asked.

"I've seen pictures of the—the—you know." I nervously looked at my friends.

"Body," Ellwood supplied.

"Body? Mr. Taylor's body? Oh, my heavens." Mr. Bean looked stressed out and under the bad lighting the bags under his eyes were more pronounced.

"The cart may have been how the murderer moved Mr. Taylor."

"Oh dear, oh dear," Mr. Bean said, his gaze going to each of us.

"Okay, Mr. Bean, what I want to do is see if this bin, or cart—or whatever—is in one of these rooms."

"Good golly, child! Shouldn't you let the police do this?" he looked upset at the prospect of doing anything out of the ordinary.

"The local police said it was suicide. I have to convince the sheriff that it wasn't. I need something to strengthen my case. I find the cart, or whatever was used to move Mr. Taylor's body down here and into the bathroom, it might have the murderer's fingerprints on it. Or some trace evidence."

"Really?"

"Would you mind opening up these doors? Let's check and see if there isn't something inside."

He pulled out his large ring of keys, they jangled and made a racket while he looked through them. "I don't mind saying this makes me terribly nervous."

"You keep my secret, Mr. Bean, and I won't say who helped me find it. If we find it," I said.

Mr. Bean opened up the first door and we went from one empty office to another. None revealed anything large enough with wheels that could have been used to move a body. Mostly there were old cardboard boxes in them, some old desks, chairs, and file drawers that looked older than me.

"Looks useless," Brett said.

"Bastard must have taken it back up with him," Ellwood said.

"We've got one more door. This is a closet," Jimmy said, unlocking one last door. It was dark inside. He pulled a string on a single light bulb above. Expecting to see nothing, or at the very most the usual contents of a closet, like mops brooms pails and such, we stared instead at something large flat-topped and gray with wheels. My pulse quickened. This was exactly what I was looking for. I could hardly believe my luck!

"Oh my gosh!" I said a thrill going through me.

"This it?" Mr. Bean reached in.

"Don't touch it!" I said, grasping his arm. "If this is it, it might have fingerprints on it from the killer." Although I highly doubted it.

"Oh. That's right." Mr. Bean retracted his hands and put them against his chest and brushed the palms down his shirt a few times, as though he might have gotten them dirty. "Holy cow. How did you know?"

I shrugged. Maybe I did have some sort of super sleuth sense.

"Now what?" Ellwood wondered.

I turned to Mr. Bean. "You don't happen to have some disposable gloves on you, do you?"

He reached for his back pocket. "I do. Always carry a pair." He held a pair of blue Polyurethane gloves in his hand. "I never know when I might need them."

I took them from him and slipped them on.

"What are you going to do?" Brett asked.

I grabbed the gray handle of the large cart trying to hold it on the farthest side, where someone wouldn't have touched it to maneuver it. Made of hard gray plastic, it was difficult to maneuver out through the doorway. I made sure the guys didn't touch it, repeating again there might be prints, or other evidence. Of course my moving it around might further jeopardized the evidence, but the killer had already moved it. Once I wrangled it out of the closet, I rolled it down the hallway, but stopped rolling and looked at the wheels. They had some sort of dust all over them.

"Look at how the wheels have tracked something along the floor," I said, pointing. They all bent to look at the floor.

"Yep," Mr. Bean said. "Looks like a powder of some sort. Maybe from a dusty floor that hasn't been in use."

I bent to examined one wheel and took a finger and swiped it. I looked at it. "It might be cleaning agent." I sniffed at it. "Smells sort of like sink cleanser. I held it to Mr. Bean and he sniffed.

"Yup. Sure does."

"I don't know where it originally came from, but one thing's for sure, it was used the way I said." I continued rolling it. "Open the door for me, Ellwood, please."

He moved ahead and pushed the men's room door open.

"I figure that the killer would have been able to push the door open, probably with his own body, and pull this through," I said, rolling the cart into the lavatory. Voice echoing, I continued my reconstruction, "I figured that he was able to roll Mr. Taylor right into the stall. Let's see if I'm right." I rolled it to the handicapped stall, opened the door and was able to push it right in.

"It fits." Mr. Bean said.

"I thought as much." I noticed the wheels had made exactly the same marks on the floor as I had seen. The new marks were more pronounced, lined up nearly side-by-side in the stall by the previous ones when it was used earlier.

"This is exactly what the killer used," I said, my voice shaky as I emerged and let the door on the stall close. My steps were a bit wobbly as I moved toward the men who were standing just inside the doorway watching my every move.

"You know that they had two children?" Mr. Bean said, his voice subdued nearly to a whisper, brow crinkled. He meant the Taylors.

I blinked, feeling the sting of tears and had to gather my resolve as I removed the blue gloves from my hands and stalked toward the waste can near the sink. "And they can't grow up thinking their father killed their mother and then committed suicide," I said, my voice rough. I was about to throw away the gloves when I noticed several pairs of whitish gloves in the waste bin, on top. I stopped my motions. I realized the first responders had probably donned them when they found Mr. Taylor, then threw them out in here. Blue Polyurethane gloves, similar to mine, were underneath these other gloves and a few paper towels. Was it possible the killer had worn similar disposable gloves?

I said to Mr. Bean, "Can you lock this bathroom?"

"Sure."

"Who has a key to open it?"

"Just me and the other four janitors."

"Any night janitors?"

"Yes."

"Is it possible to tell them to not open this because of the ongoing investigations by the police?"

"You need special police tape to keep people out," Ellwood said.

I spun on him. "Well, I don't have that, do I?"

"I can get a bit of caution tape over it. Then I'll get the word out. There's chalkboard we write notes on. I'll make a special note about not opening this door for anyone."

"Except the police. Because obviously someone opened that closet door with a key," I said, pointing down the hall.

"Should I ask around if any of my people opened it?" he asked.

"You can. But I've a feeling the killer had a key himself."

"Not that many people have access," he argued, hands on hips. His stance made me vaguely think of Weeks.

"Whoever did, or does, has access to the keys that go to all the doors in this place."

"These are old offices," Mr. Bean said after a moment of thought. "Old sets of keys might be in the main office, somewhere."

Squeezing one eye closed, I thought about that. "Then it could have been someone who worked in the office. Someone who has access to those keys. Someone who Mr. and Mrs. Taylor knew well and probably didn't feel threatened by them."

"Profile fits," Ellwood said. "Now for the motive."

I was almost sure of the motive, thinking over the last few days, what I knew about Carol, and why she was home. I moved up the hall toward the elevators, but stopped, realizing we should take that side way out again.

Jimmy had locked the door and passed me, about to take the elevator. "I'll get that caution tape up right away, Lainey."

"Thanks," I said, joining my friends. "I've gotta call Weeks. Or the sheriff's office." We retraced our steps taking the same way back up. I dialed the sheriff's office as I walked, put my cell phone to my ear and didn't have to wait long before a female voice announced, "Sheriff's office, this is Sargent Saxton, how may I direct your call?"

"Oh, hi, Maureen," I said. "This is Lainey."

"Hi, Lainey. Is everything okay?"

"Ah, well, I'm good. But I was just wondering if Weeks was in."

"No. He went home around eight." She chuckled. "Went to bed, I expect. He has to come back in tonight. Some of the guys around here went home with the flu last night. Happy I've had my flu shot. Hope everyone else has too. This thing is pretty bad." I knew Weeks had had his, insisted on by my aunt over his obstinate objections. I now wondered if he weren't thanking her profusely for making him get that shot.

"I've discovered some discrepancies concerning that so-called suicide here at Whitney College," I said.

"Really?" she sounded intrigued. "Like what?"

"I'm wondering if anyone there would be interested in my theories concerning it?"

"Ah, well, that isn't our case, I'm afraid," Maureen said.

"Whose is it, then? Who can I contact?"

"Just a second, I've gotta take another call, look this up and I'll get right back to you. Hold on."

We were outside striding toward Ellwood's car before she got back to me.

"You still there, Lainey?" Maureen asked.

"Yes."

"Okay, his name is Brandon Okert, police chief of Cedar Ridge," Maureen said.

"Where would I find his office?" She rattled the address, but I didn't have anything to write it down on, and she had to take another call. I thanked Maureen, and hung up, then repeated the address to myself as we climbed into Ellwood's car. "One-one-seven Davie Street."

"What are you rattling on about?" Brett asked.

"An address. I have to go and do something. Ellwood, my car is around the other side, if you could take me around, please?"

"Will do!" Ellwood said.

Chapter 8

Cedar Ridge boasted 360 souls, but as far as I could tell, there were very few cedar trees growing—if you counted the line along Cedar Ridge Road—and I wasn't certain where the ridge part came in. The whole downtown consisted of old buildings in need of a wrecking ball someday. The main portion of "down town" was about three blocks wide by five blocks long, with newer homes built on the outskirts, lining asphalt streets and mature oak, walnut, and maple trees, went in all four directions of the compass in their own little "subdivisions". Main businesses consisted of a laundry mat, Post Office, next to it stood a narrow bar, and a few shops situated between these main attractions, including a small grocery store on the opposite side taking up one whole white, wooden building. All of them topped with those odd fake fronts that were built in the late 1800's with nothing behind them. I was impressed they'd kept the look up, because obviously, you'd have to replace wood and paint it. I always wondered what the builder was thinking with this design. Were we to believe the building had a second and third, maybe a fourth floor? The illusion was burst once you saw there was nothing behind it.

I drove down Main Street, and found Davie Street at the fourth block and turned right, not sure if I had turned in the right direction, but I was pretty confident I would not get lost.

One set of train tracks bisected the town at this point. If a train went through at that moment, its horn would deafen a bystander, namely me. I hoped the trains didn't go through too often here.

Luckily, I found the address right away. 117 Davie Street was an old red brick building that stretched a half a block, and had a few empty windows. About a half a dozen cars were parallel parked, and since I wasn't so good at performing that maneuver yet, I pulled past a grimy looking alley, up to a white building that looked even more decrepit. A wrecking ball would definitely make a big improvement here.

I automatically locked my car door, even though I didn't think the town had that many dishonest citizens, but you never knew. Studying the windows in the second floor of the white building, it looked as though people actually paid rent here. Walking along the street with no traffic, I stepped up a crumbling curb onto a cracked sidewalk and found Cedar Ridge Police painted in black on a white sign that hung from chains above a wooden door that looked to have several coats of paint. Cedar Ridge Municipal Building – Mayor Dickie Timble - Police Chief Brandon Okert was stenciled on a large window.

I stepped up the two low steps and opened the ancient door latch and walked into what looked to be a short hall, the black and white tile in desperate need of repair twenty years ago.

Locating the correct door, I stepped into a large office space with mismatched chairs from possibly the late sixties, and one couch—a chrome frame affair with black vinyl cushions that I wouldn't dream of sitting on for fear of sticking to it. A large metal desk was positioned at one far wall with several file cabinets lined up like obedient soldiers, none of them matched, except the two black ones on the end. Currently two people were in residence.

Two large feet propped up on one corner belonged to a lanky man seated at the desk with light sandy hair trimmed around the ears, and parted on the left. He looked to be in his mid-to late twenties wearing a sand-colored police uniform. One hand held a sucker and he took it out when he spoke and waved it like a baton. The other man, heavy-set with a farmer's cap and overhauls wearing a dirty T-shirt was leaning on the desk yammering about the price of beans, and if his crop didn't produce this year, he'd be pissed because the bank would take whatever he had left. He dropped names left and right, of what I assumed were his neighboring farmers, using snide, and at times lewd language. I wished I'd come in a few moments later, but too late to turn back now.

Since the conversation didn't appear to be earth-shattering, or involve police work, I cleared my voice. I guess neither one of them had noticed my quiet entry.

The man in the light brown uniform sat up in his chair, taking the sucker out of his mouth. The man in the overhauls turned halfway around and sent me an annoyed glare.

"Can I help you, miss?" the young police chief said. If I were to guess, he couldn't be more than several years older than myself. Clean shaven with a strong chin and blue eyes, he smiled kindly in my direction.

"I'm Lainey Quilholt," I said, stepping up to his desk, and worked up my courage, despite the farmer who still glared at me. "I go to school over at Whitney." I had practiced my opening on the drive over. "I understand you handled Mr. Taylor's death investigation? He was my teacher. I'd like to speak to you about it, if you're the police chief, and are handling the investigation over at Whitney College?"

"What do you know?" the man in the John Deere hat said.

"Now, Dickie, give the lady some room, here," the police chief said. "I'm Brandon Okert. Pleased to meet you." Leaning over his desk, he put out a large hand and I pumped it.

"What do you know about the hanging incident?" the other man demanded.

It was my turn to glare at him.

"Uh, this is the mayor, Dickie Timble," Okert said.

"Hi," I said, looking the man up and down. He was mayor in a part-time capacity, apparently.

"Go ahead," Okert said. "What ever you've got to say you can say in front of the mayor here."

"Well, I believe Mr. Taylor was murdered."

"Murdered!" Timble filled the room with a belittling laugh.

I glanced at him, then at Okert gauging if I should go on, or just leave.

Surprisingly, Okert was giving me his full attention and not laughing at me. "Go on," he said. "How did you come to this conclusion?"

I carefully told them about the "pictures" made by the young man who had come across the scene in the men's john and called it in. Okert pulled a file out of a bin and opened it up. I noticed he had some photos too. They were of the suicide scene. I took them in, all upside-down to me, but when he flipped to the picture of the feet I knew he had to have seen what I had seen.

"I suppose you know who killed him," Timble glowered with a chuckle. He had a lot of miles on his face, and I stayed up wind of him since he could use some of that cologne I'd been smelling lately on certain men.

"Not yet. But he didn't kill his wife, and he didn't commit suicide," I said. "Someone wanted to pin it on him. What a better way of getting us to look away from the real murderer?"

"Oh, really? What are you, about eighteen? What could you possibly know about solving cases? Besides, this one is an open and shut case. Am I right, Brandon?" He turned to the police chief.

"Jury's out on that one, Dickie," Okert said. "I haven't heard from the coroner, yet."

"Look, you need to have the coroner really look hard at the neck. And I'm thinking he was strangled elsewhere, and moved to that stall in the men's john." I ignored the mayor who was stewing not three feet away. I wanted to ask him what he could know about solving cases, in turn, but I didn't. He hadn't pushed me far enough yet.

"I'm sure he will do just that, Miss Quilholt," Okert said, the yellow sucker was small and round, but I could tell it wasn't the big-name brand with the chocolate center. He popped it back into the side of his mouth and spoke through it. "What gave you the idea that this wasn't a suicide?"

"First of all, like I told you, he was my teacher. He was very nice, and nothing about him would make me believe he would shoot his wife, or take his own life."

"What physical evidence do you have?" Timble said in a challenge.

"The shoes, for one thing. They were on the wrong feet," I said, looking at him.

Timble turned to Okert. "Did you show her pictures from this suicide?"

Hands with palms out, Okert said, "Not me."

Timble twirled back to me. "Where did you see these so called photographs?"

Rolling my eyes I explained again how Ellwood had inadvertently taken a video of Mr. Taylor hanging in the handicapped stall.

"Good God, you kids can't just leave things as is, you gotta put things on the Internet—"

"He didn't put anything on the Internet!" I interrupted him. He hissed and rolled his eyes dramatically. At this point I figured he won his office by default—no one actually voted for him, and he was the only one staunch enough to run.

"Look, someone murdered Mr. Taylor. You need to treat this like a murder and cordon off that restroom. There may be clues all over, like in the trash. Plus, I've found the way the killer possibly transported Mr. Taylor's body."

Timble snorted. "Who do you think you are? Sherlock Holmes?"

I had to ignore Timble, but it was about as difficult as ignoring a little brat having a tantrum. Okert leaned forward, hand on his desk top, the other holding his sucker, his teeth cracked the last of the hard candy and he chewed in thought.

"Brandon, you aren't really going to entertain this girl's words, are you?" Timble said. He turned around and said to me, "Why don't you go back to your home economics classes."

Fists to my waist, I squeezed my eyes at him. "You need to get back on your John Deere tractor," I retorted.

His eyes went wide. "I beg your pardon!"

"Now. Let's just cool it," Okert had gotten to his feet, and he towered over Timble. Actually anyone who stood at six foot would be taller than the mayor. As a matter of fact, the way he slouched, he was eye to eye with me.

Timble turned to Okert. "You're not going to entertain this college student's claims, are you?"

"The shoes were on the wrong feet, weren't they?" I said.

Okert and Timble both took me in. Okert stood stone-still, staring at me. Timble pulled in a breath and let it out on a gush of an expletive.

"Language," Okert said in a warning.

Timble threw his head back with another exasperated sound, just short of another swear word.

"I'll collect a dollar from you, if you please, mayor." Okert pointed to a large, old pickle jar on the corner of his desk that could have been used by my great grandmother. It was half-full of dollars. I had to guess these were mostly, if not all, of Timble's payment into the swear jar.

Timble pulled out a fat wallet, pulled out a dollar and shoved it through the slit in the screw top. The folded dollar joined the others in the large jar. I thought it was a good way to collect a little extra fee, maybe it was donated to some charity. Maybe to Okert's sucker fund as he pulled another sucker out of his breast pocket.

"Chief, you need to go and cordon off that bathroom before someone, like the killer, gets in there and takes away any evidence," I said.

"Brandon," Timble nearly pleaded with a hand out toward me as though I were a misfit child needing to go back to the orphanage.

A new sucker appeared in Okert's mouth and he sucked on it thoughtfully. "I'm still waitin' on the examiner's report, Dickie, gall darn it."

Timble's palms flat on the chief's desk, he leaned and repeated his last claim, "What are you doing listening to a college student's wild claims for?"

"She has some good points," Okert said, folding himself back into his seat. "The shoes *were* on the wrong feet. And I don't know how the killer hoisted him up. I mean, it would take a man of considerable strength to drag him in there and then hoist him up. Taylor wasn't a string bean, exactly. He stood a little more than six foot, and when we found him, he was a good three feet off the floor."

"And nothing there for him to have stepped up on," I said.

"No." He held my gaze. It's as if we were from the same planet and Timble was the invading alien.

"What about the tawlet?" Timble said and I tried to place his odd accent.

"Toilet? You mean for him to step on?" Timble was nodding. "Nope. Too far away," Okert said. "I measured. He couldn't have reached where he was hung if he stood on the toilet, and owing to the length of cord." I was impressed that Okert had done a good job of observation and checking things out.

Timble hissed and swatted a dismissive hand at him.

"I've never worked a suicide before," Okert said almost to himself. His lips pursed as he practically kissed the sucker. I had to wonder if the sucker was substitute for another habit that he'd given up recently.

"You're forgetting Old Mrs. Owens," reminded Timble.

"Well, that was a simple one. Besides, the coroner did that one. She slipped a robe tie around her neck, tied the other end to the top of her bed post and just let her weight, what there was of it, pull it tight until she just couldn't get any air." Okert looked at me. "You simply black out. Sort of like them that do that sexual gratification thing." He snapped his fingers. "What'd ya call it?"

"Auto erotic asphyxiation?" I said.

Timble made a whimpering sound, his body sagging with his embarrassment.

"Right. Sometimes, they don't stop in time, and it's lights out for good," Okert said.

"But this was a murder/suicide!" Timble wouldn't leave it alone.

"No, sir, I don't think so," Okert said. "At any rate, Mr. Taylor's case is still open. It ain't official in the books one way or t'other until I say so."

"Oh, for crying out loud, Brandon. You gotta know when to close a case. I've got three newspapers in the area calling me every hour wanting a statement. We don't figure this out soon, they'll be here with cameras and reporters crawling all over this town lookin' for the Marriott."

Okert snickered, eyes darting to me. "As if there ever was a Marriott. We once had a hotel, but it's now mostly just apartments." He winked at me. I smiled. He had his own brand of humor.

The phone rang and Okert picked it up on the first ring. "Okert," he said, then sat up straight in the chair. "Uh-huh. Yeah." he listened for a few minutes, scribbled something down on a piece of yellow legal paper. "Right. Thank you, doctor." He hung up and looked at us. "That was the coroner. "Cause of death was asphyxiation by something tied around his neck."

"Exactly!" Timble said.

Okert held up his hand. "Not so dang fast, Dickie. Listen for once and you might just hear something new, if it'll just penetrate that thick skull of yours."

Timble looked aghast. I almost didn't cover my bark of laugh fast enough, but used the cover of a cough to keep from sounding delighted.

"What caused Chad Taylor's death wasn't the rope we found around his neck." He looked at me. "The hyoid bone in the neck was broken, of course. But the interesting thing was the lividity."

"Don't use such words when you know I don't know what they mean!" Timble complained.

"The blood pools toward gravity after the heart quits pumping it. It shows up as a darkish discoloration where the blood pools after the heart stops beating. According to the coroner Mr. Taylor's body was laying with his stomach down on some flat surface, where only a portion of the upper and lower body, and one thigh were in contact." He looked thoughtful.

"The bin I found," I said and looked up to engage his blue eyes. "Chief Okert, we need to go and cordon off that bathroom. Make sure no one disturbs anything."

Timble stormed out of the room making disparaging remarks. Okert got to his feet, grabbed a navy blue baseball cap that had the letters CRPD, acronym for Cedar Ridge Police Department. Cute.

Keys jangled in his hands and he paused and held out one hand toward the door. "Miss Quilholt, after you."

* * *

Since I had my own car, I followed Chief Okert back to Whitney College for the third time that day. My one big hope was that the killer didn't come back and find that the bathroom was locked and still had a way to gain entry. I hadn't been gone all that long. Thirty to forty minutes tops.

I parked next to Okert's white Ford Explorer with the same CRPD logo on the doors, and the word POLICE in black on the back of the vehicle along with *to serve and protect* in smaller lettering beside it.

He waited for me to join him on the sidewalk in front of the doors. "Quiet as a church without the students," he observed.

"They dismissed classes after the discovery. I have no idea when they might return."

"If this is a murder, probably not until we've solved it. Maybe in a week."

I began thinking greedily of all the time I had to read those chapters and felt guilty about it to some degree. We walked through the glass doors. I was pretty sure only janitors were still here, if that. There were a lot less cars in the lot than an hour ago at any rate.

We took the elevator down, after I showed him the way.

"How long have you been a policeman?" I asked as we descended to the ground floor.

"About four years here," he said, after pulling out the sucker. "Oh. You want a Dum-Dum?" He pulled about four suckers out of his pocket. "I'm partial to the butterscotch. But I think there's a lemon-lime one in there."

I looked at his offering and thought, why not. I took one, unwrapped it and stuck it into my mouth. It was butterscotch.

"Keeps the mouth moist, you know?" I nodded. "Course, I had to give up smoking after my son was born. I found the sucker better than chewing gum." The elevator came to an almost smooth halt, and I grasped the railing to cushion the little jar of motion. We stepped out into the now familiar hallway. I pulled out my phone to make a call to Jimmy Bean as Okert yammered on. "Named him Jeremiah, you know, after Jeremiah Johnson, the explorer. Played by Robert Redford. My favorite movie."

"I'd better call Mr. Bean so he can unlock it for us," I said and found his number, which he'd given me earlier, and called.

"Hello," Mr. Bean's voice was in my ear.

"Mr. Bean? It's Lainey. I've got Police Chief Okert here with me. We're downstairs, if you could bring the key to open the restroom door?"

"Oh, sure. Boy that was sure quick," he said.

We hung up after a few quick goodbyes.

"So, you figured out that Chad Taylor was murdered. How'd it come to you? You say you saw some pictures?" Casually Okert leaned his shoulder against the wall, hands in pockets.

"It was the guy who called the police. Name's Ellwood Blake."

"Oh. Right. Large young man with lots of hair and a beard. Sort of reminded me of that character in the Harry Potter movie—I loved those." He smiled.

"Hagred," I said.

"That's him."

"He had a video of it. I saw the video and when I looked at it a second time, a couple of things we've already discussed sent up red flags."

"Right."

"Oh! And, I found the cart which the killer had transported him on from wherever, to this restroom, and it fits right into the handicapped stall."

"You don't say."

"I found it with the help of Mr. Bean. He's the janitor here."

"Yep. I met Mr. Bean earlier."

"The murder scene's been compromised," I said.

"Understand that." He looked a little sheepish. "I've never come across an actual murder before. Had training in all the basics, o' course, but if you don't practice it in your years on the force, it's difficult to know procedurals off the top of your head."

"Maybe you'd better call the sheriff's police in?" I suggested in a conversational tone.

"I will. Just as soon as I get an idea of what we've got here."

The elevator brought Mr. Bean down to us, and in good order he unlocked the door. He said he was busy working on the third floor, doing offices and such, but if we needed it locked again, to call him. He wasn't going to stick around this time, and I bid him good-bye.

Once we stepped into the lavatory, I pointed to the stall. "The bin the murderer used to transport Mr. Taylor is in there. You might want to check the blue gloves underneath the white ones in the garbage." I was pointing at these areas as I spoke.

"You think the killer used them?" he asked.

"Hard to say. I used gloves to push the cart in here."

"Why'd you do that?"

"Didn't want to disturb the prints, if there were any."

"No. I mean why'd you move the cart?" He stepped over and looked inside the stall finding the cart pushed to the side.

"In case the killer came back and moved it elsewhere."

He nodded, twirled the sucker to the other side of his mouth with his tongue. "Hope you didn't do all this by yourself."

"I had my friends with me," I said. "You gonna call the sheriff, now?"

"I think I'd better. I can't transport this thing anywhere, plus I don't have a lab. I've got a finger print kit, that's about it. We need a forensic team in here, for sure. When we first found Mr. Taylor, it was believed it was only suicide. Now everything's different, o' course."

I gave up a big sigh. "Well, I'd better go home. I want to thank you, Chief Okert, for believing me." I stuck my hand out to him and we shook again.

"Oh, no problem." He walked me out into the hallway.

Saying our goodbyes, I moved down the hall, hand up in a wave. Thinking I had done everything possible to make sure Mr. Taylor's murderer didn't get away, I took the elevator to the main floor and began across a quiet atrium toward the far doors.

Since the building was so quiet, I thought I was one of possibly half a dozen people—including maintenance—in the building. But I found I was wrong.

The elevator doors slid open on the first floor, making me jump and hide behind a very large column. Voices halted my continuing on. I carefully peeked around the column, but I couldn't see anyone in the main area. Where had they gone?

"I want you to know you can call me any time, day or night, if you need to talk to someone," a man's voice echoed from somewhere deep within the quiet commons. His voice was soothing, comforting. Familiar.

"Thanks." A woman's voice filtered through the huge space of cement and glass. The voices seemed to be coming from the Pit. Curious because the voices sounded familiar, I slipped behind a second pillar a few feet away from the opening of the Pit and looked over a four-foot wall, and down into the Pit. There were only two people in the eating lounge below. The very large Mr. Smith, and Brianna. She stood at a table, shoving books into her backpack, her hair somewhat disheveled from when I saw her earlier. Her hands shaking as she worked the zipper shut. It was obvious to me she was taking the deaths pretty hard.

"My poor dear. You were close to Carol, weren't you?" Smith asked.

She nodded, sniffing back snot as a hand went to her bent head. I wanted to go to her, but didn't want Mr. Smith to see me, and ask why I was still here, when he knew I'd left hours ago.

"Here. Let me buy you a can of soda," Smith offered and moved with a grace that defied physics for such an obese man. Jingling pocket change, he fished out the correct change, and disappeared below the wall below me where all the vending machines were. The coins dropped noisily into the slot, and with a press of a button, the can dropped to the opening with a thud. The snap of the lid followed and he walked back into my viewpoint, the back of his baling pate shiny in the overhead lights.

"Here you go, my dear. This'll make you feel a little better," Mr. Smith said soothingly, like an old friend. Somehow his sugary voice held something behind it to me. Maybe I'd learned to dislike him for the mere reason he'd fired Carol. I promised myself to review my logic for disliking him so much on so little interaction with him. But my instincts were rarely wrong.

I ducked behind the pillar, trying to stay out of sight as they moved toward the stairs. I leaned just enough in order to watch Brianna sip her cola. She smiled gratefully at him. Smith's back to me, his hand touched her on the shoulder. "Now, I want you to drive home safely. Stay by the phone, in case there's any updates. I've announced we'll be closed at least until Sunday, and then, well, we'll see if we ever open again." He laughed at his little joke.

"Thank you Mr. Smith," she said. The two turned to the risers and climbed out of the pit.

Pressing my back to the large pillar, staying out of sight, I remained there until they were out the door and gone. I had been thinking about calling Brianna later, but now thought that I could leave my questions for her for a day or so. The dust needed to settle.

A few minutes later I emerged into the humid day—the opposite way Smith and Brianna had gone—and walked across the hot tarmac of an almost empty parking log. I climbed into my aunt's car wondering what I could learn about Mrs. Taylor's death. Or would Weeks be as tight lipped about things as usual?

Chapter 9

On my way home, I was delayed by a back-up on I-80. A real bad accident had traffic stopped or slowed for miles, and traffic was moving at a crawl. It took twenty minutes to get around with sheriff's police directing traffic. While waiting I checked messages on my phone. My aunt had left me a message that my car had been fixed, and was in the drive. Once home, I was happy to get back into my familiar ride. Noting it was nearly three o'clock, I decided to swing by my aunt's bookstore *Books 'n' Such*.

"Hi, Lainey," my aunt greeted from the register while ringing up a customer with their purchases. I floated behind her with ease, kissed her on the cheek, and disappeared into the back. My contacts had been bothering me terribly, and so I took them out in the small bathroom, and put on my glasses. Cookies on a plate had my name on them, but I only took two, and wished for some milk. Her coffee maker was perpetually filled with the dark brew, which I didn't normally drink. As compensation, I took another cookie. These were from the bakery. I took a bite. White chocolate-macadamia nut. Heavenly.

Once her customer departed, I emerged from the back and swung myself up on the counter letting my legs dangle. This wasn't frowned upon unless a customer was in the store.

"I'm sorry to hear about the teacher who died," my aunt said, patting my hand. I was so happy she did not say suicide. "What was his name?"

"Chad Taylor. That was my creative writing teacher," I said, eyes to the floor. "His wife was found shot to death." I looked up at her. My aunt's face was contorted into sadness as she cooed her lament.

"I'm so sorry. How terrible."

"I suppose it's been all over the news."

"Yes. Plus John called me a little bit ago."

"Busy day?" I asked, trying to change the subject. I took a huge bite of the second cookie in my hand. "These are sinful," I said through my cookie-filled mouth.

"Not really." She scrunched her nose and snatched one of my cookies. I gaped at her, but we both laughed. The playfulness washed right out of me and I stared at the floor again, munching and wiping cookie dust off my mouth.

"Need any help?" I asked.

"No. I'm fine," she said.

I could not work for her in the morning because of my classes, thus my aunt had hired someone to help with a few of the little things I always did. I was able to work Tuesday and Thursday afternoons, but only if she needed me.

We grew quiet. I had to talk about this.

"They called it suicide, but I knew when I saw the pictures it wasn't. I helped to make sure the police looked at it as a murder investigation. That's why I got home so late. They actually dismissed school earlier this morning."

She blinked, her head leaned a little bit. "Why am I not surprised that you helped the police with this?" She smiled, knowing how I'd helped solved Arline Rochell's murder as well as her friend's.

"I knew it when I saw that the shoes were on the wrong feet."

"Really?"

"Is Uncle John home sleeping?"

"Yes. He's got a twelve hour shift again, and I'm hoping he gets some sleep. I gave him something to help him fall asleep. Don't wake him if you go home."

"I'll just hang out here," I said moving myself off the counter, wanting to walk around the books and loose myself in the titles. I wandered into the mystery section and looked at titles. I paused and chose one *M is for Malice* by Sue Grafton. The word "malice" stuck with me as I paged through without reading the print.

"Did you hear about the accident?" my aunt said as she sauntered up beside me.

"On I-80? I was stuck in traffic. They'd already cleaned it up, but just a big back up by the time I got there."

"Terrible. Three semies and one or two cars. The girl in the car didn't make it. I think her name was Brianna."

A chill went through me. "What?" I put down the book and stood in front of her. "What was her name?"

"Brianna something. Seemed it started with a B."

"Bryde?"

"Yes. That was it."

"Oh, my god!"

"What? Did you know her?"

Tears burst to my eyes and I went to my aunt who put her arms around me. "Yes." Could this day get any worse?

When I gained control I said, "She was a girl I knew in DeWitt. She was going to school and working at the college. We were good friends, but just lost touch. I just can't believe this!" Wiping tears I found the tissues underneath the counter and blew my sloppy nose and wiped my eyes.

"Oh, you poor thing. First a teacher, and now your friend."

"This is terrible, Aunt Jessica." I wasn't sure I could handle one more thing to go wrong today.

My aunt made sympathetic noises as she pet my head.

"I'm so sorry, sweetheart," she said.

"You don't understand," I said shaking my head thinking about how Brianna was the only other person in the Bursars' office who might have known whatever Carol had come across. I needed to think this through with a clear head. Now they were both dead. What was going on? My stomach hurt, thinking there was something more sinister than I'd first suspected was at foot. I just didn't know what, and it pushed my mood in every direction. My tears stopped with these other thoughts clouding my brain.

"I need to call Brett," I said, pulling out my cell phone. When we parted, he'd said he was going home for the day, but had to work later.

"Lainey," Brett said in my ear. "Are you home yet?"

"I'm at my aunt's bookstore. Where are you?"

"We're all at *The Huddle*," he said.

"Who's we?" Wondering what happened to him saying he was going home for the day.

"Ellwood, Moon, Ham, and a few of my band members."

"The usual suspects," I said.

"What?"

"Never mind."

"Hey, Lainey, is your aunt there?"

"Yeah. Why?"

"Why don't you ask her about you going up to Dubuque with me and the band next week end?"

A knot in my stomach formed. I wasn't going to ask my aunt any such thing. For one thing, she'd ask me why I needed to go. Plus, once Weeks found out about it, he'd go ballistic. Besides, how much do motel rooms cost, anyway? I've never thought of that before as an excuse.

"I can't go," I said.

"Why not?"

"Cost of motel, food, gas…"

My aunt looked up at me and arched an eyebrow.

"I'll pay for food and gas," he said.

"Motels are expensive."

"We'll have a group rate. It probably won't cost you more than one hundred dollars."

"Sorry. Too expensive. Plus, I'm sure they'll just say no."

"Did you ask?" He was persistent.

I held the phone away from my face, making sure he could overhear us. "Aunt Jessica, Brett wants me to go spend a weekend with him and his band up in Dubuque. Is it alright?" I vehemently shook my head mouthing the word "no" to her.

"No. I don't think that's wise," she said. I gave her the okay sign with my thumb and first finger, nodding so she knew she'd said the correct thing. Not that she'd think of saying yes.

"There. Did you hear that?" I asked into the phone.

"Well, you didn't ask with any enthusiasm," he said.

I rolled my eyes, made an exaggerated expression of disbelief at my aunt. She chuckled quietly.

"I asked, I got my answer, now drop it, would you please?" my voice flat.

"Right. Whatever." I could tell by his voice he wasn't happy with me.

I lifted my mouth away from the cell phone. "Do you need me?" I asked my aunt.

She shook her head. "No. You go on."

"I'll be there in a few," I said to Brett. Sticking my phone in my back pocket, I kissed my aunt and sailed out the door. The Huddle was at the other end of town on Front Street, too far to walk, so I jumped in my car and drove across town, parked and strolled in to find a group of people at two tables that had been pushed together. Food and drinks were littered up and down the tables like there'd been a party. The fryer was going on a batch of sweet potato fries, and I was suddenly hungry for some.

Brett stood, we kissed and I said quietly, "I need to talk to you."

"Sure." We stepped away from the noise toward the back where the booths were. He sat across from me.

"You look stressed. Did you see that wreck? It was bad."

"That's what I wanted to talk to you about. My friend was in it."

"Which friend?" He grasped my hands as we stared into each other's eyes.

"Brianna Bryde," I said and had to look away as tears wanted to come again. "I saw her, you know, this morning? She looked stressed out from Carol's death. And now *she's* dead."

"That's understandable," he said. "I mean that she was stressed out. Didn't you tell me she worked with her?" I nodded.

"I can't help but think she might have known something."

"What do you mean?" He shook the hair out of his eyes.

"Carol was killed for some reason. The motive has to have something to do with the money in those accounts that were off. The one that didn't have enough money in them," I said, trying to make him understand, because he was giving me this odd look like I was off my rocker. "The check bounced. That's why she—Carol—was fired. Brianna seemed to know more about it than she was telling me, too." I was talking mostly to myself at this point.

"Lainey. Where is this going?" Brett asked suspiciously, his hands leaving mine as he sat back, a frown had grown between his brows, mouth bending down at the corners.

"Don't you see? She might have been killed by the same person."

"Oh, come on, now!" Brett said. "I don't believe you. Do you always have to find something evil behind someone's death? This was an everyday accident."

I blinked at him, surprised he wasn't backing me up. Even if he didn't believe me, he didn't have to voice it so strongly.

"You had me and Ellwood screwing around that bathroom all morning when we could have been off doing something else."

"Like what? Playing Pokemon?" I accused. There were times it was all he talked about. That or his band and the next gig, which I wouldn't be going to.

"Whatever we could have done would have been a hell of lot more interesting than that."

"And oh so important," I rallied.

"What did you do after we left you at the parking lot? Call the National Guard?"

"No. I went to the police chief of Cedar Ridge and talked to him about Mr. Taylor's death, as it was his case. While I was there the coroner called and we found out we were both right, by the way. There *was* something wrong with the way that was set up to look like a suicide. Someone murdered him. I know now that Mrs. and Mr. Taylor were murdered, most likely by the same person."

Brett shot up from the table. "Your obsessing about this stuff is really a big put off. Look. If you want to go snooping into murders, that's up to you. I've had it. I'm not playing Watson to your Sherlock. You seem to be too busy with dead bodies, men's johns, and mysterious carts to take an interest in anything else. Including me. Or us. Don't worry about having to do anything else with me, like going away for the weekend, from now on." He stalked away.

I sat there in shock. I couldn't move for a few minutes, the noise of the group louder than the music that played in the background. I felt as though no one knew I even existed, or that I was there in the building. Did that just happen? Had Brett just dumped me unceremoniously and without warning?

After a few moments, I stood on wobbly legs, turned and saw him immersed in talking to one of the band members, his arm around some blonde girl I'd never seen before.

I pulled up behind him and in his ear I said, "Looks like you've been working on a new date already. Maybe she'll go to your gig up in Dubuque." I could not get out of that place fast enough. I spun rubber when I left, heading straight home.

Yes. Apparently my day could get worse.

Entering the house, I threw my backpack on the floor of the living room and flopped onto the couch. The emotions that I'd held off came like a torrent. I hated feeling sorry for myself, but I had to get it out of my system. I'd never been dumped like this before. Actually, I hadn't gone steady more than a few weeks before this. This had lasted about four weeks, but I wasn't about to go check my calendar.

I admit all I wanted to do was mope, as I moved through the living room into the front entry room. It was a pleasant room with light green window dressings, a wingback chair next to a small table and a love seat and the little upright piano. Impressive hanging plants like a wandering Jew, pothos, and spider plants hogged what light came through in the morning. A stately peace lily took a post in the corner behind a magazine rack. My aunt had, as they say, a green thumb. Her other house plants were scattered throughout the house, but the dining room bay window looked like a local nursery had come in and set up specimens.

I plopped down in front of my aunt's piano and stared at the sheet music of Beethoven's Moonlight Sonata Op. 27 No 2. It all looked like chicken scratches right now. The notes and the notation *Adagio sostenuto* made me do a mental "huh?" I had told my piano teacher, Mr. Kingsbury, I would learn to do this piece for his class, but only the first movement. The rest of it would be impossible for me, a novice. I simply loved the mysterious tune, and was the only piano piece I knew how it went. But reading music was like learning a new language... from another planet. Why I wanted to take piano classes, I have no idea. I used to play when I was nine or ten. "Twinkle Twinkle" was the limit of my talent then, and not much better now.

Finding the piano bench uncomfortable, I moved to the green love seat and looked outside, past the purple-leafed wandering Jew plant. Of course my mind went back to everything that had just happen in the last two hours. I felt agitated, nervous energy bubbling through me, and I had no idea what to do about it. Should I go for a brisk run? Do crunches and a few sit-ups, and top it off with some jumping jacks? Clean my room? Nah.

It was then that I felt that writing everything down was the only healthy way of banishing these relentless thoughts, or at least dealing with it. I went up to my room and retrieved a steno notebook, something I'd purchased for putting down thoughts, since I had half-filled a notebook about my observations after Arline Rochelle had been murdered. I felt that something like this would small and convenient for me to carry around, instead of a larger notebook. Of course, after a while, it read like a journal. But that was alright, too.

I returned downstairs and found a comfortable spot in the front room and with my favorite pen, I began to write. I had much to add to it, and spent more than an hour getting it up to speed. I did shed a few tears about Brett dumping me, but I wiped them away, telling myself I didn't need someone so shallow in my life. I told myself that maybe he didn't really like me for myself, but what he might get out of a relationship with me. The events of the day wound up being a many paged entry, because once I began writing about something, I put in all the details. In the back of my mind, I thought I might want to try and put some of this to a future book, should I eventually get to the point where I felt I had a book to write.

It was late in the afternoon when my phone rang—the ring tone set with Moonlight Sonata—and I checked the screen. My nerves jangled a bit hopeful. It was Chief Okert.

"Hello?" I answered.

"Miss Quilholt?" he said.

"Speaking."

"We got this all wrapped up here. The sheriff's police took evidence, including fingerprints. I thought I'd let you know, too, that cart was wiped clean."

"Figures."

"They've taken it with them to go over it in the lab for trace evidence," he went on. "They also took the contents of the waste basket. Now we wait."

"Will they be in touch with you about what they find?"

"I imagine so," he said.

"Any problem letting me know what they find?"

"I don't see why not." Then he said, "By the way, I understand you were attacked just last night by someone in a clown suit?"

"Yes. His name is Sinclair. The sheriff's police came as soon as they could, but he'd been chased off by my friends. Anyway, they've an APB out on him."

"I apologize, but I wasn't working last night," he said. "I'm only part time, so I've only so many hours in one day I'm supposed to work. I would have been there right away, otherwise."

"I understand."

"Anyway, that's where we're at with Mr. Taylor's murder for now."

"Thanks," I said."I appreciate your giving me an update." We hung up, with him promising to let me know what further he learns from the investigation.

I curled up on the small love seat, hugging a plump pillow, looking over my social media, and then finding nothing interesting, I closed my eyes and fell asleep.

Noise in the living room brought me awake. Someone said, "I don't know where she is. I just got up myself."

"Lainey? Lainey, are you up there?" My aunt's voice called.

"I'm in here," I said, unfolding myself and sliding off the love seat, finding I had a stiff neck. Rubbing my neck I padded out in bare feet through the living room to join my aunt and uncle in the kitchen. Weeks was seated at the small wooden table having coffee. The aroma of breakfast would have pulled me out of sleep, if I hadn't been woken by their voices. I eased around my aunt who was at the stove cooking.

"Morning," I said to him, and he smirked at my joke.

"Morning to you. What've you been doing all afternoon, since they closed your school?"

"You know about that, do you?" I asked, evading his question.

Cup in hand he said, "I know everything."

"Naturally." I moved to the refrigerator, looking for something to eat. Finding nothing to nosh on there, I moved for the cupboards and snagged a bag of multi-grained chips. Regular potato chips weren't good enough for us.

"Snacking so close to dinner?" Weeks said. I looked up at the time. It was going on five.

"And you're about twelve hours too soon or too late to have waffles," I parried, watching my aunt bring over two huge waffles and sausage patties on a plate and set the blueberry sauce down next to him.

"Wrong." He chuckled, and dug in. The groan that came from him made me want waffles.

"I'll take two," I said.

"We're going out for dinner," Aunt Jessica said.

"We are?" I was happy to hear that.

"The Buffet," she said.

"Goodie." Although I liked The Buffet, I didn't feel too enthused about going out in public.

A sound rap on the back door had me move toward it, since I was only four steps away. A woman in uniform stood on the other side of the door. I opened it surprised to see Maureen.

"You here to pick up the boss?" I joked.

"Naw, he can walk to work, as far as I'm concerned," Maureen said, smiling. Laughing, I let her inside. "Actually, I've come to see you, Lainey."

"Me?" I backed myself against the counter and reclaimed the bag of chips, but suddenly lost my appetite, unsure what sort of news the woman officer would give me. Too many bad things had happened today. I wasn't ready for more.

"John, Jessica," she greeted, and they greeted her back.

"Want anything from the griddle? I'm about to put it out of commission, otherwise," my aunt offered.

"No thanks. Just got this over the wire, and since I've got you all here I can give it to you all at once," she said.

"Go ahead," Weeks said.

She pulled out a note pad and read from it. "At six AM, local police had a call to the Sinclair residence in New Liberty—that's about half way between here and Iowa City," she said for our benefit. "Their son, Tyler, was found in his parent's garage, in his own vehicle asphyxiated from exhaust fumes. The local police and coroner determined he ran the engine with the garage doors closed, and was dead within probably ten or fifteen minutes. They put his death at around ten or eleven last night."

There came a gasp from both myself and my aunt.

"How terrible," my aunt said. "Who was this person? I don't think I remember the name," she said.

"He was the kid making all sorts of threats on line to teachers," Weeks explained. "Last night he went after Lainey."

"Oh, my goodness, that's right!" She moved to me and put a comforting hand on my back as I leaned an elbow on the counter, hand on my forehead while shaking my head. "You okay, Lainey?"

"Wow." Was all I could say as I found a nearby chair and sank into it. Who else was going to wind up dead? How many did that make? Four?

"Thanks, Maureen," Weeks said. "Lainey, you okay?" Maureen had moved for the door, but she paused. They were all looking at me.

"Oh, I'm just peachy." I rose from the chair. "I'm going to my room for a bit." After everything that happened today, Sinclair's suicide—real, I was certain—shouldn't have bothered me. But it did. As I began up the stairs, the others continued their conversation.

"Well, there goes that theory all shot to hell," he said.

"What's that?" My aunt asked.

"We found a clown mask in the Taylor's garbage. It might have tied Sinclair to Carol Taylor's death. But not anymore."

"Sinclair was found this morning around six AM. The parents never heard him come home," Maureen said. "Plus, his clown outfit, mask with the colored hair and what-all, was found in his car along with him."

"Exactly."

"One other thing to note," Maureen went on, "the kid was taking Prozac for depression. But he was hopped up on something else. Something illegal."

"Great. That explains the crazy clown business, his on-line threats, and going after Lainey," Weeks said.

I returned to the room, they all looked up at me. "I was the one who identified him," I said. "That's why he came after me." My eyes slid to Maureen, then to my aunt. "Maybe if I'd have stayed out of it, he might have just left things alone."

"He'd put out a lot of threats to certain teachers," Maureen said, reminding me what Mr. Taylor had said about him.

"He'd been caught cheating on exams, and the school expelled him."

"I hadn't heard that," Maureen admitted.

"I got it directly from Mr. Taylor," I said. "He was concerned about how Sinclair had attacked me on school grounds." I bit my lower lip and looked down feeling tears threaten.

"He must have left the school lot that night and went home to do himself in," Week said in a quiet, thoughtful tone.

"Just remember, Lainey, he might have done something worse, if you hadn't IDed him," Maureen said. "Also, I might as well tell you, this afternoon we went and collected evidence in that lavatory at Whitman College, where Chad Taylor's body was found. Coroner's report showed that Chad Taylor was strangled, not by the rope, but something thinner. Maybe a cord of some sort. The ligature bruising was much thinner than the rope. Anyway, there was evidence the body had been moved, according to the lividity."

Weeks had stopped eating and sipped his coffee, looking at the floor. "Lividity happens in about thirty minutes," he said.

I lifted my head. "Plenty of time to go and shoot Mrs. Taylor?"

We were all exchanging looks then. But everyone's eyes pinioned me. My deductions had been right on again. Who was I, anyway? Reincarnated Sherlock Holmes? Wait. He was a character in a book.

"That gun you found in Mr. Taylor's office, it was the one that was used to shoot Mrs. Taylor, right?" I asked.

Weeks looked from me to Maureen. Maureen said, "If you don't tell her, she'll only hound us."

"Yes. It was a .38 Smith and Wesson. Used hollow points."

I screwed up my face. I didn't know what that meant.

Maureen sensed my insecurity in this area. "Hollow points don't go through the vic, they stay in the body." I nodded. "Tests showed that there was no gun powder residue on Taylor's clothes, or his hands," Maureen went on.

"Okay, obviously someone went to a lot of trouble to set this whole thing up to look like a murder-suicide, but they've been busted. I'm sure you questioned it when you looked at it closer," I said. "Why would someone shoot his wife at home, with a gun, but doesn't shoot himself, and then goes all the way to the school where he works, and hangs himself—which we've proved didn't happen—and leaves the incriminating gun in his desk drawer for anyone to find?"

"You're right, this whole thing is screwy," Weeks said and went on, "The .38 wasn't registered, so it couldn't be traced."

"Fingerprints?"

"Sure. Only Taylor's."

"Naturally." I shook my head. Weeks brushed his mustache with a finger. Quiet invaded the room. It seemed something was being unsaid.

"There's something you aren't saying," I said, reading the cop faces in the room.

It took them ten seconds of long looks back and forth before Weeks made some sort of minute nod to his deputy, and I was given the rest of it. "There was a gun owned by Chad Taylor, found in the bedroom. A cheap Glock. Nine millimeter. Never been fired. In fact, it wasn't even loaded."

I nodded. It fit with what I thought of Mr. Taylor. He probably got the gun for protection, but since they had children in the house, they couldn't take the chance that the children might find the gun and so, never loaded it.

"What have you learned about Brianna Byrde? Did they do a toxicology yet?"

Maureen's glance went from me to Weeks and back again like there was a tennis tournament going on in the room. "You know, she should really work for us."

"She does, I just don't pay her," Weeks said with an amused wink.

"Toxicology takes a little while," Maureen said. "We found no illicit drugs, or evidence she was drinking in her car. Or even using her cell phone."

"Did they look for anything else?" I asked. "Something wrong with her steering fluid? Breaks?"

"They're checking the car too. That all takes time as well."

"Think someone did her in too, Lainey?" Weeks asked. He did me a favor by not looking amused when he asked this.

"You haven't caught the murderer of Mr. and Mrs. Taylor. All of a sudden, a third death. Brianna worked with Carol. She knew there were discrepancies with some accounts. Said something wasn't right with the figures."

"What figures?" my aunt had been silent until now.

"What are you talking about?" Weeks asked.

I pulled in a breath and let it out. "I was going to have you guys talk to her, but now we can't. How convenient." I muttered the last words to myself and went on. "Carol and Brianna both worked in the bursar's office. Carol discovered that some accounts in a bank had less in them than whatever her records showed."

"How did she find that out?"

"The check she wrote out for some sort of uniforms bounced. Embarrassed, she went to the president, Mr. Smith—"

"Oh. Him," was all Weeks said, but his expression filled in his contempt.

"Mr. Smith fired Carol on Wednesday. She is killed the next morning. Her husband is also killed. Why? So that whatever Carol knew about the accounts couldn't be discovered. And on the very same day Brianna, who worked, with Carol also is dead."

"So, you think we should see what we can find out on Mr. Smith?"

"I'd say a good place to start is with the banks that the school has money in."

"Okay, so maybe Smith was skimming money out of accounts, but that's a long way from murdering someone to keep them quiet," Weeks said. "There's no proof he was there in the Taylor home."

"Yeah. Well, you've got the information," I said. "You do with it whatever you want." Suddenly exhausted I turned away. I'd had enough on my plate, a smorgasbord of events that would give anyone indigestion, a migraine and want to lock themselves away with no contact with the outside world for a week.

"Lainey?" my aunt said and I turned to look upon the somber faces. Weeks and my aunt exchanged the usual looks that would suggest they were reading each other's minds at this point.

"Until we know who's behind the murders, Jessica and I want you to be safe, and keep close to home, when you aren't going to school, that is," Weeks said.

I read between the lines. "No need to worry. Brett and I've split up." I walked out and went up to my room to get ready to go to dinner. I wasn't really in the mood to eat.

Chapter 10

"I didn't know he was your teacher," Nadine said in my ear as I lay supine on my bed with my phone laying next to my ear, propped against my shoulder, speaker phone on.

"He was my creative writing teacher," I said.

"That's really terrible," she said. "What are you doing now?"

"Nothing."

"I'd ask you to come over, but I'm shopping right now." I could hear different sounds in the background—people's conversation, laughing, music. The general noise you'd hear in a mall.

"Where are you? The mall?"

"Yeah. I'm trying to find a nice outfit for my date with Franklin, tomorrow night," she said. "Ooo. Maybe someday we could double date."

"As soon as I find another boyfriend," I said.

"What?" I repeated myself. "You broke up with Brett? How could you?" She sounded devastated, as though I were at fault. Well, my actions had caused it, but if so, better now than learning later Brett really didn't like me for me.

"It was the other way around, actually," I said. "He didn't like playing second to my investigating murders."

"What? Wait—" There was muffled sounds for a moment. Then the distinctive sound of clacking hangers came.

"If you're busy we can talk later," I said.

"No. No. You breaking up with Brett—this is like, I don't know. I'm just bummed."

You're bummed? Think of how I feel, I wanted to say.

"What happened?"

I launched into a short version, which I'd given my aunt, who showed much more empathy than Nadine was at this moment.

"Not only that, just to top it all off, remember Brianna Byrde?"

"Who?"

"Brianna, the girl I knew from DeWitt," I said.

"No."

"I introduced you to her the other day," I explained.

"Sure." *Clack, clack, swoosh.*

"Anyway, she was in a car wreck this afternoon. I came home right on the tail end of it."

"Oh, wow. Is she okay?"

"No. She's dead."

Nadine made a little scream and I had to pull the phone away from my ear, actually laid it on my chest while she got done with her over-reaction. Where had she picked up this type of behavior? I'd never heard her do that before. Maybe if it was about a guy she was wild about, but this reaction was something new with her. Something she must have picked up elsewhere.

I lifted the phone to hear some more swishing. Maybe it was her walking, I wasn't sure.

"You there?" she asked.

"Yeah." I rolled over. Three feet away, my Nerfs and teddy bears were lined up on a book shelf, along with a few books I'd bought from the bookstore the past few years. Mostly romances. I reminded myself I needed to read mystery novels. The one I'd seen earlier sounded like a good one. My thoughts were suddenly lost in what would happen to Mr. Taylor's creative writing class at this point.

Then Nadine's voice broke through the fog.

"Huh?"

"You okay?"

"No. I really need to go. I'm tired."

"It's only seven-thirty!" she said.

"I'll talk to you later, Nadine." I tapped my phone and then made sure the ringer was off.

A knock came to my door.

"Lainey?" my aunt's voice came through the door as she partially opened it.

"Yeah?" Sitting up, I hugged a pillow to myself.

My aunt stepped in and closed the door as though there were a crowd of reporters just outside wanting to push their way in and ask more stupid questions. *College student investigates murders at a local college, boyfriend says he's done with her obsessive behavior over solving grisly crimes. The full story at ten...*

"How are you doing? Were you on the phone just now?" she asked.

"It was Nadine. I just couldn't talk to her tonight. She's just too..."

"Happy?" My aunt sat on the end of the bed giving me that concerned look.

"Yeah." I sighed, wrapping my arms around my knees, leaning my cheek against the pillow I now had a strangle hold on. "She's apparently going out with someone new this weekend. She was at the mall when she called, picking out something to wear."

"I'm so sorry about what happened today, sweetie," she said, patting my bare foot. Her hand was warm on my skin, and the warmth of her touch reminded me of our bond. We had both grieved when my mother—her sister—and father died in the flood. She knows when I'm down. Today I wasn't just down, I'd been kicked in the stomach and thrown to the wolves. At least, that's how I felt.

"I'm sorry I was such a poop at dinner. I'm sorry I didn't eat very much and you paid for the meal," I muttered dismally, chin on folded hands over my smashed pillow.

She made a little gasp and a dismissive wave. "Don't worry about it." She rubbed my ankle a little. "Are you more upset about the murders, or about breaking up with Brett?" she asked. "Or is it everything?"

Good question. I had to ponder this for a moment. "I'm not sure how I feel about Brett." I managed a small smile. "Boys are such morons." She laughed, agreeing with me. "I mean, it wasn't like I loved him, or anything. He was just a guy I liked. We went out, had good times when we did." I paused and looked up at her. "Right now I just want to hate him."

"That's understandable." She chuckled. "That's normal, and you'll be able to get over him after a while. It might take a few days, maybe a few weeks, but you'll get over him. And then there will be other guys who you like and like you back. Then there'll be that special someone that really flips your world."

I smiled. "Is that how it is with you and Uncle John?"

"Well." She chuckled lightly. "It wasn't at first. I wasn't even interested in him. I thought him to be arrogant, pig-headed, and self-righteous."

"Really?" I laughed, surprised.

"Yes. But then, I guess he wore me down." She paused, closed one eye in thought, then shook her head. "He had something about him, deep down, that began to come through. When he first asked me out, I thought he was just joking. I went out with him a few times, and found out his outer personality isn't anything like the inner one. He sort of puts on this outer shell that other people see."

"Tough cop act. I think I've seen that," I said and we both chuckled.

"Anyway, his having been divorced, with three girls, now all of them living further away, and me a widow and no children—" She tickled my foot and I jerked it back with a burst of laughter. "Except for you. We were both looking for the same thing.

Companionship, a trusting relationship that would last. We love each other. I can't imagine being with anyone else, now."

I smiled. "That sounds like what I'd like. Someday."

She nodded. "Someday it'll happen. Don't just settle. Too many people settle and find that they aren't really compatible."

I laid my head down on my folded arms. "Finding someone like that sounds like it might be impossible."

"Just let it happen," she said. "If you go out intending to find that someone, it never works. Fate usually steps in and seems to be a better matchmaker than Cupid." She rose to her feet.

My chuckle died. "You know what?" I said after a moment, raising my head. "I've decided I don't want to give Brett that sort of power over me. I'm done moping about him dumping me."

"Good," she said, her hand patting mine and we both intertwined our fingers.

"I've gotta live my life the way I feel I should. If it's profiling a murderer, then so be it."

"Is that what Brett was so upset about?"

"Partially." I said with hesitation. "He didn't like how much time I devoted to it. Like today." I chuckled lightly. "Called me Sherlock."

"Oh. He complimented you, at least." We both chuckled. "What was the other thing? Did it have something to do with what you asked me while you were on the phone with him? What was that about?"

I had told her all about the break-up at dinner, but left out certain details. "He and his band have a gig up in Dubuque and wanted me to come along—for the whole weekend. You know, stay in a motel. I kept putting him off, not asking you if I could go, because I knew you'd say no, but also, I really didn't want to go and be pressured."

She knew what I meant about being "pressured".

"How do you know I'd say no?" she said.

I shrugged. "I don't know. I mean, understanding that I'm considered all grown up, now, I wasn't really sure, but I needed to just give him an excuse."

"And he broke up with you over that?"

"That and my getting so involved in the murder of Mr. and Mrs. Taylor." I'd also told her about how involved I became with Mr. Taylor's death, beginning with Ellwood telling us he had seen Mr. Taylor's body and called the police. I explained how later, when I watched his video, I discovered the shoes were on the wrong feet, and how I talked Ellwood and Brett into going back to the crime scene with me. When I told her how I went to see Chief Okert and then went back to the lavatory once again to show him what I had found, she couldn't believe how I had hounded it like a bulldog reporter might, or a good detective.

"You have a gift, Lainey. John sees it. He's said to me a number of times that you may want to look into taking certain classes in criminology."

"It has crossed my mind. In fact I've even thought about looking into the FBI Academy." I really wasn't sure I could go to that extent.

"Really?"

I shrugged.

She caressed my hand. "You've always been able to analyze things, including your emotions. I don't know where you get that."

"You forget I'm a Virgo." She laughed. It was a private joke. I didn't hold with what any zodiac sign signified, and she knew it. My smile grew. "Maybe it comes from Uncle Ed." She laughed again.

"Well, you may have that part figured out, at least."

After a few seconds of staring at my toes I said, "I'm hungry."

"How about I pop one of those frozen pizzas in the oven?"

"That one with black olives and tomatoes?"

"Sure."

After eating forbidden frozen pizza—with everything on it—my evening consisted of trying to play at least through the first page of *Moonlight Sonata* without making mistakes. Aunt Jessica crocheted in the wing chair nearby, listening, and coaching me. After an hour, and tiring of our individual pursuits on the creative level, we migrated to the living room where we watched some mindless programs. Popcorn was popped for the occasion. My aunt drank white zinfandel, while I chose something low calorie, non-alcoholic in the bubbly waters category. Around eight-thirty, Weeks called my aunt and they spoke for a while. When she hung up she passed along the news that they'd found nothing wrong with Brianna's car, but were still waiting on toxicology reports from the coroner. I couldn't help thinking the coroner had been pretty damned busy lately. I imagined he was up to his elbows—literally—in dead bodies.

At a little after nine-thirty, our yawns got the best of us and we tottered off to bed. I didn't think I could sleep, but the next thing I knew morning sun slanted through my blinds and I rolled over feeling incredibly lazy. That's until the amazing aroma of frying bacon and the hot griddle grabbed me by the stomach. In five minutes I was dressed and downstairs at the kitchen table, my tongue hanging out.

"I thought we could enjoy waffles this morning," my aunt said. "Since you were eyeing them so much last night."

"I'll eat two," I said, putting out napkins and place settings for the two of us.

We were nearly done eating when someone knocked on the front door. We looked at one another wondering who that could be, since anyone who knew us always came to the back door.

"I'll see who it is," my aunt said, getting up. I swabbed the last piece of waffle through the remainder of maple syrup on my plate when I heard her greet whoever it was. The distant male voice sounded slightly familiar, but I couldn't place it.

"Lainey? It's for you," my aunt called as she strolled halfway through the living room.

My stomach fluttered, wondering who this man was who wanted to see me. I knew it wasn't Brett. He would have called, and I sure didn't expect him to be coming to see me right after breaking up. Besides, it wasn't Brett's voice. It was slightly nasally. As I strode into the living room, I went through more reasons I was happy it wasn't Brett. Besides, I'd had no messages on my phone this morning. Which, in a way was a blessing. But my butterflies wouldn't abate.

Stepping through the living room, I eyed the tall, lanky man standing just inside the door. He wore a light tan police uniform—not dark brown like the sheriff's police.

His slim build, uniform, plus baseball cap nailed it.

"Police Chief Okert!" I said, somewhat surprised. "What are you doing here?"

"Hope I'm not interrupting breakfast," he said, pulling off his cap, and holding it in his hands.

"Not at all. Come in," I said. My aunt was standing at the living room doorway, watching and listening. Okert stepped further into the parlor, and I shut the door. I introduced him to my aunt.

Okert gave her a nod. "Ma'am." Then slid his eyes to me.

"What brings you here?" I asked. I would have expected him to call me, instead.

"I would have called, but since I live just north of here, and was on my way to work, I thought I'd just stop by," he said. "I hope you don't mind?"

"No. That's fine." I said, waiting.

"Well, the news is there were no fingerprints of anyone of any significance found in the bathroom, or on anything we found," he said. "Uh, at Whitney College, that is. No one we could pinpoint might be a suspect, at any rate, and all had alibis anyway."

"Okay. You, of course, did elimination pints?"

His mouth half opened, it turned into a smile and split his face. "I'll be. You know about them, too?" I nodded. "We did."

"Including those of Ellwood?" I said.

"I should hope so," he said. "Although, I didn't do the finger-printing. The sheriff's police did, so you might want to check with them."

I figured that they would have done so.

"Also, did you know that they can take fingerprints from the inside of those cleaning gloves?"

"Uh, seems I'd heard that. Yes," I said.

He nodded. "Anyway, the cart had been wiped clean, but trace fibers and hair samples indicate that Mr. Taylor was, indeed in contact with it. Meaning hair, or fibers on the cart had matched those of Mr. Taylor. But others did not."

"I see." I nodded, looking down in thought.

"One thing of note," Okert said cautiously. I looked up. "A piece of cord was found in the wastebasket. It was determined to be a cord from blinds. You know, because of that little bell-shaped thing at the end?"

"What color?"

"White, or beige." His eyes darted from me to my aunt and back again. He made a nervous chuckle. "Sort of difficult to come up with the color. I mean it wasn't white-white, but sort of an off white, or—"

"—Beige," I finished. I tried to think if I had seen any beige blinds at the school. No window dressings on the windows I had seen. Probably offices had such window treatments.

"Could it have come from his office? Mr. Taylor's? Did he have a window with blinds?"

"That's yet to be checked out. I won't be doing that, since the powers that be say I've spent way too much time on this and they want me to return to my usual duties."

"Speeding and parking tickets?" I guessed.

"Yep." He gave me a three-finger salute with a chuckle. "You got it."

"Anything else?"

"I also checked out Jim Bean," he said and a quirk of a smile bent his lips.

"Why did I think of a fifth of whiskey when you said that?" my aunt asked. We all chuckled.

"Because it sounds like Jim Beam. The whiskey," he said.

"Right," she said.

"Why did you do that? Check him out?" I asked.

"Because he's a janitor, and had keys to all locks on doors in the college," Okert said.

"Well, yes, but Mr. Bean has no motive. What reason would he have to kill Mr. Taylor?" I argued.

Okert shrugged. "You never know."

"No. I think everything started with Mrs. Taylor," I said. "Something she knew, or learned because of her job. Something the killer desperately wanted to keep from getting out. He needed to protect this information."

Okert leaned his shoulder up against the door frame. "Okay. But why kill the husband?"

"Easy. Don't you sometimes tell your wife about things? Share your day? Who else would be privy to secrets that maybe you wouldn't tell another soul? Something that might be questionable, or damaging? Even dangerous?"

Eyes down, fingers to chin, he nodded deeply. "I see your point."

"And anyway, we're looking for someone with considerable strength. Mr. Bean is, what, five nine at best?"

Okert snorted. "Yeah. I see your point." He straightened, and replaced the ball cap on his head. "Well, I just thought I'd swing over here. Let you know what was discovered."

"Well, thank you for stopping by with this," I said. "I really appreciate it."

"No problem at all, Miss Quilholt." He turned to reach for the door handle. "Ma'am, nice meeting you," he said with a flick of fingers to his cap.

"Likewise," my aunt said with a smile, lifting her hand in a wave.

When he was gone, I turned to my aunt.

"Well, Lainey, you've certainly got policemen stopping by keeping you up to date on these murders. Makes me wonder if the FBI might just be knocking on the door next."

I laughed. "The chief was just being very nice to let me know what was found and what wasn't in that men's john. He was surprised when I had noticed the thing with the shoes, and my claiming it was a murder, not a suicide, and a few minutes later the coroner called which agreed with both our suspicions it was murder."

"This cord from some blinds, do you think it might have been used on him?"

"Yes. Definitely, since there's no windows in that lavatory, mostly because it's underground." That one thing was a slip-up by the murderer. I hoped he had been sloppy in a few other places. But as luck would have it, we'd have to dig a bit deeper.

My aunt and I got ready to go to the bookstore. Since I had nothing better to do, I decided to come in and help with the store.

Mrs. Diamond was waiting for us to open up. This was the first time I'd met her. Her job was to do the vacuuming and generally straightened up for a couple of hours during the morning. Her gray hair was worn to her shoulders, pinned back from her face. I put her at sixty-four, or -five. She had gentle light blue eyes, a quiet voice and deep wrinkles around the eyes and mouth and a bit heavy around the middle. She wanted only to work a few hours in the morning until she went home to take care of her husband who had suffered a stroke a few months back. While she was at the store, he was with either a therapist or a nurse. She told me to just call her Jenny.

Because Jenny was basically doing my old job, I made a trip to the post office for my aunt with bills and mail. It was a bright sunny day, after the fog had burned off. I mulled over all the new information from Okert about Mr. Taylor's murder while I walked. I didn't even look up when a couple of Harley's flew down the road. I resumed pondering things, looking down at my feet while I walked.

"Well, Miss Lainey! What a pleasant surprise!"

I looked up, just three steps ahead of me was the tall man with cloud-like white hair on his head and a white mustache.

"Uncle Ed!" I strode up and gave him a hug around the neck, and kiss on the cheek as he pressed one on mine. He was somewhat surprised by this, as we usually kept our greeting a tad more cordial.

"What's this, my dear?" he said when he gently pulled me away from him and saw my tears. "Aw. Now what's happened?"

I held a hand up. "Wait here. I have to go into the post office and mail these," I said with my hand filled with various letters and bills to mail. Uncle Ed waited for me. He was really my great uncle, but would not allow me to call him "great uncle", as he didn't want to acknowledge his age. For a man in his seventies, he was probably more fit than most men in their fifties. He owned a riverboat called *The Miss Twila*, and had gotten it all spiffed up to take tours on the Mississippi, and did his Mark Twain impersonations to entertain passengers.

Exiting the building, I found Uncle Ed seated on one of the many benches scattered up and down Front Street, which is the main thoroughfare. Plopping down next to him, I caught the whiff of his lit cigar, which was between his fingers. The hands were large, age spotted, and made me want to draw the shadows along the knuckles, and the veins that stood out along the back of it. For some reason, I wish I had my sketch book and pencil. I made a mental note of doing exactly that sometime soon.

"Now tell me. What's wrong?"

"You have an hour?"

"As a matter of fact, I do," he said. "My time is yours."

I launched into all that had happened only yesterday, which in the back of my mind seemed like all of it couldn't have happened in just one day. It didn't take an hour to tell, but it did take a good fifteen or so minutes to relate. He made a shocked sound when I told him about the death of my teacher, and his wife. Hummed appropriately at my discoveries about Mr. Taylor's murder scene. And when I told him about my friend's auto accident he shook his head saying, "That's just terrible. Her poor parents." He had lost his daughter in just such a way, years ago.

When I was done with telling him everything, including my break up with Brett, he put an arm around me in a consoling way. I waited as he drew in a deep breath, let it out and drew another one.

"First of all, your beau is a jackass. And did you love him?"

I blinked at him. No one had ever asked such a thing so outright. "No."

"Good. That's good." He patted my hand. "Now, I would not even suggest you regret either knowing him, or dating him, nor do I suggest you ever return to him, no matter how much he begs."

I chuckled. "That won't happen. I promise."

Smiling, he leaned slightly toward me and said low, "He'll find someone who deserves him."

I laughed and nodded. "Already happened."

"Good. Move on. Don't give him another thought." He paused and looked out across the street. Took a puff of his cigar and let a stream of smoke through his lips, aiming it away from me. "As to these other things. These murders. My advice is be cautious and alert to the unusual, especially when it comes to those who know you've been involved in the discovery of these facts you've uncovered." He took another puff. "Do you have any ideas on who might have done these horrifying things?"

I paused. I was hesitating saying that I did. The very person my mind brought up was most prominent, and yet I had no proof whatsoever of his involvement. In fact I'd been questioning why this person was starring in the roll of "murderer" in my head. "I need the motive to make sure. And a few other things."

"And the motive is important, of course." He nodded, watching traffic pass by.

"It's one of three things that help in the investigation," I said. "The other two are opportunity and means."

"Ah." He nodded. He leaned again and said. "Liars are also good suspects."

I agreed. "But how would I discern a lie, especially if I don't know someone? Or they're pretty good at it?"

"A pretty good liar has performed his art over the years and perfected it," he said thoughtfully. "But all liars get caught at some point. One of my favorite quotes from the eminent Mr. Twain is: 'If you tell the truth, you don't have to remember anything.'"

"That's true," I said. In other words, a liar could be caught in a lie by not remembering what they had said about something in a prior conversation. It was how police sometimes catch the guilty. It was why they questioned people separately and repeatedly.

He continued, "'A lie can travel half way around the world while the truth is putting on its shoes.'"

"I like that one too," I said as we enjoyed the clever quotes of Mark Twain.

"Now," he said, patting my knee. "You feel any better, my dear?"

"Much." I beamed up at him. "Are you putting on a show later on?"

"Tonight," he said. And the loud horn of *The Miss Twila* belched not very far away.

"Are the tours going well?" I asked. I had not seen him in weeks, he'd been so busy with his boat tours and shows, plus, I'd started college.

"Yes. Very well." He laughed. "I'm actually making money and might have to pay some of it back to Uncle Sam." His mustache fluttered as he made a huffing sound.

"I think on that subject I'll leave." I stood up, ready to depart.

"I may have to invite myself over for a Sunday dinner with you, the lawman and my other niece." I was considered a niece along with my aunt.

"I think you should do that!" I encouraged. "I miss seeing you and Uncle John at odds at the dinner table."

He laughed heartily at that. Raising his hand he said, "Then I will make it a point to come. Tell your aunt to set an extra place!"

"I will!"

When I returned, much happier than when I'd left. I found Jenny shifting a whole section of books to make room for a new author. Poe, our self-proclaimed mascot, was balanced on top of the bookshelf supervising the whole operation, emitting little meows trying to get our attentions. I dove right in, pulling books off shelves and we managed to move enough books in the mystery section to make room for twelve of the new title. We had another box of the same book, but wouldn't overwhelm the area with just one author.

The author's name was Tristan Harcourt. The title of his mystery book was "A Killing at Brightwood College". I found myself staring at the dark, ominous cover—a hangman's noose hung from a tree in the foreground, with a dark-looking mansion in the background, and it was night time—the title, cover and the description had caught me like a child looking at the biggest lollipop in the store. Was this kismet or what? When Jenny and I were done working on shelving a half a dozen of Mr. Harcourt's books into the space (I read on the AUTHOR'S PAGE Harcourt lived in Massachusetts with his wife and three boys), I grabbed one and brought it up front.

"Aunt Jess, I've gotta have this one." I plopped down the hard cover book on the counter. It was over 350 pages long. A nice sized book to allow me to be swallowed up for the weekend, if I didn't do my homework (presuming school would ever resume someday).

"Hmm, yes. I thought it had an interesting title," she said, picking it up and looking at it.

"The cover sort of grabbed me," I added.

She lifted it to look more closely and looked up at me with those almost startled blue eyes. "Are you sure—"

"Definitely!"

"I'll add it to your tab."

"Great." I privately chuckled at my "tab". It was just taken out of my pay, in other words. I knew she would put it alongside my handbag below, and so I left it with her. I was reminded that Mr. Taylor had told us to read a lot of the types of books we would like to write. The idea was to get to know how to write one ourselves. He suggested it might inspire us to write that "Great American Novel". I decided to write a dedication to him on the inside of this book. A determined verve coursed through me as I knew exactly what I would write.

I finished my day with my aunt and we went home together, with Poe antsy to get back to his cat hotel my aunt had indulged in buying not long ago just for him (and it seemed to keep him occupied and out of the kitchen). Weeks thought the cat jungle gym with three levels to climb or jump up to, with a little house at the top where he could hide and snooze was a bit much. But he didn't argue when my aunt said he'd be less of a pest to him when he got home. I hadn't heard him complain lately about it.

I couldn't wait to get home to read Harcourt's book. While I waited for Aunt Jessica to shut things down in the store, I opened it up to the title page, took my favorite pen and wrote: *To*

Mr. Chad Taylor, (and his wife Carol), I will always remember you as a great teacher who encouraged me to write. I will do everything in my power to bring your murderer to justice. Lainey Quilholt

I put the date below my name.

Once we were ready to go, I climbed into the front seat with my aunt. Poe always sat in the back window, where a piece of carpet was placed just for him to feel comfortable while watching traffic from his end. I always wondered what he thought of cars. Were they large versions of dogs, or something too big for him to pursue and maul?

I opened the book to Chapter One and began to read.

"I've told you for the last time, Ken, I'm not going to bed with you!" Ann Woods informed, staring across the desk from the heavy-set, balding man with a comb-over.

Kennith Smiles chuckled, the gray-white beard spreading across his face as he reached into a drawer. "You know, Ann, I've given this a lot of thought. Your drinking while on the job has become really out of control." She sputtered incoherently at this bald lie. "And I may have to speak to the board about this." His hand came up holding a gun. Ann's eyes had gone wide from his accusation, but wider yet when she saw him brandish the gun. Why would the administrator of Brightwood College need a gun in his desk drawer?

"I don't drink on the job!" she finally stated for the record and stared at the gun as he popped out the cartridge and began popping out the bullets while he spoke. She didn't know what sort of gun it was, but it was black and ugly.

"I think we need to come to some sort of understanding, Ann," he said, his words punctuated by the heavy noise of the gun as he moved it around on his desk, like he was a child playing with a toy. He replaced the ammunition into the cartridge. He popped the cartridge back into the gun and settled it in front of himself on his desk, then folded his hands on the desk, just as if they were having

a very normal discussion. Ann had never seen a gun before. She was certain it was real. There was no question about it. What was he doing? Was he threatening her?

His blue gaze lifted to her. "I usually keep my gun in my car. I brought it with me today to keep it close." He patted it, still smiling. "You know, I go to target practice every weekend. I've become quite good."

"If you're threatening me—"

He made a belittling sound. "Threaten you? With a gun? Come, come, Ann. I thought that we had an understanding. Tell you what. After work we should go have that drink and afterwards, well… who knows? A little bit of scratching of backs never hurts anyone."

When she said nothing either way he added, "It would go a very long way in my not mentioning your drinking on the job to anyone."

Ann rose out of the chair, leaned forward, her hands on either side of the desk as she said in a low growl, "You can just kiss my ass." She whirled around and was out of Smiles office, working not to run, but her steps were quick, her heals clicking loudly along the gray linoleum, each step echoed with her heartbeat.

In need of solace, she reached her husband's office. She knocked, and turned the doorknob, but it was locked.

"Shit," she muttered to herself and took a deep breath, checking his schedule on the door. He had a class right now. If she were a smoker, she'd head out the back door to sneak a smoke, to hell with the no-smoking policy. But as it was, she needed a drink badly. How ironic the asshole accused her of drinking while on the job, when she had never done so, but now it was a necessity to calm her nerves.

The car stopped, and my aunt opened her door. I looked up shocked we were home already. I hadn't even noticed her turning, stopping and driving up the little streets of town to reach home.

"Lainey, that must be a good book, you haven't said a word, or even looked up the whole way."

"It is," I said, closing the book, but holding my place with a finger. I should have grabbed a marker, but didn't think of it. We stepped up to the back door and my aunt moved to unlocked the door, at the same time Weeks pulled it open startling us. He had a tin tray in his hand covered with tin foil.

"Oh." They both said at the same time with startled looks, and then chuckled.

"You're up?" she asked, stepping inside.

"Just waiting for you to get home," he said. "I thought I'd grill hamburgers, if that's alright." He pulled back the foil to show us the raw burgers on the tray. "Got them today when I got off work. This is the good stuff. Not the garbage they ground elsewhere. Call 'em Pub Burgers."

"Sounds good," Aunt Jessica said.

He showed me the burgers. I didn't know much about hamburger, I just enjoyed it on a bun with everything except mustard on it.

"Sure," I said. "I'm always hungry."

"I thought you'd want breakfast," my aunt said.

"Nah. I'm going in later tonight."

Head down, I sailed through the kitchen. Poe darting ahead of me, he angled to his bowl of food.

"Bug. You want one or two burgers," Weeks called to me. "Bug" was the shortened version of his pet name for me, which was "Lainey-bug". He only used it at home and never in front of company. With the exception of Uncle Ed, of course.

I stopped long enough to say over my shoulder, "One. No onion on mine."

"Okay. They'll be coming up quick."

I bounded up the stairs, anxious to get back to the story. I dumped my purse on the end of the bed, flopped down and began reading where I left off and became engrossed in the story, the characters, and the dark old mansion where this school was.

About ten pages later, the aroma of the grill came through vents of my air conditioner, causing me to realize I was starved. I marked my spot in the book with a bit of scratch paper, noting I'd finished the first two chapters. I put it down lie back and stared up at the ceiling, wondering how I had come across a book like this. It almost spoke to me. The character, David, being a writer, and his wife working in the office. Just like Carol and Chad Taylor. What a coincidence!

That's when a little voice began murmuring in my ear, *Motive... Motive... what the hell is the motive?* Not the motive in the book, but about the actual murders of the Taylors. I replayed the things discussed with Okert. A secret? Or something learned by Mrs. Taylor had everything to do with both their murders.

Turning my head, I looked for my notebook. It was across the room on my desk. I was too lazy to get up, knowing if I did the thoughts would vanish. I turned my head and found a pen on my bedside table and grabbed it up and opened the book where I'd left off. In the blank space where the print stopped I wrote: *Why was Mrs. Taylor killed? Did she know something about the murderer? Something he did? Did it have to do with money, or something else? Why was Mr. Taylor killed? Same reason? Or to guarantee no one was left who might know about whatever it was the murderer didn't want to get out.*

And what about Brianna? Murder? Or Accident?

Chapter 11

"Lainey!" the shout came from downstairs.

"Coming!" I yelled back, having slipped on my sandals and shorts. The afternoon had become the usual hot and muggy for this time of year. I was anxiously waiting for cooler, dryer fall-like temperatures to invade, noting it would not be soon enough for me. Summer had been long and hot. Besides, I had some new fall sweaters and boots I wanted to wear as soon as the leaves fell off the trees.

Weeks had our hamburgers on buns along with baked beans and chips on colorful plastic plates. All the condiments arranged in the center of the kitchen table to load on whatever you wanted. I would not touch the onions, thank you.

"We aren't eating outside?" I asked, slathering mayo over my bun.

"Too buggy," my aunt said.

"Yeah. There's only so much a bug candle can handle. Pass the pickles," Weeks said.

Setting down the ketchup, I grabbed the open jar of spears, plucked one out with my fingers and set the jar closer to him.

"Lainey! Use a fork, please," my aunt admonished.

"Sorry." Shoulders hunched, I made a face at my *fax pas.* I found Weeks' amused glance and he winked at me. No foul. He probably would have done the same thing, but he wisely used his fork to stab the end of one and extract it from the brine.

"I hear that Okert came to see you. Gave you the updates on what was discovered in that washroom over at the college?" Weeks said, and then took a huge bite of the burger stuffed with tomatoes, onion and lettuce, oozing ketchup and mustard.

I was still chewing on my mouthful, but nodded. Licking my lips, I grabbed my napkin, and found that my hands had ketchup and mayonnaise all over them. I grabbed another from the holder and wiped my face and hands. Can't take me anywhere.

After a swallow of ice tea, I said, "I asked if he could let me know what they found."

"What's the news?"

I looked up at him from my sandwich. "You don't know?"

"I've been asleep all day," he said.

"I thought you said you knew everything," I teased, then bit into my burger, enjoying the savory flavors coming together in my mouth.

"Smarty pants," he said.

"Oh, this is good beef, dear," My aunt said, asking what the company who made them were. The conversation about the beef went on as we chewed on our burgers, pickles and chips.

I finally said, "One very interesting item found was a window blind cord in the wastebasket."

"Good. That's a mistake by the perp."

"I'm told they are looking for the blinds it came from." Grabbing my spoon, I scooped through the beans on my plate and shoved a spoonful into my mouth.

"I see. So, this may be what was used to strangle him with?"

"Okay, you two." My aunt had to put a stop to our shop talk at the table. We tended to get out of control. New rule at the dinner table was no talk of murder and mayhem.

"Sorry," we both said.

From there on, dinner topics were everything but murder, and therefore anything interesting. I snarfed everything down while my aunt and Weeks conversed on the leaky faucet in the downstairs bathroom to the latest rumors my aunt had picked up in the shop—mostly attributed to Jennifer—to when his hours would be back to normal.

"Hopefully everyone will be over the flu in a few days. Maybe by Monday. So, we'll have to keep this up through Sunday at least." He paused and said. "I'll tell you, I'm making it a new policy that all my deputies get a flu shot every year from here on out. This is nuts."

His words jarred a memory from me. "Oh, by the way, Uncle Ed says he wants to come for Sunday dinner." They stared at me like I'd belched loudly.

"Hey, don't kill the messenger," I said.

"Well, that would be nice. I don't think we've seen him in weeks," my aunt ventured quietly.

"Just what I *don't* need on Sunday," Weeks said and earned a frown from my aunt.

"We haven't seen him for a long while, dear," my aunt said more sternly, giving him "the look".

"Yes, yes. And I could go on not seeing him for another few weeks," Weeks said, then he winked at me.

"Think of it this way, Uncle John, you can eat and can leave for work right away. No uncomfortable after-dinner conversations," I said. We smirked at one another. This was always fun.

"Well, there's that," he said. My aunt swatted him in a playful way and he play-acted as though he were mortally wounded. I chuckled at their antics. At times they were like teenagers.

Weeks' phone rang at his elbow. He picked it up. "Weeks." He listened, made his usual monosyllable sounds into the receiver, said "Thanks," and hung up. He looked at me. "Toxicology report on your friend's in."

"Wow. That's fast," I said.

"I'm told the girl's father is someone important. But anyway..." Eyes darting to my aunt, he said, "But I'll bring you up to speed after dinner."

"Sounds good. Meet me in the parlor," I said and snickered at the look I got from my aunt.

"You don't need to go that far away," she said.

"We don't want to upset you," Weeks said in mock sincerity.

"Whatever," she said, eating the rest of her sandwich daintily.

I helped my aunt with dishes, which consisted of cleaning off the goop left on our three plates, then she washed them in the sink while I dried. Afterwards I met Weeks in the living room where he was reading the paper.

"Busy day for Mr. Shaw and his paper. Could hardly get all of the accidents, deaths and murders on the front page." Weeks laughed. I knew for a fact that he didn't like Allen E. Shaw, Nadine's father, who owned and ran *The Montclair Herald,* our local newspaper. Often Weeks would be mis-quoted in the paper, or report something Mr. Shaw was told not to release.

He folded and put the newspaper down on the coffee table and leaned forward, arms leaning across his thighs, fingers loosely laced. I plopped into a matching wing chair on the other side of the dormant fireplace. My aunt had placed a very vibrant plant there that seemed to enjoy the non-sunny spot.

"Okay," he began in a low tone, as though we were about to swap secrets of the highest order. "They found the drug chloral hydrate in her system."

I twisted my mouth. "I'm sorry—"

"Knock out drops," he clarified. "Usually used as a date-rape drug."

"Drops?" I said. "As in liquid form?"

He nodded. "Yes."

"So, it could be given in a drink?"

"Exactly."

"How long before it goes to work?"

"Not long. Minutes. The person might feel a bit groggy at first, but they knock you out completely." He snapped his fingers. "Like that."

"Oh. Wow." Nodding, my gaze went to the floor, thinking. The images of Briana leaving with Smith, and him buying her a soft drink out of the machine beforehand came back vividly. I could still hear that distinctive sound of the tab being snapped back on the can. Chills ran up and down my spine. "This is something I've kept to myself, up until now," I said looking up at him.

"What? Tell me. Believe me, I will keep it in confidence. No one will know you told me."

"Okay. I was about to leave for the last time that day on Thursday," I began.

"The college?"

"Right. I was crossing that big open area, the commons, or whatever they call it." He nodded. "I heard two people coming out of the elevator. Because I didn't want anyone to know I was still there, after all that time, I hid behind one of those big pillars. I saw it was the school president, Mr. Smith, and Briana. She must have been crying, because she was blowing her nose, and he was saying something to her, trying to calm, or console her, I guess. He offered to buy her a drink down in the food area. He bought a soda from the vending machine. I heard the can drop into the bin. Right away, I heard him snap the top. I thought it sort of odd, at the time. I mean, why would someone open the can for the person who is going to drink it?"

"Your aunt has trouble opening pop cans, so I do it for her," Weeks said, giving Smith the benefit of the doubt.

"Okay. But he hands it to her. They go out the door, his arm's sort of across the back of her shoulders, soothing her with words."

"What was she upset about?"

"She worked with Carol."

"Ahhh."

169

"I'd had a little chat with her earlier that very morning." I went on, "She was saying some things that I'd intended to speak to her about in more detail, later on. Then, boom, she's dead. No one can ask her what she knew about Carol leaving, or being fired. I only know this. That Carol may have uncovered something to do with bank accounts that may have had money taken out, and nothing had been noted in her accounts, or files, or whatever. Brianna said Carol had said she would be speaking to someone about the discrepancy in the accounts."

"You said that before, about money in accounts." He nodded and sat back. "That's easy to look into."

"I hope you can get to the bottom of it. But even if you find something odd, how do you know who took the money out?"

"Again, you'd be surprised by how a bank teller can remember a client that comes into the bank and withdraws or moves money around. But, since it's—" he flicked his wrist and glanced at his watch "—after five, and it's Saturday, I'm unable to question anyone at the bank. We'll have to wait until Monday."

I nodded, my breath catching in my throat while my dread took on a whole new form. If Smith had put the chloral hydrate in Briana's drink before she drove home, and this caused her to pass out, and caused the accident in which she died, then it was murder. If Smith had murdered Brianna, as well as both Mr. and Mrs. Taylor. Whatever he was protecting, someone had better find out and soon.

"Whatever you do, Lainey, you be careful," Weeks said, palms pressed together like he was about to pray, pointing with two index fingers toward me.

"I will."

"This Cooper Smith guy, or whoever he is, I haven't been able to find any records of him beyond four or five years back before he began working at the college."

"Really?" I blinked with astonishment. How does one do this, was my first thought. "You've looked into him? Already?"

"Yes. I'm thinking he's taken an alias. Why, I have no idea." He looked at his watch. "Well. I've gotta go." He rose.

"Thanks for telling me about this," I said.

"No problem. I have no idea when your school will open up again for classes, but for sure, we've got a big problem with Smith. If he had anything to do with any, or all of these murders, or events, I can only say we are dealing with a very dangerous character."

I was way ahead of him. I nodded, hands sliding up over my bare arms, feeling that chill again.

Soon after Weeks had left, I returned to my room. Only this time I sat at my desk, with the intentions of doing serious study. My psychology book had been sitting there taunting me since coming home on Thursday. So, I opened it up and began reading. Interesting stuff about brain function and why, or how we make decisions. This followed up what was discussed in class on Tuesday when Ellwood had answered the question in class about a choice of saving five people by shoving one person across the tracks in front of a moving trolley. A totally bogus situation, but Ellwood made it clear he was simply above it all by cracking jokes, and later on telling me the hypothetical question was bogus anyway, so, what did it matter how he had answered.

But I disagreed with his flippant attitude. Was he merely being funny, or putting aside the seriousness of giving a well thought-out answer? The fact that I hadn't had a chance to answer the question in class no longer bothered me. What now bothered me was how Ellwood had just happened to be the one to discover Mr. Taylor's body, and returned to us maybe an hour later looking slightly drained. Sure, he'd had to answer questions by the police, but from all appearances, he seemed non-emotional. Plus, he had made a video of Mr. Taylor's body in the stall. I was certain he had fully intended to post it on social media to see what sort of rise he would get out of people who viewed it. My only regret was that I hadn't quizzed Ellwood more about how he came to be there at that moment to discover the body. I wondered why I hadn't noted the time he'd made that video.

Was his being there purely coincidence? I wondered about it now. Funny how you tend to give friends an automatic benefit of a doubt. I was now feeling suspicions about *everyone.*

I thought of how much strength it would have taken to hoist another man's body up in order to make it appear as though he had hung himself. That was the other thing this all hinged on. I certainly wouldn't be able to do it. It would take a rather large person with upper body strength to do this. My sense was that Smith was our killer, but I now wondered if they didn't have help.

Motive was only one-third of the puzzle. Means was another one-third. Opportunity was the last piece to fit into the whole jig-saw puzzle. Setting aside motive for the time being, my attention was now on means. Since Jimmy Bean was such a small man, such a gentle man, the very thought of him doing such a horrifying thing was ridiculous. I'd told Okert so right away. So, he was not a suspect.

Whoever had killed Mr. Taylor had to be strong enough to lift a man who weight at least one eighty to two hundred pounds. I tried to imagine Ellwood hoisting Mr. Taylor's body up on a rope. I could see him doing this. I then put Mr. Smith into that picture. As obese as he was I had trouble seeing him doing this without having a cardiac arrest from all the exertion. The motivation to kill someone can be very strong, and someone with limitations would find a way to do it. I thought he would have devised a way in which to hoist the other man. The cart had everything to do with it, I was certain. Being that the cart would have the body at least half-way up, might make it possible.

Turning my attention to Mrs. Taylor, who was shot, I wondered who was killed first. If the Taylors were killed by the same person, they would have to know exactly where the Taylors lived, known their movements, and/or their schedule, and known that Mrs. Taylor would not be going to work that day. This person owned a gun and was able to get from one place to the other within the allotted time in order to carry out both murders. I had learned that there had been an hour window of time in which first Mrs. Taylor was shot and died, to when Mr. Taylor had been strangled. The lividity of Mr. Taylor's body indicated that perhaps all the set-up or prep had to be done ahead of time. Mr. Taylor had been on that cart for a while. Perhaps hidden in another part of the lower section, in one of those locked rooms, while the killer went out and shot Mrs. Taylor. He then came back to set up the suicide, which might have taken longer than shooting Taylor's wife. But he acted quickly, precisely, and with premeditation.

From what was established, Mr. Taylor's body was lying dead on that dirty bin for at least thirty minutes. Within that window of time, from possibly the moment he was killed to when he was hoisted up on the rope something else must have happened. I considered that perhaps the killer had to rest between those rigorous moments of pushing the cart with Mr. Taylor's body into the elevator, and into that subbasement washroom. I didn't think he rigged the body with the noose around his neck and hung him right away. The visual in my head of this upset me, and I had to pause in thinking about that for the time being.

The last thing Weeks had told me about Mr. Smith is that he—as Cooper Smith—didn't exist prior to five years ago, which means he had to have changed his identity, for whatever reason, a few years back. Which to me (and probably to Weeks, too), leads me to believe that maybe his real identity was something that the police, or even the FBI may be interested in. In which case his fingerprints would be very valuable for identification.

Taylor's killer had been careful to not his leave fingerprints. He'd worn gloves. That brought up another memory of watching Mr. Smith use his hanky in order to touch the buttons to summon the elevator. At the time, I'd put it down to someone with an inordinate fear of germs. But now, I had other thoughts on that. Like a fear of leaving any fingerprints at all. Anywhere. I had to wonder why someone would guard his fingerprints so closely. I thought about his giving Briana that cola before the two of them left the building that day. If he had been the one to put chloral hydrate into her drink, causing her to black out, and had also murdered the Taylors, he was a very dangerous man. I wondered what it would take to bring him down. And who. Certainly not me, and I didn't think it would be Weeks. I don't know why I thought that, I just did.

These and other thoughts nagged at me and I couldn't study any longer. I took up my phone and found Week's number and hit send.

He answered on the second ring.

"Lainey? What's up?"

"The soda pop can in Breanna's car? If you guys still have it, make sure to dust it for fingerprints."

"Done and done."

"I figured," I said. "But I couldn't study thinking about that."

"Fine. Now maybe you'll study."

"Right."

* * *

On Sunday we opened the store at noon, as usual. Jenny did not work on Sunday, which was fine with us. I helped to put out the usual arrangement of cookies, which were free along with the coffee. My aunt had also placed small packets of coffees, teas, specialty treats and dip mixes, and made it an experimental promotion, because she sold these items too. People enjoyed the flavored coffee today, which was blueberry, and in my opinion tasted less like coffee and more like blueberries. I drank two cups with a calorie free sweetener and a bit of half-n-half and had a caffeine buzz the rest of the day. The hottest seller of the day was the hazelnut flavor, but some liked French vanilla, which to me seemed to taste similar. Some of the locals knew a good thing and streamed in for the freebies. I often questioned this free thing, but my aunt seemed to feel that she was giving back to people of the town, no matter if they could pay or not. I had to admire her generosity. Today, however she had a tip jar nearby, and some people threw in a dollar, or change, thanking her. This would go back into buying the cookies and other offerings the next time.

The afternoon slugged by, with only a trickle of people who came to browse or buy. Then someone I recognized came through the door. Thin, she had almost gaunt features, as though she'd lost a lot of weight from a long stay in the hospital. Her iron gray hair cut short and nicely styled. I tried to place her and it dawned on me. She never did tell me her name that day in the office. She was looking through the music selections, and had chosen something. I couldn't see the artist's name on the cover because her hand covered it.

Striding up I said, "Hi."

She turned, her smile creating numerous creases around her mouth and eyes. "Lainey? What a surprise to see you here," she said.

"I work here. I'm sorry, but I don't know your name. You never did say," I said, referring to when we spoke in the office at Whitman. She was the woman who had known my mother.

"Helen. Helen Graham." Her pale somewhat crepe-y-skinned hand went out to me and I shook it. Her hand was cool, but soft.

"I'd like to introduce you to my aunt," I said, seeing my aunt taking a turn into the aisle. I made the introductions. "Helen used to work with my mother at Darby Insurance."

"Oh, yes. How do you do," my aunt said as they shook hands.

"A terrible thing, what happened to the Taylors. Oh, I can't even begin to imagine what's to become of their children," she said.

"Someone will step in," my aunt said, smiling, giving me a knowing wink.

"I'm sure. Just as you have." Her gaze went from her to me and back again.

"Aunt Jessica is my godmother," I said.

"How wonderful," Helen said brightly.

"So, you're enjoying our town?" my aunt steered the discussion away from the dreary.

"Yes. My daughter-in-law lives nearby, I'm meeting her for dinner at the Blue Hampton Inn. I'm a bit early, but thought I'd browse through the shops."

"Glad you did," my aunt said, spying the CD she had in her hand. "That's the latest by Josh Groban, but we have more up front, if you'd don't find what you're looking for here. We also have free cookies and our coffee of the day is blueberry crumble. Let us know if you need any help." My aunt was so relaxed at making a customer feel at home, and yet didn't hover, you'd barely know from her little sales pitch she'd subliminally tried to sell you something. My shyness kept me to the line, "May I help you?" and when they said no, I'd walk away.

"Thank you." The two women made polite noises as my aunt parted.

I smiled at Helen, and edged away, but then thought of something and turned back. "Uh, Mrs. Graham?"

"Please, call me Helen, dear," she said.

"Helen," I said. "Uh, do you have any idea if classes will be back in session tomorrow?"

"I've had one email this morning that it's under consideration. If so, they will have comfort dogs in the school available to everyone who has been affected by this terrible tragedy." Her hand went to her sunken chest. I caught the glimmer of various rings, including a wedding band and a large diamond. "That much I do know." She smiled broadly, the large teeth showing were angled forward and made me think of a parrot somehow.

"Will students get an email to notify us?" I asked.

"It will most likely be put up on our website, so check that sometime tonight, or early tomorrow morning."

"Okay. Thanks," I said, and stepped away, but was caught by what she said next while still fingering through the CDs.

"Such a mess. Reminds me of when Dr. Fay died."

"Who?" I said, feeling a nudge in my curiosity department. I was careful to not push, as she looked uneasy, and her dark eyes darted around herself as though not sure about saying what she was about to say.

"Yes. About two years ago," she spoke low. "It was summertime. Anyway, Dr. Fay was our president. He was involved in a fatal car crash. Funny thing about it," she said thoughtfully, "it was a one vehicle accident." She shrugged.

A zip of a chill went through me. "Really? Helen, what do you remember about it? If you don't mind my asking?"

"Yes, well, it was strange. He just went right off the road. He was only a few miles from home, too. He lived near the college, you see, maybe only five miles away. He was almost home, and went right off one of those ramps that come off of the Interstate, just west of here. He was crossing over, and—" She shook her head, seeming to be unable to go on.

"Bad weather?" I asked.

"No. Clear and dry. But it was at night, so possibly a deer ran out in front of him—that's what the local constable said, anyway." She made a little *humph* sound. "If you ask me something seemed fishy to me," she said out the side of her mouth. If the subject wasn't so serious, I'd have chuckled at her animation. "He was not a drinker, and they didn't find anything wrong with his car, either."

"Did they do an autopsy?" I asked.

She shook her head. "I guess there was no reason to look further beyond the fact he hadn't been drinking or anything." She paused for a moment. "The only thing he drank was mineral waters. He didn't even drink coffee, if you can believe that. He was a wonderful man." She smiled with a memory, looking down. "He played classical music in the office." She looked around the shop, then said again off the side of her mouth, as though someone here would even know who she was speaking of. "Much better than the one we got now."

"Mr. Smith?"

"Yes. He was an assistant at first, then went to vice president within a short time, and right after Dr. Fay's death, he became president by virtue of no one available to take over, except him."

"Really?"

She lifted her shoulders in a shrug. "Yes. I'm not sure what the board was thinking of hiring him, but—" She shook her head, eyes pressed closed for a long suffering second. "At least he's still on probation."

"He's that bad?" I asked.

She tilted her head to the side. "You know what? I've said too much. I don't like talking ill of people. Especially my boss."

I leaned a little closer and said, "I understand, but, you were my mother's friend. You must have shared office secrets with her." I could hardly believe my audacity.

She moved closer, voice low and said, "No one is certain where Mr. Smith came from, really. Some say he's from Ohio. Others say he was out of the country for ten or more years. Traveled to Europe, South America. He can speak five languages."

"Really?"

She shrugged. "At least that's what I've been told. I also seem to recall that someone said he was once a lawyer. Something to do with business."

I nodded. "So, he has credentials."

"Oh, yes. Almost over-qualified, as they say." She laughed, it was a husky smoker's laugh. A former smoker, I guess, because she did not stink of it.

I decided I liked and trusted her and said conspiratorially, "I've been helping the police with Mr. Taylor's murder."

Her eyes went wide and her mouth fell open. "Murder? Where did you get that he was murdered, my dear?"

"Believe me, you'll hear about it soon, since you haven't as yet," I said, grasping her thin wrist firmly but with the gentleness I might have used on a bird's wing. "I've talked to the local police chief who was in charge of the investigation—" I had to stop myself from revealing everything I knew. That would have been a big mistake. The killer might learn what we knew, if this should get out, and I couldn't *prove* who the murderer was, but it had to be someone in the building because of the keys he would have had to obtain in order to access those rooms in the basement. "Anyway, they're proceeding with a murder investigation, now."

"Really?" she breathed, sounding astounded by the news.

"So, I don't know who it's up to on opening the school," I ended my earth-shattering news. "I really can't say more."

"I understand. And thank you for telling me, Lainey, dear. I hope whoever did this can be caught and brought to trial."

"I do too," I said. "For both Mr. and Mrs. Taylor's sakes."

After returning home for the night, I found myself drained. I checked the school's site and sure enough, there was a message that school would be open in the morning. It had a note about the comfort dogs being in the school throughout the week. I didn't know what a comfort dog was exactly, but probably they would be gentle and something to pet and feel comforted by. I'd heard of it before, but had never experienced it.

Chapter 12

Knowing that school was resuming, I made a point of reading the chapters I was supposed to read, and made a half-hearted stab at my math. I hated math. I didn't understand why we had to repeat everything we had already done in high school. If it wasn't for the fact that I wanted to get a degree in something, I wouldn't have gone to college. I was still not sure I'd stay in college. I'd never liked the rigid school schedule, homework, teachers, or most of the students—at least the ones who were immature. My only hope was that perhaps they would find a suitable teacher for our creative writing class and I could continue to learn more about writing.

I was up before my alarm woke me, which is frightening in and of itself. I scrubbed my face, brushed my hair and teeth, dressed and headed down for breakfast. My aunt was up bustling around the kitchen. The smell of oranges permeated the room.

"Wow," I said, glancing at the juicer filled with homemade orange juice. "This is unusual. Who's sick?"

"Your uncle had a sore throat when he came home in the middle of the night. I'm taking a tray up for him. Help yourself to whatever you want." She was placing a large glass of OJ on the tray along with some oatmeal with some grapes and a few other items. I didn't know Weeks was an oatmeal type of guy. His motto was if it didn't move on four legs, or fly when it was alive, he didn't want to eat it. I would ask him what the waffles were before they became waffles. Maybe they had wings.

I didn't blame Weeks, I wasn't much for oatmeal and so grabbed my usual box of cold cereal, a bowl, spoon and milk, and poured myself a glass of orange juice, and added a banana for good measure. Placing my phone next to my bowl I noticed I had a new text message. It was from Nadine. I read it. She was basically telling me there was school today.

I wrote back, "Y I KNOW." She probably thought she had her finger on the pulse of what went on at school, but she wasn't the only one. While I ate, we went back and forth, the usual mundane stuff. She hoped to see me at lunch. "WL C", I wrote back. She wanted to tell me about her date with Franklin. Of course.

We went back and forth about that, and I wondered why we'd have to see each other at all. I really didn't know what difference it made if I was talking to her over the phone, or text messaging, she still rambled on and on. I finally finished my breakfast and told her I had to go and get ready. I was ready, except for gathering up my books and such into my backpack, but needed to get off the phone.

I drove carefully to school, remembering that Brianna had been driving home and had perished on this very road only a few days ago. My list of suspects were not long. In fact, after ruminating about it this the whole weekend, there was only one name on it. The problem was proving it. It was obvious to me that one person had killed all three: Brianna, Mr. and Mrs. Taylor all for the same reason, or related to the main reason.

Prior to leaving the house, I checked with the school site to see if my writing class was canceled. No news on that anywhere. I thought to call Ellwood, since I'd put his phone number into my phone's memory, but wasn't sure I really wanted to call and learn it was canceled. Since I was running late (and never used my phone while driving), I decided I'd like to be happily surprised it wasn't canceled, and maybe they had someone to take over for Mr. Taylor. Of course, no one would be able to take his place, in my mind.

I did the usual driving around for several minutes finding nowhere close, so I parked about a half a football field away in the back lot, and hiked to the building. I entered through the glass doors, the very ones that Brianna had gone through for the last time with Mr. Smith. I didn't normally come in this way, and wasn't sure if it wasn't pre-ordained. Looking around, it was as though nothing of major significance had happened last week. All the students were milling about as they had the week before. I saw no dogs at all, and so I made my way to my first class, which was creative writing on the first floor. The door was open, and about the same amount of people who usually came to it were all there. Except I didn't see Ellwood.

I sat down next to a guy with glasses. I couldn't remember his name.

"I'm surprised this wasn't canceled," he said, almost sounding upset that it wasn't.

"Me too," I said. "I can't believe they could find someone so soon."

"Me too, but I've heard rumors that someone will be taking it over."

I looked at him and introduced myself, offering him my hand to shake.

"Kennith Evans," he said. "Say, aren't you the freshman?"

I screwed up my mouth. "Yes. Just don't say that so loud."

"How'd you get in this class, anyway? I tried to get in last year, but had to wait until my sophomore year." It sounded like he was miffed.

"I had a special letter from a teacher," I said. It wasn't exactly a lie. The teacher had been Mr. Taylor's teacher. Couldn't be helped if I was related.

"A teacher? You must know someone higher up than I did. I couldn't get in even with my teacher's good word in for me."

"Well, I guess I do, uh, did," I said and left it at that. I didn't like the fact he sounded as though I'd cheated in order to get into this class. I was willing to think he'd get over it by lunch time.

We waited five minutes after the hour of seven when someone partially opened the door, but didn't come in. A man's voice spoke to someone unseen in the hallway. We all got expectantly quiet. Then he walked in. Actually his large stomach appeared before the rest of him did.

Mr. Smith strode in wearing a dark brown suit complete with a vest, his shirt was the color of peanut butter, and his silk tie matched his ensemble precisely. He had to have a tailor in order to have the suit fit him so well.

I was a little shocked to see him here as though he were a teacher. My face became warm as I remembered him buying that can of pop for Brianna. He was the last person to see her alive that day. It was all I could do not to jump up and scream, "Murderer!" because I was convinced he did her and the Taylors in.

He smiled as he walked in, greeting us like he'd been here from the very beginning and we were all friends. I resented that smug smile. He set down a pile of what looked to be hand-outs which were so thick, he divided them in two piles, the larger of the two stacks of material might have been eight inches tall. I noticed the cover on each had different color sheets. One was green the other was yellow with only a title on each one.

"As you all know, Mr. Taylor met with tragic death, last week, and is the reason we were closed for the last part of the week." He allowed a pause here, expecting us all to groan or make some sort of noise. Someone coughed. Two girls across from me put their heads together. If Ellwood had been here, he might have said something snide. Probably best he wasn't here. "I've made some calls over the weekend, and through the usual venue, we've got someone who is happy to take over this class, but he was unable to come in today on such short notice. However, you'll be seeing him on Wednesday. His name is Mr. Glenn Bascom who holds an MBA and I'm certain will take you all under his wing where writing is concerned." He paused as he moved a few things around on the mostly empty desk. "I do have some hand-outs for you today. Could I have two of you come up and hand these out, please?"

Since I sat front and center, I stood, as did Evans. We didn't look at each other, but went around the table at opposite ends, stepped up to the desk and grabbed the closest pile of hand-outs. Mine was titled, "Crafting Unforgettable Characters". Evans began on one side of the room and I started handing out on the other, making sure both myself and Evans got one as I passed our table. There was no hurry, since the class wasn't going to consist of much else.

When this task was finished, Smith said, "I have nothing else for you today, however, it may behoove you to read on through the next chapter or two, just to keep up with whatever Mr. Bascom may have in mind for you when he gets here." He reached into his vest and withdrew a very expensive looking gold pocket watch. Upon examining it, he said, "That'll be all for today." The noise of everybody getting up nearly drowned out his next words as he spoke loudly, "Would Lainey Quilholt please see me before she leaves? Lainey Quilholt?"

My heart leapt into my throat. Our eyes met. *Yish*. With shaking hands, I gathered my things. My legs were a tad rubbery as I went up to the front of the class where he stood.

"Ms Quilholt?"

"Yes." I waited expectantly.

"I've been told you had a run-in with Tyler Sinclair?"

"Yes. He attacked me in the parking lot," I said, thinking this incident felt so minute compared to the murders. I'd practically forgotten all about it.

"I feel so terrible about this. Please let me convey my apologies on my oversight of not being more punctual in saying how terrible I feel about what he did to you. Were you hurt?"

I pressed my lips together. I wanted to say, *You were probably busy thinking up ways to murder people.* If his attempt at being nice to me was intended to short circuit any bad feelings I might have for him, he was sorely mistaken. But then, he didn't know that I suspected him in any of this.

"No. I'm fine. He took out my windshield with a baseball bat."

"Oh, my… I'm sorry. Did your insurance cover it?" His dark eyes sparkled, and his lips easily slipped into a smile when I said that it had. He extended a hand to me—the gentlemanly way to escort a lady—and the other motioning out the door, very much like he had Brianna that day. We stepped out into the quiet hall. At this point his cologne overwhelmed me and I had to step away. I didn't want to look at him, and it took all the nerve to do so.

"If there's anything I can do for you, just let me know," he said.

My lips pressed together and I had to say something. "Can you answer a few questions for me?"

"Certainly."

"Who's in charge of hiring and firing here?" I asked.

"Well, I am, of course."

"Then can you tell me why you fired Carol?"

I saw no visible change in his expression, not even a flinch. "I didn't fire her, she put in her resignation."

"Really?" I said, my voice in a tone that said I didn't believe him. Which I didn't, because Brianna told me she'd been fired.

"And how do you know this, may I ask? How is it any of your concern?" His face had transformed from cordial to slightly irritated, now.

"It was something I'd heard," I wasn't about to tell him who had told me. Not like he could do anything more to Brianna now.

"Well, rumors do get around, don't they?" he said and took a step away. "I wouldn't believe everything you hear, my dear. Have a good day." With that he stepped on down the hallway, wanting to cut off further interrogation, no doubt. He did not waddle, as one would expect, which amazed me. He carried himself quite well for someone of his girth with a self-assured and dignified baring. He turned swiftly at a corner and was gone.

I had wanted to catch him in a lie, or anything that sounded a little off from the facts as I knew them. Unfortunately, he was wily as they get. I figured no matter what I'd asked, he had a ready answer for it, as he had in this case. A good liar practiced their skills continuously. It dawned on me then that I would have a hard time catching him in any lie, because I wasn't a trained police officer, or profiler who knew the subtle things a liar does, such as jerking movements, or looking down—which he had done neither, that I had noticed. Although I wondered about his claim that Carol Taylor had put in her resignation. Did it really matter at this point? He probably could present such a document to this effect, he might even be a very good at forging anyone's signature when he had to.

I began up the hallway when I thought about Ellwood. Why wasn't he here today? I took out my phone and went down my list, found him and made the call. It rang four times and I thought it would go to his messages.

"Hello?" His voice sounded groggy.

"It's Lainey," I said. "Where are you?"

"I'm at home. In bed. Why?"

"Didn't you know that classes resumed this morning?"

"No, I didn't." There were noises in the background, a muffled purring. He had a cat?

"Well, we're getting a new English teacher for our writing class."

"Oh, yeah? Who?"

I grimaced. I'd forgotten the name nearly as soon as it was said. "I can't remember. But the principal handed out some sheets. Should I get you copies?"

"Yeah. Sure." There was more noise. "You said the principal handed out sheets?"

"I meant the president. Sorry." For some reason I had reverted back to high school. "Are you coming to school?"

"Yeah. I'll be there in a bit."

"Okay. See you later, then." When I hung up I had to wonder why no one else had called him or let him know about school being in session.

I returned to the creative writing room, grabbed one of each of the handouts. I wanted to look through the other one called "Writing Prompts". It was the thicker of the two. I flipped to the last page—one hundred and sixty-two pages. Wow. I flipped back to table of contents. I liked some of these prompts. One was "Eavesdropping". That one I could get behind easily enough.

Wanting to get to a quiet spot, like the library, to look these over, I quickly shoved Ellwood's set into my backpack and headed out. I spent the rest of that first hour looking through the handouts, but in the back of my mind thinking about how oily Mr. Smith seemed, showing how concerned he seemed to be over my dealings with Sinclair.

My morning droned on. After math, I went to my English class and bumped into Nadine. She was hanging on the arm of a tall blond guy with light blue eyes.

"Hi! Have you met Franklin?" she said.

"No," I said. "How do you do?"

He made a deep nod. "Hello."

"Are you busy for lunch?" she asked me.

I hesitated for the slightest second and Franklin said, "Now, Nadine, maybe she has something else to do. Or someone else to have lunch with." I wasn't sure how Nadine would take that from someone she'd just begun seeing. Didn't faze her.

"Oh, you're right." Nadine looked back at me. I must admit Franklin had put sparkle into her eyes and a bounce in her step. Plus, she was now wearing her short hair curled under at the ends, and I detected a little make-up.

"He's right, I'm busy," I said, not wanting to commit to having lunch with them as a third wheel. I'd grown sick of being that third wheel with her and Wendy back in high school. They'd talk among themselves, giggle at inside jokes I wasn't privy to. It was just too much work to being that third person. And here she had a guy, and I didn't. It would just get too awkward.

"Oh, you've found someone to replace the dirt bag? Good for you!" Nadine said. It took me a moment to understand what she meant.

"Not exactly," I said quickly to quiet Nadine's jump to conclusion. "Actually, I've got a class. Bye." Before she could pull me into another conversation I didn't want to have, I excused myself and went to my English class up the hall. The assignment was to read a book and write a two-page report on it. I was ahead of the game here.

By the end of Econ—which we all jokingly referred to as nap-hour, I was ready for lunch and maybe some quiet time.

I didn't feel like going to the lunch room—where I might run into people I knew and didn't want to see (like Brett)—I went down into the Pit, chose a few items not really good for me—a candy bar, barbecue chips, and a root beer.

Behind me I heard a woman's voice gasp, "Oh, Brett, you silly!" I made the mistake of turning around to see exactly what I was trying to avoid. Brett Rutherford sat at a nearby table smooching with the same girl I'd last seen him with. This only made me want to roll my eyes, but when his gaze shot to me, I felt the betrayal behind it. I think he had already been cheating on me with her. They seemed way too chummy for only a few days' time. But then, I wouldn't know, since I wasn't eager to wind up in the backseat with him.

Picking up my backpack, with my food items clutched in my hands, I stormed away. My anger too transparent to hide before I realized my mistake.

I stepped out into the warm day, seeking quiet, and solitude (and shade), in hopes of gathering my resolve to not be bothered by the fact that Brett had so quickly replaced me within a few days. Correction, she had been there at our parting, and he was attentive to her as soon as he told me he was through with my odd obsessions. So, there was a line of girls willing to go out with the handsome guitar player. As soon as he was finished with one, he'd go to the next in line. Such was my luck with men. I should just get over him. He certainly was over me.

I tore open the candy bar and took a huge bite and barely tasted the caramel and chocolate nougat along with the peanuts. I snapped open the can of soda, and remembered when I last heard this sound. Who was I kidding? My anger at Brett's duplicity morphed into anger toward the murderer. I made a brave attempt to stem it. But my resolve was weak. My emotional fiber had taken a hit on all sides. Not only had my boyfriend dumped me, but two people I knew were now dead, plus a third. Murdered, actually. Which is worse than just dying from a disease or some sort of accident. I knew it would take longer to get over Brett, but in the face of the fact we had a murderer on campus, I tried to shift my thinking. Unfortunately, it didn't happen. I felt alone, and sorry for myself.

I moved through the little courtyard, the trickling of the water in a nearby fountain of constant white-noise. I found a spot nearby, under a shade, and dumped my crap on the stone seat. Birdsong became a somber concerto somewhere above as I eased my body to the stone bench. I leaned and put my elbow to a knee, hand to support my chin, I let the tears dribble down my face. It was the first time I'd allowed such emotions surface since the very day everything had happened. I knew coming back to school the first day would be difficult. I now knew it was a bad idea. Brett acted as though dumping me had been his intention the whole while, he didn't look upset when he saw me just now. In fact, it was as though he didn't know me.

Mind made up to simply go home for the day, I began gathering my things. But a new sound caught my ears and I stopped to listen.

The familiar flute music soothing, I knew what it was. Logic told me who was playing the instrument, but my soul was caught up in the floaty feel of the light musical notes. Even the bird above had stopped to listen, as though not wanting to add or take away from its magic and beauty.

Closing my eyes, I sat for a while listening. Like a healing balm to my soul, I needed to bathe in it. Somehow the ethereal flute music eclipsed all the bad emotions and filled me with hope. My breath came easier as a puff of breeze fluttered my hair across my face. Like a siren song, it called to me. I rose and stepped toward the sound. Rounding the pool in the center of the courtyard, beyond the cedar hedge, where an elegant statue stood, I found the American Indian seated with legs crossed on a similar bench barefooted. He had a long face, handsome, now that I made note of it, realizing I'd never really took in his handsome features before. He looked as though in his realm, almost as though he had dreamed everything here into existence. Including me. In every case when I'd seen Nate Blackstone he had been fully clothed, looking like a normal, everyday student. Nothing over the top, nothing to hold my interest, or even make my heart pitter-patter. Today, he had taken off his shirt, because of the heat, no doubt, and his brown skin glistened in the sun. Yes, my heart had skipped a beat when I saw him half naked. Today, his hair was unfettered, and it shimmered like a glorious horses mane, fluttering in the breeze.

I realized his eyes were closed, and I was glad he hadn't seen me. I hoped to leave without his noticing me, but I couldn't move, I was so transfixed by this gorgeous being. I had no inkling how beautiful he was before this moment. Older than myself, of course, and, supposedly dangerous, and thus out of bounds for me to even entertain any sort of a relationship besides friendship. And yet there I stood, like a moth lured to the flame of a candle.

When the song was finished, Nate's eyes were still closed and he slowly lowered the flute to his side, lifted his face to the sun and whispered—breathed—something in another language. I had to guess that it was a prayer of some sort. I couldn't disturb him now. I back peddled, working to exit quietly the way I had come by inching my foot back. Lowering my toes slowly to the stone, then my heal, and shifted my weight back. Lifting the other foot, I twisted my body in order to exit swiftly, but the voice stopped me.

"The hand of fate keeps bringing us together," his deep voice resonated in my ears and I froze like a deer finding myself in a set of high beams. I turned back and looked over at him. He had opened his eyes and looked straight at me.

"I'm sorry. I didn't mean to interrupt—"

"You haven't interrupted a thing," he said. "Please, come sit with me." He motioned to the bench across from him.

Hesitating for a brief two seconds, I padded across the stone walk and eased onto the smaller ornate cement bench. "I'm not following you, or anything," I said, hoping I sounded sincere.

He smiled. "Nor am I following you." That had been the other unsaid thought. I smiled, letting a breath of titillation out. "I was about to go home for the day."

"And yet you came out here, outside. To be alone?"

I nodded. "I was making up my mind." I looked down at the partially eaten candy bar in one hand, and the open pop in the other.

His dark eyes searched beyond me as though he wanted to be careful as to what he said next. "It's sometimes hard when everyone else has moved on and you're still trying to get past it all."

I cocked my head. "You a mind reader, or something?"

"Just observant," he said, the barest of a smile.

I twisted my mouth trying to think of a comeback. None came.

"You were with the young man. I believe his name is Brett Rutherford?"

"Yes."

"He isn't with you. You are alone and sad." He shrugged. "I can't help but see that."

"No crime there," I said and cringed inwardly on saying the word crime.

"Nope."

I lowered my gaze trying to think of something to say at this awkward point. A dozen things came, but they were all either obvious statements, or silly.

"So, you're free now?"

"Lunch period," I said, dismally looking away. Or did he mean was I "free" as in dating others? I didn't know.

"That's not a very good lunch," he observed, nodding toward my food choices.

"No. But I didn't feel that hungry."

"I haven't eaten either. I've got a free period. Want to eat with me?"

"Sure." What was the harm? In fact, I could see how this would work. I walk in with a good-looking hunk, it would show I was definitely moving on. Even if Brett didn't see me, others would, and it would get back to him. Good.

He gathered up his things and began putting them away. "I'll meet you at the door."

I nearly raced to grab my things on the other side of the bushes. In a few minutes we met at the glass door leading through the gallery. Although Nate had pulled his shirt back on (there were rules about shoes and shirts), he'd left it unbuttoned.

Not just a few girls noticed this, believe me, as we strode along and headed into the cafeteria.

Something occurred to me, and I wanted to say this before we got to the table. "Uh, just want to go on record and say I'm not on the rebound."

Nate slid eyes to me. "Of course you're not. But there's no problem two friends can't go to lunch together, is there?"

"No. Not at all." I beamed back at him. There. That wasn't so hard, was it? I just wanted him to know I wasn't going to use him to get back at Brett. Although, if I were aiming to do so, I couldn't choose a better guy to wave under Brett's nose. But I wasn't. Really. If Brett should happen to see us together, or someone told him they'd seen me with the handsome Native American, who was I to worry? Rumors are just rumors, after all. My Uncle Ed at this point would likely quote Mr. Twain and say, " 'Rumor will die itself if you will only give it three days.' " I wanted to believe that, but in today's world, the Internet was capable of keeping such things alive indefinitely.

I stood nearby while Nate chose more pizza I thought was legal for one guy to eat, and paid for it. I was almost going to tease him about his choice of food, since he'd said something about my choices earlier, but I didn't know him that well and so I didn't.

"Don't you want anything to eat?" he asked.

"I'm fine." I wasn't fine. I was hungry. The pop and candy bar were stupid choices, and my money was nearly gone, so I didn't think I could afford even a wedge of pizza.

We found a spot to sit inside the low-lit cafeteria next to the brick wall. A single light above us lent enough light to see by, and the outer edges of our table seemed to be in the dark, making me feel as though we were isolated. I noticed how they'd achieved this with the recessed single bulb above. Looking around, others were either studying alone, or eating.

Across the room someone caught my eye. They waved. It was Nadine and Franklin. Oh boy. Now the rumors would surely fly.

Nate picked up one of the large pieces of pizza and set it on a napkin and put it in front of me. "Here. Eat it. Don't argue." He had a way about him.

"Thanks," I said and picked it up, happy he'd offered because the aroma of it was driving me crazy. We ate in silence, looking everywhere but at each other. This was silly. Who was going to breach the silence first? Obviously not the Indian.

"People are gonna talk," I said.

"Let them," he said leaning in for another bite of a new wedge of pizza.

"You're a few years older than me," I said.

"I'm twenty-five."

"Right. My uncle will have a cow and a half, he learns we sat with each other for lunch."

A crooked smile reached his lips as he wiped the grease from them. "Does that concern you the most? Or was there something else that bothered you more?"

I squinted at him. What was he some sort of double-talker? "Sorry. I don't know what you mean."

"If I asked you on a date, what would you say?"

I felt this odd thrill go through me. I had no such thought in my head whatsoever. "Wow. I mean, I don't know. I'd have to tell my aunt and uncle who I'm going out with. My uncle has told me you have a—" I looked around. There was no one close enough to hear me. "You have a record."

"He didn't lie."

"And that you're dangerous."

"Only to those who want to fuck with me."

I blinked, not expecting to hear that sort of language from him. Obscene language was frowned upon in my aunt's house. The word "hell" was okay, but definitely not that one. "Okay," I finally said. "What did you do? Hold up a convenience store?" It was a joke. Or maybe I was serious.

He sat back and eyed me. "I stole some candy and a bottle of pop once in a convenient store. I wasn't armed. I was fifteen. I just shoved it in my coat pocket and was caught by the owner."

I frowned. "That's it?"

"Yes."

"You wouldn't be fudging the truth, would you? Because I can certainly have someone look it up."

"I know that. Go ahead and ask." Hunched over, he looked away, eyes darting across the dining room.

"Anything else?" I prodded.

His glance swung back on me. He didn't blink much, and it was almost uncomfortable. Like a wolf staring at you, looking into your soul.

He let out a sigh as he looked down at his big hands. "I've been in fights." He looked back up at me. "You don't go around being Indian without some asshole trying to start Wounded Kneed again."

I nodded. "So, you've had to fight? No weapons?"

He lifted his hands, which I noted were somewhat scarred across the knuckles, the edges of the nails blackened from working on engines. "These and my feet are my only weapons."

"What? You mean you've a black belt?" The word karate was implied.

"Something like that. Learned it from an uncle who is second degree. Which, by the way, is pretty high. He learned it in the Marines, he went to Viet Nam. Then in training."

"Army?"

"Marines." Right. He'd said this, and I'd somehow missed hearing it.

"I see." This time I blinked and directed my gaze down to the uneaten pizza before us. "I'd like to go out with you, Nate," I finally said, flipping my hair back to gaze back into his dark eyes. They looked like just-dipped chocolates to me.

"Good." He leaned, picked up the last slice and offered it to me. I shook him off. I was full. Or, rather my stomach was so full of butterflies I couldn't eat another bite. I didn't know how I was going to fly this past Weeks, but if he had some secret document against Nate, I wanted to know about it. I wasn't about to put my reputation at stake just for a date with someone. But if Nate was telling the truth about him being fifteen when this happened—which was ten years ago, and he'd been a minor—then I couldn't see any reason why I shouldn't be able to date him.

Art class went by like a therapeutic massage. Drawing had always been one of those things that relaxed me, and it was now a proven fact that it did relax people when they filled in those line drawings. At least I wasn't thinking about Brett any more. Maybe I *was* going out with Nate on the rebound. Oh, well. Who cared?

I drove home both happy and in suspense about how my being asked out on a date with Nate would go over with both my aunt and uncle. Especially my uncle, the sheriff.

Chapter 13

My aunt's car was in the drive when I got home. My butterflies were back, but for a different reason.

"I need to speak to Uncle John," I said to my aunt the minute I came through the door.

"Oh, honey, you can't. His sore throat isn't any better. If anything, it's worse. I took him to the doctor. Said it wasn't strep, at least. But he's on penicillin."

I slumped, letting the swear word come out as a hiss.

"Why? What's the matter?" she asked.

"I'm sorry he's feeling bad. I need to talk to him, but this can wait."

"Are you sure?"

"Well," I glanced up at her and swiped my hair out of my face. I needed to find my barrette to hold it all back. "You need to know too, of course."

She wrung out the dish cloth in her hands, folded it and draped it over the oven handle. She stepped across the kitchen and sat down. "Sounds important. Sit." Her hand went out to offer the chair opposite her, as though I were an old friend visiting.

Oh, yes. The sit-down-and-tell-me-all-about-it, like when I was younger having teenager social anxieties and angst. Well, things hadn't changed, really.

I sat and began with explaining who Nate Blackstone was, reminding her that he had come out to the park that day we nailed Arline's killers. "He's the one who fixed my battery," I added.

"Oh, yes." She nodded holding a cup of tea in front of her face.

"Well, he asked me out."

"I see. And you want to go out with him."

"Well, it's just a date." I shrugged. "He asked me today."

"That's fine. I'm sure it'll be fine with John."

A funny, wavering smiled crept onto my lips. "He knows who Nate is," I said. "He might not like the idea."

"Oh, really?" She made a thoughtful glance at the clock for some reason. "He's been sleeping on and off all afternoon."

"It's not for tonight," I said. "So..." I trailed off with a one-shouldered shrug.

"I see. When?"

"I don't know. We didn't get that far. It was just a casual asking, like 'do you want to go out sometime?' type of thing."

"I see."

I scrunched my nose. "He drives a Harley." I was easing into all his bad attributes.

She blinked and her mouth crimped into a smile. "You going in for the wild guys now?" She was teasing.

"Yes. Next it will be the intellectual, and after that I'll go for the nature-geek." We both laughed.

"It's always good to experiment," she said through her chuckle.

After our giggles died, I became serious again. "He's also older." I paused to let that sink in.

My aunt smiled wider. "Age doesn't matter so much as how you get along. You know that I'm older than John?"

"I think you told me that once. What did you do? Rob the cradle?" It was my turn to tease.

"Yes. They call me a cougar in certain circles."

We laughed. At that point Poe chose to jump onto the table with a big meow, as if putting in his opinion. We both sputtered at him. I grabbed him and pulled him into my lap to give him attention, getting him to purr as he looked up at me.

"How much older?" I asked.

"About five years," she said, still holding her cup and sipped, then asked. "How about this young man, Nate?"

"Well, it's not quite a decade." I squeezed my eyes at her, trying to ease into this. I hadn't even thought about how much older Nate was than me. Not only could he go into a bar and I couldn't, but by the time I turned 62, he'd be—oh, never mind!

She cocked her head, indicating for me to quit beating around the bush.

"He's twenty-five."

"I see." She was keeping her opinion to herself.

"I know that's eight years. But it's only one date. I just want to get to know him better." I knew it wouldn't matter that much to mention it but I did anyway. "He's Native American."

"Really?" Her facial muscles went from surprised to wondering. "Oh. Now I remember him." After a moment she said. "Lainey, I trust your judgment of people. I don't have a problem with your seeing this Nate fellow."

"Cool. Thanks. Now to ask Weeks," I said.

"I'll bring it up."

I rolled my eyes. "You may want to wait. The news may kill him. They probably need him at the sheriff's office pretty bad by now."

She laughed as she got up and emptied her cup in the sink and washed it out. I set Poe down, and he walked off like a well pampered king and darted to his food bowl. My aunt stepped out of the room and I went searching for cookies and was rewarded with my favorites and poured myself a glass of milk. This would ward off stomach growlies until dinner time. I snarfed down my cookies and drank my milk and rinsed out the glass.

"Who's in charge today at the sheriff's office?" I called out as I stepped into the doorway between the kitchen and dining room and leaned a shoulder into it. My aunt was watering her plants in the bay window of the dining room.

"That would probably be Maureen," she said turning from a huge spider plant with little spidies hanging from their thin green branches.

"I'll bet she's probably up to her ears." I went back and grabbed my backpack near the table. I strode back into the hallway, my mind working on my dilemma with telling Weeks about Nate. "Uh, let's just hold off telling Uncle John about Nate. I don't want him to yell and hurt his throat even more."

"Okay," she chuckled.

"What's for supper tonight?" I stood in the hallway, trying to decide which I wanted to do first. Dump my books in my room, find my barrette, or make the call. I supposed I could do all three, and make the call upstairs.

"I haven't decided. Since John can't join us, I'm thinking something simple. I've got some chicken soup in the freezer. I'll see if he can handle it."

"Poor guy," I said. "Tell him I hope he gets better soon."

"I'll pass it along."

I took the steps up to my room, dumped my heavy bag on my small bed and pulled out my cell phone. I called the sheriff's office, using the one in my contact log. Weeks' personal number was my emergency button, now. After that business with Sinclair, I'd entered his personal number into my ICE (in case of emergency), which I then only had to press one button and it would call his number automatically.

The phone rang three times and a male voice I didn't recognize answered. I asked if Maureen was there, or available. He said she was out at the moment, but he could leave a message. I made sure he wrote down my name and number, and for her to get back to me as soon as she could.

An hour later, while I was working on my homework my cell phone rang. It was Maureen.

"Lainey? I got your message. What's up?"

"Hi, we didn't kill John, honest," I said.

She chuckled. "I expect he's laying in bed soaking up all the attention."

"Yep. I think the masseuse is due any moment to give him a back massage," I joked. She laughed.

"In that case he should be good to go in a day or so," she said. "Was it strep?"

"No, thank goodness! But it's a bad sore throat. We're thinking of feeding him intravenously at this point."

"Oh, I hope it doesn't come to that," she said, chuckling.

"Not quite yet, but we do have that option."

"I suppose he's contagious, then?"

"I'm not going within ten feet of his room," I said.

"Good plan."

"Hey, I was wondering about this one thing I discussed with John about checking with the bank—or banks—that have accounts for Whitney College. Uncle John was going to do that today, but of course, he's sick."

"Oh, gosh. We're really busy, what with so many people out right now."

"What a time to be sick, right?"

"Exactly. Even with the skeleton crew I have now we aren't doing too bad, but if anything unexpected happens, we'll be up the creek without a paddle."

"I hear you. But that's only one thing I wanted to have you check on. There's one other thing."

"What would that be, Lainey?"

"I don't know if you know Nathan Blackstone?"

"I believe I do."

"I've been told he's somewhat dangerous."

"Well. That' depends upon what you deem as dangerous."

"Okay, let's just say I'm thinking of going out with him. Should I have any concerns?"

"Just a second." I could hear her tapping on the computer, probably bringing up anything current on Mr. Blackstone. "Okay I've got him living at the homeless shelter and rides a Harley. He has no wants or warrants—not even speeding tickets—but he may have some priors, but nothing here. In other words, he hasn't done anything here that's had us looking in on him." She paused and said, "You do know he's not originally from this area."

"I figured. Where's he from?" I was curious, of course.

"In northern Minnesota, from Red Lake."

"Oh. Is that a reservation?"

"Yes. I'm sure it is."

"He's going to Whitney, right now. He seems like a nice guy," I said. "But my uncle doesn't like him."

Maureen laughed. "There's not that many men John takes a shine to unless he's wearing a badge, and a few of them he's not crazy about." We both chuckled on that.

"I just wanted to make sure that whatever he's done isn't serious. At least find out if he's someone I need to worry about stopping near banks, or liquor stores."

"Yeah. Hey, I'm sorry to cut you short, but somethings come up."

"Okay, Maureen, thanks for calling me back."

"No problem, I'll let you know about both things tomorrow, or as soon as I can."

"Okay, bye." We hung up at the same time. Maybe she hung up before I got my goodbye in. Didn't matter. From what I gathered, if Nate was so dangerous a guy, Maureen would have known about that. I had a feeling it was Weeks being overly protective of me.

Turning to my studies, I devoted an hour to each subject until dinner time, except for my creative writing—that I wanted to tackle after dinner—save best for last, right? I held off working on my math until last, of course. I was so bad at it, I'd taken a basic math class, even that was hard. I was afraid I'd get so far and just say nuts with this and give up and get an F.

I was tempted to read my new book, but was able to reclaim some self-control and told myself to wait until tonight when I was ready for bed. I was proud of myself on that count. Like waiting until I ate all my dinner before desert. I looked for my barrette, didn't find it, but figured it would show up someday. Things get lost in a house. I couldn't remember where or when I'd taken it out.

At around 5:45 the aroma of what must have been chicken soup cooking derailed my intentions of working on more math problems—oh, well—and I turned off my light and went down-stairs.

My aunt wasn't one to take short cuts often, especially when she had the day off from her shop. When she'd said chicken soup, earlier, I didn't think she'd meant she was going to cook a whole chicken for soup from scratch, but by golly that's exactly what she'd done. The thought of having hot soup for dinner on a muggy September evening wasn't exactly my idea of fun, but my aunt could make the best soup from scratch and it would be hard to pass it up. I had a vision of it in my head as I jaunted down the stairs and breezed into the kitchen.

"How's my uncle?" I asked as I rounded the corner into the kitchen.

"Still alive," my aunt reported with a smirk while stirring the soup. "This is ready, if you're hungry."

"Sure." I didn't have to set the table, as my aunt had already set things up at the kitchen table. The soup bowls were on the counter, ready to receive the hot soup. It looked like home-baked bread on the table along with real butter. My aunt sometimes used real butter, or a non-butter substitute, for those of us who had cholesterol concerns. Since neither of us had those concerns, we would indulge in fatty butter.

My aunt filled three bowls with the soup, and set my steamy bowl on the table. "There you go, Lainey. I'm going to let his cool before I take it up to him." She set another bowl in her place across from me.

"Fine by me. I think I'll let mine cool as well." That's when my cell phone vibrated in my pocket. Lifting my buttock, I reached back, slipped out my phone and opened it to answer it.

"Hi, Lainey, it's Maureen."

"Oh, hi!" I said surprised she was calling back so soon.

"Listen, um, we can't look at the bank accounts of the college," she said and I caught from her tone there was some dark, underlying reason.

"Oh?" I didn't know if it was prudent of me to prod her as to why, so I left it hanging.

"At the moment it's best I didn't say why."

"O-kay," I said. "No problem."

"Lainey, John wouldn't be able to take a call, would he?" she asked.

"Well—" I looked over at my aunt and pulled the phone away from my face. "It's Maureen. She wants to know if John can take a call?"

"I'm not sure. Let me go and see, tell her if so, he'll call her back. Is it important?" she asked.

I drew the phone back to my face. "Maureen, if it's important, he might be able to call you, but my aunt hasn't gone up there yet."

"Oh. Okay."

"She said if it's important, he can call you back."

"Sure. That'd be fine. Tell him it's semi-important."

"Okay. Anything else?"

"Not right now, no."

"Okay. Well, I guess I'll let you go." We said goodbye and I shut my phone and slipped it into my back pocket. "She said it's 'semi-important'."

"With police business, a hangnail is semi-important," she said drolly, and wiped her hands on a dishtowel. "Well, I'll take this up to him now. Maybe he'll make the call and by the time he's done the soup will be cooled."

I watched her set up a tray for Weeks, and take it up to him. Meanwhile curiosity was killing me. What reason would the police not be able to look into any bank accounts they wanted to for an investigation? Something was afoot, and I really couldn't fathom what it might be. This was going to bug me until I learned more. But how would I do that?

Chapter 14

I spent a few hours after dinner reading over all those handouts from my writing class. Then I came down and practiced *Moonlight Sonata* while my aunt sat in her usual chair sewing with a thread and needle. I was amazed she never pricked a finger, and didn't use a thimble. If I even looked at a needle and thread, I'd puncture myself and bleed all over the place. While I played, she suffered through my mistakes, and still said I was doing better. I somehow doubted that.

After a half hour of that my back was suffering and I stretched and then stood. It was going on ten by then.

"I think I'll go to bed, Aunt Jessica," I half-yawned.

"Good idea," she said, glasses perched on her nose allowing her to see the close-up work.

I stopped and eyed what she was doing. She was sewing a button on one of Weeks' shirts, and it nudged a memory from me, but I couldn't bring it up.

"What are you fixing now?" I asked, pausing next to her.

"John's buttons on his sleeves are always falling off, I thought I'd reinforce a few. Saves me from having to sew them later on, or find buttons that match, because he always loses them."

A memory involving a button wanted to bubble up to the surface. It was a half-memory. Sort of like a dream you have that's there, but like smoke, vanishes before you get it clear in your mind.

"I'll probably come up after you," she muttered as I made my way through the living room.

I paused and said, "You aren't sleeping in the same sick bed with Uncle John, are you?" I asked.

"Oh, no. I'm using the guest room," she said.

"That's wise."

"I've wiped everything down with antiseptic in the bathroom, too."

"Good." Since we all three used the same bathroom upstairs, I'd moved all my make-up downstairs in the guest powder room so I wasn't hogging too much time messing with vanity issues in the morning. But at night we all used the upstairs bathroom. Too bad there wasn't a shower too in the first floor lavatory. It saved on my hogging the bath for forty-five minutes to an hour—according to Weeks.

My aunt turned out the light on her table and went to the front door to double check the locks. "Could you check the back door, Lainey?"

"Sure." I went through the kitchen and checked the door's locks, making sure the deadbolt was engaged, then I made sure the door to the garage was locked. Not that our town had that many burglaries, but Uncle John was adamant about our locking up the house at night.

I made my way back to the hallway, and paused. It was one of those things like when you walked into a room, but forgot why you went in there, and then you have to retrace your steps to remember what you came in there for.

My aunt stepped into the hallway and stopped to look at me. "What's wrong, Lainey? You look like you're thinking about something real hard." That was when it hit me.

"Aunt Jessica, has Uncle John ever lost a button on his shirt, like around the middle, about here?" I asked motioning to my belly.

"No. I can't say he ever has." She chuckled. "He's always unbuttoning his shirt sleeves and rolling them up. I'm sure that loosens the thread on the buttons and that's why they eventually fall off."

The memory of seeing Mr. Smith's missing button on his shirt around his middle came to me full-blown just then. I had to focus on how the missing button had looked. The green threads were frayed. Almost as if the button had been yanked off, or torn off somehow.

"Oh, wow." My hand rested on the newel of the staircase, my head bowed, eyes unfocused in thought.

"What is it, Lainey? What's wrong?"

"I don't know if anything's wrong. Maybe something for a change might be right."

"Now you aren't making any sense at all," she said.

"Maybe—" I looked up at her. "I wonder if Maureen would still be at the station?"

"You could call and see."

"I think I will." I raced up to my room to get my phone. I made the call and Maureen answered.

"Hi, Maureen, it's Lainey. Sorry to keep bothering you," I said, my hand grasping a pencil and tapping it mercilessly on my notebook with nervous energy.

"No problem. What's up?"

"I know you said that you're no longer in charge of some of these murders?"

"Right."

"But would it be possible to find out if a button was found at either Mr. or Mrs. Taylor's murder sites?"

"Well, I don't know. Let me think a moment."

"It would be a green button. Or maybe olive green?"

"I'd have to get back to you on that. The forensic people aren't here at the moment."

"Make a note of it, please."

"What have you remembered?"

"I remember that Mr. Smith was missing a button on his olive green shirt the very day of the Taylor's murders. It would be a shirt button from about where his pants come on him." And him being so rotund, I had assumed—then—he could have caught it on anything. But I now wondered where that button had fallen, and when he might have noticed it. *If only buttons could talk.* Surely he couldn't have tried to retrace his steps back to the murder sites, taking a chance he'd be caught there—especially at the Taylor home.

"I see," Maureen's voice interrupted my internal voice. "Okay. Even though we had to turn over evidence, I'm sure that Frank would remember if he'd found such a thing or not."

"Great. Thanks. Good night—oh wait!" I'd nearly forgotten.

"What?"

"Say, did you by any chance get the fingerprints off a pop can from Brianna's accident?"

"Brianna?"

"Bryde, the girl who was killed in the accident on the Interstate."

"Oh-h, her. Um. I don't know, since I didn't handle that one. I'll make a note of it," she said.

"Smith's fingerprints might be on it, as well as hers. And, of course the chloral hydrate."

"Right. I would think this all went to state homicide," she said.

"State homicide?" I said, thinking a moment. "That's good, then."

"Is that all?"

"For now." I was already thinking on other stuff and wanted to get off the phone. We finished our business and said goodnight. Yawning, I drifted over to my bed. I eyed Tristan Harcourt's book "A Killing at Brightwood College" and was glad I'd called Maureen. Even though she couldn't answer my initial question, I was reminded to ask her about something else. That can of soda, which I was certain Smith had put the chloral hydrate into, had gone into evidence. I hoped they were able to get his fingerprints, but it was only if Smith's prints were in a database in any law-enforcement files would it do any good to point to him. What would be called trace evidence. The toxicology had shown up in her system (I didn't know her father had sway over the people who did autopsies, but apparently he did. I thought that I remembered him being a judge, which would make sense.) I went over the facts that linked Smith to the murders: Fact One—I saw Brianna with Smith before the two left the college back on Thursday.

Fact Two—Brianna died from falling asleep at the wheel because of the chloral hydrate she'd consumed.

Fact Three—the missing button on Smith's shirt that day. If one was found similar to the rest of the buttons on his shirt, would put him at one of the murder sites, they had him deadbang—something Weeks like to say when he had a suspect in his sights.

Unless the button was found, there was no physical evidence to link him with the Taylor's murders. Then, of course they would have to prove that was his button, and he was there, would be another problem, but that would be up to the DA to prove.

All circumstantial evidence. But my witnessing him with Brianna right before she left, giving her the can of soda would be good, should it come to trial and I testified.

* * *

The house was silent when I woke. I wondered why as I lie half-awake waiting for the usual sounds of my aunt and Weeks getting up. Then, I remembered Weeks was sick and most likely not getting up at his usual ungodly time of five-thirty a.m. in the morning. I didn't want to get up, yet, but I had to. My brain began to function, unfortunately, and I knew it was Tuesday. My brain went on to remind me what classes I had, as though happy to sneer at me that I had piano class and I knew I was nowhere near good enough to even be in that class. And it also reminded me I had history class tonight. This train of thought went on further to remind me the last time I went to that class Sinclair had attacked me. That was a full week ago. My how time flies.

A telling creak in the steps told me my aunt was up. It was hard to avoid that step, so I always knew when she was up, and this served as my alarm clock, since I slept light.

I threw the blankets off myself and found my clothes in the half-light and slipped them on. Just as I reached the door I heard Weeks coughing and it sounded like he was in the bathroom. I stepped out into the hall, hung a left and went downstairs to the other bathroom where I had a spare toothbrush and other necessities. After about fifteen minutes I was refreshed and ready for my day, whatever it brought me.

Listening to the coffee brew on the counter, and surrounded by its aroma, I opened drawers and cupboards and prepared for my simple breakfast of cereal. I plopped into a chair, poured milk over the crunchy bites and dug in.

Poe had similar thoughts, and his crunching on his kibble made it sound like we were extremely hungry. Either that, or we were walking through dry leaves on an October day.

My aunt entered the room two minutes later. I had no idea where she'd been after making the coffee, but then she may have gone back upstairs to dress. I'd heard the shower running above me while I'd been in the bathroom below, and assumed it was Weeks, but for all I knew it might have been my aunt.

"Good morning," she said brightly.

"Morning," I said. "How's your honey?" I smiled at my wise crack.

"Oh, he's better, no fever, but I've forbidden him to go to work today. Maybe tomorrow. As it is, his throat isn't much better."

"Right, you don't want him infecting those who are left at the station."

"Exactly what I said to him. He seemed to think about it and agreed with me."

"Good to hear his brain functions haven't been compromised."

She chuckled at my joke as she poured herself a cup of coffee. Since it was Tuesday, my aunt didn't open up shop.

"I forget, is this your short day?" my aunt asked.

"It's short in the morning, but I have night class."

"Oh, that's right."

"I'll be home for lunch," I said, finishing up my bowl of cereal by drinking the milk out of the bowl and swiping my mouth with the back of my hand. Without comment, my aunt pulled a napkin out of the holder and handed it to me. I took it and dabbed at my wet mouth and hand.

I took my bowl and spoon to the sink, dutifully rinsed them, and headed back upstairs to grab my stuff. While I was in my room, I could hear Weeks making noises in their bedroom. Coughing and thumping noises. I wasn't sure what he was up to in there. Surely he wasn't doing push-ups—which he did do every day, including fifty crunches. But I doubted he was in any shape to do his floor exercises.

I met my aunt halfway down the stairs as she carried two steamy cups of coffee in each hand.

"Have a good day, Lainey," she said.

"Thanks. Tell Uncle John the world will wait for him."

She barked out her laughter as I reached the bottom of the steps. In a few minutes I left the house feeling positive. Hoping for only good things to happen.

The drive to school was somewhat relaxing, especially since I listened to one of my many CD's, trying to sing along. I didn't even want to think about piano class and the teacher, Mr. Kingsbury, with his white hair, and stern light blue eyes as he watched me make goofs when I played. Well, I tried not to think about it, yet I did.

It takes about fifteen minutes to get to the college from my house, depending on traffic. Most of my drive was on I-80, so I sailed along until I had to turn off and slow down through Cedar Ridge. Although the main road didn't go through the town, the speed was 40 mph, and I thought of Police Chief Okert who patrolled the town's roads all by himself. I passed a gas station and spotted Okert's black and white parked behind the building on a gravel drive, just waiting to go after the first car to go over the speed limit. Wasn't gonna be me!

I drove on about a half a mile to the lights at the corner where I would turn right, onto another road and then a quick left into the college's parking lot, which was large enough to accommodate a small football stadium at capacity. I wasn't sure if it ever became full, but I, along with two thousand other students, chose to park in one of the closer lots near the three story white building. The sun shimmered off all the glass in the parking lot and the building. As I angled into a spot, I could make out the atrium in one large section of the entrance. There was glass above it, letting in more light. I remembered being impressed by its huge dimensions when I first entered it. Ficus trees grew as large and as tall as outdoor trees. The dense growth of Norway pines, ferns and rubber plants evoked the thought of a jungle, and I fully expected to hear the calls of exotic birds and animals, maybe see a monkey or two hanging from the tops of the trees. My imagination could go on, if I let it.

I found my way down hallways, and to my classroom for my psychology class. A lone seat at a table next to the wall suited me and I quietly settled in. This class was so beyond me I wanted to be a wallflower and just listen. Even though I'd read a few chapters, I still wasn't grasping things.

Our teacher, Mr. Ashcroft, stepped in and got right to work telling us to please turn to page fifty-eight. I heard people groan as they opened to that page. I turned and found this was another chapter beyond where I'd read. Not fair!

"Who can tell me a little bit about Rhetoric?" Mr. Ashcroft said.

Someone raised their hand, he called on them and they yammered on about Aristotle's Rhetoric. Obviously, this person had taken Rhetoric at some point in school, and speech, as he was very eloquent in getting the point across. When he was done talking about Aristotle's work on rhetoric, and Mr. Ashcroft praised him, he asked, "What are the three means of persuasion according to Aristotle's Rhetoric?"

The same person was the only one who could volunteer this information and the teacher called on him.

"Ethos, Pathos, and Logos."

"The definitions? Anyone else?" he asked looking around the classroom.

Good grief, I sighed to myself as I flipped through the section, and finally came to the part where it had the three words he'd just uttered, read something quick and I raised my hand, hoping I wouldn't sound lame. I only raised my hand because participation counted toward your grade. I forget how much, but maybe it was something like ten percent.

"Miss Quilholt?"

"Um, ethos has to do with your morals, and, well, I guess ethics?" I said, feeling my whole insides quake. I hated participation in front of an audience.

"Very good. Yes. Anyone else?"

Others must have found the page because other hands went up and he called on someone else. Having had my moment of pathos, I let my heart rate and BP settle down.

"Yes, Mr. Blake?" At first it didn't even register who "Mr. Blake" was until I heard his familiar, slightly nasally voice from the back of the class.

"Yeah, this is your basic brainwashing the audience thing, whether it's in writing, a play, or oral argument. The point is you're trying to persuade your audience to believe your argument. Like protesters in the street, or Oral Robers." The room giggled.

"Ah, very good, Mr. Blake," Mr. Ashcroft said.

I turned around, looked back to see a large man wearing thick-framed glasses, with a shaven face and dark hair cut just below the ears, parted in the middle. It took a moment, but recognition hit me like a cold, wet towel. Ellwood didn't look anything like the person I remembered from last week. *That's Ellwood? He cleans up good!*

"Okay, who can tell me about *pathos*?" Mr. Ashcroft asked.

And on it went for the hour and half of class. Ellwood got in nearly as much time speaking as the teacher, and having sucked all the air out of the room, finally Mr. Ashcroft dismissed a little bit early, telling us we would have a quiz next time we met. Having become better at packing my things away before the end of class, I only needed to slip my book into my backpack—which was less weighty as I didn't need my laptop today. I nearly slipped out unnoticed, but heard someone say my name. I looked back to see Ellwood gaining on me across the room in three strides.

"Everything okay?" he asked.

"Sure," I said. What could be wrong?

"Hey, Ellwood, if you ran like your mouth, you'd be in great shape," someone said as he passed us.

Not one to let an insult go unchallenged, Ellwood boomed, "If I was a bird, I'd know who to shit on, Bellamy!"

Walking on, and without looking back, Bellamy raised a fist and up went the one-finger salute.

"Oh, that's right. That's your IQ, isn't it!" Ellwood shouted over the heads of everyone.

Boys.

"I've got piano, Ellwood," I said, trying to rush off. "I don't have a lot of time."

He wore a black T-shirt with white letters that said, I'M SORRY – DID I ROLL MY EYES OUTLOUD?

Cute.

"I'll walk you half way," he said, and we milled slowly through the crowd. "I hear you and dumbass broke up."

"Old news," I said, not wanting to discuss it.

"Lainey!" someone screeched. I looked through a parting sea of bodies to see Nadine emerge from the crowd like a dolphin jumping out of the ocean in front of me. We hugged.

"I haven't seen you, or talked to you, in like forever," she said. It wasn't "forever", but only a few days ago, I was pretty sure.

"We aren't in high school any more," I said in explanation, watching her tall, lanky boyfriend sidle up to us, beaming a white smile. He could be used as an advertisement for toothpaste, I thought.

Franklin, who was at least as tall as Ellwood, but probably one hundred and fifty pounds lighter said, "Hey, Lainey."

To Franklin I said, "Hi." To Nadine I said, "We've got more classes, homework, and less time."

"Dude," Ellwood said to Franklin, and did one of those complicated handshakes with Franklin. "What's the buzz?"

"Not much. How about you?" And off they went into their own conversation.

"I'm sorry I haven't called, either," Nadine said, glowing. "Are you going out with anyone new?" She glanced at Ellwood.

"I might be," I said cautiously. I didn't feel like telling her who, at the moment. I didn't think it would go much further than one or two dates, but there were ears around. Mainly her's and Ellwood's.

"Anyone we know?" she said, leaning close.

"You might. But I'd rather not talk about it right now. I'll call you." I looked at my phone clock. "I really need to get going. Maybe we'll get together sometime?" I was already backing away.

"Sure. Later," she said.

I turned away, and began a quick walk that turned into a jog. Now that the crowd in the hallway had diminished, it was easier to make a quick get-away.

"Lainey. Wait up." Ellwood ran to catch up, like a large dog, wanting to drool over me. What was up with him? Hair cut and shaved, like he cared what people thought of him.

"What are you doing tonight?" He asked out of the blue, and I stumbled on my own two feet. Why was I surprised?

"Got history class."

"What about tomorrow night?"

"I've got a date." I said it, but wasn't sure at this point when I'd be going out. I just wanted to have the excuse to give him. Now I understood why he'd cleaned himself up. I hope he hadn't done this just for me, but for his own self betterment. His personality needed to be worked on, and I feared that was a lost cause.

"Ah." He nodded, his hair bobbed, and he had to tame it behind his ears with both hands.

We came to the end of the hall where I had to turn and go upstairs. I had no idea where he needed to go.

"Well, we'll be seeing you," he said, turned and walked off in a bouncy stride.

"Sure." I waved, and climbed the stairs. It was five minutes until the hour by the time I reached the music wing. I lingered in the hallway, listening to someone play a soothing melody on the piano. It was well performed, no mistakes, and beautifully executed. I fully expected to see one of the students in the advanced piano course when I peeked into the room which held the baby grand and other instruments.

I peered in, hoping not to be noticed, and found a tall man with black hair blunt cut to his shoulders bent over the keyboard, his long fingers dancing along the black and white keys as though he owned them. The music came, not from the piano, but from his soul. Even as I had questioned who this could be, the answer was now shocking me and I had to step inside the large room to make sure.

It was Nate Blackstone. He wore the usual faded denims, but had on a green and silver striped, button down shirt. How was it possible he not only could play the Native American flue with such majesty, but also the piano with such mastery, as though he were a reincarnation of Mozart himself?

I crept up to within a few feet behind him, still awestruck by the fact he was playing the piano. Was there some reason I kept bumping into him? Was it fate? Or was his being where I would be planned by him, for whatever reason. I remembered he had been playing his flute in this very room, last week, same day. I wished to know the reason for our paths continuing to cross like this. But I wasn't about to slap fate in the face.

A few minutes later, the song ended. He sat up and smoothly let his hands drop to his thighs. Not wanting to startle him, I clapped softly.

He turned, his black eyes seemed to stab me, then they softened.

"Oh. Hi," he said.

"Where did you learn to play like that?" I had chills going up my back and down my arms as I stepped over to him.

"My mother."

"Really?" I was still astounded. "You sounded magnificent!"

"I'm not so sure about that," he said, rising and stepping away from the piano.

I looked at the piano. There was no sheet music anywhere. "How did you play that without music in front of you? You must know that piece really well."

"I don't read music," he said. "I heard this once in a movie. *The Cider House Rules.*"

"What do you mean you heard it in a movie? Once!" I was aghast. "How do you do that?"

He shrugged, a small smile bent one side of his mouth. "I don't know. I can listen to a piece of music and repeat it exactly. Sort of a parlor trick."

My mouth stretched in absolute disbelief. "I can't even play when I have music in front of me."

He chuckled lightly. "I think it has to do more with the fact you're trying too hard. If you know how it goes, just play it."

It was my turn to chuckle. "As if!" He got up from the piano bench.

The sound of conversation filtered from the hallway, making me look. Students were heading to the piano class down the hall.

"Oh, my class is about to start. I need to go." I moved, but he caught the sleeve of my arm and I was pulled back. Startled, I looked up into those dark eyes that looked like black mirrors.

"I'm waiting for your answer," he said.

It took me about five seconds before it dawned on me what he meant.

"Oh. It's yes. What night?"

"How about Wednesday night?"

"Perfect! I can do that." Half of me was aware that the hallway had emptied, my eyes darted to the large wall clock that showed it was a minute past the hour. The other half of me—the *pathos*—realized my heart rate had gone up, and my underarms felt damp.

"Can I call you tonight?"

"I'd love it," I said, moving toward the door. "Oh. Did I give you my number?"

"Yes. I've got it," he said.

"Okay." I raised my hand in a wave. "See you."

His hand went up, palm out. I jogged out of the room, down the hall, slid to my cubicle where my own electric piano was and sat down, panting. I guess I should take up jogging again. Quickly, I pulled out my sheet music, then I stopped and remembered what Nate had said about knowing how the music goes and just playing it. That maybe seeing those notes on a sheet, and all the funny squiggles and lines made me feel inferior to the piece. I knew how it went in my head. Why couldn't I just play it?

Mr. Kingsbury was already going to the first person in line to play their piece. We could hear what was said and the music, once we put the headphones on. I quickly grabbed mine and listened to the teacher. I noticed he wore no coat today, but a blue pin-stripe button down shirt and no tie and black slacks with a black belt. We could see each other, as our cubicles were arranged in a circle, and he sat in the middle. All of us sat in front of a set of keys, which was somehow hooked up to the sound system.

David Combs was playing his piece. Chopin's *Nocturne*, which was the easiest piece I'd ever heard played, and wish I had chosen it instead. Combs still managed to hit a wrong key midway, but finished nicely. Mr. Kingsbury made comments, telling Combs he'd done much better this time around, but said he could go a little slower. "It's a nocturne, we don't rush through a nocturne."

Anne Locke was next and she played something by Brahms. Another slow work. I'd closed my eyes and brought up the image of Nate at the piano. I thought about going out with him on Wednesday night, wondering if I'd have to get on the back of his motorcycle. I wasn't real crazy about that loud thing. I didn't even have a helmet. He probably didn't either.

Wait. He had looked different to me. Why?

My name was being called, coming directly into my ears. I opened my eyes and realized it was my turn to play.

For the second time in less than an hour my armpits were warm and damp, but for a different reason.

"Sorry," I said.

"I believe you have the *Moonlight Sonata* by Beethoven?" Mr. Kingsbury prompted.

"Yes." I placed my hands on the keys.

He said, "Where's your sheet music?"

"Ah, I don't need it." Immediately I heard little gasps of wonder go through our class of nine people.

Heart pounding, I wondered if I could pull this off. I took a few deep breaths and let them out slowly through my mouth. Relaxation techniques I'd learned from my therapist, back when I needed to go to her after my parents had died. Instead of visualization, I had to hear the music in my head before I played it. It wasn't hard, really, as I knew the piece by heart, at least in my head. With my hands to the keyboard, I began. I didn't look anywhere but at the keyboard, and tried to pretend I was alone, in my aunt's house, playing her small piano.

Moments later, I played the last notes and was done. There was silence and I had to wonder if my headset was turned off. Then Mr. Kingsbury said, "Wonderfully performed, Lainey. Very well done!"

I blinked with surprise as everyone in the class began lightly clapping.

Wow.

The class lasted a total of an hour and a half, we each got ten minutes to perform, but usually the pieces didn't last all of ten minutes, and some lasted a little longer. It gave Mr. Kingsbury time at the end of each of our performance a moment to comment. If any of us needed special help, we could speak to him after class, or make an appointment.

Happily, at eleven-thirty, I picked up my bag and let myself out of the enclosed cubicle.

"Good job, Lainey," David Combs said to me as I passed him. I then heard a barrage of the same complements as I eased toward the door. I made similar kind comments to each person in turn.

Mr. Kingsbury stopped me and asked to see me before I left. I waited until all the students were gone, and he came up to me and said, "I'm working with a small group, trying to get a quartet together, I have one piano solo, and I was wondering if you'd be interested."

Shocked, I nearly pinched myself. I quickly got over his high praise, could see myself going through the stress of trying to perform something difficult in front of an audience. My excitement was deflated quickly. "I'm really not ready for that, Mr. Kingsbury, but thank you."

"Well, if you change your mind, let me know."

I thanked him again and left the room. My footsteps light as I went down the stairs, eager to get home, riding the high from both, my performance in my piano class, and knowing I'd have a date with Nate this week. I was so happy I nearly didn't hear someone say hello to me. But when they said, "Lainey, where are you off to in such a hurry?" I turned to find Mr. Bean carrying something in his arms. It was in an oblong box, possibly four feet long that might have been five or six inches wide, and a few inches thick.

"Huh? Oh, Mr. Bean. Uh, Jimmy. Sorry." I chuckled. "I just nailed playing *Moonlight Sonata* in my piano class just now. I'm wowed." As well as a few other things going right for a change. I eyed the box a couple of times. I could just make out the writing on it, but it didn't click at the moment.

"You hard at work, like always?" I asked him.

"Of course. Gonna get this blind put into Mr. Smith's office, then, I'm going to lunch. Think I'll go get me a burger at the place in town. I hear it's pretty good. Never been there before."

"I recommend it," I said. "They make the burgers and fries fresh, not sitting in heating trays."

"That's what I want. Thanks," he said with a nod.

"No problem. Well, have a good day, Jimmy." We parted, and I was halfway to the doors when the hammer came down on my head—figuratively speaking—and I twirled around just in time to see Mr. Bean get on the elevator with that new blind.

I ran across the atrium, darting around two comfort dogs and a small crowd of people who looked at me like maybe I'd lost my marbles. Up the stairs, my legs pumping almost as fast as my heart. Good thing it was only one flight, but darned if I wasn't winded by the time I got to the second floor, in the lobby before the office. I'd actually beat the elevator by a few seconds so I was able to head him off. I was panting again. Yeah. I need to get back to jogging. I was so out of shape, if I needed to run away from a killer, I'd be dead before he killed me.

Mr. Bean stepped out of the elevator, and I pushed him back a few steps. "Wait. What color is that blind?"

"What?" He looked down at the box, confusion riddling his brow. "Beige. Why?"

"You said this was going into Mr. Smith's office?"

"That's right?"

"What happened to his other blind?"

"Oh, the cord snapped off. Had to replace the whole darned thing." He chuckled.

"Where is the old one?" I asked carefully.

"I haven't taken it down, yet. Why?"

"When you do, don't throw it away." I looked over my shoulder, into the office where the various secretaries worked. I saw Helen. She saw me and waved. I waved back.

"What on earth are you saying, Lainey? Why such an interest in an old blind?"

"Hide it. Just put it in a very safe place and don't let anyone know about it. Okay?"

"But why?" He still smiled, seeming to think I had gone off my rocker.

"Because, it may have been the murder weapon. I mean the cord, that is," I said.

The color drained out of his face. "You're joking me!" At least he didn't shout, but anyone might have heard him.

"No. Just do this one last thing for me, Mr. Bean. I beg you." I grasped his upper arm and looked pleadingly into his baby blues. "Don't worry, I'll call the police and someone will be coming to see you about it. Just don't give it up unless it's Officer Okert, or one of the sheriff's police. Ask to see their identification, if you aren't sure." I looked back into the office and saw Mr. Smith's door open and the large man himself filled it. He looked right at us and my blood went cold.

"I've said all I can, just do as I've asked. Please? Gotta go!" I jumped into the elevator, hit the button that closed the doors and then pressed the 1 button. Down I went, finding my hands shaking like I'd just done something horrendous.

Chapter 15

I surged through the back door of the house, dumping my backpack on a chair in the hallway, next to the land-line phone—which we barely used these days.

"Aunt Jessica?" I called out. Her car was here, but I didn't know where she was. She could have been visiting a neighbor, or taking a walk. When I didn't hear her call back, my gaze went up the stairs. I had to tell Weeks about what I'd just learned. Who else could I tell, if not him?

I grabbed my backpack, charged upstairs, and tossed it onto my bed. I paused in the hallway listening for any sound from the bedroom two doors down. After a moment, I heard Weeks cough.

Gathering my nerve, I went up to the door and knocked quietly, just in case he was asleep.

"Who is it?" came his raspier than usual voice.

"It's me. Lainey," I said. "I don't want to bother you if you don't feel up to it."

"No, come on in," he invited.

I turned the knob gently like it might click too loudly, and stepped inside. The light was low because the shades were drawn, and he didn't have a light on. He reached over and turned on a small bed lamp beside him. The red shade cast an eerie maroon glow on things. The room smelled like vapor rub ointment.

"Hi, Lainey, what's up?" He had on white pajamas with dark red vertical pinstripes, but the lamp's glowing shade made them look pink. Although I'd seen Weeks in his pj's and his robe before, to see him confined to bed in this weakened state was something new. I remembered my father, from time to time, having a head cold, and my mother, too. But seeing a strong, robust man like Sheriff John Weeks sick in bed was somewhat discomforting.

Uncomfortable about seeing dark chest hairs peeking from the V of his pj top, my gaze went up to his head and face. There were dark circles under his eyes, and his hair was matted on one side and stuck out on the other and it nearly made me chuckle, but I covered my mouth and turned it into a cough.

"I hope you aren't getting sick, Lainey. Maybe you shouldn't be here," he said.

"No. I'm good. Really." I pushed on, because if I didn't say something right now, he'd be shooing me out. "I think I've found where the blind cord came from. I mean what office the cord came from that was used on Mr. Taylor. It came from Mr. Smith's office."

His lips parted and then closed as did his eyes for a span of five seconds. I didn't know if he was struggling with his sore throat or trying to put thoughts into words, so I waited. In a low rasp he said, "If I had the power to make Smith disappear, I would. But I can't. And I can't ask you to stay home from school—" He coughed. "—and I can't share with you anything I know—" more coughing, and he grabbed the tall glass of ice water with a straw next to him on the bed stand. He sucked about an inch of water down.

"It comes from high up," he said. "I'm no longer in the loop, in fact. So, just please promise me—" *cough* "—you'll stay—" *cough, cough* "—away from Smith—" He went into another coughing jag and because of it, I knew our conversation was over.

"Okay, Uncle John. I promise to keep away from Mr. Smith," I said, my hand was turning the door knob behind me.

Weeks had grabbed up a wad of tissues and held them to his mouth with one hand, the other waving wildly at me while he kept coughing.

Quickly, I backed out into the hallway and closed the door to leave him alone. I felt terrible about having been the one to cause this bought of coughing. I was all the way downstairs when I realized I hadn't brought up my going out with Nate. In his condition, I didn't want to press my luck. He might cough up a lung. I decided that since I was eighteen, I should be able to go out with whomever I wanted without anyone's permission. I mean, it was just one date. Right?

I went directly into the downstairs bathroom and washed my hands thoroughly, brushed my teeth, gargled with perox-ide (I know, but it's a staple here), and looked at my reflection. I opened the drawer to brush my hair and there was my barrette. *Why hadn't I seen it in here before?* I wondered as I plucked it out and fixed it into my hair at the back. I went downstairs.

"How's John?" my aunt asked from the kitchen.

"Oh, there you are."

"I was over at the Davis's," she said. "They had over abun-dance of cucumbers and tomatoes and gave me some."

I peered at the wicker basket of vegetables. There were also beans and a few yellow squash as well. "Cool. Last I saw, he was having a rough time. Maybe I shouldn't have bothered him."

"Oh, he'll be alright. He's got everything he needs. I'll check in on him later." She didn't seem concerned, and so I felt relieved about that. However, I didn't like the answer I'd gotten from Weeks. I wanted to tell someone about the blind that wouldn't shrug me off. I thought of calling Maureen, but they were short-handed. I'd only get the run around with her—or whoever an-swered. That's when I thought of Police Chief Okerts. I grabbed my phone and looked through my contacts as I walked through the house.

"What do you want for lunch?" my aunt asked.

"Just a sandwich," I answered as I put my call through and hoped Okert wasn't in the middle of writing a traffic ticket.

"Okert," the man's voice came like a rush in my ears.

"Hi, Chief Okert," I greeted. "It's Lainey."

"Lainey! How's it going?" he said in his usual easy way.

"Oh, fine. My uncle's sick, however. Got a sore throat, so he'll probably be out for another day or two."

"Sorry to hear that. What can I do for you?"

"I'm sorry to bother you about this, but I was coming from a class today and bumped into Mr. Bean." Okert made the usual sounds as I went on with my narrative telling him about the blinds being replaced in Smith's office, and why, and that I'd asked Jimmy to put the one he replaced somewhere safe.

"I see," Okert said.

"I was told that this is out of the sheriff's police's hands. I'm guessing it might be in the hands of the state?"

"It might be," he said. I could hear him move his sucker around in his mouth, the hard candy clicking against his teeth, and visualized him enjoying the usual butterscotch flavored *Dumdum*.

"I'd really feel better if someone had that blind with the cut cord in their possession before the suspect figures out that he may want it to disappear."

"Yep. That's exactly what I was thinking," he said. "I can go and get that. I think I've got Jimmy's number here. I'll give him a call and maybe during my lunch break I'll run over there."

"I'd really appreciate that, thanks."

"Oh, no problem, Lainey. This will help in the investigation, whoever it is looking into it. I'll just hold on to it until I find out whoever wants it."

"Good." We hung up and I felt better, but I worried about Mr. Bean, knowing that other people who came close to the truth had been murdered.

"How was school? Did you get through piano class?" my aunt asked.

"Oh, yes. I nailed it," I said, smiling from ear to ear as I sat down to the kitchen table. My aunt had all the fixings out on the table.

"Good for you."

"I'm going out Wednesday night," I said.

"Okay." She smiled. "With your young—er, *older*—man?"

"Nate." I snickered as I slathered the mayo on my whole wheat bread. "I never got the chance to tell Uncle John. He began coughing and I really didn't want to push it."

She chuckled. "Probably better to let it slide. If it comes up I'll just say you had a date."

"He'll want to know who with."

"I'll tell him. If he gets mad, there's nothing he can do."

"Oh, yes he can. He can put an APB out on us."

She laughed again. We joked about it through the first part of lunch. Then I told her what happened in piano class and how Mr. Kingsbury asked if I'd be interested in joining a musical group. She was quite proud of me.

My afternoon consisted of reading in my history book, so I'd be up-to-snuff on that. Not that I'd retain anything. I hated dates and numbers. It wasn't like I'd need to know who the 15th president was for getting a job. And as for crunching numbers in a job a calculator was used, or a cash register.

Those six hours went by like a flash, and I was having dinner with my aunt, one moment, and going out the door with my backpack the next. My drive to school was uneventful, but I couldn't help my concern over Mr. Bean, and his hiding the old blind somewhere, and maybe our killer finding out about it.

Pulling into the parking lot, the large white building of Whitney dominating my visual field, when my cell phone rang. I was already picking up my phone to answer it. "Hello, Lainey?" I knew Okert's voice right away.

"Yes." Driving with one hand, my eyes darting from it to where I was going, like most other of my ilk. I usually didn't touch my cell phone until I was parked, but this sounded important.

"I got in touch with our friend, Jim Bean. He gave me the blinds. I then contacted the sheriff's office, and someone from the state crime lab came and got it. Gave me a receipt for it. So, that's in the right hands for now."

"Oh, good. I worried all day about Mr. Bean being okay."

"He was fine last time I saw him."

"No one knows you and him got together?"

"No. Funny thing, we actually ate lunch together at Burger Boy. I caught him just as he was finishing up his job, taking the old blinds down and putting new one up. So, he just brought it with him."

"Oh, I hope no one saw." I almost said Smith, but I held back.

"Naw. We parked in the back, next to one another and I put it in my trunk. He was careful not to put his prints on it, too. Very good man, Mr. Bean. We talked about going fishing one of these days."

"Good for you!" I said, pulling into a slot, after driving through two rows of cars one-handed. My foot on the break, I said, "Just a second, I have to do something here." I set the phone down, put my car into park and turned off the ignition. "Okay, I'm back. Listen I've got class now. But I thank you for telling me how things went."

"Sure, no problem. Well, you have a good night, now," he said.

"You too," I said brightly. I gathered all my things, beeped my car lock, and strode through the parking lot. The one good thing about night classes was the offices were closed. I wasn't thinking about running into anyone I really wanted to see, as my mind was busy thinking about everything else.

My phone made that silly sound when someone was text messaging and I pulled it out of my back pocket to look.

"DU U HV NIGHT CLASS?"

I saw that it was from Nate, and my heart fluttered. It took me a moment to figure out what his text meant. Oh. He was asking if I had night class.

"Y." I messaged back.

"WHERE R U??"

"@ WHITNY."

"WHERE?"

"WEST WING." I wrote.

"IM COMING 2 U," he wrote.

I wasn't sure but I think he said he was coming toward me. I looked up, and through the many people who cluttered the main lobby, saw someone heading my way—the only person who was, in fact. His black hair, tall lean frame made me smile as we came together.

"Hi," I said.

"Hi. I forgot what day it was, and that we both had night classes," he said.

"Well, it worked out, I guess," I said. He offered me his arm and I looped my hand through it.

"How did piano class go?"

"I did what you said, and nailed it."

"Good for you!"

"What class do you have?" I noticed he had his faded jeans and a blue T-shirt with a faded picture of an eagle flying over mountains. Then I noticed he'd cut his long hair. I didn't know if I should say something, since I'd seen him earlier with the hair cut and said nothing about it.

"My automotive class."

"You get out at nine, like me?"

"Yes. I'll meet you right here," he said as we stopped. "My class is in a different building." He pointed. "Across the lot."

"Oh. Right."

We said our goodbyes, waved and I had to pull my mind out of thoughts about Nate, and our future date. We had a lot to talk about.

I headed around the corner, and down a hallway, with just minutes before my class. Odd how night classes tended to be less populated, and it made it easier to get to my class. Problem was, I'd forgotten which room history was in. Having only been there once, and afterwards being frightened by a clown in the parking lot tended to erase any memories of what room I'd been in.

I paused near a classroom, and slipped off my backpack to get out my class schedule, hoping it was still in there somewhere. I envisioned it in a crumpled ball at the bottom. But it wasn't there. I had a lot of pockets and zippers to go through. I didn't even recognize anyone in this hallway, so people going into any of the rooms was of no help.

I was bent over rifling through my backpack, looking for my schedule when I saw someone's shoes step into my periphery. They were black wingtips, and the cuff of his gray slacks had me momentarily caught by the motion as I noticed a slight bulge near his ankle when his right foot swung forward and stopped abruptly. I looked up and saw a tall man about to close the door to his classroom.

"Hello," he said in a medium deep voice as I straightened. "Can I help you?"

"Not sure. I'm looking for my history class." I looked into his striking steel blue eyes. He didn't look familiar, so I knew it wasn't this room.

"History?" There was the barest hint of a smile which deepened the crow's feet at the corners of his eyes. If I had to guess, I'd put him at around forty, athletic-trim, as though he worked out, and square-jawed, six-two, broad shouldered. His gray suit was nicely brought together with a no-nonsense tie and a light blue shirt with a matching pocket square.

He made a little chuckle. "I'm new too," he said.

"I've got my class schedule here, somewhere." I used my knee to hold up my heavy bag to riffle through it again while I balanced on one foot. My books from today's classes were still in it, plus my history book. I teetered on one foot, and had to put it down.

"Who's the teacher?" he asked.

My mouth stretched with my inability to answer that question. "I've only been in it once."

He held up one finger. "One moment. Let me see..." He took out a very small cell phone. It was black, a folding variety. He opened it and pressed a key and spoke into it. There was an answer almost right away.

"Rodgers," came a man's voice from it.

"I've got a student here, she's looking for her history class. Any idea what room?"

"Try one eighteen."

"Thank you." He looked back at me. "One eighteen." He pointed up the hall. "I believe down there."

"Thanks," I said, already moving down the hallway. I slipped through the door of 118, found many empty spots available at eight-foot tables, noting that there were only about a dozen people here, we'd all be able to spread our crap out around us without bothering anyone next to us. The teacher strode in after I'd gotten myself set up.

Three hours of class went by painfully slow, probably because I was anticipating seeing Nate afterwards. Once class ended, I shot out of the room, having grabbed the closest place near the door. I waited near the east doors where he said to wait for him. I figured it would take him a while to join me, because, hey, he was in automotive. Might have to wash up afterwards. Maybe change clothes.

Dark as coal outside the windows with parking lot lights glowing like empty stars. I entertained myself watching large moths flutter around and around a nearby sodium vapor light through the pane of glass where I leaned against the stone steps going up. At one light something much larger was fluttering, and I was pretty sure it was a bat getting easy meals.

"I hope you're not lost again," the voice caught me by surprise, and I knew exactly who it was before I turned.

"Oh. Hi." My heart had bucked in my chest. We both chuckled.

"Sorry. Didn't mean to startle you," he said, smiling. It was one of those closed-mouth sort of smiles. Warm, yet revealing little. I noticed it didn't really reach his eyes this time. They were still the cold steel-blue, and perhaps a little darker in this light. The pupils were more dilated. "Waiting for a ride?" He glanced around. No one was left, just the two of us. It was quiet without all the voices and the sound system with constant music turned off.

"Not exactly," I said, not seeing it was necessary to give him my motive for standing around.

"Then, you're alright?"

I squinted at him suspiciously. "Yeah. I'm fine." Thanks for asking.

"I'm Glenn Bascom." He held out a strong-looking hand.

"Lainey Quilholt." I shook his proffered hand.

"I'm taking over for Mr. Taylor."

My eyes went wide. "Really? I was in his class."

He wore a very sober expression. "I'm sorry about what happened." Of course he would know what had taken place here and why he was taking over the class.

"Well, then, have a good evening, Ms. Quilholt." He turned swiftly on the ball of his foot, with the file folder tucked under his arm and stepped away. I watched him go, my mind dredging up when I'd seen his pant legs earlier, with the almost unnoticeable bulge on the outside of his right ankle. My curiosity had my eyes go there again as he walked away. I couldn't see anything from this angle, but I wondered what would one have there at the ankle which would make a slight bulge. Something that they wouldn't want revealed, yet handy to get to when the need arose. I easily came up with the answer. A small gun. Tucked away and out of sight.

A teacher with a gun. That was new. But maybe there were a few teachers who'd begun carrying an equalizer after everything that had happened.

A little chill went through me. How many teachers had begun bringing weapons into the classroom, I wondered.

Before I could ponder this further, Nate's voice infiltrated the place where my mind had gone.

"Hi. Sorry it took so long," he said, striding up to me, his hair shimmering under the lights above. "C'mon. I'll see you to your car."

He grasped my hand and we strode across the atrium together. "I'll have to remember to park on this side of the building, next time."

"So, you've just got automotive classes?" I asked.

"It's an automotive technology degree. I'll be working on it for several more months. But at least I was able to move in with my cousin, and I no longer have to stay at the homeless shelter any more."

I hadn't even thought about that. "That *is* good, then." I swung the hand that was clasped in his. We walked like that for a while. I hadn't even thought about him having to sleep in a homeless shelter before this. But it was brought up before. I remembered that it was Maureen who'd said where he was staying.

"I'm moving in tonight, so, I've got tons to do." We stepped out into the night. The air was cooler and refreshing.

I remained quiet, as I didn't know if asking questions about where and with whom wasn't too nosy. I mean, where would he have kept anything he owned? Possibly he had things in a storage facility. He didn't volunteer anything, either. I wasn't one for trying to open a person up, so thought better of delving into his personal life. I figured he would tell me what he wanted me to know. Eventually.

I directed him to my car, where we paused and I dug out my keys. "Thank you for walking me out." I hit my remote and the lights on my car all flashed on.

"No problem." He opened the door for me.

"Hope you get moved in," I said, stepping toward the opening of my car.

"I'll have help." He didn't lean toward me, as if to kiss me. I was happy about that, this was awkward enough, and when I thought about it, we hadn't officially gone on a date, yet. I settled behind the wheel.

"Drive careful," he said.

"I could drive you around to where ever you're parked."

"No. That's alright. I've left a few things behind, and I've gotta grab them. I'll probably see you tomorrow. In school."

"I'd like that," I said, turning the key, and he closed the door for me. I watched him step away, and I backed out of my spot. The parking lot was practically deserted. I waved, he put up his big hand, and I drove off.

I didn't see the car that had lingered in the parking lot, closer to the building, but by the time I turned out of the college lot, a set of headlights were in my rearview mirror. I stopped at the light, waiting for it to change, and turned on my signal. The car behind me also had his left turn signal on. I hadn't seen anyone else in the parking lot when I left, but then, I'd been distracted.

The light changed, I took my turn, and stepped on the gas, to get some distance away from the car behind me. I glanced in my rearview, and could see the car was sedan style, some make and model I wasn't sure of at that quick of a glance. The headlights were the fancy LED ones that created lines and angles, instead of full headlights. Once we were away from the intersection with the overheads, no lights around us, all I had was darkness, and a set of headlights in my rearview mirror. I slowed for the speed trap through Cedar Ridge, but punched it once I got beyond the town limits and nearly had my little Honda to sixty-five. Noticing that the car had backed off some, I let off the gas and let my speedometer slow back to fifty-five and set the cruise. It wasn't more than five minutes later, and I was on the Interstate where more cars drove. Safety in numbers, I hoped. I wove in and around vehicles, losing the car which had originally followed me. My heart rate was slowing, seeing that I'd been imagining someone tailing me. Maybe I was overly paranoid, but who could blame me after what happened to Brianna, and two others? I wasn't so sure I was safe from their killer.

No one followed me off I-80, and my paranoia abated. Although I did pick up another car along the main route through town, but I saw the telltale police light rack on top. If the sheriff's police were following me home, that was fine by me. The police car took the same turns I did, and when I pulled into my aunt's drive, the car pulled over and someone got out.

I stepped around the front of my car, watching the figure move in my direction. I knew it was a woman by her movements and build.

"Hi," I called out, unable to see their face, as they were in the shadows. They came closer.

"Hi, Lainey." It was Maureen.

"Wow. Long day for you," I said.

"Pulling a double shift." She stepped into the pool of back porch light.

"Oh, that must suck," I said. "Everything okay?"

"As good as it can be. Just waiting for John to get better." Her hands went to her hips, which was difficult for all the paraphernalia that cops carried there. "I thought that was you driving back from school. Everything okay?"

"Sure." I appreciated everyone's concern, but I wasn't a child that needed everyone looking out for me. "Why?"

"No reason," she said. "Oh, uh, update on what we know about Nate Blackstone."

"Yes?"

"He's moving in with someone. Name's on the tip of my tongue," she said, her head dipping.

"No problem. I saw him tonight, and he told me. I really don't need you to look into this for me anymore."

"No problem. But just so you know, there was some trouble up north, in Minnesota. I thought I'd pass it along. He'd been in a fight. Five guys jumped him. They had knives, bats."

"Wow. He get hurt bad?" I asked, startled.

"Just some scratches and bruises. Not as bad off as the other guys. He sent two to the hospital. One guy just dropped dead about a month later. No one knows if that had anything to do with the fight—he hadn't even gone into the hospital that night. So who knows? That was about five years ago." She paused and I had nothing to say to this. "Let's just say your Mr. Blackstone can handle himself in a fight, fair or not."

"He wasn't charged with anything?"

"Charges were dropped, as there were eye witnesses who saw the other men—who were white, by the way—jump him."

"Wow. Where did you say this happened?"

"Up north, where he's from."

I nodded. "I see. Thanks for that."

"No problem." She half turned and then said, "Oh, by the way, I did tell you that we're off the Taylor case, as well as the Bryde case?"

"You did. Or someone did."

"I can't remember if I'm comin' or going, I'm so dead on my feet."

"I guess the state took it on, huh?" I tried to find out exactly who had these cases.

She made one of those half-grunt, half-chuckles. "Let's just say higher-ups have it under control. You needn't worry about any of it."

We were staring across my aunt's backyard at each other. Words weren't exchanged, but a dozen thoughts were going through my head. "Any reason someone would follow me out of Whitney College parking lot?"

She licked her lips, then made a sucking sound through her teeth. "I'm going to pass on that one for now."

"I'm being watched," I said. "Why?"

"The element that killed those people is still at large."

Element?

"Who's following me? It didn't look like a state-issued car to me."

She held a hand up. "Lainey, you've gotta leave it alone for now. Really."

I was squinting again, thinking about a teacher who may be carrying a concealed weapon on his ankle. I made a stab. "FBI?"

"No comment. I'm going home and get some sleep." She turned away, her hand held up. "I've said too much."

"You didn't say enough, Maureen. But thanks anyway." I couldn't help my smile. Maureen had just done a double shift, and I knew one shift was twelve hours. No wonder she was a bit punchy. I don't know how they managed such a day and still remained level headed. As it was, she'd forgotten what we'd discussed earlier today.

Maureen trudged back to her car. My insides were jumping as I headed for the back door, noting lights were on inside. The stove light the only one on in the kitchen, as I locked the door behind me. I set my backpack down near the stairs, and saw one light on in the living room. Weeks was in a recliner wearing a robe over his pajamas, and an afghan over him. My aunt was curled up on the couch reading. She pulled off her reading glasses.

"How was class?" she said low.

"Fine." I stepped quietly in, thinking I shouldn't wake Weeks up, but his eyes parted enough to level me with a stare. "You're up. Are you better?"

"Sick of being sick," he said, still sounding and looking rough.

"He was tired of being in bed, so we came down here," my aunt said. "So, what's up? Everything okay?"

"I was followed from Whitney tonight."

My aunt looked startled. Weeks kept the usual cop's poker face.

"Why didn't someone tell me that the FBI was involved in the killings at Whitney?"

Chapter 16

My aunt gave a sound of surprise. Weeks didn't say anything, or twitch a muscle. He aggravated me to no end.

"What are you talking about, Lainey?" my aunt said, her hand to her throat having forgotten all about the book.

I gave them the condensed version of my drive home, telling them about the car that followed me, and then how Maureen seemed to pick me up in town and followed me home. I skipped the part where we spoke in the yard, just before I came in. If Weeks wasn't sharing, I wasn't either.

"Oh, my goodness." My aunt looked over at Weeks and said, "Is it true? Is the FBI following Lainey? Why would they do this?"

Weeks motioned with his hand for her to settle down.

"So, why is the FBI involved?" I asked. Maybe if we doubled down the question he might answer.

"I don't know, and I wouldn't tell you if I knew," Weeks finally said.

"Figures," I said with an exasperated huff, hands flopping at my thighs.

"Just do what I told you."

"What's that?"

"Stay away from Smith."

"They're after him, aren't they?"

"No comment."

I blew out a breath, my eyes jerking toward the ceiling trying to calm myself, my hands went to my hips. "Okay. Fine." I wasn't about to let this end here. "I'll tell you what I suspect." I'd put a scenario together in my head as I drove home. "An FBI agent is now teaching at Whitney. I know he's wearing a piece on his ankle." I slid my eyes to my aunt's face and judging by her blank look, she didn't know what a "piece" was. "He's carrying some sort of gun on his ankle," I said. She made the appropriate shocked sound and her eyes went larger, and then daggered a look at her husband.

"He has the looks of one, you know, someone with just normal features, nothing stands out, except his cold eyes. Barely smiles. Tonight—oh, this is good. Wait until I tell you." I had my hands up, palms out. "I was trying to find my history class, and couldn't find my schedule. He was about to close the door on his classroom, and asked if he could help me. I told him I didn't know which room my history class was in. He pulled out something that looked like a cell phone—I'm not sure it was, though—and talked to someone named Rodgers over it. This Rodgers fellow knew exactly where my history class was in one second as though he had my class schedule in front of him." I paused. "What do you think? They're monitoring everything, including my moves. If so, why?"

Weeks sent me a stare. "Lainey, I don't know anything beyond the fact that the FBI are looking into something there at the college. We can't touch any of this anymore, so you might as well just leave it be for now."

"Don't tell me you don't know why they're following me," I said, not willing to accept his blatant denial.

"Don't worry about that. Just stay away from Smith."

"Right. How do I do that when I'm going to class with all these people near me?"

"The FBI being near you should be of no concern," he said.

"And Smith?" I realized my voice had gone up about half an octave.

"If Smith gives you any problems, or if he tries to get you alone, like take you to his office, hit your emergency button on your cell phone and run." My aunt exchanged grim expressions with me.

"It's that serious?" she asked him. He answered while I considered everything he'd just said.

The emergency button on my cell phone went directly to his cell phone. "If he asks me to go to his office, I'll tell him to call you. No way he can make me go," I said, pulling out my phone and checking for the text that had just come in. It was Nate, wanting to know if I'd made it home. I text messaged him back ,"YES". I would call him when I finished up here.

I looked up at Weeks. He hadn't replied to what I'd said just now. I decided to let it drop. "By the way, Maureen needs you to get back to work. Did you know she did a double shift today?"

"All of them are taking turns. She'll have the day off tomorrow." he said. "I plan on going in tomorrow."

"Good to know," I said. "Good night." I slipped out of the living room as they wished me a good night, and swooped to pick up my backpack while the call to Nate's phone went through. He picked up before I reached the top of the stairs. I realized I had forgotten about telling Weeks I was going out with him.

Oh well.

Nate and I did the usual small-talk for a few minutes. He was about to move, and that required two hands. I asked him where he would be moving to.

"In town, here. On the west side."

"You'll have to show me some time."

"Sure. Maybe tomorrow night we could swing by, if there's time."

"No hurry," I said, not sure if seeing his apartment would be such a good idea on a first date.

"True. Well, gotta load the truck."

"Truck?"

"U-Haul. I've got things in storage."

"Oh. Yeah. Okay." We signed off, knowing we'd see each other at some point tomorrow.

I was too distracted to read any chapters for school, and was pretty tired, so decided to get ready for bed. I had an early day tomorrow. But when I crawled into bed, my mind had too much to think on. I glanced over and saw the book on my bed side table and picked it up. I really liked this book, it had an eerie atmosphere, and the characters were so bizarre I didn't know what they'd do next.

At this point in the story, it was similar to what I knew about the principal at Whitney—that he had killed someone to hide the fact that he was embezzling funds. His name was Pernell Garret, and similar to Smith he was large, but had a mustache and had a penchant for bow ties. He murdered a young assistant, Wesley Tuttle, but made it look like he hung himself from a tree. Wesley's distraught fiancé, Misty Dawnberry, is determined to prove he was murdered, and by whom, and at the moment, she is in a store room trying to hide from Pernell Garret. I couldn't wait to get back to the story because she was in the principal's office.

Misty managed to go unnoticed, but now has to confide in the sheriff about what she knows. He hasn't been exactly happy with her snooping around.

Sounded familiar.

I read until I couldn't keep my eyes open, and kept yawning and had to turn out the light. I fell asleep thinking about the book, but comparing it to real life. I dreamt that I was in Mr. Smith's office trying to hide from him. Something was in my hair, and I took it out, but I couldn't remember what it was. It was something that would keep me safe, because Smith had a gun aimed right at me.

Early in the morning I could hear Weeks rousing himself and stumbling into the hall. Minutes later his gargling in the bathroom and taking a shower interrupted my plans to snooze more. I looked at my bedside clock and noted the time was five minutes after five. I rolled over and tried to fall back to sleep. I might have drifted off, but it seemed only a few minutes later I had to hit my alarm, roll out of bed, and get ready for my day. By the time I came down to breakfast (which was scrambled eggs, toast and orange juice), Weeks had gone to work.

"He wanted to get an early start," my aunt said, and with mirth added, "We'll see just how long of a day he does."

"I think with today's medicines he might be able to pull off a ten hour day," I said, getting my plate half-filled with eggs.

Twenty minutes later, I had my backpack loaded into the car and left with plenty of time to get to school. Earlier, I'd gotten a text from Nate asking when I was leaving, and I told him I was about to leave now. So, off I went on a bright, sunny day, noticing the leaves were just beginning to change. Autumn wouldn't be far off. I didn't want to think about winter.

About ten minutes later, I turned off of the Interstate and drove the bumpy state road through Cedar Ridge, following some junky truck that had some interesting bumper stickers. One said "In Rust We Trust". Well, that must have been true, since it was doubtful the tailgate would last another year. And another lovely sentiment: "Real Men Drive Trucks". I was surprised there weren't a pair of "balls" hanging from the back just to drive home that sentiment. Maybe they fell off. I've seen "real" women drive pick-ups as well as eighteen-wheelers. I just hoped this guy wasn't going where I was. He needed an attitude adjustment bad.

Ten minutes later, I pulled into the college parking lot hearing a loud growly noise behind me. Checking my rear view mirror, I saw a man on a Harley following me. How long had he been there, I had to wonder. Of course, once he got closer, I knew it was Nate. He pulled up beside me as I parked and turned his engine off. I powered down my window and said, "Hey, there's a law against following women around."

He laughed and dismounted from his steed, stepped over and opened my door.

"Good morning, sunshine."

I stepped out of my vehicle and looked up at him. He made no move to put his arms around me. Why was I expecting it? I was finding a lot of things different about Nate than with any other guy who wanted to woo me. He wasn't possessive, that's for sure, and he was a gentleman.

I turned and grabbed my backpack from the back seat and slung it over my shoulders.

"Let me carry that for you," he said, holding out his big hand.

"Sure." I handed it over and he carried it by the strap at his side.

"You've got a lot of stuff in here," he said.

"All of it necessary," I returned. He only smiled, and didn't tease me, which is what I'd expected. We walked through the lot toward the large building that was Whitney College. We had a hike to get to it. The parking lot was so full, I wasn't sure where all the kids fit inside, but they managed to disappear into classrooms.

"I didn't realize until now you've cut your hair," I said, hoping he'd forgive my white lie. It was a day late, but I thought I'd better say it before the moment was gone.

"Oh. Yeah. It was that, or get it stuck in the engine. It's what I want to do now, so I had to make a choice."

"Well, it looks cool," I said.

"Thanks." I was hoping he was okay with cutting his hair, since he was Native American, and I knew that some would never cut their hair because of religious reasons.

"What class do you nave right now?" he wondered.

"Creative writing."

He was quiet then. I wasn't sure if he knew that the original teacher was the one who had been found dead last week, but I let it pass. I was itching to bring a new subject into the void. I wanted him to know, maybe in case it would bother him too.

"I'm being followed," I said, my eyes darting around the lot. We were about fifty feet from the building. The sun glimmered on all those panes of glass, and I had to shade my eyes.

"By who?"

I stopped and so did he. Looking up into his bitter-chocolate eyes I said, "Promise not to laugh?"

"Why would I laugh? You're serious, right?"

"Very." He waited. "And you can't tell anyone. I'm telling you this in all confidence."

"I won't say a word to another soul. Your secret is safe. Now, tell me." His brows had grown together.

"The FBI."

The surprised look passed. He said, "Why are the fibbies following you?"

"I couldn't get a straight answer to that." I stepped along, and his long strides brought him at my side again. "What I think is it's something to do with the president of this college." I glance up at him. "You know who that is?"

"Not really."

"His name is Smith." I pressed my lips together as we came to the doors and he opened it for me. "I need to tell some-one—which is you—about everything I know. But not here." My gaze panned through the open space of the atrium and down to the Pit where students milled about. "Tonight would be better."

He nodded. "I agree, but now you have my curiosity up. And—" He had stopped in his tracks. I turned and stepped back to him. "If it's the Feds, then something is seriously wrong."

"It is. Three murders. For all I know, the same person who murdered them may have murdered before and the Feds have caught up with their suspect."

"Any idea who?"

"Already said who," I muttered. We were talking in low tones.

We gazed at one another for a long moment. "The teacher of the creative writing class, which I'm going to now, he is one."

"One what?"

"Fibbie." I said low, using his word. My eyes darted around as several people stalked passed us. Their voices filling the air, and our voices were like falling leaves in the wind.

"You know this how?"

"Can't say here. I'll tell you tonight."

He nodded, showing me he got it.

Without a word, we continued across the atrium, and hung a left down a hall. Nate left me at the door of my first class, but not before Ellwood sauntered up to us.

"Hey, chief. What's up?" He put a bear paw on Nate's shoulder and shook him a little bit, making Nate's black hair shimmer.

"If you don't know, I'm not telling," Nate said and turned to me and said, "See you, later, Lainey." I saw the look on Ellwood's face as he got that Nate was now my suitor. I'll admit my face felt warm under that sort of scrutiny, and I quickly ducked into the classroom ahead of Ellwood.

The tall man who had taken over the class, who called himself Mr. Bascom, was at the white board writing something out. I found a table and knew that Ellwood would sit right next to me. Which he did.

"So, you and the chief?"

"Please, don't call him that. His name is Nate."

"Just joking," he said, seeming to take my rebuke without being put off by it. "So, he's your date tonight?"

I smiled at him as I straightened up from placing my bag down on the floor next to me. Need I say it?

Mr. Bascom turned to the class in an impressive dark gray suit, with a dove gray shirt, dark tie and matching pocket square which looked like spun silver. His gaze went across the room, settled on me, and having spotted me, darted his glance to Ellwood. Having ascertained that I was not under any apparent danger from Ellwood—or so it would seem—he looked down at his notes on the desk before him and launched into how to make your characters believable. He discussed this at great length and depth. I have to say, I was impressed with his understanding of how to write. If he were an FBI agent, he had to have had creative writing, or at least English Lit, in his background of college courses. It may have been why he had been chosen for this assignment, and had been called from wherever he was originally from (Washington DC was the headquarters for the FBI, but certain other divisions were located at Quantico, Virgina—I'd looked this up last night, wanting to get a basic knowledge of my protectors, but agents can be called from any local branch from any state, even my own, Iowa). Which made me wonder, if Mr. Taylor hadn't been murdered, would the FBI now have infiltrated Whitney? Or be aware of Smith's whereabouts? My mind pondered these things, rather than the lesson at hand. Holding my pen in my fingers, hands curled under my chin and elbows on the table, trying to look as though I was absorbing whatever Mr. Bascom was saying. Instead, my brain was working out what Smith could have done that warranted FBI involvement. Of course, I was only speculating that it was Smith who they were after. It could have been any number of other people, but none struck me as needing the fibbies on their ass as much as I felt Smith did. Income tax evasion was a thought, here, but wouldn't that come under the IRS? Offshore bank accounts and such things were the new thoughts racing through my mind in that thread.

There was a short pause in Mr. Bascom's lesson as he moved from his notes to the board. He had just scrawled something on the board, was in the middle of a word, and his head turned toward the door two seconds before a light, almost polite, tap came. Bascom did not rush to open the door, nor did he acknowledge it. He put down his marker on the little shelf, and turned around to face us. His eyes speared me as the door opened and in walked Smith. Or rather his stomach first and then the rest of his body.

"As I've pointed out before, 'Keep your friends close and your enemies closer'," Bascom said, looking straight at me. I was pretty sure he hadn't said any such thing at all, even though I wasn't listening to the lesson.

Smith said to him, "I'm sorry to interrupt, Glenn, but I need to see a student."

"Of course." Without missing a beat, Bascom said to the class, "Who can tell me who said that line? 'Keep your friends close and your enemies closer'. Anyone?"

"Lainey, Quilholt?" Smith had already speared me with his beady eyes. Flicking his fingers in the universal 'come with me' signal. He said unnecessarily, "Come with me, please."

"Anyone?" Bascom repeated the same line about enemies and friends, again catching my gaze. A thrill went through me as I found myself wondering what Bascom was saying—which was so out of context from his lesson—and from what Smith wanted with me. Was he warning me? I could only take it as such.

"Michale Corleone," Ellwood said. "In *The Godfather Part Two.*"

"Correct," Bascom said.

"Collect your books and bag, please, Miss Quilholt," Smith said to me, as I stood.

My face went warm, as did the rest of my body. I did as was told, but felt myself bristle. As I stood with my things, I glanced at Bascom. I might have been imagining it, but Bascom looked more than just worried. Here he was, in the middle of his lesson and the threatening individual, Smith, had just yanked me from class. Why, I had no idea, but his stern face and voice had me unnerved. Bascom had his hand in his pocket. Was he reaching for his small cellphone, or whatever it was which was connected to someone named Rodgers? Or his gun? No. His gun was at his ankle. I had this vision of Bascom going into a one-knee stance, grabbing his little gun and firing it at Smith. From that point there was a gun battle. People screaming dove the ground…

But, of course, my imagination had gone way over board.

As I walked out of the class room, passing Smith who held the door for me, I had my phone in my hand, my thumb over my panic button, ready to send for the troops if necessary.

Out in the hallway, I turned to Smith who let the door shut, voices within being cut down to a murmur.

"What's this all about?" I asked.

"It was brought to my attention that you are not a sophomore, which is required before you can take this course," he said, his own face had turned slightly crimson in a splotchy way.

"A teacher I know sent Mr. Taylor a letter with glowing remarks about my English skills, and it was up to him as to whether or not to take me into his class." I wasn't about to go into the details. Even as I spoke, my hands were shaking, and I wasn't certain if I didn't, by accident, hit the panic button on my phone. I hoped that this was all Smith was aiming to do at this point. Kick me out of a class.

"I'm sorry, but that won't do. You're hereby dismissed from this class, Miss Quilholt."

I frowned at him, thinking what business was it of his, and how did he find out? Then I remembered that short little confrontation with Kennith Evans in class a day ago who had somehow realized I was only a freshman, and seemed affronted. I didn't like tattletales like that. It was none of his business, and if Taylor were still here, we'd all have it out, and I'd be reinstated.

But little did I know that things would become more unraveled as the day progressed. The proverbial ball of twine was unraveling day by day, hour by hour, minute by minute.

I turned away, my nerves jangling.

"Miss Quilholt, I think you and I need to have a little talk," Smith said.

I whirled around, my phone still in my hand. I was ready to both hit my panic button and run back into Bascom's room, and dare the man to physically take me out of there.

"We've said all there is to say," I said. "If you have a problem with that, you can speak to my uncle."

"Uncle?" He made an indignant scoff, and I swear it made his belly jiggle. "What if I call your father?"

"My mother and father are both dead. If you knew so much about me, you'd know that, wouldn't you?" I walked backwards, aiming my words at him. "If you want to call someone, my uncle is the sheriff of this county. You met him last week." The confused and somewhat flustered look on his face said I'd hit my mark and I turned around to walk as if I weren't afraid, the fight or flight in me having been stirred up. I patted myself on the back for not giving into my instincts and marched down the hallway. Not looking back, as I so wanted to, I continued into the atrium, and down into the Pit where I thought I deserved to sulk to some degree. A chocolate candy bar had my name on it in one of the vending machines. I put my money into the slot, made my choice, and got my reward. I sat down and text messaged Nate about what had just happened. I was certain he was in the middle of his class, and would not be able to get back to me for a while. After sending the text, I called my aunt, and told her what happened. She was appalled, of course, wondering why he, Smith, would do such a thing.

"I don't know," I said. "But I think a student, who found out I was only a freshman, went to him and made some sort of complaint."

"Well, that's just ridiculous."

"Could you tell Uncle John what happened, just so he's in the loop? I want him to be aware of it." I eyed all the people in the Pit with me, trying to see if there was anyone who didn't seem to belong, someone older than eighteen to twenty-five, watching me. I didn't notice anyone hiding behind a pillar or large palm, and so, I figured I was safe from spies for the moment.

"Of course. I was going to call him in a little while, anyway," she said. "Other than that, is everything okay?"

"Other than being embarrassed by this, yes. I'm fine." I didn't want to tell her that I nearly hit the panic button. What a mess that would have been. After some small talk about what she was up to, we rang off.

I thought that my time would be best suited by studying, instead of fuming. But not here. It was way too noisy. I gathered up my backpack and off I went to find peace and quiet. The library had too many people at the tables. Plus, all those books was just too tempting to leave alone. I opted to go to the cafeteria, where I was certain a quiet corner in a booth could be found, and was rewarded again. I settled myself in as though I'd be there all day. My books all out and gathered around me like a fortress. I then pulled out my notebooks, rifling through them until I yanked out the one I wanted. I opened the steno notebook to where I'd left off. I wrote down what had just happened, and jotted down that quote that Bascom had said in class: "Keep your friends close and your enemies closer". It didn't matter who it was attributed to, what mattered was Bascom was trying to subtly intimate to me, with his unfaltering gaze and that one sentence, that Smith was my enemy. Duly noted.

When I finished writing everything down, I looked around the cafeteria. It was roomy, and divided by a short brick wall that had fake ivy and other such fake plants spilling over it. At least, they looked like fake plants, for all I knew they might have been real. My gaze ventured past the wall to the next section, which had only one couple sitting at a table. They were both on the plus side. Then I realized that Smith was seated opposite a young lady with blond hair, perky blue eyes and a nice smile, the dimples were extra. Smith was smiling, looking perky himself. It almost appeared as though they were flirting with each other. Their laughter filtered to my section, but I couldn't quite hear what was being discussed. Me, being snoopy, and sneaky, I shoved my books and things back into my bag. I walked directly toward the exit, but once I was out of sight behind the wall, I ducked back in, and sat at a table at the very end where I could over hear some of their conversation. After their mirth came to a trickling end, Smith asked Miss Dimples where she had worked before. Ah, he was interviewing her for a job. Who's job, I wondered. Brianna's or Carol's? I listened for a few minutes. Looked at my watch and realized I had to get to my math class, all the way up on the 3rd floor, so I scooted out of there, hoping that Smith hadn't seen me leave, which he well could have, as he was facing the right direction, and the wall only covered me a portion of the way. But my back to him, and his attention was somewhat kept by Miss Dimples.

Math was, as usual, boring and confusing. I tried to look interested, but there was only so much I could do. After that it was English—my only other favorite class—and finally I had a whole hour of Econ, where I could again catch up on my social media. Nate had text messaged me back, wondering what was going on. Ellwood, of course, asked, "WHAT HAPPENED 2 U?"

There were twelve similar texts from other people, including Ellwood and Nadine. Wow. So much concern. It's great to be loved. I worked to secretly text everyone back. Half the class didn't pay much attention and were on their devices, so I didn't feel so bad.

I hated Econ.

Once that class was over, I drifted back down to the cafeteria, finding five more people asking me where I was through social media, many of which were in my writing class. I quickly sent them a message as I walked and tried not to bump into other people doing the same exact thing. Before I knew it I entered the throng of people in line for lunch.

"Lainey," someone breathily called my name. I turned. It was Nate. I shoved my phone into my back pocket.

"Hi," I said, grabbing a tray, plate and flatware. He did the same, scooting right along with me.

"So, what happened?"

I knew I would get this all day long. "I was taken out of my creative writing class because someone figured out I was a freshman, not a sophomore, which is required."

"But how did you get into that class to begin with?"

"Long story, but I'd gotten another teacher's input, and Mr. Taylor had no problem with me being a freshman."

We both opted for the fried chicken, potatoes and gravy. I went with the corn, because the green beans looked like they'd been cooking for days. We took our respective meals into the cafeteria, and suddenly there was a crowd around a large round table, calling to me. Ham and Ellwood, who stood a head above the others, motioned us over.

We strode in and around other tables of lunch-goers. I was barraged with questions all at once.

"I thought something horrible had happened," Ellwood's voice won out. "I didn't know what to think when he took you out of the class."

"I'm a freshman. Smith suddenly found out through someone in my class."

"Who? I'll kill him," Ellwood smacked a meaty fist into his other meaty palm.

"It doesn't matter."

"What's it to him, anyway?" Ellwood said and I shrugged.

There were mutterings like ,"What a jerk." "Stupid rules!" "Just jealous."—the last was from me.

Nate and I sat down to our meals. Everyone else had already eaten, or were just hanging out. But now they were making noise, yelling and generally being annoying. I secretly wished they would all leave. My gaze went up and found Nate's dark eyes staring back at me. He made a slight motion with his eyes and head to the side. I nodded. We both got up and moved to a booth. Did anyone notice? No. We ate in peace as the group carried on about how they would take care of Mr. Smith and his policies. Some were in the Student Association. I hoped they weren't going to meddle in something that didn't concern them.

Chapter 17

I got an A on my drawing for art, which didn't surprise me, as I'd always been able to draw and get A's in art. My happy mood continued as I drove home, noting with great joy I was not being followed by a strange car. With my window down, I looked up at the sky. Half of it was clear blue and the other half was covered in clouds that looked like spilled cottage cheese. I was home before three and knew if I wanted to be prepared for my psychology class tomorrow, I'd best read the assigned chapter and do the homework, because tonight I would not be home.

It was quiet in the house because both my aunt and uncle were at work. I had the house to myself. My aunt already knew I was going out, and I wondered if she had mentioned this to Weeks, so I called, because the suspense was killing me. We went through our usual hello's and how's-things-going banter, and I asked, "Did you get a chance to tell Uncle John who I was going out with?"

"I told him you were going out with a young man," she said.

"Young?" I laughed.

"Young to me."

"Did he ask who, or what his name was?"

"He did, and boy, you know, I just couldn't remember his name." I heard her snap her fingers in the background.

"Oh, boy, you're slick. How long are we going to be able to keep this from him?" I wondered aloud.

"Not for long, but for tonight, at least, he's clueless."

I thanked her and we eventually hung up.

Earlier, Nate and I had discussed when he would pick me up. He said he'd be by at six. "What should I wear?" I'd asked him.

"Whatever you want. Casual, but nice."

"Okay. I like casual," I'd said when we parted and went in opposite directions at school.

Although I had three hours before my date—which I was nervous about—I tried to do my homework but found I couldn't concentrate. By four o'clock, I found myself looking through my closet for a nice shirt. Not a T-shirt, but something nicer. I chose a short sleeved one that had a flowery print, but not too flowery, and decided on my faded jeans, and sandals. I jumped into the shower and afterwards curled the ends of my hair, found my barrette and clipped my hair back off my face. I didn't want it flopping into my face while I ate—wherever we went to eat, as he never said.

At quarter till six, I nervously paced the floor of the living room, looking out the windows, waiting for Nate. I figured I'd hear the rumble of his motorcycle, but still, I couldn't help myself. I figured I would get out of the house before Weeks came home, because I figured he'd be doing a 12-hour shift, since everyone else had to step up while he was sick.

I looked at my phone for the time, and then at the clock on the fireplace mantle. I thought I heard a car door slam. Five minutes before six, a knock came to the front door. I opened the door to my tall and slim visitor. It was Nate. He wore light brown Chinos and a light blue button shirt with the sleeves rolled up. I noticed his large watch, which was silver and contrasted nicely against his brown skin.

"Wow, you are very punctual," I said with merriment.

"Ready to go?"

"Yes. Just let me lock up," I said, grabbing my purse, and turned to make sure the door had locked behind me. I'd had plenty of time to make sure I had keys to get back in, later on. But the back door would probably be open, and if it wasn't too late, my aunt would be sitting up, waiting for me. Or not.

I turned and we stepped down the walk together, me not even registering that I hadn't heard the sound of a loud Harley Davidson. Looking to the curb, I saw a dark blue fastback Mustang with the classic hood waiting for us like a faithful steed.

"Wow! Is that yours?" I asked.

"Mine and my cousin's. I'm using it tonight," he smiled. "You're not disappointed I didn't bring my iron horse, are you?" I caught the teasing way in which he said it.

"Not at all," I said watching him lean and open up the door for me. The interior was all black upholstery. I settled in and admired it, noting the black stick shifter between the front seats. The seat seemed to fold around me, and I noticed the dash was very simple compared to newer cars. Chrome dials for the radio, and there was no CD player, but it looked like a cassette player above the radio.

He got in beside me.

"What year is this?" I noticed the round chrome dials for the speedometer, and tachometer, and smaller ones for various other gauges.

"It's a 'sixty-eight. We built it from the ground up," he said with pride as he palmed the steering wheel and made a turn down the next street. "It's got a six-point-four liter V-8 engine with a four-speed manual transmission." With the turn, the wheels chirped as he fed gas and let up on the clutch like a race driver. "This is like the one featured in *Bullitt* with Steve McQueen."

"Okay, you lost me at the six-point-four liter engine," I said. "And I've never heard of either the movie or Steve McQueen."

"Your loss," he said with a smirk.

I couldn't help my smile. He seemed more talkative than in our past moments. Maybe because the subject was something he loved—cars. Correction. *Fast* cars.

"Wait until I open it up on the high way."

"Oh, boy," I said.

"I've made dinner reservations for seven. I think we can make."

"Where are we going? It's only six o'clock now!"

Again the crooked smile. "You'll see."

"Surprise must be your middle name."

He chuckled.

The sun was sinking low in the sky, creating long shadows across lawns and streets as we wound through town until we headed out on the Interstate.

"I think I want to tell you something about my cousin," he said after a while of listening to music on the FM dial and not talking.

"Uh-oh. He isn't a girl, is she?"

"No." He chuckled. "He's actually my half-brother."

"Oh?"

"His name is Brian."

"Brian–?" I waited for the last name.

"North. Brian North. My mother and father divorced when I was twelve. My mother's white, my father is Pottawatomie. She remarried a few years back. I lived with my father on the Rez, until I was eighteen, then joined the Marines." He paused and looked over at me. "It's hard being part white. Everyone on the reservation knew I wasn't full-blooded. But it's just as hard being part-Indian in white man's world."

I nodded. "I'm sure."

"I did three years with military, and went to one year of college, dropped out. I was having trouble keeping a place. Money was tight. I found my mother, but since she was remarried and had children with her new husband, I felt like an intruder, so I could only stay with her for a while. I moved out, tried different jobs, but I couldn't get ahead, having to pay rent and all. Anyway, I knew I had to go to school in order to get anywhere, I decided on getting an automotive technology degree, because engines is all I really know. I seemed to have picked up how to fix engines when I was young."

"I see. That's really good. So, you saved your money to go to school?"

He nodded. "I'm using the GI bill for the school, had to pay for books and supplies out of my own pocket. But I also had to save up for rent. That's why I was in a homeless shelter. That's also why I hooked up with my half-brother, as he lives here, and he's going to college too. We decided to go in together on rent."

"That's good, then."

"I have a part time job as a mechanic, but once I get the degree, I'll make a lot more."

"Nice."

There was a pause. "I've told you my story. Now it's your turn."

"Ah. I knew I'd have to participate somewhere along the line." He chuckled. "My parents died in a flood, two years ago, now almost three, actually."

"I'm sorry for your loss." He looked over at me with concern.

"Thank you." Getting past that one story was getting a little bit easier, I decided.

"Where did this happen?"

I told him the whole story about my being on vacation with my parents in the Rocky Mountains, and how we were driving down the Big Thompson River Canyon Road, it began to rain hard. The river flooded and our Jeep was swept away. I somehow became separated from my parents and managed to climb to high ground. I was found the next day by a helicopter/paramedics crew.

"That must have been hard on you," he said.

"It was. Things you wouldn't even think of. For instance, it took me a while to even look at a river or lake, or be by one. I went into therapy after moving in with my aunt. For a long time, I couldn't even look or go near the river, nearby."

"The Mississippi. All that water. I can't blame you."

"Then gradually I could look at it, but not ride in a car beside it. Heaven forbid I should go *across* the bridge."

"But you did, eventually?"

"Not until a year later. And I had to close my eyes." I smiled. "Now I can keep my eyes open but I can't look down. It still scares me. Which is funny, but I can get on a boat, no problem."

"Probably because you associate the car with the water and flood."

I nodded. "That's what my therapist said."

"So, your aunt took you in."

"It worked out. She's really great. Cool, in fact."

"It's good when you can turn to a relative. I lived with an uncle for a while. My father's drinking... it was bad."

"Is that why your mother left?"

"Yes. And I know I was messed up for a while. My uncle taught me many things, and talked me into going into the service. I had to cut my hair then too."

"Ah." I nodded.

"I haven't been back home, except once, when my sister got married." He paused. "I went to the wedding and at the reception there was trouble. I was attacked by five guys. They were at another wedding party, in the same hotel and they were drunk as hell."

"Wow. What happened?" I knew that he'd beat them up, according to what Maureen had told me, but I didn't want him to know I'd checked up on him, and felt somewhat guilty about it.

"They didn't know that I have a black belt and was in military training for combat. Plus, I wasn't going to be their punching bag. I was a little drunk, too, but they were a lot drunk. It didn't take long to convince them I could defend myself." He smiled. "It was over pretty quick once I knocked two of them down, and disarmed the others with my flying feet."

"Didn't someone call the police?"

"They did, but by the time they came, and witnesses from both wedding parties told them I had been attacked, I wasn't the one hauled off to jail, for a change."

While we talked, the miles swept by. Before I knew it we were in a small town and Nate pulled into a parking lot of a Chinese restaurant called *The Lotus*.

He got out and since I knew he wanted to open the door for me like a gentleman—which wasn't always what Brett had done, or other guys I've gone out with—I waited for him to do so and angled out.

"This looks like a nice place. I had no idea this was here."

"I used to work here," he said, walking beside, and slightly behind me.

"Really?" I looked back up at him.

"I started out busing tables, and then worked up to waiting tables."

"I wouldn't have guessed it."

We stepped in through a foyer and a pretty Oriental woman in a black dress with the Mandarin collar smiled, but as she took Nate in, she smiled more broadly when she seemed to recognize him and stepped forward to take his hand in both of hers.

"Oh, Nathan, how nice to have you back, and as a customer!"

"Hi. Nice to be back as a customer." They both chuckled. He turned to me and introduced us. "I'd like you to meet Lainey Quilholt, my date. This is Miko Chan, one of the owners."

I shook her hand as we exchanged pleasantries.

"Mike is here," she said.

"Oh, good. He owes me money," Nate said and again they laughed.

She half turned picking up two menus from the counter, and strolled through the restaurant. A number of people were enjoying their meals. Along the wall were booths, and the open area had tables and chairs. She took us to a closed off area which boasted a huge frosted glass pane depicting a crane in water poising to strike a fish in the water at his feet. I gazed at several orchids growing along the wall.

"I give you the special seating," Miko said.

"I'm grateful," Nate said. As she placed the menus on the table he gave her a slight bow and she did the same to him.

"Enjoy." She walked away in little steps, barely moving her hips.

"She's a sweet lady," I said.

"Yes. But when things aren't done right, watch out. She can be a dragon," Nate said. I chuckled.

"How long did you work here?" I sat down in the chair he pulled out for me. I was enjoying being treated like a lady tonight. The tables were set with white table clothes and black napkins with silver napkin rings. A small lit candle was placed in the center of each table, and the lighting was dimmed to about half, to give the couples the air of intimacy, I supposed.

"About a year and a half. Before I came to Montclair."

"Well, since you worked here, what do you suggest?"

"Mongolian beef is good. Unless you'd like to do the buffet?"

"I love buffets."

"Well, then, we'll do that as soon as we get our drink orders in."

A young Chinese man with large eyes and a small nose made his way to our table. Nate was up out of his seat to greet him.

"Red Brother! What are you doing here, man?" the young man asked. They shook hands and gave each other the manly beating on the backs as they came together. I could see they were close friends.

"I've brought my date, thought I'd see how the place is doing without me," Nate said.

"Well, as you can see, we're barely staying afloat," the man joked. They laughed.

Nate turned to me. "This is Lainey Quilholt, and this is Mike. His real name is too impossible to pronounce, so we just call him Mike," Nate said.

I shook hands with him. "Hello, Mike. I'm happy to make your acquaintance."

Mike leaned forward, close to me and said, "I don't mind saying what's a good looker like you doing shackled to this dumb carp."

Oh-ha-ha. The two guys were big chums, I could tell by the way they went out of their way to insult each other a few times after that.

"Anyway, where are you living, man? You took off six months ago and we haven't heard from you. Thought that maybe they finally caught up with you and threw away the key."

Nate threw me a look. "He's joking. I have to say I learned a lot from this guy to keep me out of trouble."

"Well, I can say you haven't changed much. Except your hair. What happened to the hair, man?"

"Had to cut it. Living the white man way, now."

"Sucks, man."

"I'm going to school, down near Montclair. Taking auto mechanics. Want to earn more than a few bucks an hour, you know."

They went back and forth some more. Talking about people I had no idea who they were and finally Mike asked us for our drink orders. I went with iced tea, and Nate had a soft drink. I wasn't sure if he would drink a beer, but maybe knowing he was driving me back home, he chose to not go that route. Before Mike went to the next table and we got up, he said, "You're meal is on me, tonight, man. Enjoy."

"Thanks," Nate said.

"I owe you." Mike had stopped between our table and the next to say this to us.

"You do," Nate agreed. They chuckled again. I had no idea what Mike owed Nate, but if it got us a free meal, who was to argue with that?

"You want to hit the buffet?" Nate asked, waiting for me to get up.

"Yes. I'm starved," I said getting out of my chair.

We walked out of the intimate dining room and went over to the buffet. It was pretty big. Plus there was what they called a Mongolian stone where you pick out the raw meat and raw veggies and they cooked it for you on a hot, flat stone. It looked interesting, but too many people were lined up for it, so I took my chances with the fare under the silver domes, or in the heating bins.

Once we had our plates filled, we went back to our table and our drinks were waiting for us. I could hardly wait to dig in and we only made noises on how good the food was as we ate.

A few other people who worked there stopped at our table to talk to Nate, and there was more conversation between Nate and the crew than between him and me. Which was alright, as I'd run out of easy—or safe—things to ask him. I tried to imagine him in the black pants, white shirt and black tie and vest that the male servers were wearing. I could see him as a really tall dude among the smaller Chinese people who worked here. It was obvious they genuinely liked Nate, and that was saying something to me. One particular pretty woman—who wasn't Chinese, but worked as a waitress—swung by to say hi. Her name was Kelly, and she seemed to be a bit more than friendly with him and I had to wonder if he'd dated her once, or twice. She barely looked my way when he introduced me. After listening to her working her charms on him, I was happy she had to go back to wait her tables way on the other side of the restaurant.

"Wow. Did you date her once?" I asked.

"You could tell?" He almost winced.

"No. I just figured her eye-batting and touching you was the usual behavior for most of the female servers here." Of course it wasn't, but I tend to get snarky and sarcastic when I was jealous or pissed off.

"I guess you caught me. Yes. I dated her. Once. That was enough. She was so full of herself." He shook his head. "I couldn't stand her after an hour and couldn't wait to take her home and get rid of her. I didn't even kiss her."

"I guess she didn't get the idea you weren't into her, huh?"

He shrugged. "Some women don't know when to give up hounding a guy. She was one of the reasons I had to move so far away and not tell anyone where I'd moved to."

It was probably why he didn't tell her exactly where he'd moved to when she asked, prodding him to call her. He made no such promise.

We both went up to get a second helping, I went for desserts, more than the food, and we spoke about his working and living here.

"I actually lived above the restaurant," he said to me pointing upward.

"Oh, wow. Then, you had no excuse to be late to get to work."

He laughed. "That sort of sucked. But then again, I couldn't afford anywhere else. I was barely able to save up for college and rent. I wound up at the homeless shelter only because I was waiting on the apartment to become available so Brian and I could move in."

Twenty minutes later, we were ready to leave, and said good-night to nearly everyone who worked there before we got out the door (avoiding Kelly).

We were both relaxed and I noticed the night air had cooled down quite a bit. My arms were uncovered and I ran my hands over them as we walked.

Noticing my discomfort, Nate said, "You cold?"

"Just a little."

Since he didn't wear a coat, he put an arm around me as we stepped off the curb. It was the first time he'd actually done so. He was so much taller than myself, my head came to just under his chin. We were halfway through the lot—he had parked the vintage Mustang further away, to keep from getting door dings, he'd told me—and I felt him stiffen and we stopped.

I looked up at him. He was looking toward the car. There were plenty of lights in the lot, but the Mustang just happened to not be parked directly under one. When we got here it had been light, but now it was dark and a pool of light would have been preferred.

"Lainey, go back inside."

"What?"

"Just go. Tell Mike there's trouble in the parking lot. GO!"

His urgency made me start. I didn't argue and moved swiftly away, back toward the restaurant, but looked back to see him moving low through the parking lot, like he wanted to sneak up on someone. Then, for a moment, I didn't see him at all. I moved quickly toward the building but paused at the glass door entrance to look back when I heard some sounds. There was some sort of commotion suddenly near the Mustang. A couple of shadowy figures were moving in a way I associated with fighting. I didn't understand what was happening, but something was going on. I turned toward the doorway and someone exited. It was Mike.

"Hey, where's your date?" Mike smiled.

Worry etched his brow when I blurted, "Somethings going on," I said. "Nate told me to go back in and tell you there's trouble. He parked the Mustang way out there." I pointed. "I—"

The sound of a fight came to our ears. Mike didn't hesitate, but ran like he had jets on his butt, and he was soon at the altercation near the car. I could see both he and Nate's high kicks at someone, or a couple of someones. Then, the people dashed off.

Miko stepped out of the restaurant along with a few other people who worked there.

"What is happening?" Miko asked.

"I think someone was tampering with Nate's car. But I don't know," I said.

Mike strode back. "Everything's okay, now. He's checking out the car," he said to me. Lifting his gaze to Miko he said, "Someone was trying to break into Nate's car. I'm sure in two minutes they would have hotwired it and it would have been gone." Turning back to me he said, "He said he'd pull around and pick you up."

"Is he okay?" I wondered, because there definitely was some sort of confrontation.

"Oh-ha-ha!" He found this funny. "Didn't you know? Nate has a black belt in kung fu. It would take more than two men to tangle with him." I did know this, as a matter of fact.

"What if they'd had a gun?" I countered.

"Even that might not be enough to keep him from taking them on," Mike said.

In a moment, amid the chattering in Chinese behind me, Nate drove up and came to a stop in front of the restaurant, the blue paint job seemed to glow purple in the lights above.

"That is one cool car," Mike said, leaning in as I moved to round it to get in. Nate had reached over and unlocked it and pushed the door open from his side for me.

"It's not mine, but I did work on it with my half-brother," Nate said as I settled into the front seat beside him. "So, every once in a while I get to borrow it."

"It's a good thing you didn't lose it for him."

"No way, man," Nate said, moving his hand to the shift knob in the center of the front seat, revving the engine.

"Well, you take it easy," Mike said, stepping back. "Don't be a stranger!"

Waving, Nate pulled away.

I waited until we were out on the road before asking him what happened.

"Two guys were going to steal the car."

"How did you see that? I sure didn't," I said.

"They were keeping low. But I saw one trying to jimmy the lock."

"And how did you stop them?"

He looked over at me and gave me a smile. "I've got training on how to sneak up on people. And then—"

"You've a black belt in kung fu?"

"That and other things."

"But there were two of them."

"There was a moment when one had a knife. Then, Mike came charging in. That's when they beat it."

"You aren't going to call the police?"

"Naw." He paused a moment. "I don't call police. They'll somehow turn it all around and try to say I did something."

"Cautious."

"As long as I've got the car back and get you back in one piece, that's what's important."

"I can't argue with your priorities." I said as we drove out of town. Earlier, we had agreed to have him drive me back home after dinner, since this was a school night. He didn't argue about that. He was tired from moving his belongings into the apartment. Add to that, his ordeal of protecting the car from thieves. He dropped me off at the front door, like when he'd picked me up, and walked me to the door.

"I had a nice time," I said, pausing at the door. The porch light was on. I had no doubt that by this time Weeks would have learned exactly who I had been out with. I wasn't looking forward to having a discussion about it once I said goodnight and walked inside.

There was that awkward moment where I wasn't sure if he would kiss me goodnight, and I didn't want to assume or look as though I expected it. I smiled up at him. He bent and kissed me on the cheek.

"Goodnight, Lainey. I think we should do something like this again," he said quietly in my ear, giving me chills up my spine in a good way. His hand had come up to touch my face lightly.

"Oh, that's a good sign that you at least kissed me," I said, trying to be flippant, remembering what he'd said about the young lady he worked with, who had to horn in on our date to ask him to call her.

He smiled and then bent and kissed me on the lips. I hadn't expected that.

Taking a step back, he said, "I'll see you tomorrow."

"Yes. See you tomorrow," I said, waving.

He stepped away and walked down the sidewalk to his car. I waited until he got to it. We waved to one another once more.

Once he drove off, I opened the front door, noting it was unlocked. It wasn't very late and so lights were on in the living room, where I found my aunt and Weeks sitting on the couch. I bit my lower lip, wondering what sort of greeting I'd get.

"Lainey, you didn't stay out very late," my aunt said, looking up from the book she was reading.

Weeks turned to look up at me over the rim of his reading glasses.

"It's a school night," I said.

"You go out with Nate Blackstone?" Weeks asked.

"I did. He's very nice," I said, waiting for a tongue lashing in the least.

"He didn't take you on his Hog?" I saw him throw a smirk at my aunt.

"No. He had a nice retro Mustang."

Weeks nodded, and glanced back to his newspaper, as though that was more interesting.

"How was dinner?" my aunt asked.

"Great. We went to a Chinese place where he used to work. He knew everyone who worked there. And he got the whole meal free."

"That's nice," my aunt said.

When no more questions came I eased out of the room, certain my aunt had to have worked hard to keep her husband calm, and not give me grief from going out with someone he deemed unsafe.

If walls could talk.

Thoughts on my date and the things we talked about filled my head as I readied for bed. I couldn't relax for a long while, but then drifted off and slept soundly until morning when my alarm woke me.

I felt more groggy than normal. I figured it was the weird dreams I'd had, or something I ate last night.

My aunt was in the kitchen with a cup of coffee, sitting at the table when I came in. We greeted each other a "good morning", and exchanged a few other pleasantries. I had to know the answer to my most burning question.

"Did you have to work on Uncle John so he didn't give me the fifth degree when I came home?" I had to know.

She smiled, looking pleased with herself. "You'd be amazed what a wife can do to keep a man from saying things he shouldn't."

"Thanks. I thoroughly checked up on Nathan beforehand. I mean, I went to Maureen to see if there was anything I should know about him, and she said he had no wants, warrants, not even a speeding ticket. Everything that happened to him, was at least five years ago, and his biggest mistake was when he was still a teenager."

"I understand. As long as you had a nice time."

"I did." Minus the attempted carjacking, everything went fine, my thoughts came. Better to keep that to myself.

"You want something special this morning?"

"No. Just cereal." Going up on my toes, I pulled out a bowl, grabbed my cereal, and then a spoon while we spoke.

"You have enough money?" she asked.

"Oh, good thought. I don't know." It was good to have another person to remember things for you. I checked . I had about a dollar and some change left in my wallet. She gave me a ten.

I knew that Nate had a full day and I would not be seeing him at lunch since I had a short day. He would probably text me later on.

Between classes, Nate did text me, saying he'd had a nice time last night. I replied saying the same. He wanted to see me this weekend. I messaged back, asking him to call me later on, reminding him I had a night class.

I was too happy to let Ellwood's crass and dark humor in psychology bother me. I was able to answer a question, and that counted toward my grade.

I had a half-hour to kill and so went into the cafeteria and decided I needed a piece of chocolate cake and some milk. I wasn't expecting to bump into Helen but I saw her two people ahead of me in line. I watched her pay and then leave to look for a table. She wasn't with anyone, so when I finished paying I arrowed to her table.

"Hi, mind if I join you?" I asked.

She looked up at me with surprise. "Oh, please do." She motioned for me to be seated.

I arranged my snack on the table, and set my tray aside. A busboy swept in and took both our trays. She had coffee and a sweet roll.

"Food isn't bad here," I said, opening up the conversation.

"Depends on what you have," she said, making a face.

"I take it you've had the worse?"

"Don't go near the chipped beef. I have no idea what the white sauce is, but it tastes like glue and I don't mind saying it will give you the worse gas!" She put her hand on her stomach. She and I both laughed at that.

"Well, I'll definitely keep away from the chipped beef!" We were still chuckling as I picked up my fork and dove into my piece of chocolate cake. The frosting was heavenly.

While we ate there was the usual avoidance of eye contact which caused me to look elsewhere around the cafeteria. Only a smattering of people in here at this hour. I noticed a few familiar faces I knew from various classes, but didn't know their names. I glanced across the room and found a pair of eyes had been on me, and as soon as my gaze caught theirs they glanced away, their coffee cup poised near their mouth. It was Mr. Bascom, the new teacher for my creative writing class. He sat in a booth, and I could see him, but not the person he sat with. Only a large arm in a dress coat. It wasn't until the man got up and went to refill his coffee cup—and it was a ceramic cup, not the usual throwaway ones that everyone else used—that I saw who it was. Smith. Turning, his eyes were lasers and darted to me like I was a target. He noted that I sat with Helen. I wasn't sure what he made of our sitting together. Then I began thinking of how I'd had lunch with Brianna one day and the next thing, she had died in the car crash, which was no accident.

I turned back to my cake, working to act as though being seen by Smith didn't bother me. But it did. Before this morning, I had suspicions to dwell on and was willing to allow the police—or the FBI—to handle things. But now that he'd irked me by pulling me out of my favorite class, I felt I had a score to settle. I *knew* he'd killed Brianna and the Taylors. I'd bet my life on it—figuratively speaking, of course. And he was sitting there having a nice chat with the new teacher, enjoying his coffee and whatever else he was enjoying. I truly hoped that someone was watching him. But then, if Bascom was really an FBI agent, maybe he already *was* watching Smith. I envisioned Bascom somehow getting Smith's fingerprints from that cup he seemed to carry around with him. I thought he was overly protective of having his prints anywhere someone might be able to lift them. He had brought his own cup into the lunchroom, which I thought was on the overly protective side. There were no ceramic cups here—at least none I saw. Helen had one of the paper cups with the heat cozy wrapped around it. Call me crazy, but I was certain he wanted to keep his fingerprints off anything someone could collect. How I hoped this was true.

I further wondered as to why the FBI would be interested in Smith. What could he have done prior to this to come under their scrutiny?

Sucking on the straw in my milk, I watched Smith maneuver his bulk back into the booth, talking amicably with Mr. Bascom. I wondered about specific clues that might link Smith to the murders. Like fingerprints, maybe on that blind that was to be discarded, but now was with the police.

"Who is Mr. Smith sitting with?" Helen asked, seeing my keen interest. "I don't believe I recognize him."

"Oh, that's the substitute teacher for Mr. Taylor's class." I thought it odd she didn't know who he was.

"Oh. Yes. Now I remember him. Such a tall fellow. He seemed quiet. Or maybe the word here is reserved." Her eyes glittered at me with her smile.

"I didn't get a chance to get to know him," I said.

"Oh? Why's that?"

"Smith pulled me from the class because I'm not a sophomore. Only sophomores can take the creative writing class."

She made a *humf* to that. "He doesn't waste much time, I'll give him that."

I looked a question to her. Was it coincidence she and I seemed to be on the same page where Smith was concerned?

"He's already looking for someone for Brianna's position in the Bursars office."

"Brianna? Has he already hired someone for Mrs. Taylor's job?"

She shook her head slightly and sipped her coffee. "Not yet. But I'm not sure he's going to, as far as I know. I haven't seen it in the internal hiring posts. I would think those would be up as were the other positions."

"He can't have an assistant to that position do the things Mrs. Taylor did," I speculated.

"Oh, he can do anything he wants." Helen's lopsided smile radiated scorn. Then she said something under her breath. I had to turn my attention back to her from my covert watching the two men.

"What was that?" I said.

She was shaking her head. "I miss Dr. Fay. He used to have the most fabulous parties at his house during the holidays," Helen said wistfully. "Sometimes he had a few here, just on a whim to pamper us."

"Parties? They were pretty good?"

"Oh, my yes. The Christmas parties were fabulous. Once he held it at his house. Oh, it was a beautiful house, believe me! It looked like a castle! Just huge!"

"So, he was rich?"

"I'd have to say so, since he went to the Cayman Islands every year. We speculated where Edward had gotten all his money, because on his salary, well, it certainly wasn't possible. We thought that maybe it was his wife's money. Something about her being in high-end real estate sales. His house was definitely in the half-a-million range."

"Wow. Then, Mrs. Fay is now a widow?" I said, not knowing how long ago Dr. Fay had left this world.

She batted the air dismissively. "Oh, she died a number of years ago. I mean before he did. I believe it was ovarian cancer."

"So, she had money," I said. "And he inherited it all."

"So, it was rumored, yes." She paused, looking up slightly. "It isn't nice to speak ill of the dead."

"I know, but anything you say I won't repeat," I prompted, noting the look on her face.

"Well," she said, her dark eyes darted around, and she leaned in. "Don't say I said this—"

"Of course not—"

"The rumor was she wanted a divorce." Her tone was gossipy.

"Really?" I sat back. "But then she became sick?"

"She had chemo, and it only made her sick, and they could do nothing, as it was caught too late. Went all over her body."

"Wow. How terrible."

She leaned back. "Yes. I only heard this through someone who heard it through a friend of the family."

"So, he got the house?"

"And her money."

"Wow."

"At least this is what came down through the grape vine."

"So, I wonder who inherited Dr. Fay's wealth?"

"Mostly it went to the children," she said. She leaned slightly toward me again, eyes glancing to Smith over in the booth as though she worried he could hear us all the way across the room. But he wasn't even looking at us. "Now Edward's brother, Donnie Fay, is a lawyer. I spoke with him at the funeral, and he more or less said that his brother's car accident seemed suspicious."

I made a *humf* sound.

"Donnie was Edward's executor of his will." She leaned even closer to me, one hand on the table, her fingers tapping it as she went on. "Some questioned where some of Edward's wealth had come from." She paused and let her head dip as though thinking about saying more. "There was also something about some secret account that had been hacked into and drained." She sat back and shook her head. "No one could figure out how, who, or where that money went."

"Weird." I thought about it. "So, there was some secret account, and no one knows where that money came from. But someone knew about it. Obviously."

She nodded. "I think Donny did some digging."

"And he noticed some or all of it was taken out? Before or after Dr. Fay's—uh—death?"

A crooked smile made deep lines on one side of her face. "Funny you should ask that. I asked the same question of Donny, and he just clammed up."

"Got too close to the truth, I'd say." We mused on this point a while. "I wonder how someone could have gotten into that account."

"Well, you know, in today's world, anybody can steal a person's identity, get account numbers, or pin numbers, the whole enchilada," she said in a scathing way, her hand batting the air. "Once they have your social security number, you're finished."

"Yeah. So I've heard. I can't believe how dishonest people are." She looked around again. "There was also the fact that Dr. Fay's laptop disappeared."

"Really? Well, there you go. A good hacker can crack most passwords," I said.

Smith and Mr. Bascom got up from their booth and we both watched in silence as the two men walked out of the lunch room and parted company, apparently laughing at some joke one or the other had made.

"Interesting how well Mr. Smith dresses, as though he's got money," I said, hoping to get her to open up more about him.

"Yes. A very nice dresser," she said. "I've seen the tags, you know, in his coats? Very expensive."

"You said the salary of the president isn't all that much?"

"Not really. I mean, it's good. Don't get me wrong."

"But he'd have started at bottom salary, not at the top, I'm guessing," I said.

"Oh, yes. It's about eighty grand."

I hadn't known how much a college president's salary was. "Not bad. How does one get such a job?" I was mostly joking.

Helen sat back, her eyes darted from Smith back to me. Then she pulled a breath in through her nostrils and let it out almost noisily and said, "You kill your predecessor and take over."

Chapter 18

My conversation with Helen had my brain going warp speed over things I'd learned about Mr. Smith, and his predecessor, Dr. Edward Fay. Trips to the Cayman Islands? A house that is beyond a small college president's means? And finally an account that seems to have been hacked into and drained, possibly before Fay's death, *and* his personal laptop stolen. All of it was ingredients to a boiling soup of intrigue. As it was, I was so interested in the last president, I'd forgotten to ask her what she knew about Smith. But I figured if Weeks, who is sheriff, didn't know where he came from, she'd know even less. My guess was Smith kept that information very close to the vest, as they say. The very fact that the FBI was looking into him had me more than just nervous.

After piano class, I checked my phone and saw I had a message from Nadine. Since I was done for the day, I listened to her message. It sounded dire. "Hi, Lainey. Call me when you can. I'll be free at eleven-thirty. Call me. It's important."

I couldn't imagine what this was about, but since it was now a little past 11:30, I called her. After the first ring her voice was in my ear.

"Lainey. Oh, thank God!"

"What is it?" I said, finding a chair off in the corner of a hallway. "Sounds dire."

"It is. Hang on." There was a pause, I could hear voices in the background and then muffled sounds and finally she said, "I'm back. Hey, uh—" she made a nervous chuckle and said. "I did the nasty with Frank."

Shocked by this, I couldn't say anything at first. Then I went with, "Don't call it that. Sounds crude."

"Okay, we had sex."

"When?" I was still trying to process that meek little Nadine had had sex with a guy. But Frank seemed docile too. What was it they said about shy people? You just can't judge a book by the cover.

"It was over the weekend. Sunday night. Oh, God, I'm so scared." Her voice went up into a tight squeak.

"Why? You did use protection, didn't you?"

"Uh. I don't know."

"What do you mean you don't know?"

"I mean, I just don't remember. Heat of the moment sort of thing."

"You aren't on the pill and you don't know if he used a condom?" I said wondering where my friend's mind had gone. Well, duh. Heat of the moment sort of thing. We'd talked about this sort of thing during our high school years. A lot. I had been adamant on not having sex before I married. I felt it was easy enough to do, just don't get carried away and don't get into the back seat with a guy. Or a hotel room, as I thought of Brett's request of me. If the guy dumps you, then you know he wasn't serious about you at all, but just wanted sex.

"Yeah. I don't think he used a condom," she said.

"And you could get STD," I pointed out.

"Oh, God! That's why I called you. I'm a mess. How will I tell my parents?"

"First of all, you've only done it once."

"So, you think I won't get pregnant?"

"That's not what I said. You'll want to get one of those pregnancy test kits."

"Oh, yeah. Right. Didn't think of that."

"I'm heading home. Are you still in class?"

"In between. But I've got classes all day. I don't know how I'll keep my mind on anything, and I have a test in geometry."

"Look, worrying about this isn't going to make a difference in what will, or hasn't happened. But what you'll have to do is have a serious talk with your boyfriend. Make sure he understands the seriousness of this situation."

"Right. Listen, I've gotta get to class. I'll talk to you later. Thanks bunches!"

"Okay. Bye."

I hung up and took a deep breath. I wasn't sure how Nadine was going to get through the next few days, but I hope the seriousness of what she'd done got through to her. We'd taken the sex education classes in junior high and high school—which were mandatory—and they told us *everything*, so I couldn't believe Nadine had ignored everything we'd been told. But, then again, if I'd found someone so attractive would I be able to resist? Nate came to mind, but he was older, and possibly more responsible. ... *heat of the moment.* Okay. Definitely had to keep Nate at arm's length. At least he hadn't been aggressive. Yet.

I went home just to drop off my books and swung by *Books n' Such*, hoping I could order a sandwich from the sandwich shop and have it delivered at the store.

Jenny and my aunt were conversing over a book my aunt held.

"Hi," I said and their greetings chimed out.

"How were classes this morning?" Jennifer's gentle blue eyes took me in.

"Fine," I said, spirits up.

"Everything go well on your date?" she asked.

"Oh, yes. Fine." I had no idea she was in the know about my date. I turned to my aunt. "I'm going to order something from the sandwich shop. You guys want anything while I'm on the phone to them?"

"No. You go ahead, Lainey," my aunt said while Jenny merely shook her head and strode away, down a book aisle to replace the book they'd been talking about.

"How are my favorite nieces?" Uncle Ed's voice boomed as he strolled into the store, the ringing of the small bell unable to compete with his theatrically trained voice.

We hailed him back.

"Oh, I like how you call them both 'niece'," Jennifer said breezing toward the front of the store. "Can I be a niece too? I feel so left out." She stepped right up to Uncle Ed, beaming hopefully. Shifting the unlit cigar to his other hand, he happily put an arm around her. "Of course, niece number three."

"Jennifer," she said.

He laughed as he repeated her name.

"My husband and I used to come see your Mark Twain performance at the old theater. We so enjoyed it," Jennifer said.

"Well, thank you, dear lady. How is Dale, anyway?" he said.

"Oh," she said on a long sigh that had her stepping away from him slightly. "Some days are good, others aren't so good."

"That's too bad. I sure miss him down at the fire barn on poker night. He could bluff the pants off of anyone there, including me!"

Jennifer laughed. "I'm sure he misses it too, he just doesn't remember too much now."

They went back and forth about the theater, how it was too bad it had burnt down, and she asked him about how his boat tours were doing. Once that topic was picked to death my uncle exclaimed, "My, but it's a nice day. Sky is clear, autumn is in the air." Hand out, he moved toward our counter. We all agreed with him on the nice day.

"Oh. Nearly forgot." He reached into the inside of his coat pocket and pulled out an envelope. "Lainey, this just came to me in the mail. I thought you'd be interested." He handed me the thick envelope that was already opened, addressed to him. I found the colorful pages inside boasting of a writer's conference, and a winter writer's retreat. My eyes became big and then my excitement dwindled as I found the cost of each event was rather steep. More than I could find in my savings, for sure.

"Oh, thanks, Uncle Ed. But I can't afford any of these things. Nice of you to show this to me, though."

"Nonsense!" He straightened, both hands gripping the lapels of his white jacket, the cigar clutched between two fingers of his right hand. He said, "You choose which one, and I will pay for it. An early Christmas gift to you, Lainey, m'dear."

"What? Really? Wow," I said amidst the gasps of my aunt and Jennifer and his nodding confirmation. A chill of thrill going through me.

My aunt leaned over my shoulder and looked at it. "Uncle Ed, are you sure?" We exchanged looks at the price of the retreat. It was probably more than what my aunt could rake in from the store in two weeks. I certainly didn't have fifteen hundred dollars.

"Very much. I haven't attended any of these things in years. I thought that perhaps it was time I give Lainey here a leg up." He leaned and with a wink added, "I'll just take it out of the little savings I started for you."

"Thank you, Uncle Ed." I reached over to him and gave him a one-arm hug around the neck as he bent to allow it. "I'll let you know, after I've decided which one to go to."

He pointed to the green page with the writer's retreat on it. "That one is good if you want to get away and just write. There'll be one or two seasoned novelists in attendance, and you'll get your own room, or cabin, depending upon where it's held."

"What's the conference about?" I pointed to the blue page. The conference was to be held in Iowa City, on campus of the university there.

"It helps inspire you in your writing, gives you information on where to send your material to. To put it in a nutshell, a bunch of windy people get up and talk." We all chuckled at that. "I think I've quit going because of the politics involved. I couldn't stand a few of the people who attended, and others, well, they just had such big heads, you could barely get in the door because there wasn't any room." Chuckles again.

"Thanks. I'll give it some thought," I said, noticing the conference was during Thanksgiving weekend. I wasn't sure I wanted to go to that one, for a lot of reasons. But the getaway to write sounded more like something I might be able to do, since it was scheduled for after Christmas and New Year, while I was still off on winter break from school.

"How are you doing in the writing class? Learning anything?" he asked me.

"Well, I've been taken out of that class," I said sadly, placing the fliers back into the envelope he'd given me. I slipped it into my purse underneath the counter.

"What do you mean, taken out? How?" He seemed to bristle at that.

I clicked my tongue. "Someone in the class realized I wasn't a sophomore, and he must have ratted me out and went to Mr. Smith. He came into the class on Monday and took me out saying I wasn't supposed to be in the class because only sophomores can take it."

"I never liked him," Uncle Ed bristled, saying this almost to himself. "I was the only one who did not vote him in for president of the college," he said this more loudly. "I thought he was a mutton-headed jackass, and I said so."

I looked up at him, stunned. "You mean you sit on the board of trustees for my college?" I asked, still shocked. My aunt seemed to take this in stride. Why hadn't anyone told me this?

"Yes. Of course! It was one reason you got into that class in the first place," he said.

"When Mr. Taylor told me you'd put in a good word for me, I had no idea you had such power."

"I still do," he said, through the cigar around clenched teeth. "The man seemed too disingenuous. Plus, his history was full of holes. Claims he was traipsing around Europe and South America before that. When I asked what he did there, he was very vague about it. I could never find anything to confirm it."

"Uncle Weeks said he couldn't find anything about Smith, or on what he did five years prior to when he came to the college."

"Yes. I felt he moved up a bit too quickly," my uncle said.

At this point, my sandwich had arrived. I paid the young man and asked Uncle Ed if I could talk to him outside while I ate my lunch. He was right, it was a beautiful day and I felt like getting some fresh air. But I needed to speak with him. Weeks was beyond talking to about these things because his power had been stripped where Smith was concerned.

While I ate, I told uncle Ed in detail that Mrs. Taylor found some accounts that were being skimmed. I told him I thought that Mrs. Taylor was fired because of what she knew, and then killed the next day along with her husband to keep them both quiet. He listened quietly, taking it all in. I went on to tell him I was ninety-nine percent sure that the FBI were looking in on Smith, and that the murders might be one of the things they were investigating.

"I didn't know about any of this." Both hands resting on the bench on either side of his hips, looking down at the sidewalk as though in thought. The breeze eddied through his soft, white hair while I took a few bites out of my sandwich. How many times had we sat at this very bench and I'd told him something in confidence?

"I'm telling you this in total confidence," I said. "I'm not even supposed to know."

"I understand." He patted my knee.

He seemed to make a decision and pulled out his cell phone. In a moment, he spoke to someone named Al. "What's this I hear you were caught climbing out of the widow's window at two AM?" Then he laughed, and I hoped the party on the other side laughed too. "You polecat!" There was more bantering, my uncle had a colorful way of speaking to others, and never did he utter a real swearword while he did so. But much of what was said could be taken as playful insults.

He was quiet as he listened for a moment, his smile fading. "Okay, I'll do that. No. I've called about another more serious matter," he said. "Right. I will see you in a few minutes. I'm having lunch with my lovely niece." He laughed and then said good bye.

"Who was that?" I asked, finishing up the tuna sandwich on whole wheat.

"That was Al Donovan, who is head of the board of trustees. I think Mr. Smith needs to be taken out of class, as well." He smiled.

"Don't tell anyone about the FBI. I'm sure if they are involved with this, and Smith is behind either the murders, or the disappearing money—or both—they need to catch him doing something incriminating."

He nodded and got up. "I won't mention the FBI, but I've been wanting to speak to Mr. Donovan about Mr. Smith's appointment, how wrong it felt when we voted, and now during these terrible problems at the school. He's only an interim president, and I think we might be able to put him on administrative leave. After that, maybe he'll be locked up in jail for a time." He winked at me.

"Just be careful what you say in order to do it. I don't want you to get into trouble. And you can't tell anyone your source."

He smiled all the more broadly and patted my hand. "I never give up my sources, Miss Lainey." He got up and was walking away before I could finish my thoughts. I hoped he wasn't acting in haste.

Chapter 19

WHERE R U?
IN PARKING LOT.

I was reading my phone's text message from Nate. He wanted to meet me at school. He had class too. We hadn't had a chance to talk all day. He had to drive to Mason City today to get parts for one of the cars they were working on in class tonight. He explained it as a class project, and so he had had little time to chat with me. I apparently couldn't compete with a car.

WHICH 1? Nate asked in the text.

LOT A, I answered.

B THERE IN 1

OK

I had pulled into a slot, not very far from the building, grabbed my stuff and got out. The sun was behind clouds as it headed to the western horizon. Once I had retrieved my bag, I began looking for Nate. I then heard the rumble of a Hog. Looked like I was going to ride on the back of his motorcycle for the very first time.

He pulled up, hands on the handles, feet flat on the ground. "Hop on."

I couldn't help my smile. I felt like a kid getting on a pony. Pack on my back, I straddled the beast behind him and he said "Hold on" so I wound my arms around his middle and off we went. We wound through the parking lot, and he deposited me at the door. I waited until he parked it over in the spot just for motorcycles not twenty feet away. Now that was handy.

We walked in and the noise level went up with people talking, music playing in the Pit.

"Which way is your class?" he asked.

"Upstairs." We climbed the stairs as we were early yet.

"Did you get the parts you needed?" I asked.

"Yes. We're overhauling a transmission. Intricate stuff."

"I'll bet." I was glad he didn't bore me with those intricacies, because I wouldn't have known one part from another.

We strode down the hall, passing closed doors. Only one door was open, and that was where Mr. Bascom was teaching. My room was one up from his room. I couldn't help but peek into the room. He was at the board writing something. People were still drifting into the classroom. His head turned, and our eyes met briefly before he turned away first.

I had yet to tell Nate I suspected Mr. Bascom was an FBI agent. I really didn't know that he was, but he had to be something. I was certain he wasn't just another teacher filling in.

"Hey, where's your mind?" The question startled me and I came out of my thoughts with a little start. I realized I walked past the door to my history class and looked back at Nate. Covering my humility with a chuckle I stepped back over to him. He pulled me closer and I looked up at him.

"We definitely have to go out this weekend," he said, tapping my chin.

"Sure," I said, "Let's just not get into trouble again."

"No fun in that." We both chuckled. He looked at his watch. "I'd better go. I don't want to be late. Transmissions are a bitch."

"So I've heard."

He bent and kissed me on the cheek and I turned my face into it. He took the invitation and kissed me on the lips. It was a quick kiss and he looked down at me. "I think we *will* get in trouble if we keep this up."

I bit my lower lip, chuckling, feeling a blush coming on. He stepped away, hand up in a wave. I waved back. I wanted to get to know him better, but I had to remind myself about what trouble Nadine was in. She'd called me three times during the day, once about going to find the pregnancy test and once before and then after she'd taken it. Negative. What a relief. I told her she'd probably have to take another one to make sure, since this one came out negative.

My eyes lingered on Nate, he passed Mr. Bascom's class. He slowed his pace as he turned his head to peer in. He must have remembered what I'd said about Bascom. Or, had I told him what I suspected about him? I couldn't remember at this point.

Stepping into my history classroom, I found a spot by the wall, but not in the back. This class was mostly lecture. Having gotten my book out, I noticed the blackboard had a note stating that Mr. Kulp was going to be a few minutes late, and to wait and not leave.

Some of the guys in the back had begun horsing around. Ignoring it, I opened up my book to review the chapter we'd been assigned.

Laughter erupted. Some girls were making sharp yelps.

"Oh, how mature," a girl from across the way said, turned in her seat. She had something in her hand. Snapping it, the rubber band shot toward the guys, but was poorly aimed and died on the floor a foot away from the closest guy. I was a little surprised at the antics. I'd expect this sort of behavior from Ellwood, not others. But, then these guys were freshmen, and were antsy without anything to do, and no supervision just asked for trouble to begin.

I had turned away when I felt something hit me and landed on the book in front of me. Laughter. Oh, cute. I picked up the rubber band, was about to shoot it back at them when the teacher walked in and plopped a stack of files and books down on his desk in the front. Quickly, I automatically slid the rubber band over my wrist. I wanted to be armed for the next time.

"Good evening, class. Sorry I'm tardy, but I forgot something and had to turn around to get it at the house." Mr. Kulp was tall and thin, possibly the far side of forty, closing in on fifty.

Class came to order and Mr. Kulp talked about the Civil War. Interesting stuff, and we all were writing things down. Then, a young woman—she looked like a student—walked in and handed Mr. Kulp a note. He thanked her and looked up at the clock.

"I see it's time to take a brief break," he said, and everyone was up and going out the door. I stayed put, as I didn't need to use the lady's room.

"Miss Quilholt?" Mr. Kulp stepped over to me and handed me a note. "I didn't read it, only that it was for you," he assured.

"Oh." I took the note which was folded over. On the outer side it had my full name written out. "Thanks," I said. He stepped away and went out the door. I opened the note.

Lainey,
I have new information.
Come to room 309 when you get a chance.
It's important.
Helen

I looked for some other words to help me decipher this note.

New information? About what?

It was handwritten in a cryptic style that slanted severely to the left, yet went in a straight line across the page. I studied it as I rose and walked out of the room. What was Helen doing at school at this hour? Why was it so important she needed to see me? She had my phone number, she could have called and left me a message. I had my phone out, having obediently shut it off, as our teachers all require us while in class, and turned it on to check for any messages.

No messages.

I passed Mr. Bascom who stood out in the hall. We exchanged hello's, and he showed little interest in where I was heading.

I checked the room numbers and found I was heading in the wrong direction, so I back tracked.

"Are you lost, again, Miss Quilholt?" Mr. Bascom asked with a small smile.

"Oh, just looking for room three-o-nine," I said.

"I believe it's up the hallway." He pointed. "But there's no other classes going on at this time."

"Oh, I know. I'm meeting someone," I said over my shoulder.

Room 309 was at the end of the hall. The stairs were just around the corner from it. I tried the door. It was locked.

What was the deal? Was this a joke? Why would anyone pull such a joke? My mind automatically thought of Evil Clown Guy. But he was dead. Besides, how would anyone know that Helen was my friend?

My skin began to crawl as I looked up and down the hallway. People were way at the other end, using the washrooms.

I had been scrolling down my contacts and found Helen's number and hit send. It began to ring. It went to voice mail, but I never had a chance to say anything when someone stepped out from the stairwell. In the dim light I saw his rotund shape and nearly jumped out of my skin.

"Miss Quilholt, if you'll come with me," Smith said. I was about to turn and bolt, but saw that he was holding something in his hand. I'd never looked down the barrel of a gun before, and this was a first. My blood ran cold and my insides were doing flips. My knees almost turned liquid.

"Put the phone away and come with me," he said more sternly.

I closed my phone, but while keeping eye contact with him, my thumb found the emergency button on the outside and I pressed it. This would go directly to Weeks.

Throat dry, I walked down the steps, with Smith slightly behind me and to the side, the gun in my ribs.

"What are you doing?" I asked, because I really didn't know.

"This isn't about you, my dear. I've got plans and things are getting a little sticky right now. Just be quiet, don't make a sound or call out to anyone, and if everything goes smoothly, I'll let you live."

Oh, God. The last words you ever want to hear from someone with a gun pointed at you.

In a moment, we were on the second floor and moving swiftly down the hallway. In a few more moments, he opened the door to the office with a key and ushered me inside, past the secretary's station, and to his door.

I stopped and looked at him.

"Inside." He waggled the gun, which was pointed to the ceiling, but nevertheless, deadly.

I went inside as instructed and watched him lock the door.

"So we won't be disturbed." Smiling, he breezed through the room as though he hadn't a care in the world. "Have a seat," he offered as though we were old friends. I sat in one of two leather upholstered seats and watched him move through the room, every motion deliberate. He open a lower desk drawer and pulled out a large black briefcase. Setting it on the desk, he opened it.

"Really, Miss Quilholt, I was puzzled at first by some of the things you did. I thought there was no way you, a mere college student, could become such a nuisance to me, but you have."

"I'm sorry?" I said. Not meaning I was sorry, but that I didn't understand.

Turning to the wall, he removed a large picture of a country scene and set it down on the floor revealing a safe. He proceeded to open it.

"I had no idea your uncle, for instance, sat on the board of trustees of this college."

"I had no idea either, until today," I said more to myself than to him.

"And your tampering in Chad Taylor's death."

"Murder, you mean," I corrected him.

He turned with chubby hands full of bundled bills. The denomination of which I wasn't able to see, but I had to guess they could have been twenties, or fifties. Ready-to-use-cash. Unless he was going to take it out of the country and simply stash it in some off-shore account. He made three such trips. He closed the safe and replaced the picture on the wall.

"I was going to be gone by Christmastime, but everything got pushed up," he said. "Unfortunately I had to make plans to leave sooner than I'd expected, but no problem. I have everything I need." Out of the top drawer he took out a small booklet, which I suspected was a passport, and threw it into the briefcase. A few other things went into the briefcase, and he closed it. My glance went to the coffee cup, thinking about using it to fend him off. Too late to get prints off it. The FBI probably knew who this guy was by now, anyway.

"Where do I fit into all this?" I thought that I might as well ask. One of the first things I learned from Weeks was to keep your kidnapper talking.

He looked straight at me for the first time. His smile was infuriating.

"You, my dear, are my ticket out of here."

"I'm your hostage? Why? You can leave whenever you want," I said, hands out, really not crazy about becoming a hostage. "Who's to stop you? Certainly not me."

He chuckled, face flushed from his movements around his nicely appointed office. He went to a recessed bookcase and pulled out a book and took something out of the pages and put it into a pocket, and replaced the book carefully. I had no idea what that could have been, maybe another passport with an alias.

"No, no. You see, Mr. Bascom, or whoever he *really* is, is definitely an agent with the FBI," he said.

I was worrying the rubber band around my wrist, thinking if only I had a spit wad—or something more deadly—I'd be able to stop him, and maybe buy time to get away.

"Too many questions asked about where I live, what I do with my past time. How well did I know Edward Fay—the past president. Besides, I know the type. His mannerisms, style of dress, those eyes of his." He shook his head, jowls shaking dangerously, and made that sound like he'd suddenly become cold.

"Why me?" I asked.

"You and Helen became too cozy. Helen favored Dr. Fay. She's probably told you a few things about him, no doubt."

"No. I'm sure she didn't. She knew my mother." It was only a half-lie. I had been thinking about Dr. Fay's visits to the Caribbean. It was very possible he, himself, was skimming money from the school over the years and keeping it hidden in various accounts. When I'd heard about an account that had been hacked into and the family wondering what happened to "all the money", I had to wonder about Dr. Fay's wealth myself.

"You made a few mistakes along the way," I said, trying to keep him busy. I didn't want him to leave the building too quickly, and have me in his car, where he could keep the gun on me and no one had a chance to get close to us. I glanced at the clock on the wall. It was 8:16. By now my history class would have resumed and Mr. Kulp would be wondering about my whereabouts, since I'd left my book and book bag, after having been given that note. I also knew that if Weeks had gotten my emergency call, he'd have men headed in our direction. I wasn't sure, but thought that ten minutes had passed since I'd been abducted.

Smith turned around and placed two large, pudgy hands on his desk. Yes, I could see he had strength enough to pull a rope to hang a man in a men's john. "Be very careful, my dear, anything you say will be used against you, and I dare say after killing a half a dozen people in my life, one more wouldn't matter."

Wow. He killed six people?

His threat was too real. Meanwhile I was racking my brain trying to think of what I had on my person that could be used as a projectile. I reached up to itch my head and my fingers found it on the back of my head, holding my hair in place. Casually, I unclipped my hair clip and brought it down in my hand, hiding it from him. The rubber band still around my wrist from class was easy to pull off without his notice as he was still moving around the room. He took out yet another gun. A big shiny one. I had no idea what it was, but it had a large barrel. Something that would not only kill me, but probably go through a door like a WMD.

"You'll drive, of course," he said, shoving the larger gun into his coat pocket Keys jingled in that pocket. That's when he grabbed the smaller gun, which he'd had while bringing me here. He lifted the briefcase with all his money. "Time to go."

I readied myself before I stood. My aim would have to be perfect. At least in the general area of his big, round head, but I wanted to hurt him bad and draw blood if I could. If I was lucky, maybe blind him. I could not dare miss. I needed enough time to get to the door, unlock it and hopefully run like hell.

My fingers shook like someone with palsy as I fitted the open clip into the rubber band. I took a deep breath, trying to steady myself. I didn't want him to see what I was about to do, so stayed seated until he came forward, hiding it partially between my knees, below his level of sight behind the desk.

With the open barrette in place over the rubber band, I stood, made a move as though I were his willing hostage, but turned back around, swiftly lifted my hands, arms parallel like I was about to shoot an arrow from a bow. I aimed at his large head and snapped the rubber band. I didn't waste time to see if it had hit him—his yelp told me it had. I was across the room, as he was swearing a blue streak, groaning and rolling on the floor. The hair clip had really hurt him. Maybe I poked him in the eye—good! But I hoped the lighter thump on the carpet had been the gun. Seconds seemed like minutes as I unlocked the door and yanked it open and shot out of there screaming at the top of my lungs.

That's when a tall man with black hair swept past me— "Down! Out of the way, Lainey!"

I ducked against the counter in the outer office, identifying Nate as he charged through the door, threw a high kick with one foot and something thudded to the ground—again. He performed a quick pirouette and kicked his other foot and down the obese man went with a heavier thud.

Suddenly a number of men were in the outer office, some with jackets with the letters FBI or IRS in gold on their backs. The man in a finely tailored suit coat leaned over where I had knelt behind the counter. I looked up into a pair of steel blue eyes.

"Lainey, are you alright?" It was Mr. Bascom—or whatever his real name was. He held out a hand and I took it. He pulled me to my feet.

"I'm okay. Not everyday I get into a mess like this one," I muttered. My eyes went to where Nate stood as he waited until the officers cleared a path for him to slip out of the room.

My heart—which was in my throat—was going like a race horse's, but it was slowing down.

"That was close," Nate said, looking first at Mr. Bascom, then at me.

I felt some sort of knowing pass between the two.

"Yes. It was a good thing I told Randy Kulp to keep an eye on you," Mr. Bascom said to me. "When he told me you hadn't returned to class, and had left all your books there, I knew something had happened. I wondered why you were looking for that room number."

"He tricked me with a note. I thought it was from Helen Graham," I said.

Suddenly five sheriff's police and two state policemen entered the already crowded outer office.

"Lainey! Lainey, are you alright?" Week's wide shoulders cleared a path toward me.

"Yes. I'm alright," I said.

"I got your emergency signal and got my men out here pronto."

"I'm fine, now. But I have to thank Nate and Mr. Bascom, here," I said, feeling weak, as the adrenaline rush drained. I leaned on the counter. Nate found an office chair and rolled it over to me. I sat down, thanking him.

Bascom stepped away to speak to his men, still dealing with Smith, opening up his briefcase, no doubt, and searching him.

"What happened to his face?" someone was saying.

I looked up to see they had Smith in handcuffs, hands behind his back, blood ran over his face. One of the IRS guys found something to swab up the blood.

"Oh, I did that," I said smiling. "I needed something to stop him, knowing he was going to use me as a hostage. I didn't want to get into his car."

"What did you use? A knife?" Nate asked.

"No. Just a barrette and a rubber band."

Weeks and Nate exchanged grins.

"I know why everyone else showed up," I said to Nate. "Why did you come in like Bruce Lee?"

Hands on hips, Nate pulled in a breath, looked at the ceiling and let it out, his head sank and he studied the floor now. "You might say I was inducted," he said finally. "Embrey and another agent came to me and took me aside. You see, I'm trained in MMA—mixed martial arts—in the Marines. They saw my military record, and persuaded me to keep an eye on you." He looked at me.

I frowned. "You went out with me just to keep me under surveillance?"

"No. I didn't know this until the other day. I asked you out way before that."

"So, how is it you knew to come here, now?"

"I had a message from Bascom that you were missing. I left class, explaining I had an emergency, and met him in the main building. He somehow knew where you'd be. I'm glad he knew, because I wouldn't have guessed."

"You took quite a risk, chum," Weeks said. "You weren't even armed."

"Not with a weapon," Nate said with a small shrug. "Just my skills."

"He is dangerous," I said, my brows wagging at Weeks.

"As long as he only fights the bad guys I have no problem with him," Weeks said.

Chapter 20

"That was a very fine meal, Mrs. Weeks," Nate said. He sat next to me at our dining room table. My aunt had made an excellent stew for Sunday dinner and everyone was here, including Uncle Ed, who had been watching his mannerisms, for some strange reason.

He had pulled me aside earlier and said "Lainey, I hope what I did about Mr. Smith didn't cause that mad man to grab you."

"No. It was other things, Uncle Ed," I assured. "Although he was a bit surprised to find out you were related to me and sat on the board of trustees."

"I've been feeling horrible about it ever since I heard he tried to abduct you," he said.

"Everything came out alright." I had learned that my aim had been perfect when I shot the barrette at Smith. It hit him in the forehead, leaving a pretty deep gash which needed at least three stitches.

"I promised to wait until after dinner to tell everyone the details about Smith, and his atrocities," Weeks said, looking across to his wife for some sort of permission.

"I'll just make the coffee. Anyone up for cherry pie?" My aunt stood and lifted her plate, and I grabbed mine and Nate's.

"I'll have a slice," Uncle Ed said.

"Me too," Weeks said. "Let me take your plate in for you, Ed."

"Coffee and pie Nate?" my aunt asked.

"Yes. I'll make room," he said with a big smile. He had the whitest teeth.

I was embarrassed that I would be the only one having milk with the pie. I noted, however, when wine was offered as the drink with the meal, Nate refused it, and drank water, instead. I was sort of happy about that.

Weeks and I brought in the plates from the dining room, clinking cutlery into the sink to be loaded into the dishwasher.

"You and Uncle Ed are getting along swimmingly," I said to Weeks.

He looked back at his wife while she was at the other end of the kitchen making coffee. "He and I have made a truce, at least when he's in the house. Elsewhere its a free-for-all."

I laughed. Then I asked the one question I needed to. "So, you don't have any problem with my dating and seeing Nate?" I asked.

"No. I'm trusting you are an adult and can make your own choices. Besides, he came through like Batman." Weeks was a big fan of the Batman movies, and believe me, he had all the DVD's to show for it.

"Thank you," I said as we stepped back into the dining room.

We settled back into our chairs. Nate found my hand and clasped his over mine and I smiled at him.

Placing elbows on the table, Weeks clasped his hands together and began to tell us what he'd learned from the FBI and other investigators.

"His real name is James Brad Cooper. He was from San Bernardino, California. He worked in a corporate law office. He was there for five years and was caught embezzling. He was arrested, but got out on bail. He skipped bail, and left the country. It's fuzzy exactly where he went, but it is thought he went somewhere down in South America. After a few years, agents tracked him there, got close, and he must have somehow known they were on to him, so he fled to Europe. After this, at some point, they think whatever money he had—I'm told it was two million—dries up, because he's living the high life, right? He comes back into the country as Cooper Smith."

My aunt brought in a large tray laden with coffee cups and plates of pie wedges. The coffee smelled really good. I helped her get the pie and coffee served to everyone. I had the only glass of milk.

"Thank you, hon," Weeks said to my aunt, picked up his cup and took a sip.

We all thanked my aunt, and the piece of pie with the red cherries oozing out of the flaky crust was too much for us to resist, and everyone dug in. We were all in gastronomic ecstasy for a few minutes while we ate.

Resuming the tale, Weeks went on. "Let's see. Where was I?"

"You told us Smith had gone into hiding over in Europe and ran out of money, and came back here," I prompted.

"Ah, right. So, he returns to America—under another false name and passport—and tries to find someplace remote, where the FBI wouldn't think to look. Not a city, because that's the first place they'd begin looking. Oh, I forgot to say, he'd gained a lot of weight, had a mole removed from his right cheek, and had a nose job. Just enough to look a little different from his mug shot. Shaved a beard, too.

"So, he finds a small town where he can fit in, which, unfortunately, was here. No one's real sure, but Dr. Fay may have known him from way back in college, as they both were born and lived in San Bernardino at about the same time, although Fay had about ten years on Smith."

"We can't ask him because he's dead," Uncle Ed said.

"Exactly. If they were in contact with each other, it's hard to know," Weeks said. "Someone might know, but I'm not privy to that information."

"What was their thoughts on Dr. Fay having siphoned money from the college?" I asked.

"That seemed to fit, because for one thing only Fay was able to access those accounts, and it would seem that whatever money was coming in from various events, and whatnot, didn't match what was in the accounts when the IRS began checking things for years past. Of course he would have opened new accounts and hid them under a shell corporation."

"A sham company," Uncle Ed said, his long white mustache fluttering. "Foolish, to begin with, and it's horrible what happened because of someone's greed."

We all mumbled agreement with that.

"The feds do believe Smith may have killed Fay in order to both take his position, but also, it's thought that Fay may have caught Smith skimming from an account of his." He was chuckling. "Two crooks trying to take advantage of one another."

"That explains his expensive life-style and trips to the Caribbean every so often," I said and added, "I spoke with Helen Graham. She knew him the best and spoke highly of him, but she had no idea he was also skimming accounts."

"I'm not clear on how Smith became president of the college, Uncle Ed." I looked his way.

"We couldn't find anyone with the proper credentials who wanted such low pay to do the job. Smith was the only applicant. We put him in temporarily. He knew that as soon as we had someone with the right degree, background and training, he would no longer be in that position."

"Obviously Smith had to work fast if he wanted to get as much money out of these accounts as he could before he was pushed out of a job where he could access these accounts."

"And Mrs. Taylor was in charge of paying for certain things, and when she found that an account was way low, she went to Smith," I said.

"The very last person she should have gone to," my aunt said.

"So, Smith killed her and her husband to keep them hushed up, and killed Brianna because she was Kay's assistant," I went on with this sad account of Smith's actions.

"That's what we're figuring at this point."

When the pie and coffee was gone, and the subject was hashed over a few more times, we got up from the table. Uncle Ed wanted to get home, claiming he would take a nap, as he had a dinner tour to do tonight.

Nate had brought his motorcycle, and offered to take me for a little ride. My uncle wasn't agreeing with my going on his motorcycle without a helmet.

"That's why I brought one, hopefully it's the right size," Nate said.

We stepped outside, and he had the helmet on the back of the seat. It was silver with a visor. I tried it on while my aunt and uncle looked on. My uncle only marginally approved of this. Nate started up his Hog, and I waved to my audience on the front lawn. We drove uptown and went out onto the open highway. My insides were tumbling with the thrill of it. It was freeing to be on the back of a motorcycle, feeling the cool air on my face, sun in my eyes, and a guy I had yet to get to know all his mysteries.

Epilogue

To date I can only report what facts I'd been able to gather, or wheedle out of my sources, like Weeks, Brandon Okert, Helen Graham, and even some tidbits from Jimmy Bean, the janitor of our college.

After her dismissal by Smith from her job, Mrs. Taylor called, oddly enough, the IRS, and this is how they became involved, along with the FBI. Whatever they spoke of, I was not privy to.

Item: the blind Jimmy Bean had been ask to replace had been the one from which a cord was either cut, or torn from and used to strangle Mr. Taylor.

Item: the button—the missing green one I noticed on Smith's shirt that day, which looked to have been torn or pulled from it—was, indeed, found in the Taylor's home, underneath Mrs. Taylor, proving that the button had to have fallen at the time of her death from whomever shot her. It was speculated that she may have grasped his shirt at the moment he shot her, as the shot was at very close range. The gun which shot her was untraceable, even though found in Mr. Taylor's desk—which was determined to be a plant.

Item: the clown mask, which was left outside the Taylor home in a garbage bin, was a feeble attempt to misdirect the police, make them think this was Sinclair's doing, which it could not have been, since he had committed suicide the night before.

Probably, Smith had a moment of brilliance the night before as he planned his moves for the next morning. It's not known where he'd gotten the mask, but I'd learned from Moon that one was missing from the drama department. Coincidence? I think not.

Item: a call came to Smith's personal phone from Mr. Taylor's the night before his and his wife's murders. It lasted approximately five minutes. What was discussed between the two can only be guessed at. But it's reasonable to assume this is what got the wheels turning, and Smith began plotting to kill the two, since he felt threatened.

I was told that Smith never confessed to anything and got himself, in Weeks' words "one hell of a lawyer"—and not a local one either. The trial won't be for a while yet, but my eye witness testimony will hopefully help in linking Smith to Brianna's murder. As it is, he is facing various charges, not in the least of which is a charge of kidnapping yours truly. I must confess, I don't relish the thought of going in front of a court room answering questions from Mr. Smith's bulldog lawyer in front of a room full of people, and retelling my harrowing account. But it would be satisfying to know the man who killed my friends will go to jail for a very long time. I vowed this to Brianna's parents—who were, understandably, broken up over her senseless death—after the funeral that I would make sure to do my utmost to see justice done.

And, yes. Mr. Smith's fingerprints were part of the FBI's ability to track Mr. Smith aka Brad Cooper of San Bernardino, California to Whitney College. I have no idea how, or who, had collected them, as Smith was very careful about leaving either his personal coffee cup, or his fingerprints, anywhere. He was also wanted in the murder of a corporate lawyer, and one of his ex-wifes—whom I understand was about to testify against him in a trial prior to his disappearance years ago.

As to whether or not he somehow killed Dr. Fay has not been determined. However, there is some talk of exhuming Dr. Fay's remains to test for possible drugs in his system.

I think it was the week after all this happened, in my psychology class where we began studying personality disorders. The teacher made handouts, as it was rather involved. But I found that there was one personality disorder that described Smith's personality to a "T". He was a sociopath who had no remorse, and showed no guilt over what he had done, and was willing to hurt others if it helped him continue in getting whatever it was he wanted. He was charming, to a point, and I felt he could manipulate others for his own personal gain. Smith had obviously done so with Dr. Fay, getting into position of trust and finding a way to embezzle funds from the college. As of this writing, I have not heard that Dr. Fay's same activities have been uncovered. But give it time, I tell myself. People who are willing to talk, will.

For me, running into such a monster in everyday life was one I would never forget. Especially coming so close to such an evil person, and possible death at his hands. I considered myself lucky to have people around me who love and want to protect me. Weeks later, when I allowed myself to think about all this, I realized that was the second time I had actually cheated death.

For the Taylors, and Brianna, death came too soon. I consider myself the lucky one, and am dealing with depression over it. I've been visiting my therapist again. Making sense of such things is nearly impossible. But with help from others, I'm muddling through it and working to get back to a normal life.

Oh, on a bright note, I am still dating Nate Blackstone. We're taking it slow, and have not committed to each other, other than taking one day at a time.

# # #

About the Author

Imagine if you will a young impressionable teenage girl, running home from school to watch the dark soap opera, "*Dark Shadows*". Imagine also, same girl a little older, staying up—or trying to—to watch the old B&W classic horror flicks—her favorite, of course, is *Dracula*.

That little girl was me. I had a crush on Dracula, but never liked that he was hunted down and killed. I always thought he should have the woman he loved, after all, he went to so much trouble in getting her. If I had written the play, it would have gone 180 degrees the other way. I spent an inordinate amount of time digging up anything on vampires I could throughout high school and college—which probably earned me the Weirdo Award... but I didn't care.

Before Anne Rice, or Charlaine Harris, vampire fiction was under the overall Horror banner. I read Stephan King, Dean Koontz, and James Hubert. There was no such thing as "paranormal romance", or "urban fantasy". Not very long ago, certain authors (like those above and may more—women, all), were able to dash away the male-driven idea of making a vampire so... unwanted. Only a woman would put a vampire in bed with a woman. And it was about time. But my writing is more urban fantasy style, even though I manage to marry romance, horror, adventure, and mystery into my books.

I took a creative writing course in high school (a very long time ago), and was so excited I'd found my true calling and told my teacher I wanted to become an author. She told me to pick a different vocation because my spelling was horrible and my grammar not much better.

I didn't follow her advice. So glad I was determined to prove her wrong.

I got more out of the same course in college—the teacher didn't pick at such things. He encouraged me/us, and I was first published in ByLine Magazine. But I wanted to write long fiction. In the early years, I must have written a million pages (not at all good), in longhand, and typed—practicing to become a writer. I went to a writer's conference or two, read books and magazines on how to write. I've published poems, short stories and articles for various publications. I first self-published "Spell of the Black Unicorn" in 2008. My Sabrina Strong first book was taken by another publisher, who went on to publish the first three books in the series. I now write for Creativia, and as of 2016, have five in the series published.

I love to create worlds you can taste, smell and feel with main characters you can identify with, fall in love with, lust for, and villains you may love to hate. My vampires are never cardboard baddies. They've all got their own personalities, needs, hates, and

idiosyncrasies. I refused to fall into the pre-teen vampire fiction, and instead delve into the gritty, sometimes violent, dark and sexual world of vampires. I wasn't about to castrate a vampire for his lust for blood. That's the basic appeal a male vampire has for women—those very significant psychological reasons for adoring Dracula et al. And I've added the need for sex to be just as strong, thus upping the strong tie between the two needs.

An outdoors person, self-made naturalist, and love to go on road vacations with my husband. A chronic rule breaker, I chose to write fantasy/urban fantasy, because I wanted to do whatever

I desired with my characters. When I write darker fiction/horror, my work is more similar to Hitchcock and Rod Sterling, with surprise endings. When I go into the longer works I tend to be more of a combination of Josh Wedon, Charlaine Harris, and Kim Harrison.

My hobbies include crocheting, bird watching, nature watching/hiking. I live on a re-planted prairie/wetlands, which my husband of 30 years is manager of. I also dabble in crafts of some sort. I've nearly finished the 8th book of the Sabrina Strong series. Currently I'm working on a murder mystery (my first without vampires or anything odd), and "Dhampire Legacy", which I'd begun several years ago. These I hope to have finished at the end of the summer, along with #6 Sabrina Strong book.

Books by the Author

Lainey Quilholt Mysteries
    Party to a Murder
    An Invitation To Kill
Sabrina Strong -Series
    Ascension
    Trill
    Nocturne
    Caprice
    Crescendo
    Requiem

Spell of the Black Unicorn
Spell of the Dark Castle
The Cat Whisperer
Vampire, My Own

Lightning Source UK Ltd.
Milton Keynes UK
UKHW020008221020
372003UK00003B/249